Please turn the page for more reviews....

By Ken Follett:

A DANGEROUS FORTUNE
NIGHT OVER WATER
THE PILLARS OF THE EARTH
LIE DOWN WITH LIONS
ON WINGS OF EAGLES
THE MAN FROM ST. PETERSBURG
THE KEY TO REBECCA
TRIPLE
EYE OF THE NEEDLE
A PLACE CALLED FREEDOM*
THE THIRD TWIN*
THE HAMMER OF EDEN*

*Published by Fawcett Books

THE
HAMMER
OF
EDEN

a novel

KEN
FOLLETT

FAWCETT CREST • NEW YORK

A Fawcett Crest Book
Published by The Ballantine Publishing Group
Copyright © 1998 by Ken Follett

"Smoke on the Water." Words and music by Jon Lord, Ritchie Blackmore, Ian Gillan, Roger Glover, and Ian Paice (Deep Purple) © 1972, reproduced by permission of B. Feldman & Co. Ltd. trading as Hec Music, London WC2H 0EA.

"There but for Fortune" by Phil Ochs, © 1963 Barricade Music ASCAP, quoted by kind permission of Barricade Music, a division of Rondor Music International.

www.randomhouse.com/BB/

Fawcett is a registered trademark and Fawcett Crest and the Fawcett colophon are trademarks of Random House, Inc.

ISBN 0-449-00677-8

This edition published by arrangement with Crown Publishers, Inc.

Printed in Canada

First Fawcett Crest International Edition: April 1999
First Fawcett Crest Canadian Edition: November 1999

10 9 8 7 6 5 4 3 2 1

CONTENTS

PART ONE

Four Weeks

When he lies down to sleep, this landscape is always on his mind:

A pine forest covers the hills, as thick as the fur on a bear's back. The sky is so blue, in the clear mountain air, that it hurts his eyes to look up. Miles from the road there is a secret valley with steep sides and a cold river in its cleft. Here, hidden from strangers' eyes, a sunny south-facing slope has been cleared, and grapevines grow in neat rows.

When he remembers how beautiful it is, he feels his heart will break.

Men, women, and children move slowly through the vineyard, tending the plants. These are his friends, his lovers, his family. One of the women laughs. She is a big woman with long, dark hair, and he feels a special warmth for her. She throws back her head and opens her mouth wide, and her clear high voice floats across the valley like birdsong. Some of the men quietly speak a mantra as they work, praying to the gods of the valley and of the grapevines for a good crop. At their feet, a few massive tree stumps remain, to remind them of the backbreaking work that created this place twenty-five years ago. The soil is stony, but this is good, because the stones retain the heat of the sun and warm the roots of the vines, protecting them from the deadly frost.

Beyond the vineyard is a cluster of wooden buildings, plain but well built and weatherproof. Smoke rises from a cookhouse. In a clearing, a woman is teaching a boy how to make barrels.

This is a holy place.

Protected by secrecy and by prayers, it has remained pure, its people free, while the world beyond the valley has degenerated into corruption and hypocrisy, greed and filth.

But now the vision changes.

Something has happened to the quick cold stream that used to zigzag through the valley. Its chatter has been silenced, its hurry abruptly halted. Instead of a rush of white water there is a dark pool, silent and still. The edges of the pool seem static, but if he looks away for a few moments, the pool widens. Soon he is forced to retreat up the slope.

He cannot understand why the others do not notice the rising tide. As the black pool laps at the first row of vines, they carry on working with their feet in the water. The buildings are surrounded, then flooded. The cookhouse fire goes out, and empty barrels float away across the growing lake. Why don't they run? he asks himself; and a choking panic rises in his throat.

Now the sky is dark with iron-colored clouds, and a cold wind whips at the clothing of the people, but still they move along the vines, stooping and rising, smiling at one another and talking in quiet, normal voices. He is the only one who can see the danger, and he realizes he must pick up one or two or even three of the children and save them from drowning. He tries to run toward his daughter, but he discovers that his feet are stuck in the mud and he cannot move; and he is filled with dread.

In the vineyard the water rises to the workers' knees, then their waists, then their necks. He tries to yell at the people he loves, telling them they must do something now, quickly, in the next few seconds, or they will die, but though he opens his mouth and strains his throat, no sounds will come out. Sheer terror possesses him.

The water laps into his open mouth and begins to choke him.

This is when he wakes up.

1

A man called Priest pulled his cowboy hat down at the front and peered across the flat, dusty desert of South Texas.

The low dull green bushes of thorny mesquite and sagebrush stretched in every direction as far as he could see. In front of him, a ridged and rutted track ten feet wide had been driven through the vegetation. These tracks were called *senderos* by the Hispanic bulldozer drivers who cut them in brutally straight lines. On one side, at precise fifty-yard intervals, bright pink plastic marker flags fluttered on short wire poles. A truck moved slowly along the *sendero*.

Priest had to steal the truck.

He had stolen his first vehicle at the age of eleven, a brand-new snow white 1961 Lincoln Continental parked, with the keys in the dash, outside the Roxy Theatre on South Broadway in Los Angeles. Priest, who was called Ricky in those days, could hardly see over the steering wheel. He had been so scared he almost wet himself, but he drove it ten blocks and handed the keys proudly to Jimmy "Pigface" Riley, who gave him five bucks, then took his girl for a drive and crashed the car on the Pacific Coast Highway. That was how Ricky became a member of the Pigface Gang.

But this truck was not just a vehicle.

As he watched, the powerful machinery behind the driver's

cabin slowly lowered a massive steel plate, six feet square, to the ground. There was a pause, then he heard a low-pitched rumble. A cloud of dust rose around the truck as the plate began to pound the earth rhythmically. He felt the ground shake beneath his feet.

This was a seismic vibrator, a machine for sending shock waves through the earth's crust. Priest had never had much education, except in stealing cars, but he was the smartest person he had ever met, and he understood how the vibrator worked. It was similar to radar and sonar. The shock waves were reflected off features in the earth—such as rock or liquid—and they bounced back to the surface, where they were picked up by listening devices called geophones, or jugs.

Priest worked on the jug team. They had planted more than a thousand geophones at precisely measured intervals in a grid a mile square. Every time the vibrator shook, the reflections were picked up by the jugs and recorded by a supervisor working in a trailer known as the doghouse. All this data would later be fed into a supercomputer in Houston to produce a three-dimensional map of what was under the earth's surface. The map would be sold to an oil company.

The vibrations rose in pitch, making a noise like the mighty engines of an ocean liner gathering speed; then the sound stopped abruptly. Priest ran along the *sendero* to the truck, screwing up his eyes against the billowing dust. He opened the door and clambered up into the cabin. A stocky black-haired man of about thirty was at the wheel. "Hey, Mario," Priest said as he slid into the seat alongside the driver.

"Hey, Ricky."

Richard Granger was the name on Priest's commercial driving license (class B). The license was forged, but the name was real.

He was carrying a carton of Marlboro cigarettes, the brand Mario smoked. He tossed the carton onto the dash. "Here, I brought you something."

"Hey, man, you don't need to buy me no cigarettes."

"I'm always bummin' your smokes." He picked up the open pack on the dash, shook one out, and put it in his mouth.

Mario smiled. "Why don't you just buy your own cigarettes?"

"Hell, no, I can't afford to smoke."

"You're crazy, man." Mario laughed.

Priest lit his cigarette. He had always had an easy ability to get on with people, make them like him. On the streets where he grew up, people beat you up if they didn't like you, and he had been a runty kid. So he had developed an intuitive feel for what people wanted from him—deference, affection, humor, whatever—and the habit of giving it to them quickly. In the oilfield, what held the men together was humor: usually mocking, sometimes clever, often obscene.

Although he had been here only two weeks, Priest had won the trust of his co-workers. But he had not figured out how to steal the seismic vibrator. And he had to do it in the next few hours, for tomorrow the truck was scheduled to be driven to a new site, seven hundred miles away, near Clovis, New Mexico.

His vague plan was to hitch a ride with Mario. The trip would take two or three days—the truck, which weighed forty thousand pounds, had a highway speed of around forty miles per hour. At some point he would get Mario drunk or something, then make off with the truck. He had been hoping a better plan would come to him, but inspiration had failed so far.

"My car's dying," he said. "You want to give me a ride as far as San Antonio tomorrow?"

Mario was surprised. "You ain't coming all the way to Clovis?"

"Nope." He waved a hand at the bleak desert landscape. "Just look around," he said. "Texas is so beautiful, man, I never want to leave."

Mario shrugged. There was nothing unusual about a restless transient in this line of work. "Sure, I'll give you a ride." It was against company rules to take passengers, but the drivers did it all the time. "Meet me at the dump."

Priest nodded. The garbage dump was a desolate hollow, full of rusting pickups and smashed TV sets and verminous mattresses, on the outskirts of Shiloh, the nearest town. No one would be there to see Mario pick him up, unless it was a couple of kids shooting snakes with a .22 rifle. "What time?"

"Let's say six."

"I'll bring coffee."

Priest needed this truck. He felt his life depended on it. His palms itched to grab Mario right now and throw him out and just drive away. But that was no good. For one thing, Mario was almost twenty years younger than Priest and might not let himself be thrown out so easily. For another, the theft had to go undiscovered for a few days. Priest needed to drive the truck to California and hide it before the nation's cops were alerted to watch out for a stolen seismic vibrator.

There was a beep from the radio, indicating that the supervisor in the doghouse had checked the data from the last vibration and found no problems. Mario raised the plate, put the truck in gear, and moved forward fifty yards, pulling up exactly alongside the next pink marker flag. Then he lowered the plate again and sent a ready signal. Priest watched closely, as he had done several times before, making sure he remembered the order in which Mario moved the levers and threw the switches. If he forgot something later, there would be no one he could ask.

They waited for the radio signal from the doghouse that would start the next vibration. This could be done by the driver in the truck, but generally supervisors preferred to retain command themselves and start the process by remote control. Priest finished his cigarette and threw the butt out the window. Mario nodded toward Priest's car, parked a quarter of a mile away on the two-lane blacktop. "That your woman?"

Priest looked. Star had got out of the dirty light blue Honda Civic and was leaning on the hood, fanning her face with her straw hat. "Yeah," he said.

"Lemme show you a picture." Mario pulled an old leather billfold out of the pocket of his jeans. He extracted a photograph and handed it to Priest. "This is Isabella," he said proudly.

Priest saw a pretty Mexican girl in her twenties wearing a yellow dress and a yellow Alice band in her hair. She held a baby on her hip, and a dark-haired boy was standing shyly by her side. "Your children?"

He nodded. "Ross and Betty."

Priest resisted the impulse to smile at the Anglo names. "Good-looking kids." He thought of his own children and almost told Mario about them; but he stopped himself just in time. "Where do they live?"

"El Paso."

The germ of an idea sprouted in Priest's mind. "You get to see them much?"

Mario shook his head. "I'm workin' and workin', man. Savin' my money to buy them a place. A nice house, with a big kitchen and a pool in the yard. They deserve that."

The idea blossomed. Priest suppressed his excitement and kept his voice casual, making idle conversation. "Yeah, a beautiful house for a beautiful family, right?"

"That's what I'm thinking."

The radio beeped again, and the truck began to shake. The noise was like rolling thunder, but more regular. It began on a profound bass note and slowly rose in pitch. After exactly fourteen seconds it stopped.

In the quiet that followed, Priest snapped his fingers. "Say, I got an idea. . . . No, maybe not."

"What?"

"I don't know if it would work."

"What, man, what?"

"I just thought, you know, your wife is so pretty and your kids are so cute, it's wrong that you don't see them more often."

"That's your idea?"

"No. My idea is, I could drive the truck to New Mexico while you go visit them, that's all." It was important not to seem too keen, Priest told himself. "But I guess it wouldn't work out," he added in a who-gives-a-damn voice.

"No, man, it ain't possible."

"Probably not. Let's see, if we set out early tomorrow and drove to San Antonio together, I could drop you off at the airport there, you could be in El Paso by noon, probably. You'd play with the kids, have dinner with your wife, spend the night, get a plane the next day, I could pick you up at Lubbock airport. . . . How far is Lubbock from Clovis?"

"Ninety, maybe a hundred miles."

"We could be in Clovis that night, or next morning at the latest, and no way for anyone to know you didn't drive the whole way."

"But you want to go to San Antonio."

Shit. Priest had not thought this through; he was making it up as he went along. "Hey, I've never been to Lubbock," he said airily. "That's where Buddy Holly was born."

"Who the hell is Buddy Holly?"

Priest sang: " 'I love you, Peggy Sue. . . .' Buddy Holly died before you were born, Mario. I liked him better than Elvis. And don't ask me who Elvis was."

"You'd drive all that way just for me?"

Priest wondered anxiously whether Mario was suspicious or just grateful. "Sure I would," Priest told him. "As long as you let me smoke your Marlboros."

Mario shook his head in amazement. "You're a hell of a guy, Ricky. But I don't know."

He was not suspicious, then. But he was apprehensive,

and he probably could not be pushed into a decision. Priest masked his frustration with a show of nonchalance. "Well, think about it," he said.

"If something goes wrong, I don't want to lose my job."

"You're right." Priest fought down his impatience. "I tell you what, let's talk later. You going to the bar tonight?"

"Sure."

"Why don't you let me know then?"

"Okay, that's a deal."

The radio beeped the all-clear signal, and Mario threw the lever that raised the plate off the ground.

"I got to get back to the jug team," Priest said. "We've got a few miles of cable to roll up before nightfall." He handed back the family photo and opened the door. "I'm telling you, man, if I had a girl that pretty, I wouldn't leave the goddamn *house.* " He grinned, then jumped to the ground and slammed the door.

The truck moved off toward the next marker flag as Priest walked away, his cowboy boots kicking up dust.

As he followed the *sendero* to where his car was parked, he saw Star begin to pace up and down, impatient and anxious.

She had been famous, once, briefly. At the peak of the hippie era she lived in the Haight-Ashbury neighborhood of San Francisco. Priest had not known her then—he had spent the late sixties making his first million dollars—but he had heard the stories. She had been a striking beauty, tall and black haired with a generous hourglass figure. She had made a record, reciting poetry against a background of psychedelic music with a band called Raining Fresh Daisies. The album had been a minor hit, and Star was a celebrity for a few days.

But what turned her into a legend was her insatiable sexual promiscuity. She had had sex with anyone who briefly took her fancy: eager twelve-year-olds and surprised men in their sixties, boys who thought they were gay and girls who did not know they were lesbians, friends she had known for years and strangers off the street.

That was a long time ago. Now she was a few weeks from her fiftieth birthday, and there were streaks of gray in her hair. Her figure was still generous, though no longer like an hourglass: she weighed a hundred and eighty pounds. But she still exercised an extraordinary sexual magnetism. When she walked into a bar, men stared.

Even now, when she was worried and hot, there was a sexy flounce to the way she paced and turned beside the cheap old car, an invitation in the movement of her flesh beneath the thin cotton dress, and Priest felt the urge to grab her right there.

"What happened?" she said as soon as he was within earshot.

Priest was always upbeat. "Looking good," he said.

"That sounds bad," she said skeptically. She knew better than to take what he said at face value.

He told her the offer he had made to Mario. "The beauty of it is, Mario will be blamed," he added.

"How so?"

"Think about it. He gets to Lubbock, he looks for me, I ain't there, nor his truck, either. He figures he's been suckered. What does he do? Is he going to make his way to Clovis and tell the company he lost their truck? I don't think so. At best, he'd be fired. At worst, he could be accused of stealing the truck and thrown in jail. I'm betting he won't even go to Clovis. He'll get right back on the plane, fly to El Paso, put his wife and kids in the car, and disappear. Then the police will be sure he stole the truck. And Ricky Granger won't even be a suspect."

She frowned. "It's a great plan, but will he take the bait?"

"I think he will."

Her anxiety deepened. She slapped the dirty roof of the car with the flat of her hand. "Shit, we have to have that goddamn truck!"

He was as worried as she, but he covered it with a cock-sure air. "We will," he said. "If not this way, another way."

She put the straw hat on her head and leaned back against the car, closing her eyes. "I wish I felt sure."

He stroked her cheek. "You need a ride, lady?"

"Yes, please. Take me to my air-conditioned hotel room."

"There'll be a price to pay."

She opened her eyes wide in pretended innocence. "Will I have to do something nasty, mister?"

He slid his hand into her cleavage. "Yeah."

"Oh, darn," she said, and she lifted the skirt of her dress up around her waist.

She had no underwear on.

Priest grinned and unbuttoned his Levi's.

She said: "What will Mario think if he sees us?"

"He'll be jealous," Priest said as he entered her. They were almost the same height, and they fit together with the ease of long practice.

She kissed his mouth.

A few moments later he heard a vehicle approaching on the road. They both looked up without stopping what they were doing. It was a pickup truck with three roustabouts in the front seat. The men could see what was going on, and they whooped and hollered through the open window as they went by.

Star waved at them, calling: "Hi, guys!"

Priest laughed so hard, he came.

The crisis had entered its final, decisive phase exactly three weeks earlier.

They were sitting at the long table in the cookhouse, eating their midday meal, a spicy stew of lentils and vegetables with fresh bread warm from the oven, when Paul Beale walked in with an envelope in his hand.

Paul bottled the wine that Priest's commune made—but he did more than that. He was their link with the outside,

enabling them to deal with the world yet keep it at a distance.
A bald, bearded man in a leather jacket, he had been Priest's
friend since the two of them were fourteen-year-old hoodlums, rolling drunks in L.A.'s skid row in the early sixties.

Priest guessed that Paul had received the letter that morning and had immediately got in his car and driven here from
Napa. He also guessed what was in the letter, but he waited
for Paul to explain.

"It's from the Bureau of Land Management," Paul said.
"Addressed to Stella Higgins." He handed it to Star, sitting
at the foot of the table opposite Priest. Stella Higgins was
her real name, the name under which she had first rented
this piece of land from the Department of the Interior in the
autumn of 1969.

Around the table, everyone went quiet. Even the kids
shut up, sensing the atmosphere of fear and dismay.

Star ripped open the envelope and took out a single sheet.
She read it with one glance. "June the seventh," she said.

Priest said reflexively: "Five weeks and two days from
now." That kind of calculation came automatically to him.

Several people groaned in despair. A woman called Song
began to cry quietly. One of Priest's children, ten-year-old
Ringo, said: "Why, Star, why?"

Priest caught the eye of Melanie, the newest arrival. She
was a tall, thin woman, twenty-eight years old, with striking
good looks: pale skin, long hair the color of paprika, and the
body of a model. Her five-year-old son, Dusty, sat beside
her. "What?" Melanie said in a shocked voice. "What is
this?"

Everyone else had known this was coming, but it was too
depressing to talk about, and they had not told Melanie.

Priest said: "We have to leave the valley. I'm sorry,
Melanie."

Star read from the letter. " 'The above-named parcel of
land will become dangerous for human habitation after June
seventh, therefore your tenancy is hereby terminated on that

date in accordance with clause nine, part B, paragraph two, of your lease.' "

Melanie stood up. Her white skin flushed red, and her pretty face twisted in sudden rage. "No!" she yelled. "No! They can't do this to me—I've only just found you! I don't believe it, it's a lie." She turned her fury on Paul. "Liar!" she screamed. "Motherfucking liar!"

Her child began to cry.

"Hey, knock it off!" Paul said indignantly. "I'm just the goddamn mailman here!"

Everyone started shouting at the same time.

Priest was beside Melanie in a couple of strides. He put his arm around her and spoke quietly into her ear. "You're frightening Dusty," he said. "Sit down, now. You're right to be mad, we're all mad as hell."

"Tell me it isn't true," she said.

Priest gently pushed her into her chair. "It's true, Melanie," he said. "It's true."

When they had quieted down, Priest said: "Come on, everyone, let's wash the dishes and get back to work."

"Why?" said Dale. He was the winemaker. Not one of the founders, he had come here in the eighties, disillusioned with the commercial world. After Priest and Star, he was the most important person in the group. "We won't be here for the harvest," he went on. "We have to leave in five weeks. Why work?"

Priest fixed him with the Look, the hypnotic stare that intimidated all but the most strong-willed people. He let the room fall silent, so that they would all hear. At last he said: "Because miracles happen."

A local ordinance prohibited the sale of alcoholic beverages in the town of Shiloh, Texas, but just the other side of the town line there was a bar called the Doodlebug, with cheap draft beer and a country-western band and waitresses in tight blue jeans and cowboy boots.

Priest went on his own. He did not want Star to show her face and risk being remembered later. He wished she had not had to come to Texas. But he needed someone to help him take the seismic vibrator home. They would drive day and night, taking turns at the wheel, using drugs to stay awake. They wanted to be home before the machine was missed.

He was regretting that afternoon's indiscretion. Mario had seen Star from a full quarter of a mile away, and the three roustabouts in the pickup had glimpsed her only in passing, but she was distinctive looking, and they could probably give a rough description of her: a tall white woman, heavyset, with long dark hair. . . .

Priest had changed his appearance before arriving in Shiloh. He had grown a bushy beard and mustache and tied his long hair in a tight plait that he kept tucked up inside his hat.

However, if everything went according to his plan, no one would be asking for descriptions of him or Star.

When he arrived at the Doodlebug, Mario was already there, sitting at a table with five or six of the jug team and the party boss, Lenny Petersen, who controlled the entire seismic exploration crew.

Not to seem too eager, Priest got a Lone Star longneck and stood at the bar for a while, sipping his beer from the bottle and talking to the barmaid, before joining Mario's table.

Lenny was a balding man with a red nose. He had given Priest the job two weekends ago. Priest had spent an evening at the bar, drinking moderately, being friendly to the crew, picking up a smattering of seismic exploration slang, and laughing loudly at Lenny's jokes. Next morning he had found Lenny at the field office and asked him for a job. "I'll take you on trial," Lenny had said.

That was all Priest needed.

He was hardworking, quick to catch on, and easy to get

along with, and in a few days he was accepted as a regular member of the crew.

Now, as he sat down, Lenny said in his slow Texas accent: "So, Ricky, you're not coming with us to Clovis."

"That's right," Priest said. "I like the weather here too much to leave."

"Well, I'd just like to say, very sincerely, that it's been a real privilege and pleasure knowing you, even for such a short time."

The others grinned. This kind of joshing was commonplace. They looked to Priest for a riposte.

He put on a solemn face and said: "Lenny, you're so sweet and kind to me that I'm going to ask you one more time. Will you marry me?"

They all laughed. Mario clapped Priest on the back.

Lenny looked troubled and said: "You know I can't marry you, Ricky. I already told you the reason why." He paused for dramatic effect, and they all leaned forward to catch the punch line. "I'm a lesbian."

They roared with laughter. Priest gave a rueful smile, acknowledging defeat, and ordered a pitcher of beer for the table.

The conversation turned to baseball. Most of them liked the Houston Astros, but Lenny was from Arlington and he followed the Texas Rangers. Priest had no interest in sports, so he waited impatiently, joining in now and again with a neutral comment. They were in an expansive mood. The job had been finished on time, they had all been well paid, and it was Friday night. Priest sipped his beer slowly. He never drank much: he hated to lose control. He watched Mario sinking the suds. When Tammy, their waitress, brought another pitcher, Mario stared longingly at her breasts beneath the checkered shirt. *Keep wishing, Mario—you could be in bed with your wife tomorrow night.*

After an hour, Mario went to the men's room.

Priest followed. *The hell with this waiting, it's decision time.*

He stood beside Mario and said: "I believe Tammy's wearing black underwear tonight."

"How do you know?"

"I got a little peek when she leaned over the table. I love to see a lacy brassiere."

Mario sighed.

Priest went on: "You like a woman in black underwear?"

"Red," said Mario decisively.

"Yeah, red's beautiful, too. They say that's a sign a woman really wants you, when she puts on red underwear."

"Is that a fact?" Mario's beery breath came a little faster.

"Yeah, I heard it somewhere." Priest buttoned up. "Listen, I got to go. My woman's waiting back at the motel."

Mario grinned and wiped sweat from his brow. "I saw you and her this afternoon, man."

Priest shook his head in mock regret. "It's my weakness. I just can't say no to a pretty face."

"You were *doing* it, right there in the goddamn road!"

"Yeah. Well, when you haven't seen your woman for a while, she gets kind of frantic for it, know what I mean?" *Come on, Mario, take the friggin' hint!*

"Yeah, I know. Listen, about tomorrow . . ."

Priest held his breath.

"Uh, if you're still willing to do like you said . . ."

Yes! Yes!

"Let's go for it."

Priest resisted the temptation to hug him.

Mario said anxiously: "You still want to, right?"

"Sure I do." Priest put an arm around Mario's shoulders as they left the men's room. "Hey, what are buddies for, know what I mean?"

"Thanks, man." There were tears in Mario's eyes. "You're some guy, Ricky."

* * *

They washed their pottery bowls and wooden spoons in a big tub of warm water and dried them on a towel made from an old workshirt. Melanie said to Priest: "Well, we'll just start again somewhere else! Get a piece of land, build wood cabins, plant vines, make wine. Why not? That's what you did all those years ago."

"It is," Priest said. He put his bowl on a shelf and tossed his spoon into the box. For a moment he was young again, strong as a pony and boundlessly energetic, certain that he could solve whatever problem life threw up next. He remembered the unique smells of those days: newly sawn timber; Star's young body, perspiring as she dug the soil; the distinctive smoke of their own marijuana, grown in a clearing in the woods; the dizzy sweetness of grapes as they were crushed. Then he returned to the present, and he sat down at the table.

"All those years ago," he repeated. "We rented this land from the government for next to nothing, then they forgot about us."

Star put in: "Never a rent increase, in twenty-nine years."

Priest went on: "We cleared the forest with the labor of thirty or forty young people who were willing to work for free, twelve and fourteen hours a day, for the sake of an ideal."

Paul Beale grinned. "My back still hurts when I think of it."

"We got our vines for nothing from a kindly Napa Valley grower who wanted to encourage young people to do something constructive instead of just sitting around taking drugs all day."

"Old Raymond Dellavalle," Paul said. "He's dead now, God bless him."

"And, most important, we were willing and able to live on the poverty line, half-starved, sleeping on the floor, holes in our shoes, for five long years until we got our first salable vintage."

Star picked up a crawling baby from the floor, wiped its

nose, and said: "And we didn't have any kids to worry about."

"Right," Priest said. "If we could reproduce all those conditions, we could start again."

Melanie was not satisfied. "There has to be a way!"

"Well, there is," Priest said. "Paul figured it out."

Paul nodded. "You could set up a corporation, borrow a quarter of a million dollars from a bank, hire a workforce, and become like any other bunch of greedy capitalists watching the profit margins."

"And that," Priest said, "would be the same as giving in."

It was still dark when Priest and Star got up on Saturday morning in Shiloh. Priest got coffee from the diner next door to their motel. When he came back, Star was poring over a road atlas by the light of the reading lamp. "You should be dropping Mario off at San Antonio International Airport around nine-thirty, ten o'clock this morning," she said. "Then you'll want to leave town on Interstate 10."

Priest did not look at the atlas. Maps baffled him. He could follow signs for I-10. "Where shall we meet?"

Star calculated. "I should be about an hour ahead of you." She put her finger on a point on the page. "There's a place called Leon Springs on I-10 about fifteen miles from the airport. I'll park where you're sure to see the car."

"Sounds good."

They were tense and excited. Stealing Mario's truck was only the first step in the plan, but it was crucial: everything else depended on it.

Star was worrying about practicalities. "What will we do with the Honda?"

Priest had bought the car three weeks ago for a thousand dollars cash. "It's going to be hard to sell. If we see a used-car lot, we may get five hundred for it. Otherwise we'll find a wooded spot off the interstate and dump it."

"Can we afford to?"

"Money makes you poor." Priest was quoting one of the Five Paradoxes of Baghram, the guru they lived by.

Priest knew how much money they had to the last cent, but he kept everyone else in ignorance. Most of the communards did not even know there was a bank account. And no one in the world knew about Priest's emergency cash, ten thousand dollars in twenties, taped to the inside of a battered old acoustic guitar that hung from a nail on the wall of his cabin.

Star shrugged. "I haven't worried about it for twenty-five years, so I guess I won't start now." She took off her reading glasses.

Priest smiled at her. "You're cute in your glasses."

She gave him a sideways glance and asked a surprise question. "Are you looking forward to seeing Melanie?"

Priest and Melanie were lovers.

He took Star's hand. "Sure," he said.

"I like to see you with her. She makes you happy."

A sudden memory of Melanie flashed into Priest's brain. She was lying facedown across his bed, asleep, with the morning sun slanting into the cabin. He sat sipping coffee, watching her, enjoying the texture of her white skin, the curve of her perfect rear end, the way her long red hair spread out in a tangled skein. In a moment she would smell the coffee, and roll over, and open her eyes, and then he would get back into bed and make love to her. But for now he was luxuriating in anticipation, planning how he would touch her and turn her on, savoring this delicious moment like a glass of fine wine.

The vision faded and he saw Star's forty-nine-year-old face in a cheap Texas motel. "You're not unhappy about Melanie, are you?" he asked.

"Marriage is the greatest infidelity," she said, quoting another of the Paradoxes.

He nodded. They had never asked each other to be faithful. In the early days it had been Star who scorned the idea of committing herself to one lover. Then, after she hit thirty and started to calm down, Priest had tested her permissiveness by flaunting a string of girls in front of her. But for the last few years, though they still believed in the principle of free love, neither of them had actually taken advantage of it.

So Melanie had come as kind of a shock to Star. But that was okay. Their relationship was too settled anyway. Priest did not like anyone to feel they could predict what he was going to do. He loved Star, but the ill-concealed anxiety in her eyes gave him a pleasant feeling of control.

She toyed with her Styrofoam coffee container. "I just wonder how Flower feels about it all." Flower was their thirteen-year-old daughter, the oldest child in the commune.

"She hasn't grown up in a nuclear family," he said. "We haven't made her a slave to bourgeois convention. That's the point of a commune."

"Yeah," Star agreed, but it was not enough. "I just don't want her to lose you, that's all."

He stroked her hand. "It won't happen."

She squeezed his fingers. "Thanks."

"We got to go," he said, standing up.

Their few possessions were packed into three plastic grocery bags. Priest picked up the bags and took them outside to the Honda. Star followed.

They had paid their bill the previous night. The office was closed, and no one watched as Star took the wheel and they drove away in the gray early light.

Shiloh was a two-street town with one stoplight where the streets crossed. There were not many vehicles around at this hour on a Saturday morning. Star ran the stoplight and headed out of town. They reached the dump a few minutes before six o'clock.

There was no sign beside the road, no fence or gate, just a track where the sagebrush had been beaten down by the tires of pickup trucks. Star followed the track over a slight rise. The dump was in a dip, hidden from the road. She pulled up beside a pile of smoldering garbage. There was no sign of Mario or the seismic vibrator.

Priest could tell that Star was still troubled. He had to reassure her, he thought worriedly. She could not afford to be distracted today of all days. If something should go wrong, she would need to be alert, focused.

"Flower isn't going to lose me," he said.

"That's good," she replied cautiously.

"We're going to stay together, the three of us. You know why?"

"Tell me."

"Because we love each other."

He saw relief drain the tension out of her face. She fought back tears. "Thank you," she said.

He felt reassured. He had given her what she needed. She would be okay now.

He kissed her. "Mario will be here any second. You get movin', now. Put some miles behind you."

"You don't want me to wait until he gets here?"

"He mustn't get a close look at you. We can't tell what the future holds, and I don't want him to be able to identify you."

"Okay."

Priest got out of the car.

"Hey," she said, "don't forget Mario's coffee." She handed him the paper sack.

"Thanks." He took the bag and slammed the car door.

She turned around in a wide circle and drove away fast, her tires throwing up a cloud of Texas desert dust.

Priest looked around. He found it amazing that such a small town could generate so much trash. He saw twisted bicycles and new-looking baby carriages, stained couches and old-fashioned refrigerators, and at least ten supermarket carts. The place was a wasteland of packaging: cardboard boxes for stereo systems, pieces of lightweight polystyrene packing like abstract sculptures, paper sacks and polythene bags and tinfoil wrappers, and a host of plastic containers that had contained substances Priest had never used: rinse aid, moisturizer, conditioner, fabric softener, fax toner. He saw a fairy-tale castle made of pink plastic, presumably a child's toy, and he marveled at the wasteful extravagance of such an elaborate construction.

In Silver River Valley there was never much garbage. They did not use baby carriages or refrigerators, and they rarely bought anything that came in a package. The children would use imagination to make a fairy-tale castle from a tree or a barrel or a stack of timber.

A hazy red sun edged up over the ridge, casting a long shadow of Priest across a rusting bedstead. It made him think of sunrise over the snow peaks of the Sierra Nevada, and he suffered a sharp pang of longing for the cool, pure air of the mountains.

Soon, soon.

Something glinted at his feet. A shiny metal object was half-buried in the earth. Idly he scraped away the dry earth with the toe of his boot, then bent and picked up the object. It was a heavy Stillson wrench. It seemed new. Mario might find it useful, Priest thought: it was about the right size for the large-scale machinery of the seismic vibrator. But, of course, the truck would contain a full tool kit, with wrenches to fit every nut used in its construction. Mario had no need of a discarded wrench. This was the throwaway society.

Priest dropped the wrench.

He heard a vehicle, but it did not sound like a big truck. He glanced up. A moment later a tan pickup came over the ridge, bouncing along the rough track. It was a Dodge Ram with a cracked windshield: Mario's car. Priest suffered a pang of unease. What did this mean? Mario was supposed to show up in the seismic vibrator. His own car would be driven north by one of his buddies, unless he had decided to sell it here and buy another in Clovis. Something had gone wrong. "Shit," he said. "Shit."

He suppressed his feelings of anger and frustration as Mario pulled up and got out of the pickup. "I brought you coffee," he said, handing Mario the paper sack. "What's up?"

Mario did not open the bag. He shook his head sadly. "I can't do it, man."

Shit.

Mario went on: "I really appreciate what you offered to do for me, but I gotta say no."

What the hell is going on?

Priest gritted his teeth and made his voice sound casual. "What happened to change your mind, buddy?"

"After you left the bar last night, Lenny gave me this long speech, man, about how much the truck cost, and how I don't gotta give no rides, nor pick up no hitchhikers, and how he's trustin' me, and stuff."

I can just imagine Lenny, shit-faced drunk and maudlin— he probably had you nearly in tears, Mario, you dumb son of a bitch.

"You know how it is, Ricky. This is an okay job—hard work and long hours, but the pay is pretty good. I don't want to lose this job."

"Hey, no problem," Priest said with forced lightness. "So long as you can still take me to San Antonio." *I'll think of something between here and there.*

Mario shook his head. "I better don't, not after what Lenny said. I ain't taking nobody nowhere in that truck. That's why I brought my own car here, so I can give you a ride back into town."

And what am I supposed to do now, for Christ's sake?

"So, uh, what do you say, you wanna get going?"

And then what?

Priest had built a castle of smoke, and now he saw it shimmer and dissipate in the light breeze of Mario's guilty conscience. He had spent two weeks in this hot, dusty desert, working at a stupid, worthless job, and had wasted hundreds of dollars on airfares and motel bills and disgusting fast food.

He did not have time to do it again.

The deadline was now only two weeks and one day away. Mario frowned. "Come on, man, let's go."

"I'm not going to give this place up," Star had said to Priest on the day the letter arrived. She sat next to him on a carpet of pine needles at the edge of the vineyard, during the midafternoon rest period, drinking cold water and eating raisins made from last year's grapes. "This is not just a wine farm, not just a valley, not just a commune—this is my whole life. We came here, all those years ago, because we believed that our parents had made a society that was twisted and corrupt and poisoned. And we were right, for Christ's sake!" Her face flushed as she let her passion show, and Priest thought how beautiful she was, still. "Just *look* at what's happened to the world outside," she said, raising her voice. "Violence and ugliness and pollution, presidents who tell lies and break the law, riots and crime and poverty. Meanwhile, we've lived here in peace and harmony, year after year, with no money, no sexual jealousy, no conformist rules. We said that all you need is love, and they called us naive, but we were *right* and they were *wrong*. We *know* we've found the way to live—we've *proved* it." Her voice had become very precise, betraying her old-money origins. Her father had come from a wealthy family but had spent his life as a doctor in a slum neighborhood. Star had inherited his idealism. "I'll do anything to save our home and our way of life," she went on. "I'll die for it, if our children can continue to live here." Her voice went quiet, but her words were clear, and she spoke with remorseless determination. "I'll kill for it, too," she said. "Do you understand me, Priest? *I will do anything.*"

* * *

"Are you listening to me?" Mario said. "You want a ride into town or not?"

"Sure," Priest said. *Sure, you lily-livered bastard, you yellow dog coward, you goddamn scum of the earth, I want a ride.*

Mario turned around.

Priest's eye fell on the Stillson wrench he had dropped a few minutes earlier.

A new plan unfolded, fully formed, in his brain.

As Mario walked the three paces to his car, Priest stooped and picked up the wrench.

It was about eighteen inches long and weighed four or five pounds. Most of the weight was at the business end, with its adjustable jaws for gripping massive hexagonal nuts. It was made of steel.

He glanced past Mario, along the track that led to the road. There was no one in sight.

No witnesses.

Priest took a step forward just as Mario reached to open the door of his pickup.

He had a sudden disconcerting flash: a photograph of a pretty young Mexican woman in a yellow dress, with a child in her arms and another by her side, and for a split second his resolve wavered as he felt the crushing weight of the grief he would bring into their lives.

Then he saw a worse vision: a pool of black water slowly rising to engulf a vineyard and drown the men, women, and children who were tending the vines.

He ran at Mario, raising the wrench high over his head.

Mario was opening the car door. He must have seen something out of the corner of his eye, for when Priest was almost on him he suddenly let out a roar of fear and flung the door wide, partly shielding himself.

Priest crashed into the door, which flew back at Mario. It was a wide, heavy door, and it knocked Mario sideways.

Both men stumbled. Mario lost his footing and went down on his knees, facing the side of the pickup. His Houston Astros baseball cap landed on the ground. Priest fell backward and sat heavily on the stony earth, dropping the wrench. It landed on a plastic half-gallon Coke bottle and bounced a yard away.

Mario gasped: "You crazy—" He got to one knee and reached for a handhold to pull his heavy body upright. His left hand closed around the door frame. As he heaved, Priest—still on his butt—drew back his leg and kicked the door as hard as he could with his heel. It slammed on Mario's fingers and bounced open. Mario cried out with pain and fell to one knee, slumping against the side of the pickup.

Priest leaped to his feet.

The wrench gleamed silvery in the morning sun. He snatched it up. He looked at Mario, and his heart filled with rage and hate toward the man who had wrecked his careful plan and put his way of life in jeopardy. He stepped close to Mario and raised the tool.

Mario half turned toward him. The expression on his young face showed infinite puzzlement, as if he had no understanding of what was happening. He opened his mouth and, as Priest brought the wrench down, he said in a questioning voice: "Ricky . . . ?"

The heavy end of the wrench made a sickening thud as it smashed into Mario's head. His dark hair was thick and glossy, but it made no perceptible difference. His scalp tore, his skull cracked, and the wrench sank into the soft brain underneath.

But he did not die.

Priest began to be afraid.

Mario's eyes stayed open and focused on Priest. The mystified, betrayed expression barely altered. He seemed to be trying to finish what he had started to say. He lifted one hand, as if to catch someone's attention.

Priest took a frightened step back. "No!" he said.

Mario said: "Man . . ."

Priest felt possessed by panic. He lifted the wrench again. "Die, you motherfucker!" he screamed, and he hit Mario again.

This time the wrench sank in farther. Withdrawing it was like pulling something out of soft mud. Priest felt a surge of nausea when he saw the living gray matter smeared on the adjustable jaws of the tool. His stomach churned and he swallowed hard, feeling dizzy.

Mario fell slowly backward and lay slumped against the rear tire, motionless. His arms became limp and his jaw slack, but he stayed alive. His eyes locked with Priest's. Blood gushed from his head and ran down his face and into the open neck of his checked shirt. His stare terrified Priest. "Die," Priest pleaded. "For the love of God, Mario, please die."

Nothing happened.

Priest backed off. Mario's eyes seemed to be begging him to finish the job, but he could not hit him again. There was no logic to it; he just could not lift the wrench.

Then Mario moved. His mouth opened, his body became rigid, and a strangled scream of agony burst from his throat.

It pushed Priest over the edge. He, too, screamed; then he ran at Mario and hit him again and again, in the same place, hardly seeing his victim through the haze of terror that blurred his eyesight.

The screaming stopped and the fit passed.

Priest stepped back, dropping the wrench on the ground.

The corpse of Mario fell slowly sideways until the mess that had been his head hit the ground. His gray brains seeped into the dry soil.

Priest fell to his knees and closed his eyes. "Dear God almighty, forgive me," he said.

He knelt there, shaking. He was afraid that if he opened his eyes, he might see Mario's soul going up.

To quiet his brain he recited his mantra: *"Ley, tor, pur-doy-kor . . ."* It had no meaning: that was why concentrating hard on it produced a soothing effect. It had the rhythm of a nursery rhyme he recalled from childhood:

> *One, two, three-four-five*
> *Once I caught a fish alive*
> *Six, seven, eight-nine-ten*
> *Then I let him go again*

When he was chanting to himself, he often slipped from the mantra into the rhyme. It worked just as well.

As the familiar syllables soothed him, he thought about the way his breath entered his nostrils, went through his nasal passages into the back of his mouth, passed along his throat, and descended into his chest, finally penetrating the farthest branches of his lungs, before retracing the entire journey in reverse: lungs, throat, mouth, nose, nostrils, and back out into the open air. When he concentrated fully on the journey of the breath, nothing else came into his head—no visions, no nightmares, no memories.

A few minutes later he stood up, his heart cold, his face set in a determined expression. He had purged himself of emotion: he felt no regret or pity. The murder was in the past, and Mario was just a piece of garbage that he had to dispose of.

He picked up his cowboy hat, brushed off the dirt, and put it on his head.

He found the pickup's tool kit behind the driving seat. He took a screwdriver and used it to detach the license plates, front and rear. He walked across the dump and buried them in a smoldering mass of garbage. Then he put the screwdriver back in the tool kit.

He bent over the body. With his right hand he grasped the belt of Mario's jeans. With his left he took a fistful of the checked shirt. He lifted the body off the ground. He grunted as his back took the strain: Mario was heavy.

The door of the pickup stood open. Priest swung Mario back and forth a couple of times, building up a rhythm, then with one big heave he threw the body into the cabin. It lay over the bench seat, with the heels of the boots sticking out of the open door and the head hanging into the footwell on the passenger side. Blood dripped from the head.

He threw the wrench in after the body.

He wanted to siphon gas out of the pickup's tank. For that he needed a long piece of narrow tubing.

He opened the hood, located the windshield washer fluid, and ripped out the flexible plastic pipe that led from the reservoir to the windshield nozzle. He picked up the half-gallon Coke bottle he had noticed earlier, then walked around to the side of the pickup and unscrewed the gas cap. He fed the tube into the fuel tank, sucked on it until he tasted gasoline, then inserted the end into the Coke bottle. Slowly it filled with gas.

Gas continued to spill on the ground while he walked to the door of the pickup and emptied the Coke bottle over the corpse of Mario.

He heard the sound of a car.

Priest looked at the dead body soaked in gasoline in the cab of the pickup. If someone came along right now, there was nothing he could say or do to conceal his guilt.

His rigid calm left him. He started to shake, the plastic bottle slipped from his fingers, and he crouched on the ground like a scared child. Trembling, he stared at the track that led to the road. Had an early riser come to get rid of an obsolete dishwasher, or the plastic playhouse the kids had grown out of, or the old-fashioned suits of a dead grandfather? The noise of the engine swelled as it came nearer, and Priest closed his eyes.

"Ley, tor, pur-doy-kor . . ."

The noise began to fade. The vehicle had passed the entrance and gone on down the road. It was just traffic.

He felt stupid. He stood up, regaining control. "Ley, tor, pur-doy-kor . . ."

But the scare made him hurry.

He filled the Coke bottle again and quickly doused the plastic bench seat and the entire interior of the cabin with gasoline. He used the remainder of the gas to lay a trail across the ground to the rear of the truck, then splashed the last of it onto the side near the fuel cap. He threw the bottle into the cabin and stepped back.

He noticed Mario's Houston Astros cap on the ground. He picked it up and threw it into the cab with the body.

He took a book of matches from his jeans, struck one, and used it to light all the others; then he threw the blazing matchbook into the cab of the pickup and swiftly backed away.

There was a *whoosh* of flame and a cloud of black smoke, and in a second the inside of the cabin was a furnace. A moment later the flames snaked across the ground to where the tube was still spilling gas from the tank. There was another explosion as the gas tank blew up, rocking the pickup on its wheels. The rear tires caught fire, and flames flickered around the oily chassis.

A disgusting smell filled the air, almost like roasting meat. Priest swallowed hard and stood farther back.

After a few seconds the blaze became less intense. The tires, the seats, and the body of Mario continued to burn slowly.

Priest waited a couple of minutes, watching the flames; then he ventured closer, trying to breathe shallowly to keep the stench out of his nose. He looked inside the cabin of the pickup. The corpse and the seating had congealed together into one vile black mass of ash and melted plastic. When it cooled down, the vehicle would be just another piece of junk that some kids had set fire to.

He knew he had not got rid of all traces of Mario. A

casual glance would reveal nothing, but if the cops ever examined the pickup, they would probably find Mario's belt buckle, the fillings from his teeth, and maybe his charred bones. Someday, Priest realized, Mario might come back to haunt him. But he had done all he could to conceal the evidence of his crime.

Now he had to steal the seismic vibrator.

He turned away from the burning body and started walking.

At the commune in Silver River Valley, there was an inner group called the Rice Eaters. There were seven of them, the remnants of those who had survived the desperate winter of 1972–73, when they had been isolated by a blizzard and had eaten nothing but brown rice boiled in melted snow for three straight weeks. On the day the letter came, the Rice Eaters stayed up late in the evening, sitting in the cookhouse, drinking wine and smoking marijuana.

Song, who had been a fifteen-year-old runaway in 1972, was playing an acoustic guitar, picking out a blues riff. Some of the group made guitars in the winter. They kept the ones they liked best, and Paul Beale took the rest to a shop in San Francisco, where they were sold for high prices. Star was singing along in a smoky, intimate contralto, making up words, "Ain't gonna ride that no-good train . . ." She had the sexiest voice in the world, always did.

Melanie sat with them, although she was not a Rice Eater, because Priest did not care to throw her out, and the others did not challenge Priest's decisions. She was crying silently, big tears streaming down her face. She kept saying: "I only just found you."

"We haven't given up," Priest told her. "There has to be a way to make the governor of California change his damn mind."

Oaktree, the carpenter, a muscular black man the same age as Priest, said in a musing tone: "You know, it ain't that hard to make a nuclear bomb." He had been in the marines, but had deserted after killing an officer during a training exercise, and he had been here ever since. "I could do it in a day, if I had some plutonium. We could blackmail the governor—if they don't do what we want, we threaten to blow Sacramento all to hell."

"No!" said Aneth. She was nursing a child. The boy was three years old: Priest thought it was time he was weaned, but Aneth felt he should be allowed to suckle as long as he wanted to. "You can't save the world with bombs."

Star stopped singing. "We're not trying to save the world. I gave that up in 1969, after the world's press turned the hippie movement into a joke. All I want now is to save *this,* what we have here, our life, so our children can grow up in peace and love."

Priest, who had already considered and rejected the idea of making a nuclear bomb, said: "It's getting the plutonium that's the hard part."

Aneth detached the child from her breast and patted his back. "Forget it," she said. "I won't have anything to do with that stuff. It's deadly!"

Star began to sing again. "Train, train, no-good train . . ."

Oaktree persisted. "I could get a job in a nuclear power plant, figure out a way to beat their security system."

Priest said: "They would ask you for your résumé. And what would you say you had been doing for the last twenty-five years? Nuclear research at Berkeley?"

"I'd say I been living with a bunch of freaks and now they need to blow up Sacramento, so I came here to get me some radio-friggin'-*activity*, man."

The others laughed. Oaktree sat back in his chair and began to harmonize with Star: "No, no, ain't gonna ride that no-good train . . ."

Priest frowned at the flippant air. He could not smile. His heart was full of rage. But he knew that inspired ideas sometimes came out of lighthearted discussions, so he let it run.

Aneth kissed the top of her child's head and said: "We could kidnap someone."

Priest said: "Who? The governor probably has six bodyguards."

"What about his right-hand man, that guy Albert Honeymoon?" There was a murmur of support: they all hated Honeymoon. "Or the president of Coastal Electric?"

Priest nodded. This could work.

He knew about stuff like that. It was a long time since he had been on the streets, but he remembered the rules of a rumble: Plan carefully, look cool, shock the mark so badly he can hardly think, act fast, and get the hell out. But something bothered him. "It's too . . . like, low-profile," he said. "Say some big shot gets kidnapped. So what? If you're going to scare people, you can't pussyfoot around, you have to scare them *shitless.*"

He restrained himself from saying more. *When you've got a guy on his knees, crying and pissing his pants and pleading with you, begging you not to hurt him anymore, that's when you say what you want; and he's so grateful, he loves you for telling him what he has to do to make the pain stop.* But that was the wrong kind of talk for someone like Aneth.

At this point, Melanie spoke again.

She was sitting on the floor with her back against Priest's chair. Aneth offered her the big joint that was going around. Melanie wiped her tears, took a long pull on the joint, and passed it up to Priest, then blew out a cloud of smoke and said: "You know, there are ten or fifteen places in California where the faults in the earth's crust are under such tremendous, like, *pressure* that it would only take a teeny little nudge, or something, to make the tectonic plates slip, and then, *boom!* It's like a giant slipping on a pebble. It's only a little pebble, but the giant is so big that his fall shakes the earth."

Oaktree stopped singing long enough to say: "Melanie, baby, what the fuck you talking about?"

"I'm talking about an earthquake," she said.

Oaktree laughed. "Ride, ride that no-good train . . ."

Priest did not laugh. Something told him this was important. He spoke with quiet intensity. "What are you saying, Melanie?"

"Forget kidnapping, forget nuclear bombs," she said. "Why don't we threaten the governor with an earthquake?"

"No one can cause an earthquake," Priest said. "It would take such an enormous amount of energy to make the earth move."

"That's where you're wrong. It might take only a small amount of energy, if the force was applied in just the right place."

Oaktree said: "How do you know all this stuff?"

"I studied it. I have a master's in seismology. I should be teaching in a university now. But I married my professor, and that was the end of my career. I was turned down for a doctorate."

Her tone was bitter. Priest had talked to her about this, and he knew she bore a deep grudge. Her husband had been on the university committee that turned her down. He had been obliged to withdraw from the meeting while her case was discussed, which seemed natural to Priest, but Melanie felt her husband should somehow have made sure of her success. Priest guessed that she had not been good enough to study at doctoral level—but she would believe anything rather than that. So he told her that the men on the committee were so terrified of her combination of beauty and brains that they conspired to bring her down. She loved him for letting her believe that.

Melanie went on: "My husband—soon to be my ex-husband—developed the stress-trigger theory of earthquakes. At certain points along the fault line, shear pressure builds up, over the decades, to a very high level. Then it takes only a relatively weak vibration in the earth's crust to dislodge the plates, release all that accumulated energy, and cause an earthquake."

Priest was captivated. He caught Star's eye. She nodded somberly. She believed in the unorthodox. It was an article of faith with her that the bizarre theory would turn out to be the truth, the unconventional way of life would be the happiest, and the madcap plan would succeed where sensible proposals foundered.

Priest studied Melanie's face. She had an otherworldly air. Her pale skin, startling green eyes, and red hair made her look like a beautiful alien. The first words he had spoken to her had been: "Are you from Mars?"

Did she know what she was talking about? She was stoned, but sometimes people had their most creative ideas while doping. He said: "If it's so easy, how come it hasn't already been done?"

"Oh, I didn't say it would be easy. You'd have to be a seismologist to know exactly where the fault was under critical pressure."

Priest's mind was racing now. When you were in real trouble, sometimes the way out was to do something so weird, so totally unexpected, that your enemy was paralyzed by surprise. He said to Melanie: "How would you cause a vibration in the earth's crust?"

"That would be the hard part," she said.

Ride, ride, ride . . .
I'm gonna ride that no-good train . . .

Walking back to the town of Shiloh, Priest found himself thinking obsessively about the killing: the way the wrench had sunk into Mario's soft brains, the look on the man's face, the blood dripping into the footwell.

This was no good. He had to stay calm and alert. He still did not have the seismic vibrator that was going to save the commune. Killing Mario had been the easy part, he told

himself. Next he had to pull the wool over Lenny's eyes.
But how?

He was jerked back to the immediate present by the sound
of a car.

It was coming from behind him, heading into town.

In these parts, no one walked. Most people would assume his car had broken down. Some would stop and offer
him a ride.

Priest tried to think of a reason why he would be walking
into town at six-thirty on Saturday morning.

Nothing came.

He tried to call on whatever god had inspired him with
the idea of murdering Mario, but the gods were silent.

There was nowhere he could be coming *from* within fifty
miles—except for the one place he could not speak of, the
dump where Mario's ashes lay on the seat of his burned-out
pickup.

The car slowed as it came nearer.

Priest resisted the temptation to pull his hat down over
his eyes.

What have I been doing?

—I went out into the desert to observe nature.

Yeah, sagebrush and rattlesnakes.

—My car broke down.

Where? I didn't see it.

—I went to take a leak.

This far?

Although the morning air was cool, he began to perspire.

The car passed him slowly. It was a late-model Dodge
Neon with a metallic green paint job and Texas plates.
There was one person inside, a man. He could see the driver
examining him in the mirror, checking him out. Could be an
off-duty cop—

Panic filled him, and he had to fight the impulse to turn
and run.

The car stopped and reversed. The driver lowered the

nearside window. He was a young Asian man in a business suit. He said: "Hey, buddy, want a ride?"

What am I going to say? "No, thanks, I just love to walk."

"I'm a little dusty," Priest said, looking down at his jeans. *I fell on my ass trying to kill a man.*

"Who isn't, in these parts?"

Priest got in the car. His hands were shaking. He fastened his seat belt, just to have something to do to disguise his anxiety.

As the car pulled away, the driver said: "What the heck you doing walking out here?"

I just murdered my friend Mario with a Stillson wrench.

At the last second, Priest thought of a story. "I had a fight with my wife," he said. "I stopped the car and got out and walked away. I didn't expect her to just drive on." He thanked whatever gods had given him inspiration again. His hands stopped shaking.

"Would that be a good-looking dark-haired woman in a blue Honda that I passed fifteen or twenty miles back?"

Jesus Christ, who are you, the Memory Man?

The guy smiled and said: "When you're crossing this desert, every car is interesting."

"No, that ain't her," Priest said. "My wife's driving my goddamn pickup truck."

"I didn't see a pickup."

"Good. Maybe she didn't go too far."

"She's probably parked down a farm track crying her eyes out, wishing she had you back."

Priest grinned with relief. The guy had bought his story.

The car reached the edge of town. "What about you?" Priest said. "How come you're up early on Saturday morning?"

"I didn't fight with my wife, I'm going home to her. I live in Laredo. I travel in novelty ceramics—decorative plates, figurines, signs saying 'Baby's Room,' very attractive stuff."

"Is that a fact?" *What a way to waste your life.*

"We sell them in drugstores, mostly."

"The drugstore in Shiloh won't be open yet."

"I'm not working today anyway. But I might stop for breakfast. Got a recommendation?"

Priest would have preferred the salesman to drive through town without stopping, so that he would have no chance to mention the bearded guy he had picked up near the dump. But he was sure to see Lazy Susan's as he drove along Main Street, so there was no point in lying. "There's a diner."

"How's the food?"

"Grits are good. It's right after the stoplight. You can let me out there."

A minute later the car pulled into a slantwise slot outside Susan's. Priest thanked the novelty salesman and got out. "Enjoy your breakfast," he called as he walked away. *And don't get into conversation with anyone local, for Christ's sake.*

A block from the diner was the local office of Ritkin Seismex, the small seismic exploration firm he had been working for. The office was a large trailer in a vacant lot. Mario's seismic vibrator was parked in the lot alongside Lenny's cranberry red Pontiac Grand Am.

Priest stopped and stared at the truck for a moment. It was a ten-wheeler, with big off-road tires like dinosaur armor. Underneath a layer of Texas dirt it was bright blue. He itched to jump in and drive it away. He looked at the mighty machinery on the back, the powerful engine and the massive steel plate, the tanks and hoses and valves and gauges. *I could have the thing started in a minute, no keys necessary.* But if he stole it now, every Highway Patrolman in Texas would be looking for him within a few minutes. He had to be patient. *I'm going to make the earth shake, and no one is going to stop me.*

He went into the trailer.

The office was busy. Two jug team supervisors stood over a computer as a color map of the area slowly emerged from the printer. Today they would collect their equipment from the field and begin to move it to Clovis. A surveyor was arguing on the phone in Spanish, and Lenny's secretary, Diana, was checking a list.

Priest stepped through an open door into the inner office. Lenny was drinking coffee with a phone to his ear. His eyes were bloodshot and his face blotchy after last night's drinking. He acknowledged Priest with a barely perceptible nod.

Priest stood by the door, waiting for Lenny to finish. His heart was in his mouth. He knew roughly what he was going to say. But would Lenny take the bait? Everything depended on it.

After a minute, Lenny hung up the phone and said: "Hey, Ricky—you seen Mario this mornin'?" His tone was annoyed. "He should've left here a half hour ago."

"Yeah, I seen him," Priest said. "I hate to bring you bad news this friggin' early, but he's let you down."

"What are you talking about?"

Priest told the story that had come into his mind, in a flash of inspiration, just before he picked up the wrench and went after Mario. "He was missing his wife and kids so bad, he got into his old pickup and left town."

"Aw, shit, that's great. How did you find out?"

"He passed me on the street, early this morning, headed for El Paso."

"Why the hell didn't he call me?"

"Too embarrassed about letting you down."

"Well, I just hope he keeps going across the border and doesn't stop until he drives into the goddamn ocean." Lenny rubbed his eyes with his knuckles.

Priest began to improvise. "Listen, Lenny, he's got a young family, don't be too hard on him."

"Hard? Are you serious? He's history."

"He really needs this job."

"And I need someone to drive his rig all the damn way to New Mexico."

"He's saving up to buy a house with a pool."

Lenny became sarcastic. "Knock it off, Ricky, you're making me cry."

"Try this." Priest swallowed and tried to sound casual. "I'll drive the damn truck to Clovis if you promise to give Mario his job back." He held his breath.

Lenny stared at Priest without saying anything.

"Mario ain't a bad guy, you know that," Priest went on. *Don't gabble, you sound nervous, try to seem relaxed!*

Lenny said: "You have a commercial driver's license, class B?"

"Since I was twenty-one years old." Priest took out his billfold, extracted the license, and tossed it on the desk. It was a forgery. Star had one just like it. Hers was a forgery, too. Paul Beale knew where to get such things.

Lenny checked it, then looked up and said suspiciously: "So, what are you after? I thought you didn't want to go to New Mexico."

Don't screw around, Lenny, tell me yes or no! "Suddenly I could use another five hundred bucks."

"I don't know. . . ."

You son of a bitch, I killed a man for this, come on!

"Would you do it for two hundred?"

Yes! Thank you! Thank you! He pretended to hesitate. "Two hundred is low for three days' work."

"It's two days, maybe two and a half. I'll give you two fifty."

Anything! Just give me the keys! "Listen, I'm going to do it anyway, whatever you pay me, because Mario's a nice kid and I want to help him. So just pay me whatever you genuinely think the job's worth."

"All right, you sly mother, three hundred."

"You got a deal." *And I've got a seismic vibrator.*

Lenny said: "Hey, thanks for helping me out. I sure appreciate it."

Priest tried not to beam triumphantly. "You bet."

Lenny opened a drawer, took out a sheet of paper, and tossed it over the desk. "Just fill out this form for insurance."

Priest froze.

He could not read or write.

He stared at the form in fear.

Lenny said impatiently: "Come on, take it, for Christ's sake, it ain't a rattlesnake."

I can't understand it, I'm sorry, those squiggles and lines on the paper just jump and dance, and I can't make them keep still!

Lenny looked at the wall and spoke to an invisible audience. "A minute ago I would of swore the man was wide awake."

Ley, tor, pur-doy-kor . . .

Priest reached out slowly and took the form.

Lenny said: "Now, what was so hard about that?"

Priest said: "Uh, I was just thinking about Mario. Do you suppose he's okay?"

"Forget him. Fill out the form and get going. I want to see that truck in Clovis."

"Yeah." Priest stood up. "I'll do it outside."

"Right, let me get to my other fifty-seven friggin' problems."

Priest walked out of Lenny's room into the main office.

You've had this scene a hundred times before, just calm down, you know how to deal with it.

He stopped outside Lenny's door. Nobody noticed him; they were all busy.

He looked at the form. *The big letters stick up, like trees among the bushes. If they're sticking down, you got the form upside-down.*

He had the form upside-down. He turned it around.

Sometimes there was a big X, printed very heavy, or

written in pencil or red ink, to show you where to put your
name; but this form did not have that easy-to-spot mark.
Priest could write his name, sort of. It took him a while, and
he knew it was kind of a scrawl, but he could do it.

However, he could not write anything else.

As a kid he was so smart he did not need to read and
write. He could add up in his head faster than anyone, even
though he could not read figures on paper. His memory was
infallible. He could always get people to do what he wanted
without writing anything down. In school he managed to
find ways to avoid reading aloud. When there was a writing
assignment he might get another kid to do it for him, but if
that failed, he had a thousand excuses, and the teachers
eventually shrugged and said that if a child really did not
want to work, they could not force him. He got a reputation
for laziness, and when he saw a crisis approaching he would
play hooky.

Later on, he had managed to run a thriving liquor whole-
saling business. He never wrote a letter but did everything
on the phone and in person. He kept dozens of phone numbers in his head until he could afford a secretary to place
calls for him. He knew exactly how much money was in the
till and how much in the bank. If a salesman presented him
with an order form, he would say: "I'll tell you what I need
and you fill out the form." He had an accountant and a
lawyer to deal with the government. He had made a million
dollars at the age of twenty-one. He had lost it all by the
time he met Star and joined the commune—not because he
was illiterate, but because he defrauded his customers and
failed to pay his taxes and borrowed money from the Mob.

Getting an insurance form filled out had to be easy.

He sat down in front of Lenny's secretary's desk and smiled
at Diana. "You look tired this morning, honey," he said.

She sighed. She was a plump blonde in her thirties, married to a roustabout, with three teenage kids. She was quick
to rebuff crude advances from the men who came into the

trailer, but Priest knew she was susceptible to polite charm. "Ricky, I got so much to do this morning, I wish I had two brains."

He put on a crestfallen look. "That's bad news—I was going to ask you to help me with something."

She hesitated, then smiled ruefully. "What is it?"

"My handwriting's so poor, I wanted you to fill out this form for me. I sure hate to trouble you when you're so busy."

"Well, I'll make a deal with you." She pointed to a neat stack of carefully labeled cardboard boxes up against the wall. "I'll help you with the form if you'll put all those files in the green Chevy Astro Van outside."

"You got it," Priest said gratefully. He gave her the form.

She looked at it. "You going to drive the seismic vibrator?"

"Yeah, Mario got homesick and went to El Paso."

She frowned. "That's not like him."

"It sure ain't. I hope he's okay."

She shrugged and picked up her pen. "Now, first we need your full name and date and place of birth."

Priest gave her the information, and she filled out the blanks on the form. It was easy. Why had he panicked? It was just that he had not expected the form. Lenny had surprised him, and for a moment he had given way to fear.

He was experienced at concealing his disability. He even used libraries. That was how he had found out about seismic vibrators. He had gone to the central library on I Street in downtown Sacramento—a big, busy place where his face probably would not be remembered. At the reception desk he had learned that science was up on the second floor. There, he had suffered a stab of anxiety when he looked at the long aisles of bookshelves and the rows of people sitting at computer screens. Then he had caught the eye of a friendly-looking woman librarian about his own age. "I'm looking for information on seismic exploration," he had said with a warm smile. "Could you help me?"

She had taken him to the right shelf, picked out a book,

and with a little encouragement found the relevant chapter. "I'm interested in how they generate the shock waves," he had explained. "I wonder if this book has that information.".

She had leafed through the pages with him. "There seem to be three ways," she had said. "An underground explosion, a weight drop, or a seismic vibrator."

"Seismic vibrator?" he had said with just the hint of a twinkle in his eye. "What's that?"

She had pointed to a photograph. Priest had stared, fascinated. The librarian had said: "It looks pretty much like a truck."

To Priest it had looked like a miracle.

"Can I photocopy some of these pages?" he had asked.

"Sure."

If you were smart enough, there was always a way to get someone else to do the reading and writing.

Diana finished the form, drew a big X next to a dotted line, handed the paper to him, and said: "You sign here."

He took her pen and wrote laboriously. The "R" for Richard was like a showgirl with a big bust kicking out one leg. Then the "G" for Granger was like a billhook with a big round blade and a short handle. After "RG" he just did a wavy line like a snake. It was not pretty, but people accepted it. A lot of folk signed their names with a scrawl, he had learned: signatures did not have to be written clearly, thank God.

This was why his forged license had to be in his own name: it was the only one he could write.

He looked up. Diana was watching him curiously, surprised at how slowly he wrote. When she caught his eye, she reddened and looked away.

He gave her back the form. "Thanks for your help, Diana, I sure appreciate it."

"You're welcome. I'll get you the keys to the truck as soon as Lenny gets off the phone." The keys were kept in the boss's office.

Priest remembered that he had promised to move the

boxes for her. He picked one up and took it outside. The green van stood in the yard with its rear door open. He loaded the box and went back for another.

Each time he came back in, he checked her desk. The form was still there, and no keys were visible.

After he had loaded all the boxes, he sat in front of her again. She was on the phone, talking to someone about motel reservations in Clovis.

Priest ground his teeth. He was almost there, he nearly had the keys in his hand, and he was listening to crap about motel rooms! He forced himself to sit still.

At last she hung up. "I'll ask Lenny for those keys," she said. She took the form into the inner office.

A fat bulldozer driver called Chew came in. The trailer shook with the impact of his work boots on the floor. "Hey, Ricky," he said, "I didn't know you were married." He laughed. The other men in the office looked up, interested.

Shit, what's this? Priest said: "Now, where did you hear a thing like that?"

"Saw you get out of a car outside Susan's a while back. Then I had breakfast with the salesman that gave you a ride."

Damn, what did he tell you?

Diana emerged from Lenny's office with a key ring in her hand. Priest wanted to snatch it from her, but he pretended to be more interested in talking to Chew.

Chew went on: "You know, Susan's western omelet is really something." He lifted his leg and farted, then looked up and saw the secretary standing in the doorway, listening. " 'Scuse me, Diana. Anyhow, this youngster was saying how he picked you up out near the dump."

Hell!

"You were walking in the desert alone at six-thirty, on account of how you quarreled with your wife and stopped the car and got out." Chew looked around at the other men, making sure he had their attention. "Then she up and drove off and left you there!" He grinned broadly, and the others laughed.

Priest stood up. He did not want people remembering that he was out near the dump on the day Mario disappeared. He needed to kill this talk dead. He put on a hurt look. "Well, Chew, I'm going to tell you something. If I ever happen to learn anything about your private affairs, specially something a little embarrassing, I promise I won't shout about it all over the office. Now, what do you think of that?"

Chew said: "Ain't no call to get sensitive."

The other men looked shamefaced. No one wanted to talk about this anymore.

There was an awkward silence. Priest did not want to exit in a bad atmosphere, so he said: "Hell, Chew, no hard feelings."

Chew shrugged. "No offense intended, Ricky."

The tension eased.

Diana handed Priest the keys to the seismic vibrator.

He closed his fist over the bunch. "Thank you," he said, trying to keep the elation out of his voice. He could hardly wait to get out of there and sit behind the wheel. "Bye, everyone. See you in New Mexico."

"You drive safely, now, you hear?" Diana said as he reached the door.

"Oh, I'll do that," Priest replied. "You can count on it."

He stepped outside. The sun was up, and the day was getting warmer. He resisted the temptation to do a victory dance around the truck. He climbed in and turned over the engine. He checked the gauges. Mario must have filled the tank last night. The truck was ready for the road.

He could not keep the grin off his face as he pulled out of the yard.

He drove out of town, moving up through the gears, and headed north, following the route Star had taken in the Honda.

As he approached the turnoff for the dump, he began to feel strange. He imagined Mario at the side of the road, with gray brains seeping out of the hole in his head. It was a stupid, superstitious thought, but he could not shake it. His stomach churned. For a moment he felt weak, too weak to drive. Then he pulled himself together.

Mario was not the first man he had killed.

Jack Kassner had been a cop, and he had robbed Priest's mother.

Priest's mother had been a whore. She had been only thirteen years old when she gave birth to him. By the time Ricky was fifteen, she was working with three other women out of an apartment over a dirty bookstore on Seventh Street in the skid row neighborhood of downtown Los Angeles. Jack Kassner was a vice squad detective who came once a month for his shakedown money. He usually took a free blow job at the same time. One day he saw Priest's mother getting the bribe money out of the box in the back room. That night the vice squad raided the apartment, and Kassner stole fifteen hundred dollars, which was a lot of money in the sixties. Priest's mother did not mind doing a few days in the slammer, but she was heartbroken to lose all the money she had saved. Kassner told the women that if they complained, he would slap them with drug-trafficking charges and they would all go down for a couple of years.

Kassner thought he was in no danger from three B-girls and a kid. But the next evening, as he stood in the men's room of the Blue Light bar on Broadway, pissing away a few beers, little Ricky Granger stuck a razor-sharp six-inch knife in his back, easily slicing through the black mohair suit jacket and the white nylon shirt and penetrating the kidney. Kassner was in so much pain, he never got his hand on his gun. Ricky stabbed him several more times, quickly, as the cop lay on the wet concrete floor of the men's room, vomiting blood; then he rinsed his blade under the tap and walked out.

Looking back, Priest marveled at the cool assurance of his fifteen-year-old self. It had taken only fifteen or twenty seconds, but during that time anyone might have stepped into the room. However, he had felt no fear, no shame, no guilt.

But after that he had been afraid of the dark.

He was not in the dark very much in those days. The lights usually stayed on all night in his mother's apartment. But sometimes he would wake up a little before dawn on a slow night, like a Monday, and find that everyone was asleep and the lights were out; and then he would be possessed by blind, irrational terror and would blunder around the room, bumping into furry creatures and touching strange clammy surfaces, until he found the light switch and sat on the edge of the bed, panting and perspiring, slowly recovering as he realized that the clammy surface was the mirror and the furry creature his fleece-lined jacket.

He had been afraid of the dark until he found Star.

He recalled a song that had been a hit the year he met her, and he began to sing: "Smoke on the water . . ." The band was Deep Purple, he recalled. Everyone was playing their album that summer.

It was a good apocalyptic song to sing at the wheel of a seismic vibrator.

Smoke on the water
A fire in the sky

He passed the entrance to the dump and drove on, heading north.

"We'll do it tonight," Priest had said. "We'll tell the governor there'll be an earthquake four weeks from today."

Star was dubious. "We're not even sure this is possible. Maybe we should do everything else first, get all our ducks lined up in a row, *then* issue the ultimatum."

"Hell, no!" Priest said. The suggestion angered him. He knew that the group had to be led. He needed to get them committed. They had to go out on a limb, take a risk, and feel there was no turning back. Otherwise tomorrow they would think of reasons to get scared and back out.

They were fired up now. The letter had arrived today, and they were all angry and desperate. Star was grimly determined; Melanie was in a fury; Oaktree was ready to declare war; Paul Beale was reverting to his street hoodlum type. Song had hardly spoken, but she was the helpless child of the group and would go along with the others. Only Aneth was opposed, and her opposition would be feeble because she was a weak person. She would be quick to raise objections, but she would back down even faster.

Priest himself knew with cold certainty that if this place ceased to exist, his life would be over.

Now Aneth said: "But an earthquake might kill people."

Priest said: "I'll tell you how I figure this will pan out. I guess we'll have to cause a small, harmless tremor, out in the desert somewhere, just to prove we can do what we say. Then, when we threaten a second earthquake, the governor will negotiate."

Aneth turned her attention back to her child.

Oaktree said: "I'm with Priest. Do it tonight."

Star gave in. "How should we make the threat?"

"An anonymous phone call or letter, I guess," Priest said. "But it has to be impossible to trace."

Melanie said: "We could post it on an Internet bulletin board. If we used my laptop and mobile phone, no one could possibly trace it."

Priest had never seen a computer until Melanie arrived. He threw a questioning glance at Paul Beale, who knew all about such things. Paul nodded and said: "Good idea."

"All right," Priest said. "Get your stuff."

Melanie went off.

"How will we sign the message?" Star said. "We need a name."

Song said: "Something that symbolizes a peace-loving group who have been driven to take extreme measures."

"I know," Priest said. "We'll call ourselves the Hammer of Eden."

It was just before midnight on the first of May.

Priest became tense as he reached the outskirts of San Antonio. In the original plan, Mario would have driven the truck as far as the airport. But now Priest was alone as he entered the maze of freeways that encircled the city, and he began to sweat.

There was no way he could read a map.

When he had to drive an unfamiliar road, he always took Star with him to navigate. She and the other Rice Eaters knew he could not read. The last time he drove alone on strange roads had been in the late autumn of 1972, when he fled from Los Angeles and finished up, by accident, at the commune in Silver River Valley. He had not cared where he went then. In fact, he would have been happy to die. But now he wanted to live.

Even road signs were difficult for him. If he stopped and concentrated for a while, he could tell the difference between "East" and "West" or "North" and "South." Despite his remarkable ability to calculate in his head, he could not read numbers without staring hard and thinking long. With an effort, he could recognize signs for Route 10: a stick with a circle. But there was a lot of other stuff on road signs that meant nothing to him and confused the picture.

He tried to stay calm, but it was difficult. He liked to be in control. He was maddened by the sense of helplessness and bewilderment that came over him when he lost his way. He knew by the sun which way was north. When he felt he might be going wrong, he pulled into the next gas station or shopping mall and asked for directions. He hated doing it, for people noticed the seismic vibrator—it was a big rig, and the machinery on the back looked kind of intriguing—

and there was a danger he would be remembered. But he had to take the risk.

And the directions were not always helpful. Gas station attendants would say things like "Yeah, easy, just follow Corpus Christi Highway until you see a sign for Brooks Air Force Base."

Priest just forced himself to remain calm, keep asking questions, and hide his frustration and anxiety. He played the part of a friendly but stupid truck driver, the kind of person who would be forgotten by the next day. And eventually he got out of San Antonio on the right road, sending up prayers of thanks to whatever gods might be listening.

A few minutes later, passing through a small town, he was relieved to see the blue Honda parked at a McDonald's restaurant.

He hugged Star gratefully. "What the hell happened?" she said worriedly. "I expected you a couple of hours ago!"

He decided not to tell her he had killed Mario. "I got lost in San Antonio," he said.

"I was afraid of that. When I came through I was surprised how complicated the freeway system was."

"I guess it's not half as bad as San Francisco, but I know San Francisco."

"Well, you're here now. Let's order coffee and get you calmed down."

Priest bought a beanburger and got a free plastic clown, which he put carefully in his pocket for his six-year-old son, Smiler.

When they drove on, Star took the wheel of the truck. They planned to drive nonstop all the way to California. It would take at least two days and nights, maybe more. One would sleep while the other drove. They had some amphetamines to combat drowsiness.

They left the Honda in the McDonald's lot. As they pulled away, Star handed Priest a paper bag, saying: "I got you a present."

Inside was a pair of scissors and a battery-powered electric shaver.

"Now you can get rid of that damn beard," she said.

He grinned. He turned the rearview mirror toward himself and started to cut. His hair grew fast and thick, and the bushy beard and mustache had made him round faced. Now his own face gradually reemerged. With the scissors he trimmed the hair down to a stubble, then he used the shaver to finish the job. Finally he took off his cowboy hat and undid his plait.

He threw the hat out the window and looked at his reflection. His hair was pushed back from a high forehead and fell in waves around a gaunt face. He had a nose like a blade and hollow cheeks, but he had a sensual mouth—many women had told him that. However, it was his eyes they usually talked about. They were dark brown, almost black, and people said they had a forceful, staring quality that could be mesmerizing. Priest knew it was not the eyes themselves, but the intensity of the look that could captivate a woman: he gave her the feeling that he was concentrating powerfully on her and nothing else. He could do it to men, too. He practiced the Look now, in the mirror.

"Handsome devil," Star said—laughing at him, but in a nice way, affectionate.

"Smart, too," Priest said.

"I guess you are. You got us this machine, anyway."

Priest nodded. "And you ain't seen nothing yet."

2

In the Federal Building at 450 Golden Gate Avenue in San Francisco, early on Monday morning, FBI agent Judy Maddox sat in a courtroom on the fifteenth floor, waiting.

The court was furnished in blond wood. New courtrooms always were. They generally had no windows, so the architects tried to make them brighter by using light colors. That was her theory. She spent a lot of time waiting in courtrooms. Most law enforcement personnel did.

She was worried. In court she was often worried. Months of work, sometimes years, went into preparing a case, but there was no telling how it would go once it got to court. The defense might be inspired or incompetent, the judge a sharp-eyed sage or a senile old fool, the jury a group of intelligent, responsible citizens or a bunch of lowlife jerks who ought to be behind bars themselves.

Four men were on trial today: John Parton, Ernest "Taxman" Dias, Foong Lee, and Foong Ho. The Foong brothers were the big-time crooks, the other two their executives. In cooperation with a Hong Kong triad, they had set up a network for laundering money from the Northern California dope industry. It had taken Judy a year to figure out how they were doing it and another year to prove it.

She had one big advantage when going after Asian crooks: she looked Oriental. Her father was a green-eyed Irishman, but she took more after her late mother, who had been Vietnamese. Judy was slender and dark haired, with an upward slant to her eyes. The middle-aged Chinese gangsters she had been investigating had never suspected that this pretty little half-Asian girl was a hotshot FBI agent.

She was working with an assistant U.S. attorney whom she knew unusually well. His name was Don Riley, and until a year ago they had been living together. He was her age, thirty-six, and he was experienced, energetic, and as smart as a whip.

She had thought they had a watertight case. But the accused men had hired the top criminal law firm in the city and put together a clever, vigorous defense. Their lawyers had undermined the credibility of witnesses who were, inevitably, from the criminal milieu themselves; and they had exploited the documentary evidence amassed by Judy to confuse and bewilder the jury.

Now neither Judy nor Don could guess which way it would go.

Judy had a special reason to be worried about this case. Her immediate boss, the supervisor of the Asian Organized Crime squad, was about to retire, and she had applied for the job. The overall head of the San Francisco office, the special agent in charge, or SAC, would support her application, she knew. But she had a rival: Marvin Hayes, another high-flying agent in her age group. And Marvin also had powerful support: his best friend was the assistant special agent in charge responsible for all the organized crime and white-collar crime squads.

Promotions were granted by a career board, but the opinions of the SAC and ASACs carried a lot of weight. Right now the contest between Judy and Marvin Hayes was close.

She wanted that job. She wanted to rise far and fast in the FBI. She was a good agent, she would be an outstanding supervisor, and one of these days she would be the best SAC the bureau had ever had. She was proud of the FBI, but she knew she could make it better: with faster introduction of new techniques like profiling through the use of stream-lined management systems and—most of all—by getting rid of agents like Marvin Hayes.

Hayes was the old-fashioned type of law enforcement officer: lazy, brutal, and unscrupulous. He had not put as many bad guys in jail as Judy, but he had made more high-profile arrests. He was good at insinuating himself into a glamorous investigation and quick to distance himself from a case that was going south.

The SAC had hinted to Judy that she would get the job, rather than Marvin, if she won her case today.

In court with Judy were most of the team on the Foong case: her supervisor, the other agents who had worked with her, a linguist, the squad secretary, and two San Francisco Police Department detectives. To her surprise, neither the ASAC nor the SAC was there. This was a big case, and the result was important to both of them. She felt a twinge of unease. She wondered if something was going on at the office that she did not know about. She decided to step out-side and call. But before she got to the door, the clerk of the court entered and announced that the jury was about to return. She sat down again.

A moment later Don came back in, smelling of ciga-rettes: he had started smoking again since they split. He gave her shoulder an encouraging squeeze. She smiled at him. He looked nice, with his neat short haircut, dark blue suit, white button-down shirt, and dark red Armani tie. But there was no chemistry, no zing: she no longer wanted to muss his hair and undo his tie and slide her hand inside the white shirt.

The defense lawyers returned, the accused men were walked into the dock, the jury entered, and at last the judge emerged from his chambers and took his seat.

Judy crossed her fingers under the table.

The clerk stood up. "Members of the jury, have you reached a verdict?"

Absolute silence descended. Judy realized she was tapping her foot. She stopped.

The foreman, a Chinese shopkeeper, stood up. Judy had spent many hours wondering whether he would sympathize with the accused, because two of them were Chinese, or hate them for dishonoring the race. In a quiet voice he said: "We have."

"And how do you find the accused—guilty or not guilty?"

"Guilty as charged."

There was a second of silence as the news sank in. Behind her, Judy heard a groan from the dock. She resisted the impulse to whoop with joy. She looked at Don, who was smiling broadly at her. The expensive defense lawyers shuffled papers and avoided each other's eyes. Two reporters got up and left hastily, heading for the phones.

The judge, a thin, sour-faced man of around fifty, thanked the jury and adjourned the case for sentencing in a week's time.

I did it, Judy thought. I won the case, I put the bad guys in jail, and my promotion is in the bag. Supervising Special Agent Judy Maddox, only thirty-six, a rising star.

"All stand," the clerk said.

The judge went out.

Don hugged Judy.

"You did a great job," she told him. "Thanks."

"You gave me a great case," he said.

She could tell he wanted to kiss her, so she stepped back a pace. "Well, we both did good," she said.

She turned to her colleagues and went around them all, shaking hands and hugging and thanking them for their work. Then the defense lawyers came over. The senior of the two was David Fielding, a partner in the firm of Brooks Fielding. He was a distinguished-looking man of about sixty. "Congratulations, Ms. Maddox, on a well-deserved win," he said.

"Thank you," she said. "It was closer than I expected. I thought I had it buttoned up until you got started."

He acknowledged the compliment with a tilt of his well-groomed head. "Your preparation was immaculate. Were you trained as a lawyer?"

"I went to Stanford Law School."

"I thought you must have a law degree. Well, if you ever get tired of the FBI, please come and see me. With my firm you could be earning three times your present salary in less than a year."

She was flattered, but she also felt condescended to, so her reply was sharp. "That's a nice offer, but I want to put bad guys in jail, not keep them out."

"I admire your idealism," he said smoothly, and turned to speak to Don.

Judy realized she had been waspish. It was a fault of hers, she knew. But what the hell, she did not want a job with Brooks Fielding.

She picked up her briefcase. She was eager to share her victory with the SAC. The San Francisco field office of the FBI was in the same building as the court, on two lower floors. As she turned to leave, Don grabbed her arm. "Have dinner with me?" he said. "We ought to celebrate."

She did not have a date. "Sure."

"I'll make a reservation and call you."

As she left the room, she remembered the feeling she had had earlier, that he wanted to kiss her; and she wished she had invented an excuse.

As she entered the lobby of the FBI office she wondered again why the SAC and the ASAC had not come to court for the verdict. There was no sign of unusual activity here. The carpeted corridors were quiet. The robot mailman, a motorized cart, hummed from door to door on its predetermined route. For a law enforcement agency, they had fancy premises. The difference between the FBI and a police precinct house was like the difference between corporate headquarters and the factory floor.

She headed for the SAC's office. Milton Lestrange had always had a soft spot for her. He had been an early supporter of women agents, who now numbered ten percent of agents. Some SACs barked orders like army generals, but Milt was always calm and courteous.

As soon as she entered his outer office she knew something was wrong. His secretary had obviously been crying. Judy said: "Linda, are you okay?" The secretary, a middle-aged woman who was normally coldly efficient, burst into tears. Judy went to comfort her, but Linda waved her away and pointed to the door of the inner office.

Judy went in.

It was a large room, expensively furnished, with a big desk and a polished conference table. Sitting behind Lestrange's desk, with his jacket off and his tie loosened, was ASAC Brian Kincaid, a big, barrel-chested man with thick white hair. He looked up and said: "Come in, Judy."

"What the hell is going on?" she said. "Where's Milt?"

"I have bad news," he said, though he did not look too sad. "Milt is in the hospital. He's been diagnosed with pancreatic cancer."

"Oh, my God." Judy sat down.

Lestrange had gone to the hospital yesterday—for a routine checkup, he had said, but he must have known there was something wrong.

Kincaid went on: "He'll be having an operation, some kind of intestinal bypass, and he won't be back here for a while, at best."

"Poor Milt!" Judy was shocked. He had seemed like a man at his peak: fit, vigorous, a good boss. Now he had been diagnosed with a deadly illness. She wanted to do something to comfort him, but she felt helpless. "I guess Jessica's with him," she said. Jessica was Milt's second wife.

"Yes, and his brother's flying up from Los Angeles today. Here in the office—"

"What about his first wife?"

Kincaid looked irritated. "I don't know about her. I talked to Jessica."

"Someone should tell her. I'll see if I can get a number for her."

"Whatever." Kincaid was impatient to get off the personal stuff and talk about work. "Here in the office, there are some changes, inevitably. I've been made acting SAC in Milt's absence."

Judy's heart sank. "Congratulations," she said, trying for a neutral tone.

"I'm moving you to the Domestic Terrorism desk."

At first Judy was just puzzled. "What for?"

"I think you'll do well there." He picked up the phone and spoke to Linda. "Ask Matt Peters to come in and see me right away." Peters was supervisor of the DT squad.

"But I just won my case," Judy said indignantly. "I put the Foong brothers in jail today!"

"Well done. That doesn't change my decision."

"Wait a minute. You know I've applied for the job of supervisor in the Asian Organized Crime squad. If I get moved off the squad now, it's going to look like I had some kind of problem."

"I think you need to broaden your experience."

"And *I* think *you* want Marvin to get the Asian desk."

"You're right. I believe Marvin is the best person for that job."

What a jerk, Judy thought furiously. He gets made boss and the first thing he does is use his new power to promote a buddy. "You can't do this," she said. "We have Equal Employment Opportunity rules."

"Go ahead, make a complaint," Kincaid said. "Marvin is better qualified than you."

"I've put a hell of a lot more bad guys in jail."

Kincaid gave her a complacent smile and played his trump card. "But he's spent two years at headquarters in Washington."

He was right, Judy thought despairingly. She had never worked at FBI headquarters. And although it was not an absolute requirement, headquarters experience was thought desirable in a supervisor. So there was no point in her making an Equal Employment Opportunity complaint. Everyone knew she was the better agent, but Marvin looked better on paper.

Judy fought back tears. She had worked her socks off for two years and scored a major victory against organized crime, and now she was being cheated of her reward by this creep.

Matt Peters came in. He was a stocky guy of about forty-five, bald, wearing a short-sleeved shirt and a tie. Like Marvin Hayes, he was close to Kincaid. Judy began to feel surrounded.

"Congratulations on winning your case," Peters said to Judy. "I'll be glad to have you on my squad."

"Thank you." Judy could not think what else to say.

Kincaid said: "Matt has a new assignment for you."

Peters had a file under his arm, and now he handed it to Judy. "The governor has received a terrorist threat from a group calling itself the Hammer of Eden."

Judy opened the file, but she could hardly make out the words. She was shaking with anger and an overwhelming sense of futility. To cover her emotions she tried to talk about the case. "What are they demanding?"

"A freeze on the building of new power plants in California."

"Nuclear plants?"

"Any kind. They gave us four weeks to comply. They say they're the radical offshoot of the Green California Campaign."

Judy tried to concentrate. Green California was a legitimate environmental pressure group based in San Francisco. It was hard to believe they would do something like this. But all such organizations were capable of attracting nutcases. "And what's the threat?"

"An earthquake."

She looked up from the file. "You're putting me on."

Matt shook his bald head.

Because she was angry and upset, she did not bother to sweeten her words. "This is stupid," she said bluntly. "No one can *cause* an earthquake. They might as well threaten us with three feet of snow."

He shrugged. "Check it out."

Judy knew that high-profile politicians received threats every day. Messages from crazies were not investigated by the FBI unless there was something special about them. "How was this threat communicated?"

"It appeared on an Internet bulletin board on the first of May. It's all in the file."

She looked him in the eye. She was in no mood to take any crap. "There's something you're not telling me. This threat has no credibility whatsoever." She looked at her watch. "Today is the twenty-fifth. We've ignored the message for three and a half weeks. Now, suddenly, with four days left to the deadline, we're worried?"

"John Truth saw the bulletin board—surfing the Net, I guess. Maybe he was desperate for a hot new topic. Anyway, he talked about the threat on his show Friday night, and he got a lot of calls."

"I get it." John Truth was a controversial talk radio host. His show came out of San Francisco, but it was syndicated live on stations all over California. Judy became even angrier. "John Truth pressured the governor to do something about the terrorist message. The governor responded by calling in the FBI to investigate. So we have to go through the motions of an investigation that no one really believes in."

"That's about it."

Judy took a deep breath. She addressed Kincaid, not Peters, because she knew this was his doing. "This office has been trying to nail the Foong brothers for twenty years. Today I put them in jail." She raised her voice. "And now you give me a bullshit case like this?"

Kincaid looked pleased with himself. "If you want to be in the Bureau, you'll have to learn to take the rough with the smooth."

"I learned, Brian!"

"Don't yell."

"I learned," she repeated in a lower voice. "Ten years ago, when I was new and inexperienced and my supervisor didn't know how far he could rely on me, I was given assignments like this—and I took them cheerfully, and did them conscientiously, and proved that I goddamn well deserve to be trusted with real work!"

"Ten years is nothing," Kincaid said. "I've been here twenty-five."

She tried reasoning with him. "Look, you've just been put in charge of this office. Your first act is to give one of your best agents a job that should have gone to a rookie. Everyone will know what you've done. People will think you've got some kind of grudge."

"You're right, I just got this job. And you're already telling me how to do it. Get back to work, Maddox."

She stared at him. Surely he would not just dismiss her.

He said: "This meeting is over."

Judy could not take it. Her rage boiled over.

"It's not just this meeting that's over," she said. She stood up. "Fuck you, Kincaid."

A look of astonishment came over his face.

Judy said: "I quit."

And then she walked out.

"You said that?" Judy's father said.

"Yeah. I knew you'd disapprove."

"You were right about that, anyway."

They were sitting in the kitchen, drinking green tea. Judy's father was a detective with the San Francisco police. He did a lot of undercover work. He was a powerfully built man, very fit for his age, with bright green eyes and gray hair in a ponytail.

He was close to retirement and dreading it. Law enforcement was his life. He wished he could remain a cop until he was seventy. He was horrified by the idea of his daughter quitting when she did not have to.

Judy's parents had met in Saigon. Her father was with the army in the days when American troops there were still called "advisers." Her mother came from a middle-class Vietnamese family: Judy's grandfather had been an accountant with the Finance Ministry there. Judy's father brought his bride home, and Judy was born in San Francisco. As a baby she called her parents Bo and Me, the Vietnamese equivalent of Daddy and Mommy. The cops caught on to this, and her father became known as Bo Maddox.

Judy adored him. When she was thirteen her mother died in a car wreck. Since then Judy had been close to Bo. After she had broken up with Don Riley a year ago, she had moved into her father's house.

She sighed. "I don't often lose it, you have to admit."

"Only when it's really important."

"But now that I've told Kincaid I'm quitting, I guess I will."

"Now that you've cursed him like that, I guess you'll have to."

Judy got up and poured more tea for both of them. She was still boiling with fury inside. "He's such a damn fool."

"He must be, because he just lost a good agent." Bo sipped his tea. "But you're dumber—you lost a great job."

"I was offered a better one today."

"Where?"

"Brooks Fielding, the law firm. I could earn three times my FBI salary."

"Keeping mobsters out of jail!" Bo said indignantly.

"Everyone's entitled to a vigorous defense."

"Why don't you marry Don Riley and have babies? Grandchildren would give me something to do in retirement."

Judy winced. She had never told Bo the real story of her breakup with Don. The simple truth was that he had had an affair. Feeling guilty, he had confessed to Judy. It was only a brief fling with a colleague, and Judy had tried to forgive him, but her feelings for Don were not the same afterward. Never again did she feel the urge to make love to him. She had not felt drawn to anyone else, either. A switch had been thrown somewhere inside her, and her sex drive had closed down.

Bo did not know any of this. He saw Don Riley as the perfect husband: handsome, intelligent, successful, and working in law enforcement.

Judy said: "Don asked me to have a celebration dinner, but I think I'll cancel."

"I guess I ought to know better than to tell you who to marry," Bo said with a rueful grin. He stood up. "I've got to go. We have a raid going down tonight."

She did not like it when he worked at night. "Have you eaten?" she asked anxiously. "Shall I make you some eggs before you go?"

"No, thanks, honey. I'll get a sandwich later." He pulled on a leather jacket and kissed her cheek. "I love you."

"Bye."

As the door slammed, the phone rang. It was Don. "I got us a table at Masa's," he said.

Judy sighed. Masa's was very swanky. "Don, I hate to let you down, but I'd rather not."

"Are you serious? I practically had to offer my sister's body to the maître d' to get a table at this short notice."

"I don't feel like celebrating. Bad stuff happened at the office today." She told him about Lestrange getting cancer and Kincaid giving her a dumb-ass assignment. "So I'm quitting the Bureau."

Don was shocked. "I don't believe it! You *love* the FBI."

"I used to."

"This is terrible!"

"Not so terrible. It's time for me to make some money, anyway. I was a hotshot at law school, you know. I got better grades than a couple of people who are earning fortunes now."

"Sure, help a murderer beat the rap, write a book about it, make a million dollars . . . Is this *you?* Am I speaking to Judy Maddox? Hello?"

"I don't know, Don, but with all this on my mind, I'm not in the mood to go out on the town."

There was a pause. Judy knew that Don was resigning himself to the inevitable. After a moment he said: "Okay, but you have to make it up to me. Tomorrow?"

Judy did not have the energy to fence with him anymore. "Sure," she said.

"Thanks."

She hung up.

She turned on the TV and looked in the fridge, thinking about dinner. But she did not feel hungry. She took out a can of beer and opened it. She watched TV for three or four minutes before realizing the show was in Spanish. She decided she did not want the beer. She turned off the TV and poured the beer down the sink.

She thought about going to Everton's, the FBI agents' favorite bar. She liked to hang out there, drinking beer and eating hamburgers and swapping war stories. But she was not sure she would be welcome now, especially if Kincaid was there. She was already beginning to feel like an outsider.

She decided to write her résumé. She would go into the office and do it on her computer. Better to be out doing something than sitting at home getting cabin fever.

She picked up her gun, then hesitated. Agents were on

duty twenty-four hours a day and were obliged to be armed except in court, inside a jail, or at the office. *But if I'm no longer an agent, I don't have to go armed.* Then she changed her mind. *Hell, if I see a robbery in progress and I have to drive on by because I left my weapon at home, I'm going to feel pretty stupid.*

It was a standard-issue FBI weapon, a SIG-Sauer P228 pistol. It normally held thirteen rounds of nine-millimeter ammunition, but Judy always racked back the slide and chambered the first bullet, then removed the clip and added an extra round, making fourteen. She also had a Remington model 870 five-chamber shotgun. Like all agents, she did firearms training once a month, usually at the sheriff's range in Santa Rita. Her marksmanship was tested four times a year. The qualification course never gave her any trouble: she had a good eye and a steady hand, and her reflexes were quick.

Like most agents, she had never fired her gun except in training.

FBI agents were investigators. They were highly educated and well paid. They did not dress for combat. It was perfectly normal to go through an entire twenty-five-year career with the Bureau and never get involved in a shoot-out or even a fistfight. But they had to be ready for it.

Judy put her weapon into a shoulder bag. She was wearing the *ao dai*, a traditional Vietnamese garment like a long blouse, with a little upright collar and side slits, always worn over baggy pants. It was her favorite casual wear because it was so comfortable, but she knew it also looked good on her: the white material showed off her shoulder-length black hair and honey-colored skin, and the close-fitting blouse flattered her petite figure. She would not normally wear it to the office, but it was late in the evening, and anyway she had resigned.

She went outside. Her Chevrolet Monte Carlo was parked at the curb. It was an FBI car, and she would not be sorry to lose it. When she was a defense lawyer she could get something more exciting—a little European sports car, maybe, a Porsche or an MG.

Her father's house was in the Richmond neighborhood. It was not very swanky, but an honest cop never got rich. Judy took the Geary Expressway downtown. Rush hour was over and traffic was light, so she was at the Federal Building in a few minutes. She parked in the underground garage and took the elevator to the twelfth floor.

Now that she was leaving the Bureau, the office took on a cozy familiarity that made her feel nostalgic. The gray carpet, the neatly numbered rooms, the desks and files and computers, all spoke of a powerful, well-resourced organization, confident and dedicated. There were a few people working late. She entered the office of the Asian Organized Crime squad. The room was empty. She turned on the lights, sat at her desk, and booted up her computer.

When she thought about writing her résumé, her mind went blank.

There was not much to say about her life before the FBI: just school and two dull years in the legal department of Mutual American Insurance. She needed to give a clear account of her ten years in the Bureau, showing how she had succeeded and progressed. But instead of an ordered narrative, her memory produced a disjointed series of flashbacks: the serial rapist who had thanked her, from the dock, for putting him in jail where he could do no more harm; a company called Holy Bible Investments that had robbed dozens of elderly widows of their savings; the time she had found herself alone in a room with an armed man who had kidnapped two small children, and she had persuaded him to give her his gun . . .

She could hardly tell Brooks Fielding about those moments. They wanted Perry Mason, not Wyatt Earp.

She decided to write her formal letter of resignation first.

She put the date, then typed: "To the Acting Special Agent in Charge."

She wrote: "Dear Brian: This is to confirm my resignation."
It hurt.

She had given ten years of her life to the FBI. Other
women had got married and had children, or started their
own business, or written a novel, or sailed around the world.
She had dedicated herself to being a terrific agent. Now she
was throwing it all away. The thought brought tears to her
eyes. *What kind of an idiot am I, sitting alone in my office
crying to my damn computer?*

Then Simon Sparrow came in.

He was a heavily muscled man with neat short hair and a
mustache. He was a year or two older than Judy. Like her,
he was dressed casually, in tan chinos and a short-sleeved
sports shirt. He had a doctorate in linguistics and had spent
five years with the Behavioral Science Unit at the FBI
Academy at Quantico, Virginia. His specialty was threat
analysis.

He liked Judy and she liked him. With the men in the
office he talked men's talk, football and guns and cars, but
when he was alone with Judy he noticed and commented on
her outfits and her jewelry the way a girlfriend would.

He had a file in his hand. "Your earthquake threat is *fascinating*," he said, his eyes glowing with enthusiasm.

She blew her nose. He had surely seen that she was
upset, but he was tactfully pretending not to notice.

He went on: "I was going to leave this on your desk, but
I'm glad I've caught you."

He had obviously been working late to finish his report,
and Judy did not want to deflate his keenness by telling him
she was quitting. "Take a seat," she said, composing herself.

"Congratulations on winning your case today!"

"Thanks."

"You must be so pleased."

"I should be. But I had a fight with Brian Kincaid right
afterward."

"Oh, him." Simon dismissed their boss with a flap of his

hand. "If you apologize nicely, he'll have to forgive you. He can't afford to lose you, you're too good."

That was unexpected. Simon was normally more sympathetic. It was almost as if he had known beforehand. But if he knew about the fight, he knew she had resigned. So why had he brought her the report?

Intrigued, she said: "Tell me about your analysis of the threat."

"It had me mystified for a while." He handed her a printout of the message as it had originally appeared on the Internet bulletin board. "Quantico were puzzled, too," he added. He would have automatically consulted the Behavioral Science Unit on this, Judy knew.

She had seen the message before: it was in the file Matt Peters had handed her earlier today. She studied it again.

```
MAY 1ST
TO THE STATE GOVERNOR

Hi!
You say you care about pollution and
the environment, but you never do
nothing about it; so we're going to
make you.

The consumer society is poisoning the
planet because you are too greedy,
and you got to stop now!

We are the Hammer of Eden, the
radical offshoot of the Green
California Campaign.

We are telling you to announce an
immediate freeze on building power
```

```
plants. No new plants. Period. Or
else!

Or else what, you say?

Or else we will cause an earthquake
exactly four weeks from today.

Be warned! We really mean it!

                    —The Hammer of Eden
```

It did not tell her much, but she knew that Simon would mine every word and comma for meaning.

"What do you make of it?" he asked.

She thought for a minute. "I see a nerdy young student with greasy hair, wearing a washed-out Guns n' Roses T-shirt, sitting at his computer fantasizing about making the world obey him, instead of ignoring him the way it always has."

"Well, that's about as wrong as could be," Simon said with a smile. "He's an uneducated low-income man in his forties."

Judy shook her head in amazement. She was always astonished by the way Simon drew conclusions from evidence she could not even see. "How do you know?"

"The vocabulary and sentence structure. Look at the salutation. Affluent people don't start a letter with 'Hi,' they put 'Dear Sir.' And college graduates generally avoid double negatives such as 'you never do nothing.' "

Judy nodded. "So you're looking for Joe Bluecollar, aged forty-five. That sounds pretty straightforward. What puzzled you?"

"Contradictory indications. Other elements in the message suggest a young middle-class woman. The spelling is perfect. There's a semicolon in the first sentence, which indicates some education. And the number of exclamation points suggests a female—sorry, Judy, but it's the truth."

"How do you know she's young?"

"Older writers are more likely to use initial capital letters for a phrase such as 'state governor' and hyphenate words such as 'offshoot' that young writers run together to make one word. Also, the use of a computer and the Internet suggest someone both young and educated."

She studied Simon. Was he deliberately getting her interested to stop her from resigning? If he was, it wouldn't work. Once she had made a decision, she hated to change her mind. But she was fascinated by the mystery Simon had posed. "Are you about to tell me this message was written by someone with a split personality?"

"Nope. Simpler than that. It was written by two people: the man dictating, the woman typing."

"Clever!" Judy was beginning to see a picture of the two individuals behind this threat. Like a hunting dog that scents game, she was tense, alert, the anticipation of the chase already thrilling in her veins. *I can smell these people, I want to know where they are, I'm sure I can catch them.*

But I've resigned.

"I ask myself why he dictates," Simon said. "It might come naturally to a corporate executive who was used to having a secretary, but this is just a regular guy."

Simon spoke casually, as if this were just idle speculation, but Judy knew that his intuitions were often inspired. "Any theories?"

"I wonder if he's illiterate?"

"He could simply be lazy."

"True." Simon shrugged. "I just have a hunch."

"All right," Judy said. "You've got a nice college girl who is somehow in the thrall of a street guy. Little Red Riding Hood and the Big Bad Wolf. She's probably in danger, but is anyone else? The threat of an earthquake just doesn't seem real."

Simon shook his head. "I think we have to take it seriously."

Judy could not contain her curiosity. "Why?"

"As you know, we analyze threats according to *motivation*, *intent*, and *target selection*."

Judy nodded. This was basic stuff.

"*Motivation* is either emotional or practical. In other words, is the perpetrator doing this just to make himself feel good, or because he wants something?"

Judy thought the answer was pretty obvious. "On the face of it, these people have a specific goal. They want the state to stop building power plants."

"Right. And that means they don't really want to hurt anyone. They hope to achieve their aims just by making a threat."

"Whereas the emotional types would rather kill people."

"Exactly. Next, *intent* is either political, criminal, or mentally disturbed."

"Political, in this case, at least on the surface."

"Right. Political ideas can be a pretext for an act that is basically insane, but I don't get that feeling here, do you?"

Judy saw where he was heading. "You're trying to tell me these people are rational. But it's insane to threaten an earthquake!"

"I'll come back to that, okay? Finally, *target selection* is either specific or random. Trying to kill the president is specific; going berserk with a machine gun in Disneyland is random. Taking the earthquake threat seriously, just for the sake of argument, it would obviously kill a lot of people indiscriminately, so it's random."

Judy leaned forward. "All right, you've got practical intent, political motivation, and random targeting. What does that tell you?"

"The textbook says these people are either bargaining or seeking publicity. I say they're bargaining. If they wanted publicity, they wouldn't have chosen to put their message on an obscure bulletin board on the Internet—they would have gone for TV or the newspapers. But they didn't. So I think they simply wanted to communicate with the governor."

"They're naive if they think the governor reads his messages."

"I agree. These people display an odd combination of sophistication and ignorance."

"But they're serious."

"Yeah, and I've got another reason for believing that. Their demand—for a freeze on new power plants—isn't the kind of thing you would choose for a pretext. It's too down-to-earth. If you were making it up, you'd go for something splashy, like a ban on air-conditioning in Beverly Hills."

"So who the hell are these people?"

"We don't know. The typical terrorist shows an escalating pattern. He begins with threatening phone calls and anonymous letters; then he writes to the newspapers and TV stations; then he starts hanging around government buildings, fantasizing. By the time he shows up for the White House tour with a Saturday night special in a plastic shopping bag, we've got quite a lot of his work on the FBI computer. But not this one. I've had the linguistic fingerprint checked against all past terrorist threats on record at Quantico, but there's no match. These people are new."

"So we know nothing about them?"

"We know plenty. They live in California, obviously."

"How do you know that?"

"The message is addressed 'To the state governor.' If they were in another state, they would send it 'To the governor of California.' "

"What else?"

"They're Americans, and there's no indication of any particular ethnic group: their language shows no characteristically black, Asian, or Hispanic features."

"You left out one thing," Judy told him.

"What?"

"They're crazy."

He shook his head.

Judy said: "Simon, come on! They think they can cause an earthquake. They have to be crazy!"

He said stubbornly: "I don't know anything about seismology, but I know psychology, and I'm not comfortable with the theory that these people are out of their minds. They're sane, serious, and focused. And that means they're dangerous."

"I don't buy it."

He stood up. "I'm beat. Want to go for a beer?"

"Not tonight, Simon—but thanks. And thanks for the report. You're the best."

"You bet. So long."

Judy put her feet up on her desk and studied her shoes. She was sure now that Simon had been trying to persuade her not to resign. Kincaid might think this was a bullshit case, but Simon's message was that the Hammer of Eden might be a genuine threat, a group that really needed to be tracked down and put out of action.

In which case her career at the FBI was not necessarily over. She could make a triumph of a case that had been given to her as a deliberate insult. That would make her seem brilliant at the same time as it made Kincaid appear dumb. The prospect was enticing.

She put her feet down and looked at her screen. Because she had not touched the keys for a while, her screen saver had come on. It was a photograph of her at the age of seven, with gaps in her teeth and a plastic clip holding her hair back off her forehead. She was sitting on her father's knee. He was still a patrolman then, wearing the uniform of a San Francisco cop. She had taken his cap and was trying to put it on her own head. The picture had been taken by her mother.

She imagined herself working for Brooks Fielding, driving a Porsche, and going to court to defend people like the Foong brothers.

She touched the space bar and the screen saver disappeared. In its place she saw the words she had written: "Dear Brian: This is to confirm my resignation." Her hands hovered over the keyboard. After a long pause, she spoke aloud. "Aw, hell," she said. Then she erased the sentence and wrote: "I would like to apologize for my rudeness . . ."

3

The Tuesday morning sun was coming up over I-80. Priest's 1971 Plymouth 'Cuda headed for San Francisco, its built-in roar making fifty-five miles per hour sound like ninety.

He had bought the car new, at the height of his business career. Then, when his wholesale drinks business collapsed and the IRS was about to arrest him, he had fled with nothing but the clothes he stood up in—a navy business suit, as it happened, with broad lapels and flared pants—and his car. He still had both.

During the hippie era, the only cool car to own was a Volkswagen Beetle. Driving the bright yellow 'Cuda, Priest looked like a pimp, Star used to tell him. So they gave it a trippy paint job: planets on the roof, flowers on the trunk lid, and an Indian goddess on the hood with eight arms trailing over the fenders, all in purple and pink and turquoise. In twenty-five years the colors had faded to a mottled brown, but you could still make out the design if you looked closely. And now the car was a collectible.

He had set out at three A.M. Melanie had slept all the way. She lay with her head in his lap, her fabulously long legs folded on the worn black upholstery. As he drove, he toyed with her hair. She had sixties hair, long and straight with a part in the middle, although she had been born around the time the Beatles split up.

The kid was asleep, too, lying full length on the backseat, mouth open. Priest's German shepherd dog, Spirit, lay beside him. The dog was quiet, but every time Priest looked back at him he had one eye open.

Priest felt anxious.

He told himself he should feel good. This was like the old days. In his youth he always had something going, some scam, a project, a plan to make money or steal money or have a party or start a riot. Then he discovered peace. But sometimes he felt that life had become too peaceful. Stealing the seismic vibrator had revived his old self. He felt more alive now, with a pretty girl beside him and a battle of wits ahead, than he had for years.

All the same, he was worried.

He had stuck his neck all the way out. He had boasted that he could bend the governor of California to his will, and he had promised an earthquake. If he failed, he would be finished. He would lose everything that was dear to him. And if he was caught, he would be in jail until he was an old man.

But he was extraordinary. He had always known he was not like other people. The rules did not apply to him. He did things no one else thought of.

And he was already halfway to his goal. He had stolen a seismic vibrator. He had killed a man for it, but he had gotten away with the murder: there had been no repercussions except for occasional nightmares in which Mario got out of his burning pickup, with his clothes alight and fresh blood pouring from his smashed head, and came staggering after Priest.

The truck was now hidden in a lonely valley in the foothills of the Sierra Nevada. Today Priest was going to find out exactly where to place it so as to cause an earthquake.

And Melanie's husband was going to give him that information.

Michael Quercus knew more than anyone else in the world

about the San Andreas fault, according to Melanie. His accumulated data was stored on his computer. Priest wanted to steal his backup disk.

And he had to make sure that Michael would never know what had happened.

For that, he needed Melanie. Which was why he was worried. He had known her only a few weeks. In that short time he had become the dominant person in her life, he knew; but he had never put her through a test like this. And she had been married to Michael for six years. She might suddenly regret leaving her husband; she might realize how much she missed the dishwasher and the TV; she might be struck by the danger and the illegality of what she and Priest were doing; there was no telling what might happen to someone as bitter and confused and troubled as Melanie.

In the rear seat, her five-year-old son woke up.

Spirit, the dog, moved first, and Priest heard the click of his claws on the plastic of the seat. Then there was a childish yawn.

Dustin, known as Dusty, was an unlucky boy. He suffered from multiple allergies. Priest had not yet seen one of his attacks, but Melanie had described them: Dusty sneezed uncontrollably, his eyes bulged, and he broke out in itchy skin rashes. She carried powerful suppressing drugs, but she said they mitigated the symptoms only partially.

Now Dusty started to fret.

"Mommy, I'm thirsty," he said.

Melanie came awake. She sat upright, stretching, and Priest glanced at the outline of her breasts in the skimpy T-shirt she wore. She turned around and said: "Drink some water, Dusty, you have a bottle right there."

"I don't want water," he whined. "I want orange juice."

"We don't have any goddamn juice," she snapped.

Dusty started to cry.

Melanie was a nervous mother, frightened of doing the wrong thing. She was obsessive about her son's health, so she was overprotective, but at the same time, her tension made her cranky with him. She felt sure her husband would one day try to take the boy away from her, so she was terrified of doing anything that would enable him to call her a bad mother.

Priest took charge. He said: "Hey, whoa, what the heck is that coming up behind us?" He made himself sound really scared.

Melanie looked around. "It's just a truck."

"That's what you think. It's *disguised* as a truck, but really it's a Centaurian fighter spacecraft with photon torpedoes. Dusty, I need you to tap three times on the rear window to raise our invisible magnetic armor. Quick!"

Dusty tapped on the window.

"Now, we'll know he's firing his torpedoes if we see an orange light flashing on his port fender. You better watch for that, Dusty."

The truck was closing on them fast, and a minute later its left side indicator flashed and it pulled out to pass them.

Dusty said: "It's firing, it's firing!"

"Okay, I'll try to hold the magnetic armor while you fire back! That water bottle is actually a laser gun!"

Dusty pointed the bottle at the truck and made zapping noises. Spirit joined in, barking furiously at the truck as it passed. Melanie started to laugh.

When the truck pulled back into the slow lane ahead of them, Priest said: "Whew. We were lucky to come out of that in one piece. I think they've given up for now."

"Will there be any more Centaurians?" Dusty asked eagerly.

"You and Spirit keep watch out the back and let me know what you see, okay?"

"Okay."

Melanie smiled and said quietly: "Thanks. You're so good with him."

I'm good with everyone: men, women, children, and pets.

*I got charisma. I wasn't born with it—I learned. It's just a
way of making people do what you want. Anything from per-
suading a faithful wife to commit adultery, all the way down
to getting a scratchy kid to stop whining. All you need is
charm.*

"Let me know what exit to take," Priest said.

"Just watch for signs to Berkeley."

She did not know he could not read. "There's probably
more than one. Just tell me where to turn."

A few minutes later they left the freeway and entered the
leafy university town. Priest could feel Melanie's tension
rise. He knew that all her rage against society and her disappointment with life somehow centered on this man she had
left six months ago. She directed Priest through the intersec-
tions to Euclid Avenue, a street of modest houses and apartment buildings probably rented by graduate students and
younger faculty.

"I still think I should go in alone," she said.

It was out of the question. Melanie was not steady
enough. Priest could not rely on her when he was beside
her, so there was no way he would trust her alone. "No,"
he said.

"Maybe I—"

He allowed a flash of anger to show. "No!"

"Okay, okay," she said hastily. She bit her lip.

Dusty said excitedly: "Hey, this is where Daddy lives!"

"That's right, honey," Melanie said. She pointed to a
low-rise stucco apartment building, and Priest parked outside it.

Melanie turned to Dusty, but Priest forestalled her. "He
stays in the car."

"I'm not sure how safe—"

"He's got the dog."

"He might get scared."

Priest twisted around to speak to Dusty. "Hey, Lieutenant, I need you and Ensign Spirit to stand guard over

our spacecraft while First Officer Mom and I go inside the spaceport."

"Am I going to see Daddy?"

"Of course. But I'd like a few minutes with him first. Think you can handle the guard duty assignment?"

"You bet!"

"In the space navy, you have to say 'Aye, sir!' not 'You bet.' "

"Aye, sir!"

"Very good. Carry on." Priest got out of the car.

Melanie got out, but she still looked troubled. "For Christ's sake, don't let Michael know we left his kid in the car," she said.

Priest did not reply. *You might be afraid of offending Michael, baby, but I don't give a flying fuck.*

Melanie took her purse off the seat and slung it over her shoulder. They walked up the path to the building door. Melanie pressed the entry phone buzzer and held it down.

Her husband was a night owl, she had told Priest. He liked to work in the evening and sleep late. That was why they had chosen to get here before seven o'clock in the morning. Priest hoped Michael would be too bleary-eyed to wonder whether their visit had a hidden purpose. If he got suspicious, stealing his disk might be impossible.

Melanie said he was a workaholic, Priest recalled as they waited for Michael to answer. He spent his days driving all over California, checking the instruments that measured small geological movements in the San Andreas and other faults, and the nights inputting the data into his computer.

But what had finally driven her to leave him was an incident with Dusty. She and the child had been vegetarian for two years, and they would eat only organic food and health store products. Melanie believed the strict diet reduced Dusty's allergy attacks, although Michael was skeptical. Then one day she had discovered that Michael had bought Dusty a hamburger. To her, that was like poisoning the child. She still shook with fury when she told the story. She had left that night, taking Dusty with her.

Priest thought she might be right about the allergy attacks. The commune had been vegetarian ever since the early seventies, when vegetarianism was eccentric. At the time Priest had doubted the value of the diet but had been in favor of a discipline that set them apart from the world outside. Their grapes were grown without chemicals simply because they had been unable to afford sprays, so they had made a virtue of necessity and called their wine organic, which turned out to be a strong selling point. But he could not help noticing that after a quarter century of this life the communards were a remarkably healthy bunch. It was rare for them to have a medical emergency they could not cope with themselves. So he was now convinced. But, unlike Melanie, he was not obsessive about diet. He still liked fish, and now and again he would unintentionally eat meat in a soup or a sandwich and would shrug it off. But if Melanie discovered that her mushroom omelet had been cooked in bacon fat, she would throw up.

A grouchy voice came through the intercom. "Who is it?"

"Melanie."

There was a buzz, and the building door opened. Priest followed Melanie inside and up the stairs. An apartment was open on the second floor. Michael Quercus stood in the doorway.

Priest was surprised by his appearance. He had been expecting a weedy professorial type, probably bald, wearing brown clothes. Quercus was around thirty-five. Tall and athletic, he had a head of short black curls and the shadow of a heavy beard on his cheeks. He wore only a towel around his waist, so Priest could see that he had broad, well-muscled shoulders and a flat belly. *They must have made a handsome couple.*

As Melanie reached the top of the stairs, Michael said: "I've been very worried—where the hell have you been?"

Melanie said: "Can't you put some clothes on?"

"You didn't say you had company," he replied coolly. He stayed in the doorway. "Are you going to answer my question?"

Priest could see he was barely controlling his stored-up rage.

"I'm here to explain," Melanie said. She was enjoying Michael's fury. *What a screwed-up marriage.* "This is my friend Priest. May we come in?"

Michael stared at her angrily. "This had better be pretty fucking good, Melanie." He turned his back and walked inside.

Melanie and Priest followed him into a small hallway. He opened the bathroom door, took a dark blue cotton robe off a hook, and slipped into it, taking his time. He discarded his towel and tied the belt. Then he led them into the living room.

This was clearly his office. As well as a couch and a TV set, there was a computer screen and keyboard on the table and a row of electronic machines with blinking lights on a deep shelf. Somewhere in those bland pale gray boxes was stored the information Priest needed. He felt tantalized. There was no way he could get at it unaided. He had to depend on Melanie.

One wall was entirely taken up with a huge map. "What the hell is that?" Priest said.

Michael just gave him a who-the-fuck-are-you look and said nothing, but Melanie answered the question. "It's the San Andreas fault." She pointed. "Beginning at Point Arena lighthouse a hundred miles north of here in Mendocino County, all the way south and east, past Los Angeles and inland to San Bernardino. A crack in the earth's crust, seven hundred miles long."

Melanie had explained Michael's work to Priest. His specialty was the calculation of pressure at different places along seismic faults. It was partly a matter of precise measurement of small movements in the earth's crust, partly a question of estimating the accumulated energy based on the lapse of time since the last earthquake. His work had won him academic prizes. But a year ago he had quit the university to start his own business, a consultancy offering advice on earthquake hazards to construction firms and insurance companies.

Melanie was a computer wizard and had helped Michael devise his setup. She had programmed his machine to back up every day between four A.M. and six A.M., when he was asleep. Everything on his computer, she had explained to Priest, was copied onto an optical disk. When he switched on his screen in the morning, he would take the disk out of the disk drive and put it in a fireproof box. That way, if his computer crashed or the house burned down, his precious data would not be lost.

It was a wonder to Priest that information about the San Andreas fault could be kept on a little disk, but then books were just as much of a mystery. He simply had to accept what he was told. The important thing was that with Michael's disk Melanie would be able to tell Priest where to place the seismic vibrator.

Now they just had to get Michael out of the room long enough for Melanie to snatch the disk from the optical drive.

"Tell me, Michael," Priest said. "All this stuff." He indicated the map and the computers with a wave of his hand, then fixed Michael with the Look. "How does it make you *feel?*"

Most people got flustered when Priest gave them the Look and asked them a personal question. Sometimes they gave a revealing answer because they were so disconcerted. But Michael seemed immune. He just looked blankly at Priest and said: "It doesn't make me *feel* anything, I use it." Then he turned to Melanie and said: "Now, are you going to tell me why you disappeared?"

Arrogant prick.

"It's very simple," she said. "A friend offered me and

Dusty the use of her cabin in the mountains." Priest had told her not to say which mountains. "It was a late cancellation of a rental." Her tone of voice indicated that she did not see why she had to explain something so simple. "We can't afford vacations, so I grabbed at the chance."

That was when Priest had met her. She and Dusty had been wandering in the forest and got completely lost. Melanie was a city girl and could not even find her way by the sun. Priest was out on his own that day, fishing for sockeye salmon. It was a perfect spring afternoon, sunny and mild. He had been sitting on the bank of a stream, smoking a joint, when he heard a child crying.

He knew it was not one of the commune children, whose voices he would have recognized. Following the sound, he found Dusty and Melanie. She was close to tears. When she saw Priest she said: "Thank God, I thought we were going to die out here!"

He had stared at her for a long moment. She was a little weird, with her long red hair and green eyes, but in the cutoff jeans and a halter top she looked good enough to eat. It was magical, coming across a damsel in distress like that when he was alone in the wilderness. If it had not been for the kid, Priest would have tried to lay her right then and there, on the springy mattress of fallen pine needles beside the splashing stream.

That was when he had asked her if she was from Mars. "No," she said, "Oakland."

Priest knew where the vacation cabins were. He picked up his fishing rod and led her through the forest, following the trails and ridges that were so familiar to him. It was a long walk, and on the way he talked to her, asking sympathetic questions, giving his engaging grin now and again, and found out all about her.

She was a woman in deep trouble.

She had left her husband and moved in with the bass guitarist in a hot rock band; but the bassist had thrown her out after a few weeks. She had no one to turn to: her father was dead, and her mother lived in New York with a guy who had tried to get into bed with Melanie the one night she had slept at their apartment. She had exhausted the hospitality of her friends and borrowed all the money they could afford to lend. Her career was a washout, and she was working in a supermarket, stacking shelves, leaving Dusty with a neighbor all day. She lived in a slum that was so dirty, it gave the kid constant allergy attacks. She needed to move to a place with clean air, but she could not find a job outside the city. She was up a blind alley and desperate. She had been trying to calculate the exact overdose of sleeping pills that would kill her and the child when a girlfriend had offered her this vacation.

Priest liked people in trouble. He knew how to relate to them. All you had to do was offer them what they needed, and they became your slaves. He was uncomfortable with confident, self-sufficient types: they were too hard to control.

By the time they reached the cabin it was suppertime. Melanie made pasta and salad, then put Dusty to bed. When the child was asleep, Priest seduced her on the rug. She was frantic with desire. All her pent-up emotional charge was released by sex, and she made love as if it were her last chance ever, scratching his back and biting his shoulders and pulling him deep inside her as if she wanted to swallow him up. It was the most exciting encounter Priest could remember.

Now her supercilious handsome-professor husband was complaining. "That was *five weeks* ago. You can't just take my son and disappear without even a phone call!"

"You could have called me."

"I didn't know where you were!"

"I have a mobile."

"I tried. I couldn't get an answer."

"The service was cut off because you didn't pay the bill. You're supposed to pay it, we agreed."

"I was a couple of days late, that's all! They must have turned it back on."

"Well, you called when it was cut off, I guess."

This family row was not bringing Priest closer to that disk, he fretted. *Got to get Michael out of the room, some way, any way.* He interrupted to say: "Why don't we all have some coffee?" He wanted Michael to go into the kitchen to make it.

Michael jerked a thumb over his shoulder. "Help yourself," he said brusquely.

Shit.

Michael turned back to Melanie. "It doesn't matter *why* I couldn't reach you. I couldn't. That's why you have to call me before taking Dusty away on vacation."

Melanie said: "Listen, Michael, there's something I haven't told you yet."

Michael looked exasperated, then sighed and said: "Sit down, why don't you." He sat behind his desk.

Melanie sank into a corner of the couch, folding her legs beneath her in a familiar way that made Priest think this had been her regular seat. Priest perched on the arm of the couch, not wanting to sit lower than Michael. *I can't even figure out which of those machines is the disk drive. Come on, Melanie, lose the damn husband!*

Michael's tone of voice suggested he had been through scenes like this with Melanie before. "All right, make your pitch," he said wearily. "What is it this time?"

"I'm going to move to the mountains, permanently. I'm living with Priest and a bunch of people."

"Where?"

Priest answered that question. He did not want Michael to know where they lived. "It's in Del Norte County." That was in redwood country at the northern end of California. In fact the commune was in Sierra County, in the foothills of the Sierra Nevada, near the eastern border of the state. Both were far from Berkeley.

Michael was outraged. "You can't take Dusty to live hundreds of miles away from his father!"

"There's a reason," Melanie persisted. "In the last five weeks, Dusty hasn't had a single allergy attack. He's healthy in the mountains, Michael."

Priest added: "It's probably the pure air and water. No pollution."

Michael was skeptical. "It's the desert, not the mountains, that normally suits people with allergies."

"Don't talk to me about *normally*!" Melanie flared. "I can't go to the desert—I don't have any money. This is the only place I can afford where Dusty can be healthy!"

"Is Priest paying your rent?"

Go ahead, asshole, insult me, talk about me like I'm not here; and I'll just carry on fucking your sexy wife.

Melanie said: "It's a commune."

"Jesus, Melanie, what kind of people have you fallen in with now? First a junkie guitar player—"

"Wait a minute, Blade was not a junkie—"

"—now a godforsaken hippie commune!"

Melanie was so involved in this quarrel that she had forgotten why they were here. *The disk, Melanie, the damn disk!* Priest interrupted again. "Why don't you ask Dusty how he feels about this, Michael?"

"I will."

Melanie shot Priest a despairing look.

He ignored her. "Dusty's right outside, in my car."

Michael flushed with anger. "You left my son outside in the car?"

"He's okay, my dog's with him."

Michael glared furiously at Melanie. "What the hell is wrong with you?" he shouted.

Priest said: "Why don't you just go and get him?"

"I don't need your fucking permission to get my own son. Give me the car keys."

"It's not locked," Priest said mildly.

Michael stormed out.

"I told you not to tell him Dusty was outside!" Melanie wailed. "Why did you do it?"

"To get him out of the goddamn room," Priest said. "Now grab that disk."

"But you've made him so mad!"

"He was angry already!" This was no good, Priest realized. She might be too frightened to do what was needed. He stood up. He took her hands, pulled her upright, and gave her the Look. "You don't have to be afraid of him. You're with me now. I take care of you. Be cool. Say your mantra."

"But—"

"Say it."

"Lat hoo, dat soo."

"Keep saying it."

"Lat hoo, dat soo, lat hoo, dat soo." She became calmer.

"Now get the disk."

She nodded. Still saying her mantra under her breath, she bent over the row of machines on the shelf. She pressed a button and a flat plastic square popped out of a slot.

Priest had noticed before that "disks" were always square in the world of computers.

She opened her purse and took out another disk that looked similar. "Shit!" she said.

"What?" Priest said worriedly. "What's wrong?"

"He's changed his brand!"

Priest looked at the two disks. They seemed the same to him. "What's the difference?"

"Look, mine is a Sony, but Michael's is a Philips."

"Will he notice?"

"He might."

"Damn." It was vital that Michael did not know his data had been stolen.

"He'll probably start work as soon as we've gone. He'll

eject the disk and swap it with the one in the fireproof box, and if he looks at them, he'll see they're different."

"And he's sure to connect that with us." Priest felt a surge of panic. It was all turning to shit.

Melanie said: "I could buy a Philips disk and come back another day."

Priest shook his head. "I don't want to do this again. We might fail again. And we're running out of time. The dead-line is three days away. Does he keep spare disks?"

"He should. Sometimes a disk gets corrupted." She looked around. "I wonder where they are." She stood in the middle of the floor, helpless.

Priest could have screamed with frustration. He had dreaded something like this. Melanie had completely gone to pieces, and they had only a minute or two. He had to get her calmed down fast. "Melanie," he said, struggling to make his voice low and reassuring, "you have two disks in your hand. Put them both in your purse."

She obeyed him automatically.

"Now close your purse."

She did that.

Priest heard the building door slam. Michael was on his way back. Priest felt perspiration break out in the small of his back. "Think: when you were living here, did Michael have a stationery cupboard?"

"Yes. Well, a drawer."

"Well?" *Wake up, girl!* "Where is it?"

She pointed to a cheap white chest against the wall.

Priest yanked open the top drawer. He saw a package of yellow pads, a box of cheap ballpoints, a couple of reams of white paper, some envelopes—and an open box of disks.

He heard Dusty's voice. It seemed to come from the vestibule at the entrance to the apartment.

With shaking fingers, he fumbled a disk out of the packet and handed it to Melanie. "Will this do?"

"Yes, it's a Philips."

Priest closed the drawer.

Michael walked in with Dusty in his arms.

Melanie stood frozen with the disk in her hand.

For God's sake, Melanie, do something!

Dusty was saying: "And you know what, Daddy? I didn't sneeze in the mountains."

Michael's attention was fixed on Dusty. "How about that?" he said.

Melanie regained her composure. As Michael bent to put Dusty down on the couch, she stooped over the disk drive and slid the disk into the slot. The machine whirred softly and drew it in, like a snake eating a rat.

"You didn't sneeze?" Michael said to Dusty. "Not once?"

"Uh-uh."

Melanie straightened up. Michael had not seen what she did.

Priest closed his eyes. The relief was overwhelming. They had got away with it. They had Michael's data—and he would never know.

Michael said: "That dog doesn't make you sneeze?"

"No, Spirit is a clean dog. Priest makes him wash in the stream, and then he comes out and shakes himself and it's like a rainstorm!" Dusty laughed with pleasure as he remembered.

"Is that right?" his father said.

Melanie said: "I told you, Michael."

Her voice sounded shaky, but Michael did not seem to notice. "All right, all right," he said in a conciliatory tone. "If it makes such a difference to Dusty's health, we'll just have to work something out."

She looked relieved. "Thanks."

Priest allowed himself the ghost of a smile. It was all over. His plan had moved another crucial step forward.

Now they just had to hope that Michael's computer did not crash. If that happened, and he tried to retrieve his data from the optical disk, he would discover that it was blank.

But Melanie said that crashes were rare. In all probability there would be no crash today. And tonight the computer would back up again, overwriting the blank disk with Michael's data. By this time tomorrow it would be impossible to tell that a switch had been made.

Michael said: "Well, at least you came here to talk about it. I appreciate that."

Melanie would much rather have dealt with her husband on the phone, Priest knew. But her move to the commune was a perfect pretext for visiting Michael. He and Melanie could never have paid a casual social call on her husband without making him suspicious. But this way it would not occur to Michael to wonder why they had come.

In fact, Michael was not the suspicious type, Priest felt sure. He was brainy but guileless. He had no ability to look beneath the surface and see what was really going on in the heart of another human being.

Priest himself had that ability in spades.

Melanie was saying: "I'll bring Dusty to see you as often as you like. I'll drive down."

Priest could see into her heart. She was being nice to Michael, now that he had given her what she wanted—she had her head to one side, and she was smiling prettily at him—but she did not love him, not anymore.

Michael was different. He was angry with her for leaving him, that was clear. But he still cared for her. He was not over her yet, not quite. A part of him still wanted her back. He would have asked her, but he was too proud.

Priest felt jealous.

I hate you, Michael.

4

Judy woke up early on Tuesday wondering if she had a job. Yesterday she had said: "I quit." But she had been angry and frustrated. Today she was sure she did not want to leave the FBI. The prospect of spending her life defending criminals, instead of catching them, depressed her. Had she changed her mind too late? Last night she had left a note on Brian Kincaid's desk. Would he accept her apology? Or would he insist on her resignation?

Bo came in at six A.M. and she warmed up some *pho*, the noodle soup that the Vietnamese ate for breakfast. Then she dressed in her smartest outfit, a dark blue Armani suit with a short skirt. On a good day it made her sophisticated, authoritative, and sexy all at the same time. *If I'm going to be fired, I might as well look like someone they'll miss.*

She was stiff with tension as she drove to work. She parked in the garage beneath the Federal Building and took the elevator to the FBI floor. She went straight to the SAC's office.

Brian Kincaid was behind the big desk, wearing a white shirt with red suspenders. He looked up at her. "Good morning," he said coldly.

"Morn—" Her mouth was dry. She swallowed and started again. "Good morning, Brian. Did you get my note?"

"Yes, I did."

Obviously he wasn't going to make this any easier for her.

95

She could not think what else to say, so she simply looked at him and waited.

Eventually he said: "Your apology is accepted."

She felt weak with relief. "Thank you."

"You can move your personal stuff into the Domestic Terrorism squad room."

"Okay." There were worse fates, she reflected. There were several people she liked in the DT squad. She began to relax.

Kincaid said: "Get to work on the Hammer of Eden case right away. We need something to tell the governor."

Judy was surprised. "You're seeing the governor?"

"His cabinet secretary." He checked a note on his desk. "A Mr. Albert Honeymoon."

"I've heard of him." Honeymoon was the governor's right-hand man. The case had taken on a higher profile, Judy realized.

"Let me have a report by tomorrow night."

That hardly gave her time to make progress, given how little she had to begin with. Tomorrow was Wednesday. "But the deadline is Friday."

"The meeting with Honeymoon is on Thursday."

"I'll get you something concrete to give him."

"You can give it to him yourself. Mr. Honeymoon insists on seeing what he calls the person at the sharp end. We need to be at the governor's office in Sacramento at twelve noon."

"Wow. Okay."

"Any questions?"

She shook her head. "I'll get right on it."

As she left, she felt elated that she had her job back but dismayed by the news that she had to report to the governor's aide. It was not likely she would catch the people behind the threat in only two days, so she was almost doomed to report failure.

She emptied her desk in the Asian Organized Crime

squad and carried her stuff down the corridor to Domestic Terrorism. Her new supervisor, Matt Peters, allocated her a desk. She knew all the agents, and they congratulated her on the Foong brothers case, though in subdued tones—everyone knew she had fought with Kincaid yesterday.

Peters assigned a young agent to work with her on the Hammer of Eden case. He was Raja Khan, a fast-talking Hindu with an MBA. He was twenty-six. Judy was pleased. Although inexperienced, he was intelligent and keen.

She briefed him on the case and sent him to check out the Green California Campaign. "Be nice," she told him. "Tell them we don't believe they're involved, but we have to eliminate them."

"What am I looking for?"

"A couple: a blue-collar man of about forty-five who may be illiterate, and an educated woman of about thirty who is probably dominated by the man. But I don't think you'll find them there. That would be too easy."

"Alternatively . . . ?"

"The most useful thing you can do is get the names of all the officers of the organization, paid or volunteer, and run them through the computer to see if any of them have any record of criminal or subversive activity."

"You got it," Raja said. "What will you do?"

"I'm going to learn about earthquakes."

Judy had been in one major earthquake.

The Santa Rosa earthquake had caused damage worth $6 million—not much, as these things go—and had been felt over the relatively small area of twelve thousand square miles. The Maddox family was then living in Marin County, north of San Francisco, and Judy was in first grade. It was a minor tremor, she knew now. But at the time she had been six years old, and it had seemed like the end of the world.

First there was a noise like a train, but real close, and she came awake fast and looked around her bedroom in the clear light of dawn, searching for the source of the sound, scared to death.

Then the house began to shake. Her ceiling light with its pink-fringed shade whipped back and forth. On her bedside table, *Best Fairy Tales* leaped up in the air like a magic book and came down open at "Tom Thumb," the story Bo had read her last night. Her hairbrush and her toy makeup set danced on the Formica top of the dresser. Her wooden horse rocked furiously with no one on it. A row of dolls fell off their shelf, as if diving into the rug, and Judy thought they had come alive, like toys in a fable. She found her voice at last and screamed once: "DADDY!"

From the next room she heard her father curse, then there was a thud as his feet hit the floor. The noise and the shaking grew worse, and she heard her mother cry out. Bo came to Judy's door and turned the handle, but it would not open. She heard another thud as he shouldered it, but it was stuck.

Her window smashed, and shards of glass fell inward, landing on the chair where her school clothes were neatly folded, ready for the morning: gray skirt, white blouse, green V-neck sweater, navy blue underwear, and white socks. The wooden horse rocked so hard, it fell over on top of the dollhouse, smashing the miniature roof; and Judy knew the roof of her real house might be smashed as easily. A framed picture of a rosy-cheeked Mexican boy came off its hook on the wall, flew through the air, and hit her head. She cried out in pain.

Then her chest of drawers began to walk.

It was an old bow-fronted pine chest her mother had bought in a junk shop and painted white. It had three drawers, and it stood on short legs that ended in feet like lions' paws. At first it seemed to dance in place, restlessly, on its four feet. Then it shuffled from side to side, like someone hesitating nervously in a doorway. Finally it started to move toward her.

She screamed again.

Her bedroom door shook as Bo tried to break it down.

The chest inched across the floor toward her. She hoped maybe the rug would halt its advance, but the chest just pushed the rug with its lions' paws.

Her bed shook so violently that she fell out.

The chest came within a few inches of her and stopped. The middle drawer came open like a wide mouth ready to swallow her. She screamed at the top of her voice.

The door shattered and Bo burst in.

Then the shaking stopped.

Thirty years later she could still feel the terror that had possessed her like a fit as the world fell apart around her. She had been frightened of closing the bedroom door for years afterward; and she was still scared of earthquakes. In California, feeling the ground move in a minor tremor was commonplace, but she had never really gotten used to it. And when she felt the earth shake, or saw television pictures of collapsed buildings, the dread that crept through her veins like a drug was not the fear of being crushed or burned, but the blind panic of a little girl whose world suddenly started to fall apart.

She was still on edge that evening as she walked into the sophisticated ambience of Masa's, wearing a black silk sheath and the row of pearls Don Riley had given her the Christmas they were living together.

Don ordered a white burgundy called Corton Charlemagne. He drank most of it: Judy loved the nutty taste, but she was not comfortable drinking alcohol when she had a semi-automatic pistol loaded with nine-millimeter ammunition tucked into her black patent evening purse.

She told Don that Brian Kincaid had accepted her apology and allowed her to withdraw her resignation.

"He had to," Don said. "Refusing would be tantamount to firing you. And it would look real bad for him if he lost one of his best people on his first day as acting SAC."

"Maybe you're right," Judy said, but she was thinking that it was easy for Don to be wise after the event.

"Sure I'm right."

"Remember, Brian is KMA." It stood for kiss my ass, and it meant the person had built up such a generous pension entitlement that he could retire comfortably at any time that suited him.

"Yeah, but he has his pride. Imagine where he explains to headquarters how come he had to let you go. 'She said "fuck" to me,' he says. Washington goes: 'So what are you, a priest? You never heard an agent say "fuck" before?' Uh-uh." Don shook his head. "Kincaid would seem like a wimp to refuse your apology."

"I guess so."

"Anyway, I'm real glad we may be working together again soon." He raised his glass. "Here's to many more brilliant prosecutions by the great team of Riley and Maddox."

She clinked glasses and took a sip of wine.

They talked over the case as they ate, recalling the mistakes they had made, the surprises they had sprung on the defense, the moments of tension and triumph.

When they were drinking coffee, Don said: "Do you miss me?"

Judy frowned. It would be cruel to say no, and anyway it was not true. But she did not want to give him false encouragement. "I miss some things," she said. "I like you when you're funny and smart." She also missed having a warm body beside her at night, but she was not going to tell him that.

He said: "I miss talking about my work, and hearing about yours."

"I guess I talk to Bo now."

"I miss him, too."

"He likes you. He thinks you're the ideal husband—"

"I am, I am!"

"—for someone in law enforcement."

Don shrugged. "I'll settle for that."

Judy grinned. "Maybe you and Bo should get married."

"Ho, ho." He paid the bill. "Judy, there's something I want to say."

"I'm listening."

"I think I'm ready to be a father."

For some reason that angered her. "So what am I supposed to do about it—shout hooray and open my legs?"

He was taken aback. "I mean. . . . well, I thought you wanted commitment."

"Commitment? Don, all I asked was that you refrain from shtupping your secretary, but you couldn't manage that!"

He looked mortified. "Okay, don't get mad. I'm just trying to tell you that I've changed."

"And now I'm supposed to come running back to you as if nothing had happened?"

"I guess I still don't understand you."

"You probably never will." His evident distress softened her. "Come on, I'll drive you home." When they were living together she had always been the after-dinner driver.

They left the restaurant in an awkward silence. In the car he said: "I thought we might at least talk about it." Don the lawyer, negotiating.

"We can talk." *But how can I tell you that my heart is cold?*

"What happened with Paula . . . it was the worst mistake of my whole life."

She believed him. He was not drunk, just mellow enough to say what he felt. She sighed. She wanted him to be happy. She was fond of him, and she hated to see him in pain. It hurt her, too. Part of her wished she could give him what he wanted.

He said: "We had some good times together." He stroked her thigh through the silk dress.

She said: "If you feel me up while I'm driving, I'll throw you out of the car."

He knew she could do it. "Whatever you say." He took his hand away.

A moment later she wished she had not been so harsh. It was not such a bad thing, to have a man's hand on your thigh. Don was not the world's greatest lover—he was enthusiastic, but unimaginative. However, he was better than nothing, and nothing was what she had had since she'd left him.

Why don't I have a man? I don't want to grow old alone. Is there something wrong with me?

Hell, no.

A minute later she pulled up outside his building. "Thanks, Don," she said. "For a great prosecution and a great dinner."

He leaned over to kiss her. She offered her cheek, but he kissed her lips, and she did not want to make a big thing of it, so she let him. His kiss lingered until she broke away. Then he said: "Come in for a while. I'll make you a cappuccino."

The longing look in his eyes almost broke her will. How hard could it be? she asked herself. She could put her gun in his safe, drink a large, heartwarming brandy, and spend the night in the arms of a decent man who adored her. "No," she said firmly. "Good night."

He stared at her for a long moment, misery in his eyes. She looked back, embarrassed and sorry, but resolute.

"Good night," he said at last. He got out and closed the car door.

Judy pulled away. When she glanced in the rearview mirror she saw him standing on the sidewalk, his hand half-raised in a kind of wave. She ran a red light and turned a corner, then at last she felt alone again.

When she got home, Bo was watching Conan O'Brien and chuckling. "This guy breaks me up," he said. They watched his monologue until the commercial break, then Bo turned off the TV. "I solved a murder today," he said. "How about that?"

Judy knew he had several unsolved cases on his desk. "Which one?"

"The Telegraph Hill rape-murder."

"Who did it?"

"A guy who's already in jail. He was arrested a while back for harassing young girls in the park. I had a hunch about him and searched his apartment. He had a pair of police handcuffs like the ones found on the body, but he denied the murder, and I couldn't break him. Today I got his DNA test back from the lab. It matches the semen from the victim's body. I told him that and he confessed. Jackpot."

"Well done!" She kissed the top of his head.

"How about you?"

"Well, I still have a job, but it remains to be seen whether I have a career."

"You have a career, come on."

"I don't know. If I get demoted for putting the Foong brothers in jail, what will they do to me when I have a failure?"

"You've suffered a setback. It's just temporary. You'll get over it, I promise."

She smiled, remembering the time she had thought there was nothing her father could not do. "Well, I didn't make much progress with my case."

"Last night you thought it was a bullshit assignment anyway."

"Today I'm not so sure. The linguistic analysis showed that these people are dangerous, whoever they are."

"But they can't trigger an earthquake."

"I don't know."

Bo raised his eyebrows. "You think it's possible?"

"I've spent most of today trying to find out. I spoke to three seismologists and got three different answers."

"Scientists are like that."

"What I really wanted was for them to tell me firmly it couldn't happen. But one said it was 'unlikely,' one said the possibility was 'vanishingly small,' and the third said it could be done with a nuclear bomb."

"Could these people—what are they called?"

"The Hammer of Eden."

"Could they have a nuclear device?"

"It's possible. They're smart, focused, serious. But then why would they talk about earthquakes? Why not just threaten us with their bomb?"

"Yeah," Bo said thoughtfully. "That would be just as terrifying and a lot more credible."

"But who can tell how these people's minds work?"

"What's your next step?"

"I have one more seismologist to see, a Michael Quercus. The others all say he's kind of a maverick, but he's the leading authority on what causes earthquakes."

She had already tried to interview Quercus. Late that afternoon she had rung his doorbell. He had told her, through the entry phone, to call for an appointment.

"Maybe you didn't hear me," she had said. "This is the FBI."

"Does that mean you don't have to make appointments?"

She had cursed under her breath. She was a law enforcement officer, not a damn replacement window salesperson. "It does, generally," she said into the intercom. "Most people feel our work is too important to wait."

"No, they don't," he replied. "Most people are scared of you, that's why they let you in without an appointment. Call me. I'm in the phone book."

"I'm here about a matter of public safety, Professor. I've been told you're an expert who can give me crucial information that will help in our work of protecting people. I'm sorry I didn't have the opportunity of calling for an appointment, but now that I'm here, I would really appreciate it if you would see me for a few minutes."

There was no reply, and she realized he had hung up at his end.

She had driven back to the office, fuming. She did not

make appointments: agents rarely did. She preferred to catch people off-guard. Almost everyone she interviewed had something to hide. The less time they had to prepare, the more likely they were to make a revealing mistake. But Quercus was infuriatingly correct: she had no right to barge in on him.

Swallowing her pride, she had called him and made an appointment for tomorrow.

She decided not to tell Bo any of this. "What I really need," she said, "is someone to explain the science to me in such a way that I can make my own judgment about whether a terrorist could cause an earthquake."

"And you need to find these Hammer of Eden people and bust them for making threats. Any progress there?"

She shook her head. "I had someone interview everyone at the Green California Campaign. No one there matches the profile, none have any kind of criminal or subversive record; in fact, there's nothing suspicious about them at all."

Bo nodded. "It always was unlikely the perpetrators would have told the truth about who they were. Don't be discouraged. You've only been on the case a day and a half."

"True—but that leaves only two clear days to their deadline. And I have to go to Sacramento on Thursday to report to the governor's office."

"You'd better start early tomorrow." He got up off the couch.

They both went upstairs. Judy paused at her bedroom door. "Remember that earthquake, when I was six?"

He nodded. "It wasn't much, by California standards, but it scared you half to death."

Judy smiled. "I thought it was the end of the world."

"The shaking must have shifted the house a little, because your bedroom door jammed shut, and I nearly busted my shoulder breaking it down."

"I thought it was you that made the shaking stop. I believed that for years."

"Afterward you were scared of that damn chest of drawers that your mother liked so much. You wouldn't have it in the house."

"I thought it wanted to eat me."

"In the end I chopped it up for firewood." Suddenly Bo looked sad. "I wish I could have those years back, to live all over again."

She knew he was thinking of her mother. "Yeah," she said.

"Good night, kid."

"Night, Bo."

As she drove across the Bay Bridge on Wednesday morning, heading for Berkeley, Judy wondered what Michael Quercus looked like. His irritable manner suggested a peevish professor, stooped and shabby, peering irritably at the world through glasses that kept falling down his nose. Or he could be an academic fat cat in a pinstripe suit, charming to people who might donate money to the university, contemptuously indifferent to anyone who could not be of use to him.

She parked in the shade of a magnolia tree on Euclid Avenue. As she rang his bell she had a horrible feeling he might find another excuse to send her away; but when she gave her name there was a buzz and the door opened. She climbed two flights to his apartment. It was open. She walked in. The place was small and cheap: his business could not be making much money. She passed through a vestibule and found herself in his office-cum–living room.

He was sitting at his desk in khakis, tan walking boots, and a navy blue polo shirt. Michael Quercus was neither a peevish professor nor an academic fat cat, she saw immediately. He was a hunk: tall, fit, good-looking, with sexy hair, dark and curly. She quickly summed him up as one of those guys who were so big and handsome and confident, they thought they could do anything they liked.

He, too, was surprised. His eyes widened and he said: "Are you the FBI agent?"

She gave him a firm handshake. "Were you expecting someone else?"

He shrugged. "You don't look like Efrem Zimbalist, Junior."

Zimbalist was the actor who played Inspector Lewis Erskine in the long-running television show *The FBI*. Judy said mildly: "I've been an agent for ten years. Can you imagine how many people have already made that joke?"

To her surprise he grinned broadly. "Okay," he said. "You got me."

That's better.

She noticed a framed photo on his desk. It showed a pretty redhead with a child in her arms. People always liked to talk about their children. "Who's this?" she said.

"Nobody important. You want to get to the point?"

Forget friendly.

She took him at his word and asked her question right out. "I need to know if a terrorist group could trigger an earthquake."

"Have you had a threat?"

I'm supposed to be asking the questions. "You haven't heard? It's been talked about on the radio. Don't you listen to John Truth?"

He shook his head. "Is it serious?"

"That's what I need to establish."

"Okay. Well, the short answer is yes."

Judy felt a frisson of fear. Quercus seemed so sure. She had been hoping for the opposite answer. She said: "How could they do it?"

"Take a nuclear bomb, put it at the bottom of a deep mine shaft, and detonate it. That'll do the trick. But you probably want a more realistic scenario."

"Yeah. Imagine *you* wanted to trigger an earthquake."

"Oh, I could do it."

Judy wondered if he was just bragging. "Explain how."

"Okay." He reached down behind his desk and picked up a short plank of wood and a regular house brick. He obviously kept them there for this purpose. He put the plank on his desk and the brick on the plank. Then he lifted one end of the plank slowly until the brick slid down the slope onto the desk. "The brick slips when the gravity pulling it overcomes the friction holding it still," he said. "Okay so far?"

"Sure."

"A fault such as the San Andreas is a place where two adjacent slabs of the earth's crust are moving in different directions. Imagine a pair of icebergs scraping past one another. They don't move smoothly: they get jammed. Then, when they're stuck, pressure builds up, slowly but surely, over the decades."

"So how does that lead to earthquakes?"

"Something happens to release all that stored-up energy." He lifted one end of the plank again. This time he stopped just before the brick began to slide. "Several sections of the San Andreas fault are like this—just about ready to slip, any decade now. Take this."

He handed Judy a clear plastic twelve-inch ruler.

"Now tap the plank sharply just in front of the brick."

She did so, and the brick began to slide.

Quercus grabbed it and stopped it. "When the plank is tilted, it takes only a little tap to make the brick move. And where the San Andreas is under tremendous pressure, a little nudge may be enough to unjam the slabs. Then they slip—and all that pent-up energy shakes the earth."

Quercus might be abrasive, but once he got onto his subject he was a pleasure to listen to. He was a clear thinker, and he explained himself easily, without condescending. Despite the ominous picture he was painting, Judy realized she was enjoying talking to him, and not just because he was so good-looking. "Is that what happens in most earthquakes?"

"I believe so, though some other seismologists might disagree. There are natural vibrations that resound through the earth's crust from time to time. Most earthquakes are probably triggered by the right vibration in the right place at the right time."

How am I going to explain all this to Mr. Honeymoon? He's going to want simple yes-no answers. "So how does that help our terrorists?"

"They need a ruler, and they need to know where to tap."

"What's the real-life equivalent of the ruler? A nuclear bomb?"

"They don't need anything so powerful. They have to send a shock wave through the earth's crust, that's all. If they know exactly where the fault is vulnerable, they might do it with a charge of dynamite, precisely placed."

"Anyone can get hold of dynamite if they really want to."

"The explosion would have to be underground. I guess drilling a shaft would be the challenge for a terrorist group."

Judy wondered if the blue-collar man imagined by Simon Sparrow was a drilling rig operator. Such men would surely need a special license. A quick check with the Department of Motor Vehicles might yield a list of all of them in California. There could not be many.

Quercus went on: "They would obviously need drilling equipment, expertise, and some kind of pretext to get permission."

Those problems were not insurmountable. "Is it really so simple?" Judy said.

"Listen, I'm not telling you this would work. I'm saying it might. No one will know for sure until they try it. I can try to give you some insight into how these things happen, but you'll have to make your own assessment of the risk."

Judy nodded. She had used almost the same words last night in telling Bo what she needed. Quercus might act like an asshole sometimes, but as Bo would say, everyone needed an asshole now and again. "So knowing where to place the charge is everything?"

"Yes."

"Who has that information?"

"Universities, the state geologist . . . me. We all share information."

"Anyone can get hold of it?"

"It's not secret, though you would need to have some scientific knowledge to interpret the data."

"So someone in the terrorist group would have to be a seismologist."

"Yes. Could be a student."

Judy thought of the educated thirty-year-old woman who was doing the typing, according to Simon's theory. She could be a graduate student. How many geology students were there in California? How long would it take to find and interview them all?

Quercus went on: "And there's one other factor: earth tides. The oceans move this way and that under the gravitational influence of the moon, and the solid earth is subject to the same forces. Twice a day there's a seismic window, when the fault line is under extra stress because of the tides; and that's when an earthquake is most likely—or most easy to trigger. Which is my specialty. I'm the only person who has done extensive calculations of seismic windows for California faults."

"Could someone have gotten this data from you?"

"Well, I'm in the business of selling it." He gave a rueful smile. "But, as you can see, my business isn't making me rich. I have one contract, with a big insurance company, and that pays the rent, but unfortunately that's all. My theories about seismic windows make me kind of a maverick, and corporate America hates mavericks."

The note of wry self-deprecation was surprising, and Judy started to like him better. "Someone might have taken the information without your knowledge. Have you been burgled lately?"

"Never."

"Could your data have been copied by a friend or relative?"

"I don't think so. No one spends time in this room without my being here."

She picked up the photo from his desk. "Your wife, or girlfriend?"

He looked annoyed and took the picture out of her hand. "I'm separated from my wife, and I don't have a girlfriend."

"Is that so?" said Judy. She had got everything she needed from him. She stood up. "I appreciate your time, Professor."

"Please call me Michael. I've enjoyed talking to you."

She was surprised.

He added: "You pick up fast. That makes it more fun."

"Well . . . good."

He walked her to the door of the apartment and shook her hand. He had big hands, but his grip was surprisingly gentle. "Anything else you want to know, I'll be glad to help."

She risked a gibe. "So long as I call ahead for an appointment, right?"

He did not smile. "Right."

Driving back across the bay, she reflected that the danger was now clear. A terrorist group might conceivably be able to cause an earthquake. They would need accurate data on critically stressed points on the fault line, and perhaps on seismic windows, but that was obtainable. They had to have someone to interpret the data. And they needed some way to send shock waves through the earth. That would be the most difficult task, but it was not out of the question.

She had the unwelcome task of telling the governor's aide that the whole thing was horrifyingly possible.

5

Priest woke at first light on Thursday.

He generally woke early, all the year round. He never needed much sleep, unless he had been partying too hard, and that was rare now.

One more day.

From the governor's office there had been nothing but a maddening silence. They acted as if no threat had been made. So did the rest of the world, by and large. The Hammer of Eden was rarely mentioned in the news broadcasts Priest listened to on his car radio.

Only John Truth took them seriously. He kept taunting Governor Mike Robson in his daily radio show. Until yesterday, all the governor would say was that the FBI was investigating. But last night Truth had reported that the governor had promised a statement today.

That statement would decide everything. If it was conciliatory, and gave at least a hint that the governor would consider the demand, Priest would rejoice. But if the statement was unyielding, Priest would have to cause an earthquake.

He wondered if he really could.

Melanie sounded convincing when she talked about the fault line and what it would take to make it slip. But no one had ever tried this. Even she admitted she could not be one hundred percent sure it would work. What if it failed? What if it worked and they were caught? What if it worked and they were killed in the earthquake—who would take care of the communards and the children?

He rolled over. Melanie's head lay on the pillow beside him. He studied her face in repose. Her skin was very white, and her eyelashes were almost transparent. A strand of long ginger-colored hair fell across her cheek. He pulled the sheet back a little and looked at her breasts, heavy and soft. He contemplated waking her. Under the covers, he reached out and stroked her, running his hand across her belly and into the triangle of reddish hair below. She stirred, swallowed, then turned over and moved away.

He sat up. He was in the one-room house that had been his home for the last twenty-five years. As well as the bed, it had an old couch in front of the fireplace and a table in the corner with a fat yellow candle in a holder. There was no electric light.

In the early days of the commune, most people lived in cabins like this, and the kids all slept in a bunkhouse. But over the years some permanent couples had formed, and they had built bigger places with separate bedrooms for their children. Priest and Star had kept their own individual houses, but the trend was against them. It was best not to fight the inevitable: Priest had learned that from Star. Now there were six family homes as well as the original fifteen cabins. Right now the commune consisted of twenty-five adults and ten children, plus Melanie and Dusty. One cabin was empty.

This room was as familiar as his hand, but lately the well-known objects had taken on a new aura. For years his eye had passed over without registering them: the picture of Priest that Star had painted for his thirtieth birthday; the elaborately decorated hookah left behind by a French girl called Marie-Louise; the rickety shelf Flower had made in woodwork class; the fruit crate in which he kept his clothes. Now that he knew he might have to leave, each homely item looked special and wonderful, and it brought a lump to his throat to look at them. His room was like a photograph album in which every picture unchained a string of memories: the birth of Ringo; the day Smiler nearly drowned in the river; making love to twin sisters called Jane and Eliza; the warm, dry autumn of their first grape harvest; the taste of the '89 vintage. When he looked around and thought of the people who wanted to take it all away from him, he was filled with a rage that burned inside him like vitriol in his belly.

He picked up a towel, stepped into his sandals, and went outside naked. His dog, Spirit, greeted him with a quiet snuffle. It was a clear, crisp morning, with patches of high cloud in the blue sky. The sun had not yet appeared over the mountains, and the valley was in shadow. No one else was about.

He walked downhill through the little village, and Spirit followed. Although the communal spirit was still strong, people had customized their homes with individual touches. One woman had planted the ground around her house with flowers and small shrubs: Priest had named her Garden in consequence. Dale and Poem, who were a couple, had let their children paint the outside walls, and the result was a colorful mess. A man called Slow, who was retarded, had built a crooked porch on which stood a wobbly homemade rocking chair.

Priest knew the place might not be beautiful to other eyes. The paths were muddy, the buildings were rickety, and the layout was haphazard. There was no zoning: the kids' bunkhouse was right next to the wine barn, and the carpentry yard was in the midst of the cabins. The privies were moved every year, to no avail: no matter where they were sited, you could always smell them on a hot day. Yet everything about the place warmed his heart. And when he looked farther away and saw the forested hillsides soaring steeply from the gleaming river all the way to the blue peaks of the Sierra Nevada, he had a view that was so beautiful it hurt.

But now, every time he looked at it, the thought that he might lose it stabbed him like a knife.

Beside the river, a wooden box on a boulder held soap, cheap razors, and a hand mirror. He lathered his face and shaved, then stepped into the cold stream and washed all over. He dried himself briskly on the coarse towel.

There was no piped water here. In winter, when it was too cold to bathe in the river, they had a communal bath night twice a week and heated great barrels of water in the cookhouse to wash one another: it was quite sexy. But in summer only babies had warm water.

He went back up the hill and dressed quickly in the blue jeans and workshirt he always wore. He walked over to the cookhouse and stepped inside. The door was not locked: no doors had locks here. He built up the fire with logs and lit it, put on a pan of water for coffee, and went out.

He liked to walk around when the others were all abed. He whispered their names as he passed their homes: "Moon. Chocolate. Giggle." He imagined each one lying there, sleeping: Apple, a fat girl, lying on her back with her mouth open, snoring; Juice and Alaska, two middle-aged women, entwined together; the kids in the bunkhouse—his own Flower, Ringo, and Smiler; Melanie's Dusty; the twins, Bubble and Chip, all pink cheeks and tousled hair . . .

My people.

May they live here forever.

He passed the workshop, where they kept spades and hoes and pruning shears; the concrete circle where they trod the grapes in October; and the barn where the wine from last year's harvest stood in huge wooden casks, slowly settling and clarifying, now almost ready to be blended and bottled.

He paused outside the temple.

He felt very proud. From the very beginning they had talked of building a temple. For many years it had seemed an impossible dream. There was always too much else to do—land to clear and vines to plant, barns to build, the vegetable garden and the free shop and the kids' lessons. But five years ago the commune had seemed to reach a plateau. For the first time, Priest was not worried about whether they would have enough to eat through the coming winter. He no longer felt that one bad harvest could wipe them out. There was nothing undone on the list of urgent tasks he carried in his head. So he had announced that it was time to build the temple.

And here it was.

It meant a lot to Priest. It showed that his community was mature. They were not living hand to mouth anymore. They could feed themselves and have time and resources to spare for building a place of worship. They were no longer a bunch of hippies trying out an idealistic dream. The dream worked; they had proved it. The temple was the emblem of their triumph.

He stepped inside. It was a simple wooden structure with a single skylight and no furniture. Everyone sat cross-legged in a circle on the plank floor to worship. It was also the schoolhouse and meeting room. The only decoration was a banner Star had made. Priest could not read it, but he knew what it said:

> *Meditation is life: all else is distraction*
> *Money makes you poor*
> *Marriage is the greatest infidelity*
> *When no one owns anything, we all own everything*
> *Do what you like is the only law*

These were the Five Paradoxes of Baghram. Priest said he had learned them from an Indian guru he had studied under in Los Angeles, but in fact he had made them up. *Pretty good for a guy who can't read.*

He stood in the center of the room for several minutes,

eyes closed, arms hanging loosely at his sides, focusing his energy. There was nothing phony about *this*. He had learned meditation techniques from Star, and they really worked. He felt his mind clarify like the wine in the casks. He prayed that Governor Mike Robson's heart would be softened and he would announce a freeze on the building of new power plants in California. He imagined the handsome governor in his dark suit and white shirt, sitting in a leather chair behind a polished desk; and in his vision the governor said: "I have decided to give these people what they want—not just to avoid an earthquake, but because it makes sense anyway."

After a few minutes, Priest's spiritual strength was renewed. He felt alert, confident, centered.

When he went outside again, he decided to check on the vines.

There had been no grapes originally. When Star arrived there was nothing in the valley but a ruined hunting lodge. For three years the commune had lurched from crisis to crisis, riven by quarrels, washed out in storms, sustained only by begging trips to towns. Then Priest came.

It took him less than a year to become Star's acknowledged equal as joint leader. First he had organized the begging trips for maximum efficiency. They would hit a town like Sacramento or Stockton on a Saturday morning, when the streets were crowded with shoppers. Each individual would be assigned a different corner. Everyone had to have a pitch: Aneth would say she was trying to get the bus fare home to her folks in New York, Song would strum her guitar and sing "There but for Fortune," Slow would say he had not eaten for three days, Bones would make people smile with a sign saying "Why lie? It's for beer."

But begging was only a stopgap. Under Priest's direction, the hippies had terraced the hillside, diverted a brook for irrigation, and planted a vineyard. The tremendous team effort made them into a strongly knit group, and the wine enabled them to live without begging. Now their chardonnay was sought after by connoisseurs.

Priest walked along the neat rows. Herbs and flowers were planted between the vines, partly because they were useful and pretty, but mainly to attract ladybugs and wasps that would destroy greenflies and other pests. No chemicals were used here: they relied on natural methods. They grew clover, too, because it fixed nitrogen from the air, and when they plowed it into the soil it acted as a natural fertilizer.

The vines were sprouting. It was late May, so the annual peril of frost killing the new shoots was past. At this point in the cycle, most of the work consisted of tying the shoots to trellises to train their growth and prevent wind damage.

Priest had learned about wine during his years as a liquor wholesaler, and Star had studied the subject in books, but they could not have succeeded without old Raymond Dellavalle, a good-natured wine grower who helped them because, Priest guessed, he wished his own youth had been more daring.

Priest's vineyard had saved the commune, but the commune had saved Priest's life. He had arrived here a fugitive—on the run from the Mob, the Los Angeles police, and the Internal Revenue Service all at once. He was a drunk and a cocaine abuser, lonely, broke, and suicidal. He had driven down the dirt road to the commune, following vague directions from a hitchhiker, and wandered through the trees until he came upon a bunch of naked hippies sitting on the ground chanting. He had stared at them for a long while, spellbound by the mantra and the sense of profound calm that rose up like smoke from a fire. One or two had smiled at him, but they had continued their ritual. Eventually he had stripped off, slowly, like a man in a trance, discarding his business suit, pink shirt, platform shoes, and red-and-white jockey shorts. Then, naked, he had sat down with them.

Here he had found peace, a new religion, work, friends, and lovers. At a time when he was ready to drive his yellow

Plymouth 'Cuda 440-6 right over the edge of a cliff, the commune had given meaning to his life.

Now there would never be any other existence for him. This place was all he had, and he would die to defend it.

I may have to.

He would listen to John Truth's radio show tonight. If the governor was going to open the door to negotiation, or make any other concession, it would surely be announced before the end of the broadcast.

When he came to the far side of the vineyard, he decided to check on the seismic vibrator.

He walked up the hill. There was no road, just a well-trodden path through the forest. Vehicles could not get through to the village. A quarter of a mile from the houses, he arrived at a muddy clearing. Parked under the trees were his old 'Cuda, a rusty Volkswagen minibus that was even older, Melanie's orange Subaru, and the communal pickup, a dark green Ford Ranger. From here a dirt track wound two miles through the forest, uphill and down, disappearing into a mudslide here and passing through a stream there, until at last it reached the county road, a two-lane blacktop. It was ten miles to the nearest town, Silver City.

Once a year the entire commune would spend a day rolling barrels of wine up the hill and through the trees to this clearing, there to be loaded onto Paul Beale's truck for transport to his bottling plant in Napa. It was the big day in their calendar, and they always held a feast that night, then took a holiday on the following day, to celebrate a successful year. The ceremony took place eight months after the harvest, so it was due in a few days' time. This year, Priest resolved, they would hold the party the day after the governor reprieved the valley.

In return for the wine, Paul Beale brought food for the communal kitchen and kept the free shop stocked with supplies: clothing, candy, cigarettes, stationery, books, tampons, toothpaste, everything anyone needed. The system operated without money. However, Paul kept accounts, and at the end of each year, he deposited surplus cash in a bank account that only Priest and Star knew about.

From the clearing, Priest headed along the track for a mile, skirting rainwater pools and clambering over dead-falls, then turned off and followed an invisible way through the trees. There were no tire tracks because he had carefully brushed the carpet of pine needles that formed the forest floor. He came to a hollow and stopped. All he could see was a pile of vegetation: broken branches and uprooted saplings heaped twelve feet high like a bonfire. He had to go right up to the pile and push aside some of the brush to con-firm that the truck was still there under its camouflage.

Not that he thought anyone would come here looking for the truck. The Ricky Granger who had been hired as a juggie by Ritkin Seismex in the South Texas oilfield had no traceable connection with this remote vineyard in Sierra County, California. However, it did occasionally happen that a couple of backpackers would lose their way radically and wander onto the commune's land—as Melanie had—and they would sure as hell wonder why this large piece of expensive machinery was parked out here in the woods. So Priest and the Rice Eaters had slaved for two hours to con-ceal the truck. Priest was pretty sure it could not be seen even from the air.

He exposed a wheel and kicked the tire, just like the skeptical purchaser of a used car. He had killed a man for this vehicle. He thought briefly about Mario's pretty wife and kids and wondered whether they had realized yet that Mario was never coming home. Then he put the thought out of his mind.

He wanted to reassure himself that the truck would be ready to go tomorrow morning. Just looking at it made him edgy. He felt a powerful urge to get going right away, today, now, just to ease the tension. But he had announced a dead-line, and timing would be important.

This waiting was unbearable. He thought of getting in and starting the truck, just to make sure everything was okay; but that would be foolish. He was suffering from dumb nerves. The truck would be fine. He would do better to stay away and leave it alone until tomorrow.

He parted another section of the covering and looked at the steel plate that hammered the earth. If Melanie's scheme worked, the vibration would unleash an earthquake. There was a pure kind of justice about the plan. They would be using the earth's stored-up energy as a threat to force the governor to take care of the environment. The earth was saving the earth. It felt right to Priest in a way that was almost holy.

Spirit gave a low bark, as if he had heard something. It was probably a rabbit, but Priest nervously replaced the branches he had moved, then headed back.

He made his way through the trees to the track and turned toward the village.

He stopped in the middle of the track and frowned, mystified. On the way here he had stepped over a fallen bough. Now it had been moved to the side. Spirit had not been barking at rabbits. Someone else was about. He had not heard anyone, but sounds were quickly muffled in the dense vegetation. Who was it? Had someone followed him? Had they seen him looking at the seismic vibrator?

As he headed home, Spirit became agitated. When they came within sight of the parking circle, Priest saw why.

There in the muddy clearing, parked beside his 'Cuda, was a police car.

Priest's heart stopped.

So soon! How could they have tracked him down so soon? He stared at the cruiser.

It was a white Ford Crown Victoria with a green stripe along the side, a silver six-pointed sheriff's star on the door, four aerials, and a rack of blue, red, and orange lights on the roof.

Be calm. All things must pass.

The police might not be here for the vibrator. Idle curiosity might have brought a cop wandering down the track: it had never happened before, but it was possible. There were lots of other possible reasons. They could be searching for a tourist who had gone missing. A sheriff's deputy could be looking for a secret place to meet his neighbor's wife.

They might not even realize there was a commune here. Perhaps they need never find out. If Priest slipped back into the woods—

Too late. Just as the thought entered his head, a cop stepped around the trunk of a tree.

Spirit barked fiercely.

"Quiet," Priest said, and the dog fell silent.

The cop was wearing the gray-green uniform of a sheriff's deputy, with a star over the left breast of the short jacket, a cowboy hat, and a gun on his pants belt.

He saw Priest and waved.

Priest hesitated, then slowly raised his hand and waved back.

Then, reluctantly, he walked up to the car.

He hated cops. Most of them were thieves and bullies and psychopaths. They used their uniform and their position to conceal the fact that they were worse criminals than the people they arrested. But he would force himself to be polite, just as if he were some dumb suburban citizen who imagined the police were there to protect him.

He breathed evenly, relaxed the muscles of his face, smiled, and said: "Howdy."

The cop was alone. He was young, maybe twenty-five or thirty, with short light brown hair. His body in the uniform was already beefy: in ten years' time he would have a beer gut.

"Are there any residences near here?" the cop asked.

Priest was tempted to lie, but a moment's reflection told him it was too risky. The cop only had to walk a quarter of a mile in the right direction to stumble upon the houses, and his suspicions would be aroused if he found he had been lied to. So Priest told the truth. "You're not far from the Silver River Winery."

"I never heard of it before."

That was no accident. In the phone book, its address and number were Paul Beale's in Napa. None of the communards registered to vote. None of them paid taxes because none had any income. They had always been secretive. Star had a horror of publicity that dated from the time the hippie movement had been destroyed by over-exposure in the media. But many of the communards had a reason to hide away. Some had debts, others were wanted by the police. Oaktree had been a deserter, Song had escaped from an uncle who sexually abused her, and Aneth's husband had beaten her up and swore that if she left him, he would seek her out wherever she might be.

The commune continued to act as a sanctuary, and some of the more recent arrivals were also on the run. The only way anyone could find out about the place was from people such as Paul Beale who had lived here for a while, then returned to the world outside, and they were very cautious about sharing the secret.

There had never been a cop here.

"How come I never heard of the place?" the cop said. "I been a deputy here ten years."

"It's pretty small," Priest said.

"You the owner?"

"No, just a worker."

"So what do you do here, make wine?"

Oh, boy, an intellectual giant. "Yeah, that about sums it up." The cop did not pick up the irony. Priest went on: "What brings you to these parts so early in the morning? We haven't had a crime here since Charlie got drunk and voted for Jimmy Carter." He grinned. There was no Charlie: he was trying to make the kind of joke a cop might like.

But this one remained straight-faced. "I'm looking for the parents of a young girl who gives her name as Flower."

A terrible fear possessed Priest, and he suddenly felt as cold as the grave. "Oh, my God, what's happened?"

"She's under arrest."

"Is she okay?"

"She's not injured in any way, if that's what you mean."

"Thank God. I thought you were going to say she'd been in an accident." Priest's brain began to recover from the shock. "How can she be in jail? I thought she was here, asleep in her bed!"

"Obviously not. How are you connected with her?"

"I'm her father."

"Then you'll need to come to Silver City."

"Silver City? How long has she been there?"

"Just overnight. We didn't want to keep her that long, but for a while she refused to tell us her address. She broke down an hour or so ago."

Priest's heart lurched to think of his little girl in custody, trying to keep the secret of the commune until she broke down. Tears came to his eyes.

The cop went on: "Even so, you were god-awful hard to find. In the end I got directions from a bunch of damn gun-toting freaks about five miles down the valley from here."

Priest nodded. "Los Alamos."

"Yeah. Had a damn big sign up saying 'We do not recognize the jurisdiction of the United States government.' Assholes."

"I know them," Priest said. They were right-wing vigilantes who had taken over a big old farmhouse in a lonely spot and now guarded it with high-powered firearms and dreamed of fighting off a Chinese invasion. Unfortunately they were the commune's nearest neighbors. "Why is Flower in custody? Did she do something wrong?"

"That is the usual reason," the cop said sarcastically.

"What did she do?"

"She was caught stealing from a store."

"From a *store*?" Why would a kid who had access to a free shop want to do that? "What did she steal?"

"A large-size color photograph of Leonardo DiCaprio."

Priest wanted to punch the cop in the face, but that would not have helped Flower, so instead he thanked the man for coming here and promised that he and Flower's mother would appear at the sheriff's office in Silver City within an hour to pick up their daughter. Satisfied, the cop drove away.

Priest went to Star's cabin. It doubled as the commune's clinic. Star had no medical training, but she had picked up a great deal of knowledge from her physician father and nurse mother. As a girl she had got used to medical emergencies and had even assisted at births. Her room was full of boxes of bandages, jars of ointment, aspirins, cough medicines, and contraceptives.

When Priest woke her and told her the bad news, she became hysterical. She hated the police almost as much as he did. In the sixties she had been beaten by cops with nightsticks on demonstrations, sold bad dope by undercover narcs, and, on one occasion, raped by detectives in a precinct house. She jumped out of bed, screaming, and started hitting him. He held her wrists and tried to calm her down.

"We have to go there now and get her out!" Star yelled.

"Right," he said. "Just get dressed first, okay?"

She stopped struggling. "Okay."

While she was pulling on her jeans he said: "You were busted at thirteen, you told me."

"Yeah, and a dirty old sergeant with a cigarette hanging from the corner of his mouth put his hands on my tits and said I was going to grow up into a beautiful lady."

"It won't help Flower if you go in there mad and get yourself arrested, too," he pointed out.

She got control of herself. "You're right, Priest. For her sake, we have to ingratiate ourselves with those motherfuckers."

She combed her hair and glanced in a small mirror. "All right. I'm ready to eat shit."

Priest had always believed it was best to be conventionally dressed when dealing with the police. He woke Dale and got from him the old dark blue suit. It was communal property now, and Dale had worn it most recently, to go to court when the wife he had left twenty years ago finally decided to divorce him. Priest put the suit on over his workshirt and tied the twenty-five-year-old pink-and-green "kipper" tie. The shoes had long worn out, so he put his sandals back on. Then he and Star got in the 'Cuda.

When they reached the county road, Priest said: "How come neither of us noticed she wasn't at home last night?"

"I went to say good night to her, but Pearl told me she had gone to the privy."

"I got that story, too! Pearl must have known what happened and covered up for her!" Pearl, the daughter of Dale and Poem, was twelve years old and Flower's best friend.

"I went back later, but all the candles were out and the bunkhouse was in darkness, so I didn't want to wake them up. I never imagined. . . . "

"Why would you? The darn kid has spent every night of her life in the same place—no reason to think she was anywhere else."

They drove into Silver City. The sheriff's office was next door to the courthouse. They entered a gloomy lobby decorated with yellowing news clippings of ancient murders. There was a reception desk behind a window with an intercom and a buzzer. A deputy in a khaki shirt and green tie said: "Help you?"

Star said: "My name is Stella Higgins, and you have my daughter here."

The deputy gave them a hard look. Priest figured he was appraising them, wondering what kind of parents they were. He said, "Just one moment, please," and disappeared.

Priest spoke to Star in a low voice. "I think we should be

respectable, law-abiding citizens who are appalled that a child of theirs is in trouble with the police. We have nothing but profound respect for law enforcement personnel. We are sorry to have caused trouble to such hardworking folk."

"Gotcha," Star said tightly.

A door opened and the deputy let them in. "Mr. and Mrs. Higgins," he said. Priest did not correct him. "Follow me, please." He led them to a conference room with a gray carpet and bland modern furniture.

Flower was waiting.

She was going to be formidable and voluptuous like her mother one day, but at thirteen she was still a lanky, awkward girl. Now she was sullen and tearful at the same time. But she seemed unharmed. Star hugged her silently, then Priest did the same.

Star said: "Honey, have you spent the night in jail?"

Flower shook her head. "At some house," she said.

The deputy explained. "California law is very strict. Juveniles can't be jailed under the same roof as adult criminals. So we have a couple of people in town who are willing to take charge of young offenders overnight. Flower stayed at the home of Miss Waterlow, a local schoolteacher who also happens to be the sheriff's sister."

Priest asked Flower: "Was it okay?"

The child nodded dumbly.

He began to feel better. *Hell, worse things can happen to kids.*

The deputy said: "Sit down, please, Mr. and Mrs. Higgins. I'm the probation officer, and it's part of my job to deal with juvenile offenders."

They sat down.

"Flower is charged with stealing a poster worth $9.99 from the Silver Disc Music Store."

Star turned to her daughter. "I can't understand this," she said. "Why would you steal a *poster* of a damn *movie star*?"

Flower was suddenly vocal. She yelled: "I just wanted it, okay? I just wanted it!" Then she burst into tears.

Priest addressed the deputy. "We'd like to take our daughter home as soon as possible. What do we need to do?"

"Mr. Higgins, I should point out to you that the maximum penalty for what Flower has done would be imprisonment until the age of twenty-one."

"Jesus Christ!" Priest exclaimed.

"However, I wouldn't expect such a harsh punishment for a first offense. Tell me, has Flower been in trouble before?"

"Never."

"Are you surprised by what she has done?"

"Yes."

"We're flabbergasted," said Star.

The deputy probed their home life, trying to establish whether Flower was well cared for. Priest answered most of the questions, giving the impression that they were simple agricultural workers. He said nothing of their communal life or their beliefs. The deputy asked where Flower attended school, and Priest explained that there was a school at the winery for the children of workers.

The deputy seemed satisfied with the answers. Flower had to sign a promise to appear in court in four weeks' time at ten A.M. The deputy asked for one of the parents to countersign, and Star obliged. They did not have to post bail. They were out of there in less than an hour.

Outside the sheriff's office, Priest said: "This doesn't make you a bad person, Flower. You did a dumb thing, but we love you as much as we always did. Just remember that. And we'll all talk about it when we get home."

They drove back to the winery. For a while Priest had been unable to think about anything except how his daughter was, but now that he had her back safe and well, he began to reflect on the wider implications of her arrest. The commune had never previously attracted the attention of the police. There was no theft, because they did not acknowledge private property. Sometimes there were fist-fights, but the communards dealt with such situations themselves. No one had ever died here. They had no phone to call the police. They never broke any laws except the drug laws, and they were discreet about that.

But now the place was on the map.

It was the worst possible moment for this to happen.

There was nothing he could do about it other than to be extra cautious. He resolved not to blame Flower. At her age he had been a full-time professional thief, with an arrest record that stretched back three years. If any parent could understand, he should.

He switched on the car radio. At the top of the hour there was a news bulletin. The last item referred to the earthquake threat. "Governor Mike Robson meets with FBI agents this morning to discuss the terrorist group the Hammer of Eden, who have threatened to cause an earthquake," said the newsreader. "A spokesman for the Bureau said that all threats are taken seriously but would not comment further ahead of the meeting."

The governor would make his announcement after he met with the FBI, Priest guessed. He wished the radio station had given the time of the meeting.

It was midmorning when they got home. Melanie's car was gone from the parking circle: she had taken Dusty to San Francisco to leave him with his father for the weekend.

There was a subdued air at the winery. Most of the group were weeding in the vineyard, working without the usual songs and laughter. Outside the cookhouse Holly, the mother of his sons Ringo and Smiler, grimly fried onions while Slow, who was always sensitive to atmosphere, looked frightened as he scrubbed early potatoes from the vegetable garden. Even Oaktree, the carpenter, seemed quiet as he bent over his workbench, sawing a plank.

When they saw Priest and Star returning with Flower,

they all began to finish up the tasks they were doing and head for the temple. When there was a crisis they always met to discuss it. If it was a minor matter, it could wait until the end of the day, but this was too important to be postponed.

On their way to the temple, Priest and his family were intercepted by Dale and Poem with their daughter, Pearl.

Dale, a small man with neat, short hair, was the most conventional one in the group. He was a key person because he was an expert winemaker and he controlled the blend of each year's vintage. But Priest sometimes felt he treated the commune as if it were any other village. Dale and Poem had been the first couple to build a family cabin. Poem was a dark-skinned woman with a French accent. She had a wild streak—Priest knew, he had slept with her many times—but with Dale she had become kind of domesticated. Dale was one of the few who might conceivably make the readjustment to normal life if he had to leave. Most of them would not, Priest felt: they would end up in jail or institutionalized or dead.

"There's something you should see," Dale said.

Priest noticed a quick interchange between the girls. Flower shot an accusing glare at Pearl, who looked frightened and guilty.

"What now?" said Star.

Dale led them all to the one empty cabin. At present it was used as a study room by the older children. There was a rough table, some chairs, and a cupboard containing books and pencils. The ceiling had a trapdoor leading to a crawl space under the sloping roof. Now the trapdoor was open and a stepladder stood beneath it.

Priest had a horrible feeling he knew what was coming.

Dale lit a candle and went up the ladder. Priest and Star followed. In the roof space, illuminated by the flickering candle, they saw the girls' secret cache: a box full of cheap jewelry, makeup, fashionable clothes, and teen magazines.

Priest said quietly: "All the things we brought them up to consider worthless."

Dale said: "They've been hitchhiking to Silver City. They've done it three times in the past four weeks. They take these clothes and change out of their jeans and work-shirts when they get there."

Star said: "What do they do there?"

"Hang out on the street, talk to boys, and steal from stores."

Priest put his hand into the box and pulled out a narrow-bodied T-shirt, blue with a single orange stripe. It was made of nylon and felt thin and trashy. It was the kind of clothing he despised: it gave no warmth or protection, and it did nothing but cover the beauty of the human body with a layer of ugliness.

With the shirt in his hand, he retreated down the step-ladder. Star and Dale followed.

The two girls looked mortified.

Priest said: "Let's go to the temple and discuss this with the group."

By the time they got there, everyone else had assembled, children included. They were sitting cross-legged on the floor, waiting.

Priest sat in the middle, as always. The discussions were democratic in theory, and the commune had no leaders, but in practice he and Star dominated all meetings. Priest would steer the dialogue toward the outcome he wanted, usually by asking questions rather than stating a point of view. If he liked an idea, he would encourage a discussion of its bene-fits; if he wanted to squash a proposal, he would ask how they could be sure it would work. And if the mood of the meeting was against him, he would pretend to be persuaded, then subvert the decision later.

"Who wants to begin?" he said.

Aneth spoke up. She was a motherly type in her forties, and she believed in understanding rather than condemning. She said: "Maybe Flower and Pearl should begin, by telling us why they wanted to go to Silver City."

"To meet people," Flower said defiantly.

Aneth smiled. "Boys, you mean?"

Flower shrugged.

Aneth said: "Well, I guess that's understandable . . . but why did you have to steal?"

"To look nice!"

Star gave an exasperated sigh. "What's wrong with your regular clothes?"

"Mom, be serious," Flower said scornfully.

Star leaned forward and slapped her face.

Flower gasped. A red mark appeared on her cheek.

"Don't you dare speak to me that way," Star said. "You've just been caught stealing, and I've had to get you out of jail, so don't talk as if I'm the stupid one."

Pearl started to cry.

Priest sighed. He should have seen this coming. There was nothing wrong with the clothes in the free shop. They had jeans in blue, black, or tan; denim workshirts; T-shirts in white, gray, red, and yellow; sandals and boots; heavy wool sweaters for the winter; waterproof coats for working in the rain. But the same clothes were worn by everyone, and had been for years. Of course the children wanted something different. Thirty-five years ago Priest had stolen a Beatle jacket from a boutique called Rave on San Pedro Street.

Poem said to her daughter: "Pearl, *cherie,* you don't like your clothes?"

Between sobs she said: "We wanted to look like Melanie."

"Ah," Priest said, and he saw it all.

Melanie was still wearing the clothes she had brought here: skimpy tops that showed her midriff, miniskirts and short shorts, funky shoes and cute caps. She looked chic and sexy. It was not surprising the girls had adopted her as a role model.

Dale said: "We need to talk about Melanie." He sounded

apprehensive. Most of them were nervous about saying anything that might be seen as a criticism of Priest.

Priest felt defensive. He had brought Melanie here, and he was her lover. And she was crucial to the plan. She was the only one who could interpret the data from Michael's disk, which had now been copied onto her laptop. Priest could not let them turn on her. "We never make people change their clothes when they join us," he said. "They wear out their old stuff first, it's always been the rule."

Alaska spoke up. A former schoolteacher, she had come here with her lover, Juice, ten years ago, after they had been ostracized in the small town where they lived for coming out as lesbians. "It's not just her clothes," Alaska said. "She doesn't do much work." Juice nodded agreement.

Priest argued: "I've seen her in the kitchen, washing dishes and baking cookies."

Alaska looked scared, but she persisted. "Some light domestic chores. She doesn't work in the vineyard. She's a passenger, Priest."

Star saw Priest coming under attack and weighed in on his side. "We've had a lot of people like that. Remember what Holly was like when she first came?"

Holly had been a bit like Melanie, a pretty girl who was attracted first to Priest and then to the commune.

Holly grinned ruefully. "I admit it. I was lazy. But eventually I started to feel bad about not pulling my weight. Nobody said anything to me. I just realized I'd be happier doing my fair share."

Now Garden spoke. A former junkie, she was twenty-five but looked forty. "Melanie's a bad influence. She talks to the kids about pop records and TV shows and trash like that."

Priest said: "Obviously we need to have a discussion with Melanie about this when she gets back from San Francisco. I know she's going to be very upset when she hears what Flower and Pearl have done."

Dale was not satisfied. "What bugs a lot of us . . ."

Priest frowned. This sounded as if a group of them had been talking behind his back. *Jesus, have I got a full-scale rebellion on my hands?* He let his displeasure show in his voice. "Well? What *bugs* a lot of you?"

Dale swallowed. "Her mobile phone and computer."

There was no power line into the valley, so they had few electrical appliances; and there had grown up a kind of puritanism about things like TV and videotapes. Priest had to listen to his car radio to hear the news. They had come to look down on anything electrical. Melanie's equipment, which she recharged at the public library in Silver City by plugging into an outlet normally used for the vacuum cleaner, had drawn some disapproving stares. Now several people nodded agreement with Dale's complaint.

There was a special reason why Melanie had to keep her mobile and her computer. But Priest could not explain it to Dale. He was not a Rice Eater. Although he was a full member of the group and had been here for years, Priest could not be sure he would go along with the earthquake plan. He might freak.

Priest realized he had to end this. It was getting out of control. Discontented people had to be dealt with one by one, not in a collective discussion where they reinforced one another.

But before he could say anything, Poem weighed in. "Priest, is there something going on? Something you're not telling us about? I never really understood why you and Star had to go away for two and a half weeks."

Song, supporting Priest, said: "Wow, that's such a mistrustful question!"

The group was falling apart, Priest could see. It was the imminent prospect of having to leave the valley. There was no sign of the miracle he had hinted at. They saw their world coming to an end.

Star said: "I thought I told everyone. I had an uncle who

died and left his affairs in a tangle, and I was his only relative, so I had to help the lawyers straighten everything out."

Enough.

Priest knew how to choke off a protest. He spoke decisively. "I feel we're discussing these things in a bad atmosphere," he said. "Does anyone agree with me?"

They all did, of course. Most of them nodded.

"What do we do about it?" Priest looked at his ten-year-old son, a dark-eyed, serious child. "What do you say, Ringo?"

"We meditate together," the boy said. It was the answer any of them would give.

Priest looked around. "Does everyone approve of Ringo's idea?"

They did.

"Then let's make ourselves ready."

Each of them assumed the position they liked. Some lay flat on their backs, others bent into a fetal curl, one or two lay as if sleeping. Priest and several others sat cross-legged, hands loose on their knees, eyes closed, faces raised to heaven.

"Relax the small toe of your left foot," Priest said in a quiet, penetrating voice. "Then the fourth toe, then the third, then the second, then the big toe. Relax your whole foot . . . and your ankle . . . and then your calf." As he went slowly around the body, a contemplative peace descended on the room. People's breathing slowed and became even, their bodies grew more and more still, and their faces gradually took on the tranquillity of meditation.

Finally Priest said a slow, deep syllable: "Om."

With one voice the congregation replied: "Omm . . ."

My people.

May they live here forever.

6

The meeting at the governor's office was scheduled for twelve noon. Sacramento, the state capital, was a couple of hours' drive from San Francisco. Judy left home at nine forty-five to allow for heavy traffic getting out of the city.

The aide she was to meet, Al Honeymoon, was a well-known figure in California politics. Officially cabinet secretary, he was in fact hatchet man. Any time Governor Robson needed to run a new highway through a beauty spot, build a nuclear power station, fire a thousand government employees, or betray a faithful friend, he got Honeymoon to do the dirty work.

The two men had been colleagues for twenty years. When they met, Mike Robson was still only a state assemblyman and Honeymoon was fresh out of law school. Honeymoon had been selected for his bad-guy role because he was black, and the governor had shrewdly calculated that the press would hesitate to vilify a black man. Those liberal days were long gone, but Honeymoon had matured into a political operator of great skill and utter ruthlessness. No one liked him, but plenty of people were scared of him.

For the sake of the Bureau, Judy wanted to make a good impression on him. It was not often that political types had a direct personal interest in an FBI case. Judy knew that her handling of this assignment would forever color Honeymoon's attitude to the Bureau and to law enforcement agencies in general. Personal experience always had more impact than reports and statistics.

The FBI liked to appear all-powerful and infallible. But she had made so little progress with the case that it would be kind of difficult to play that part, especially to a hard-ass like Honeymoon. Anyway, it was not her style. Her plan was simply to appear efficient and inspire confidence.

And she had another reason for giving a good account of herself. She wanted Governor Robson's statement to open the door to a dialogue with the Hammer of Eden. A hint that the governor might negotiate could just persuade them to hold off. And if they responded by trying to communicate, that might give Judy new clues to who they were. Right now it was the only way she could think of to catch them. All other lines of inquiry had led to dead ends.

She thought it might be difficult to persuade the governor to give this hint. He would not want to give the impression he would listen to terrorist demands, for fear of encouraging others. But there should be a way to word the statement so that the message was clear only to the Hammer of Eden people.

She was not wearing her Armani power suit. Instinct told her that Honeymoon was more likely to warm to someone who came on as a working Joe, so she had put on a steel gray pantsuit, tied her hair back in a neat knot, and carried her gun in a holster on her hip. In case that was too severe, she wore small pearl earrings that called attention to her long neck. It never did any harm to look attractive.

She wondered idly whether Michael Quercus found her attractive. He was a dish; shame he was so irritating. Her mother would have approved of him. Judy could remember her saying: "I like a man who takes charge." Quercus dressed nicely, in an understated kind of way. She wondered what his body was like under his clothes. Maybe he was covered with dark hair, like a monkey: she did not like hairy men. Maybe he was pale and soft, but she thought not: he seemed fit. She realized she was fantasizing about Quercus in the nude, and she felt annoyed with herself. *The last thing I need is a bad-tempered matinee idol.*

She decided to call ahead and check the parking. She dialed the governor's office on her cell phone and got Honeymoon's secretary. "I have a twelve noon meeting with Mr. Honeymoon, and I'm wondering if I can park at the Capitol Building. I've never been to Sacramento before."

The secretary was a young man. "We have no visitor parking at the building, but there's a parking garage on the next block."

"Where exactly is that?"

"The entrance is on Tenth Street between K Street and L. The Capitol Building is on Tenth between L and M. It's literally a minute away. But your meeting isn't at noon, it's at eleven-thirty."

"What?"

"Your meeting is scheduled for eleven-thirty."

"Has it been changed?"

"No, ma'am, it always was eleven-thirty."

Judy was furious. To arrive late would create a bad impression even before she opened her mouth. This was already going wrong.

She controlled her anger. "I guess someone made a mistake." She checked her watch. If she drove like hell, she could be there in ninety minutes. "It's no problem, I'm running ahead of schedule," she lied. "I'll be there."

"Very good."

She put her foot down and watched the Monte Carlo's speedometer climb to a hundred. Fortunately the road was not busy. Most of the morning traffic was headed the other way, into San Francisco.

Brian Kincaid had told her the time of the meeting, so he would be late, too. They were traveling separately because he had a second appointment in Sacramento, at the FBI field office there. Judy dialed the San Francisco office and spoke to the SAC's secretary. "Linda, this is Judy. Would you call Brian and tell him the governor's aide is expecting us at eleven-thirty, not twelve noon, please?"

"I think he knows that," Linda said.

"No, he doesn't. He told me twelve. See if you can reach him and warn him."

"Sure will."

"Thanks." Judy hung up and concentrated on her driving.

A few minutes later she heard a police siren.

She looked in her mirror and saw the familiar tan paint job of a California Highway Patrol car.

"I do not fucking believe this," she said.

She pulled over and braked hard. The patrol car pulled in behind her. She opened her door.

An amplified voice said: "STAY IN THE CAR."

She took our her FBI shield, held it at arm's length so the cop could see it, then got out.

"STAY IN THE CAR!"

She heard a note of fear in the voice and saw that the patrolman was alone. She sighed. She could just imagine some rookie cop pulling a gun and shooting her out of nervousness.

She held out her shield so he could see it. "FBI!" she shouted. "Look, for Christ's sake!"

"GET BACK IN THE CAR!"

She looked at her watch. It was ten-thirty. Shaking with frustration, she sat in her car. She left the door open.

There was a maddeningly long wait.

At last the patrolman approached her. "The reason I stopped you is that you were doing ninety-nine miles per hour—"

"Just look at this," she said, holding out her shield.

"What's that?"

"For Christ's sake, it's an FBI shield! I'm an agent on urgent business and you've just delayed me!"

"Well, you sure don't look like—"

She jumped out of the car, startling him, and waved a finger under his chin. "Don't you tell me I don't look like a fucking agent. You don't recognize an FBI shield, so how would you know what an agent looks like?" She put her hands on her hips, pushing her jacket back so that he could see her holster.

"Can I see your license, please?"

"Hell, no. I'm leaving now, and I'm going to drive to Sacramento at ninety-nine miles per hour, do you understand?" She got back into the car.

"You can't do that," he said.

"Write your congressman," she said, and she slammed the door and drove off.

She moved into the fast lane, accelerated to a hundred, then checked her watch. She had wasted about five minutes. She could still make it.

She had lost her temper with the patrolman. He would tell his superior, who would complain to the FBI. Judy would get a reprimand. But if she had been polite to the guy, she would still be there. "Shit," she said feelingly.

She reached the turnoff for downtown Sacramento at eleven-twenty. By eleven twenty-five she was entering the parking garage on Tenth Street. It took her a couple of minutes to find a slot. She ran down the staircase and across the street.

The Capitol Building was a white stone palace like a wedding cake, set in immaculate gardens bordered by giant palm trees. She hurried along a marble hall to a large doorway with GOVERNOR carved over it. She stopped, took a couple of calming breaths, and checked her watch.

It was exactly eleven-thirty. She had got there on time. The Bureau would not look incompetent.

She opened the double doors and stepped inside.

She found herself in a large lobby presided over by a secretary behind an enormous desk. On one side was a row of chairs where, to her surprise, she saw Brian Kincaid waiting, looking cool and relaxed in a crisp dark gray suit, his white hair combed neatly, not at all like someone who had rushed to get here. She was suddenly conscious that she was perspiring.

When Kincaid caught her eye, she saw a flash of surprise in his expression, swiftly suppressed.

She said: "Uh . . . hi, Brian."

"Morning." He looked away.

He did not thank her for sending a message to warn him that the meeting was earlier.

She asked: "What time did you get here?"

"A few minutes ago."

That meant he had known the correct time for the meeting. But he had told her it was half an hour later. Surely he had not deliberately misled her? It seemed almost childish.

Before she had time to reach a conclusion, a young black man emerged from a side door. He spoke to Brian. "Agent Kincaid?"

He stood up. "That's me."

"And you must be Agent Maddox. Mr. Honeymoon will see you both now."

They followed him along the corridor and around a corner. As they walked, he said: "We call this the Horseshoe, because the governor's offices are grouped around three sides of a rectangle."

Halfway along the second side they passed another lobby, this one occupied by two secretaries. A young man holding a file waited on a leather couch. Judy guessed that was the way to the governor's personal office. A few steps on, they were shown into Honeymoon's room.

He was a big man with close-cropped hair turning gray. He had taken off the coat of his gray pinstripe suit to reveal black suspenders. The sleeves of his white shirt were rolled, but his silk tie was fastened tight in a high pin-through collar. He removed a pair of gold-rimmed half-glasses and stood up. He had a dark, sculptured face that wore a don't-fuck-with-me expression. He could have been a police lieutenant, except he was too well dressed.

Despite his intimidating appearance, his manner was courteous. He shook their hands and said: "I appreciate your coming here all the way from San Francisco."

"No problem," said Kincaid.

They sat down.

Without preamble Honeymoon said: "What's your assessment of the situation?"

Kincaid said: "Well, sir, you particularly asked to meet with the agent at the sharp end, so I'll let Judy here fill you in."

Judy said: "We haven't caught these people yet, I'm afraid." Then she cursed herself for beginning with an apology. *Be positive!* "We're fairly sure they're *not* connected with the Green California Campaign—that was a weak attempt to lay a false trail. We don't know who they are, but I can tell you some important things we have found out about them."

Honeymoon said: "Go ahead, please."

"First of all, linguistic analysis of the threat message tells us we're dealing not with a lone individual, but with a group."

Kincaid said: "Well, two people, at least."

Judy glared at Kincaid, but he did not meet her eye.

Honeymoon said irritably: "Which is it, two or a group?"

Judy felt herself blush. "The message was composed by a man and typed by a woman, so there are at least two. We don't yet know if there are more."

"Okay. But please be exact."

This was not going well.

Judy pressed on. "Point two: These people are not insane."

Kincaid said: "Well, not clinically. But they sure as hell aren't normal." He laughed as if he had said something witty.

Judy silently cursed him for undermining her. "People who commit crimes of violence can be divided into two kinds, organized and disorganized. The disorganized kind act on the spur of the moment, use whatever weapons come to hand, and choose their victims at random. They're the real crazies."

Honeymoon was interested. "And the other kind?"

"The organized ones plan their crimes, carry their weapons with them, and attack victims who have been selected beforehand using some logical criteria."

Kincaid said: "They're just crazy in a different way."

Judy tried to ignore him. "Such people may be sick, but they are not looney tunes. We can think of them as rational, and try to anticipate what they might do."

"All right. And the Hammer of Eden people are organized."

"Judging by their threat message, yes."

"You rely a great deal on this linguistic analysis," Honeymoon said skeptically.

"It's a powerful tool."

Kincaid put in: "It's no substitute for careful investigative work. But in this case, it's all we've got."

The implication seemed to be that they had to fall back on linguistic analysis because Judy had failed to do the legwork. Feeling desperate, she struggled on. "We're dealing with serious people—which means that if they can't cause an earthquake, they may attempt something else."

"Such as?"

"One of the more usual terrorist acts. Explode a bomb, take a hostage, murder a prominent figure."

Kincaid said: "Assuming they have the capability, of course. So far we've nothing to indicate that."

Judy took a deep breath. There was something she had to say, and she could not avoid it. "However, I'm not prepared to rule out the possibility that they really could cause an earthquake."

Honeymoon said: *"What?"*

Kincaid laughed scornfully.

Judy said stubbornly: "It's not likely, but it's conceivable.

That's what I was told by California's leading expert, Professor Quercus. I'd be failing in my duty if I didn't tell you."

Kincaid leaned back in his chair and crossed his legs. "Judy has told you the textbook answers, Al," he said in a we're-all-boys-together tone of voice. "Now maybe I should tell you how it looks from the perspective of a certain amount of age and experience."

Judy stared at him. *I'll get you for this if it's the last thing I do, Kincaid. You've spent this entire meeting putting me down. But what if there really is an earthquake, you asshole? What will you say to the relatives of the dead?*

"Please go on," Honeymoon said to Kincaid.

"These people can't cause an earthquake and they don't give a flying fuck about power plants. My instinct tells me this is a guy trying to impress his girlfriend. He's got the governor freaked out, he's got the FBI running around like blue-assed flies, and the whole thing is on the John Truth radio show every night. Suddenly he's a big shot, and she's, like, wow!"

Judy felt totally humiliated. Kincaid had let her lay out her findings and then poured scorn on everything she had said. He had obviously planned this, and she was now sure that he had deliberately misled her about the time of the meeting in the hope that she would show up late. The whole thing was a strategy for discrediting her and at the same time making Kincaid look better. She felt sick.

Honeymoon stood up suddenly. "I'm going to advise the governor to take no action on this threat." He added dismissively: "Thank you both."

Judy realized it was too late to ask him to open the door to dialogue with the terrorists. The moment had passed. And any suggestion of hers would be nixed by Kincaid anyway. She felt despairing. *What if it's real? What if they actually can do it?*

Kincaid said: "Any time we can be of assistance, you just let us know."

Honeymoon looked faintly scornful. He hardly needed an invitation to use the services of the FBI. But he politely held out his hand to shake.

A moment later Judy and Kincaid were outside.

Judy remained silent as they walked around the Horseshoe and through the lobby into the marble hallway. There Kincaid stopped and said: "You did just fine in there, Judy. Don't you worry about a thing." He could not conceal his smirk.

She was determined not to let him see how rattled she was. She wanted to scream at him, but she forced herself to say calmly: "I think we did our job."

"Sure we did. Where are you parked?"

"In the garage across the street." She jerked a thumb.

"I'm the opposite side. See you later."

"You bet."

Judy watched him walk away, then she turned and went in the other direction.

Crossing the street, she saw a See's candy store. She went in and bought some chocolates.

Driving back to San Francisco, she ate the whole box.

7

Priest needed physical activity to keep him from going crazy with tension. After the meeting in the temple he went to the vineyard and started weeding. It was a hot day, and he soon worked up a sweat and took off his shirt.

Star worked beside him. After an hour or so she looked at her watch. "Time for a break," she said. "Let's go listen to the news."

They sat in Priest's car and turned on the radio. The bulletin was identical to the one they had heard earlier. Priest ground his teeth in frustration. "Damn, the governor has to say something soon!"

Star said: "We don't expect him to give in right away, do we?"

"No, but I thought there would be some message, maybe just a hint of a concession. Hell, the idea of a freeze on new power plants ain't exactly wacko. Millions of people in California probably agree with it."

Star nodded. "Shit, in Los Angeles it's already dangerous to breathe because of the pollution, for Christ's sake! I can't believe people really want to live that way."

"But nothing happens."

"Well, we figured all along we'd need to give a demonstration before they'd listen."

"Yeah." Priest hesitated, then blurted: "I guess I'm just scared it won't work."

146

"The seismic vibrator?"

He hesitated again. He would not have been this frank with anyone but Star, and he was already half regretting his confession of doubt. But he had begun, so he might as well finish. "The whole thing," he said. "I'm scared there'll be no earthquake, and then we'll be lost."

She was a little shocked, he could see. She was used to him being supremely confident about everything he did. But he had never done anything like this.

Walking back to the vineyard, she said: "Do something with Flower tonight."

"What do you mean?"

"Spend time with her. Do something with her. You're always playing with Dusty."

Dusty was five. It was easy to have fun with him. He was fascinated by everything. Flower was thirteen, the age when everything grown-ups did seemed stupid. Priest was about to say this when he realized there was another reason for what Star was saying.

She thinks I may die tomorrow.

The thought hit him like a punch. He knew that this earthquake plan was dangerous, of course, but he had mainly considered the peril to himself and the risk of leaving the commune leaderless. He had not imagined Flower alone in the world at the age of thirteen.

"What'll I do with her?" he said.

"She wants to learn the guitar."

That was news to Priest. He was not much of a guitarist himself, but he could play folk songs and simple blues, enough to get her started anyway. He shrugged. "Okay, we'll start tonight."

They went back to work, but a few minutes later they were interrupted when Slow, grinning from ear to ear, shouted: "Hey, lookit who's here!"

Priest looked across the vineyard. The person he was waiting for was Melanie. She had gone to San Francisco to take Dusty to his father. She was the only one who could tell Priest exactly where to use the seismic vibrator, and he would not feel comfortable until she was back. But it was too early to expect her, and anyway, Slow would not have gotten so excited about Melanie.

He saw a man coming down the hill, followed by a woman carrying a child. Priest frowned. Often a year went by without a single visitor coming to the valley. This morning they had had the cop; now these people. But were they strangers? He narrowed his eyes. The man's rolling walk was terribly familiar. As the figures got closer, Priest said: "My God, is that Bones?"

"Yes, it is!" Star said delightedly. "Holy moley!" And she hurried toward the newcomers. Spirit joined in the excitement and ran with her, barking.

Priest followed more slowly. Bones, whose real name was Billy Owens, was a Rice Eater. But he had liked the way things were before Priest arrived. He enjoyed the hand-to-mouth existence of the early commune. He reveled in the constant crises and liked to be drunk or stoned, or both, within a couple of hours of waking up. He played the blues harmonica with manic brilliance and was the most successful street beggar they had. He had not joined a commune to find work, self-discipline, and a daily act of worship. So after a couple of years, when it became clear that the Priest-Star regime was permanent, Bones took off. He had not been seen since. Now, after more than twenty years, he was back.

Star threw her arms around him, hugged him hard, and kissed his lips. Those two had been a serious item for a while. All the men in the commune had slept with Star in those days, but she had had a special soft spot for Bones. Priest felt a twinge of jealousy as he watched Bones press Star's body to his own.

When they let each other go, Priest could see that Bones did not look well. He had always been a thin man, but now he looked as if he were dying of starvation. He had wild hair and a straggly beard, but the beard was matted and the hair seemed to be falling out in clumps. His jeans and T-shirt were dirty, and the heel had come off one of his cowboy boots.

He's here because he's in trouble.

Bones introduced the woman as Debbie. She was younger than he, no more than twenty-five, and pretty in a pinched-looking way. Her child was a boy about eighteen months old. She and the kid were almost as thin and dirty as Bones.

It was time for their midday meal. They took Bones to the cookhouse. Lunch was a casserole made with pearl barley and flavored with herbs grown by Garden. Debbie ate ravenously and fed the child, too, but Bones took just a couple of spoonfuls, then lit a cigarette.

There was a lot of talk about the old times. Bones said: "I'll tell you my favorite memory. One afternoon right on that hillside over there, Star explained to me about cunnilingus." There was a ripple of laughter around the table. It was faintly embarrassed laughter, but Bones failed to pick up on that, and he went on: "I was twenty years old and I never knew people did that. I was shocked! But she made me try it. And the taste! Yech!"

"There was a lot you didn't know," Star said. "I remember you telling me that you couldn't understand why you sometimes got headaches in the morning, and I had to explain to you that it happened whenever you got falling-down drunk the night before. You didn't know the meaning of the word 'hangover.' "

She had deftly changed the subject. In the old days it had been perfectly normal to talk about cunnilingus around the table, but things had changed since Bones left. No one had ever made an issue of cleaning up their conversation, but it had happened naturally as the children started to understand more.

Bones was nervy, laughing a lot, trying too hard to be

friendly, fidgeting, chain-smoking. *He wants something. But he'll tell me what it is soon enough.*

As they cleared the table and washed the bowls, Bones took Priest aside and said: "Got something I want to show you. Come on."

Priest shrugged and went with him.

As they walked, Priest took out a little bag of marijuana and a pack of cigarette papers. The communards did not usually smoke dope during the day, because it slowed down the work in the vineyard, but today was a special day, and Priest felt the need to soothe his nerves. As they walked up the hill and through the trees, he rolled a joint with the ease of long practice.

Bones licked his lips. "You don't have anything with, like, more of a kick, do you?"

"What are you using these days, Bones?"

"A little brown sugar now and again, you know, keep my head straight."

Heroin.

So that was it. Bones had become a junkie.

"We don't have any smack here," Priest told him. "No one uses it." *And I'd get rid of anyone who did, faster than you can say spike.*

Priest lit the joint.

When they reached the clearing where the cars were parked, Bones said: "This is it."

At first Priest could not work out what he was looking at. It was a truck, but what kind? It was painted with a gay design in bright red and yellow, and along the side was a picture of a monster breathing fire and some lettering in the same gaudy colors.

Bones, who knew that Priest could not read, said: "The Dragon's Mouth. It's a carnival ride."

Priest saw it then. A lot of small carnival rides were mounted on trucks. The truck engine powered the ride in use. Then the parts of the ride could be folded down and the truck driven to the next site.

Priest passed him the joint and said: "Is it yours?"

Bones took a long toke, held the smoke down, then blew out before answering. "I been making my living from this for ten years. But it needs work, and I can't afford to get it fixed. So I have to sell it."

Now Priest could see what was coming.

Bones took another draw on the joint but did not hand it back. "It's probably worth fifty thousand dollars, but I'm asking ten."

Priest nodded. "Sounds like a bargain . . . for someone."

"Maybe you guys should buy it," Bones said.

"What the fuck would I do with a carnival ride, Bones?"

"It's a good investment. If you have a bad year with the wine, you could go out with the ride and make some money."

They had bad years, sometimes. There was nothing they could do about the weather. But Paul Beale was always willing to give them credit. He believed in the ideals of the commune, even though he had been unable to live up to them himself. And he knew there would always be another vintage next year.

Priest shook his head. "No way. But I wish you luck, old buddy. Keep trying, you'll find a buyer."

Bones must have known it had been a long shot, but all the same he looked panicky. "Hey, Priest, you want to know the truth of it. . . . I'm in bad shape. Could you loan me a thousand bucks? That'd get me straight."

It would get you stoned out of your head, you mean. Then, after a few days, you'd be right back where you were.

"We don't have any money," Priest told him. "We don't use it here, don't you remember that?"

Bones looked crafty. "You gotta have a stash somewhere, come on!"

And you think I'm going to tell you about it?

"Sorry, pal, can't help."

Bones nodded. "That's a bummer, man. I mean, I'm in serious trouble."

Priest said: "And don't try to go behind my back and ask Star, because you'll get the same answer." He put a harsh note into his voice. "Are you listening to me?"

"Sure, sure," Bones said, looking scared. "Be cool, Priest, man, be cool."

"I'm cool," Priest said.

Priest worried about Melanie all afternoon. She might have changed her mind and decided to go back to her husband or simply got scared and taken off in her car. Then he would be finished. There was no way he or anyone else here could interpret the data on Michael Quercus's disk and figure out where to place the seismic vibrator tomorrow.

But she showed up at the end of the afternoon, to his great relief. He told her about Flower being arrested and warned her that one or two people wanted to put the blame on Melanie and her cute clothes. She said she would get some work clothes from the free shop.

After supper Priest went to Song's cabin and picked up her guitar. "Are you using this?" he said politely. He would never say, "May I borrow your guitar?" because in theory all property was communal, so the guitar was his as much as hers, even though she had made it. However, in practice everyone always asked.

He sat outside his cabin with Flower and tuned the guitar. Spirit, the dog, watched alertly, as if he, too, were going to learn to play. "Most songs have three chords," Priest began. "If you know three chords, you can play nine out of ten of the songs in the whole world."

He showed her the chord of C. As she struggled to press the strings with her soft fingertips, he studied her face in the evening light: her perfect skin, the dark hair, green eyes like Star's, the little frown as she concentrated. *I have to stay alive, to take care of you.*

He thought of himself at that age, already a criminal, experienced, skilled, hardened to violence, with a hatred of cops and a contempt for ordinary citizens who were dumb enough to let themselves get robbed. *At thirteen I had already gone wrong.* He was determined that Flower would not be like that. She had been brought up in a community of love and peace, untouched by the world that had corrupted little Ricky Granger and turned him into a hoodlum before he grew hair on his chin. *You'll be okay, I'll make sure of it.*

She played the chord, and Priest realized that a particular song had been running in his head ever since Bones arrived. It was a folkie number from the early sixties that Star had always liked.

> *Show me the prison*
> *Show me the jail*
> *Show me the prisoner*
> *Whose life has gone stale*

"I'll teach you a song your mommy used to sing to you when you were a baby," he said. He took the guitar from her. "Do you remember this?" He sang:

> *I'll show you a young man*
> *With so many reasons why*

In his head he heard Star's unmistakable voice, low and sexy then as now.

> *There, but for fortune*
> *Go you or I*
> *You or I.*

Priest was about the same age as Bones, and Bones was dying. Priest had no doubt about that. Soon the girl and the baby would leave him. He would starve his body and feed his habit. He might overdose or poison himself with bad drugs, or he might just abuse his system until it gave up and he got pneumonia. One way or another, he was a dead man.

If I lose this place, I'll go the same way as Bones.

As Flower struggled to play the chord of A minor, Priest toyed with the idea of returning to normal society. He fantasized going every day to a job, buying socks and wingtip shoes, owning a TV set and a toaster. The thought made him queasy. He had never lived straight. He had been brought up in a whorehouse, educated on the streets, briefly the owner of a semilegitimate business, and for most of his life the leader of a hippie commune cut off from the world.

He recalled the one regular job he had ever had. At eighteen he had gone to work for the Jenkinsons, the couple who ran the liquor store down the street. He had thought of them as old, at the time, but now he guessed they had been in their fifties. His intention had been to work just long enough to figure out where they kept their money, then steal it. But then he learned something about himself.

He discovered he had a queer talent for arithmetic. Each morning Mr. Jenkinson put ten dollars' worth of change into the cash register. As customers bought liquor and paid and got change, Priest either served them himself or heard one of the Jenkinsons sing out the total, "Dollar twenty-nine, please, Mrs. Roberto," or "Three bucks even, sir." And the figures seemed to add themselves up in his head. All day long Priest always knew exactly how much money was in the till, and at the end of the day he could tell Mr. Jenkinson the total before he counted it.

He would hear Mr. Jenkinson talking to the salesmen who called, and he soon knew the wholesale and retail prices of every item in the store. From then on the automatic register in his brain calculated the profit on every transaction, and he was awestruck by how much the Jenkinsons were making *without stealing from anyone.*

He arranged for them to be robbed four times in a month,

then made them an offer for the store. When they turned him down, he arranged a fifth robbery and made sure Mrs. Jenkinson got roughed up this time. After that Mr. Jenkinson accepted his offer.

Priest borrowed the deposit from the neighborhood loan shark and paid Mr. Jenkinson the installments out of the store's takings. Although he could not read or write, he always knew his financial position exactly. Nobody could cheat him. One time he employed a respectable-looking middle-aged woman who stole a dollar out of the register every day. At the end of the week he deducted five dollars from her pay, beat her up, and told her not to come back.

Within a year he had four stores; two years later he had a wholesale liquor warehouse; after three years he was a millionaire; and at the end of his fourth year he was on the run.

He sometimes wondered what might have happened if he had paid off the loan shark in full, given his accountant honest figures to report to the IRS, and made a plea-bargain deal with the LAPD on the fraud charges. Maybe today he would have a company as big as Coca-Cola and be living in one of those mansions in Beverly Hills with a gardener and a pool boy and a five-car garage.

But as he tried to imagine it, he knew it could never have happened. That was not him. The guy who came down the stairs of the mansion in a white bathrobe, and coolly ordered the maid to squeeze him a glass of orange juice, had someone else's face. Priest could never live in the square world. He had always had a problem with rules: he could never obey other people's. That was why he had to live here.

In Silver River Valley I make the rules, I change the rules, I am the rules.

Flower told him her fingers hurt.

"Then it's time to stop," Priest said. "If you like, I'll teach you another song tomorrow." *If I'm still alive.*

"Does it hurt you?"

"No, but that's only because I'm used to it. When you've

practiced the guitar a little, your fingertips get hard pads on them, like the skin on your heel."

"Does Noel Gallagher have hard pads?"

"If Noel Gallagher is a pop guitarist . . ."

"Of course! He's in Oasis!"

"Well, then he has hard pads. Do you think you might like to be a musician?"

"No."

"That was pretty definite. You have some other ideas?"

She looked guilty, as if she knew he was going to disapprove, but she screwed up her courage and said: "I want to be a writer."

He was not sure how he felt about that. *Your daddy will never be able to read your work.* But he pretended enthusiasm. "That's good! What kind?"

"For a magazine. Like *Teen*, maybe."

"Why?"

"You get to meet stars and interview them, and write about fashions and makeup."

Priest gritted his teeth and tried not to let his revulsion show. "Well, I like the idea that you might be a writer, anyway. If you wrote poetry and stories, instead of magazine articles, you could still live here in Silver River Valley."

"Yeah, maybe," she said doubtfully.

He could see that she was not planning to spend her life here. But she was too young to understand. By the time she was old enough to decide for herself, she would have a different view. *I hope.*

Star came over. "Time for Truth," she said.

Priest took the guitar from Flower. "Go and get ready for bed, now," he said.

He and Star headed for the parking circle, dropping off the guitar at Song's cabin on the way. They found Melanie already there, sitting in the backseat of the 'Cuda, listening to the radio. She had put on a bright yellow T-shirt and blue jeans from the free shop. Both were too big for her, and she had tucked in the T-shirt and pulled the jeans tight with a belt, showing off her tiny waist. She still looked like sex on a stick.

John Truth had a flat nasal twang that could become hypnotic. His specialty was saying aloud the things his listeners believed in their hearts but were ashamed to admit to. It was mostly standard fascist-pig stuff: AIDS was a punishment for sin, intelligence was racially inherited, what the world needed was stricter discipline, all politicians were stupid and corrupt, and like that. Priest imagined that his audience was mostly the kind of fat white men who learned everything they knew in bars. "This guy," Star said. "He's everything I hate about America: prejudiced, sanctimonious, hypocritical, self-righteous, and really fucking stupid."

"That's a fact," Priest said. "Listen up."

Truth was saying: "I'm going to read once more that statement made by the governor's cabinet secretary, Mr. Honeymoon."

Priest's hackles rose, and Star said: "That son of a bitch!" Honeymoon was the man behind the scheme to flood Silver River Valley, and they hated him.

John Truth went on, speaking slowly and ponderously, as if every syllable was significant. "Listen to this. 'The FBI has investigated the threat which appeared on an Internet bulletin board on the first of May. That investigation has determined that there is no substance to the threat.'"

Priest's heart sank. This was what he had expected, but all the same he was dismayed. He had hoped for at least some slight hint of appeasement. But Honeymoon sounded completely intractable.

Truth carried on reading. " 'Governor Mike Robson, following the FBI's recommendation, has decided to take no further action.' That, my friends, is the statement *in its entirety*." Truth obviously felt it was outrageously short.

"Are *you* satisfied? The terrorist deadline runs out tomorrow. Do *you* feel reassured? Call John Truth on this number now to tell the world what *you* think."

Priest said: "That means we have to do it."

Melanie said: "Well, I never expected the governor to cave in without a demonstration."

"Nor did I, I guess." He frowned. "The statement mentioned the FBI twice. It sounds to me like Mike Robson is getting ready to blame the feds if things go wrong. And that makes me wonder if in his heart he's not so sure."

"So if we give him proof that we really can cause an earthquake . . ."

"Maybe he'll think again."

Star looked downcast. "Shit," she said. "I guess I've been hoping we wouldn't have to do this."

Priest was alarmed. He did not want Star to get cold feet at this point. Her support was necessary to carry the rest of the Rice Eaters. "We can do this without hurting anyone," he said. "Melanie has picked the perfect location." He turned to the backseat. "Tell Star what we talked about."

Melanie leaned forward and unfolded a map so that Star and Priest could see it. She did not know that Priest could not read maps. "Here's the Owens Valley fault," she said, pointing to a red streak. "There were major earthquakes in 1790 and 1872, so another one is overdue."

Star said: "Surely earthquakes don't happen according to a regular timetable?"

"No. But the history of the fault shows that enough pressure for an earthquake builds up over about a century. Which means we can cause one now if we give a nudge in the right place."

"Which is where?" Star said.

Melanie pointed to a spot on the map. "Round about here."

"You can't be exact?"

"Not until I get there. Michael's data gives us the location within about a mile. When I look at the landscape I should be able to pinpoint the spot."

"How?"

"Evidence of earlier earthquakes."

"Okay."

"Now, the best time, according to Michael's seismic window, will be between one-thirty and two-twenty."

"How can you be sure no one will get hurt?"

"Look at the map. Owens Valley is thinly populated, just a few small towns strung along a dried-up riverbed. The point I've chosen is miles from any human habitation."

Priest added: "We can be sure the earthquake will be minor. The effects will hardly be felt in the nearest town." He knew this was not certain, and so did Melanie; but he gave her a hard stare, and she did not contradict him.

Star said: "If the effects are hardly felt, no one's going to give a shit, so why do it?"

She was being contrary, but that was just a sign of how tense she was. Priest said: "We said we would cause an earthquake tomorrow. As soon as we've done it, we'll call John Truth on Melanie's mobile phone and tell him we kept our promise." *What a moment that will be, what a feeling!*

"Will he believe us?"

Melanie said: "He'll have to, when he checks the seismograph."

Priest said: "Imagine how Governor Robson and his people will feel." He could hear the exultation in his own voice. "Especially that asshole Honeymoon. They'll be, like, 'Shit! These people really can cause earthquakes, man! What the fuck we gonna do?' "

"And then what?" said Star.

"Then we threaten to do it again. But this time, we don't give them a month. We give them a week."

"How will we make the threat? Same way we did before?"

Melanie answered. "I don't think so. I'm sure they have a way of monitoring the bulletin board and tracing the phone call. And if we use a different bulletin board, there's always the chance that no one will notice our message. Remember, it was three weeks before John Truth picked up on our last one."

"So we call and threaten a second earthquake."

Priest put in: "But next time it won't be in a remote wilderness—it'll be someplace where real damage will be done." He caught an apprehensive look from Star. "We don't have to mean it," he added. "Once we've shown our power, just the threat ought to be enough."

Star said: *"Inshallah."* She had picked it up from Poem, who was Algerian. "If God wills."

It was pitch dark when they left the next morning.

The seismic vibrator had not been seen in daylight within a hundred miles of the valley, and Priest wanted to keep it that way. He planned to leave home and return in darkness. The round trip would be about five hundred miles, eleven hours driving in a truck with a top speed of forty-five. They would take the 'Cuda as a backup car, Priest had decided. Oaktree would come with them to share the driving.

Priest used a flashlight to illuminate the way through the trees to where the truck was concealed. The four of them were silent, anxious. It took them half an hour to remove the branches they had piled over the vehicle.

He was tense when at last he sat behind the wheel, slid the key into the ignition, and turned on the engine. It started the first time with a satisfying roar, and he felt exultant.

The commune's houses were more than a mile away, and he was sure no one would hear the engine at such a distance. The dense forest muffled sound. Later, of course, everyone would notice that four commune members were away. Aneth had been briefed to say they had gone to a vineyard in Napa that Paul Beale wanted them to see, where a new hybrid vine had been planted. It was unusual for people to make trips out of the commune; but there would be few questions, for no one liked to challenge Priest.

He turned on the headlights, and Melanie climbed into the truck beside him. He engaged low gear and steered the heavy vehicle through the trees to the dirt track, then turned uphill and headed for the road. The all-terrain tires coped easily with streambeds and mudslides.

Jesus, I wonder if this is going to work.

An earthquake? Come on!

But it has to work.

He got on the road and headed east. After twenty minutes they climbed out of Silver River Valley and hit Route 89. Priest turned south. He checked his mirrors and saw that Star and Oaktree were still behind in the 'Cuda.

Beside him, Melanie was very calm. Probing gently, he said: "Was Dusty okay last night?"

"Fine, he likes visiting his father. Michael could always find time for him, never for me."

Melanie's bitterness was familiar. What surprised Priest was her lack of fear. Unlike him, she was not agonizing over what would happen to her child if she died today. She seemed completely confident that nothing would go wrong, the earthquake would not harm her. Was it that she knew more than Priest? Or was she the type of person who just ignored uncomfortable facts? Priest was not sure.

As dawn broke they were looping around the north end of Lake Tahoe. The motionless water looked like a disk of polished steel fallen amid the mountains. The seismic vibrator was a conspicuous vehicle on the winding road that followed the pine-fringed shore; but the vacationers were still asleep, and the truck was seen only by a few bleary-eyed workers on their way to jobs in hotels and restaurants.

By sunup they were on U.S. 395, across the border in Nevada, bowling south through a flat desert landscape. They took a break at a truck stop, parking the seismic vibrator where it could not be seen from the road, and ate a breakfast of oily western omelets and watery coffee.

When the road swung back into California it climbed

into the mountains, and for a couple of hours the scenery was majestic, with steep forested slopes, a grander version of Silver River Valley. They dropped down again beside a silvery sea that Melanie said was Mono Lake.

Soon afterward they were on a two-lane road that cut a straight line down a long, dusty valley. The valley widened until the mountains on the far side were just a blue haze, then it narrowed again. The ground on either side of the road was tan colored and stony, with a scattering of low brush. There was no river, but the salt flats looked like a distant sheet of water.

Melanie said: "This is Owens Valley."

The landscape gave Priest the feeling that some kind of disaster had blighted it. "What happened here?" he said.

"The river is dry because the water was diverted to Los Angeles years ago."

They passed through a sleepy small town every twenty miles or so. Now there was no way to be inconspicuous. There was little traffic, and the seismic vibrator was stared at every time they waited at a stoplight. Plenty of men would remember it. *Yeah, I seen that rig. Looked like she might be for layin' blacktop or somethin'. What was she, anyway?*

Melanie switched on her laptop and unfolded her map. She said musingly: "Somewhere beneath us, two vast slabs of the earth's crust are wedged together, stuck, straining to spring free."

The thought made Priest feel cold. He could hardly believe he aimed to release all that pent-up destructive force. *I must be out of my mind.*

"Somewhere in the next five or ten miles," she said.

"What's the time?"

"Just after one."

They had cut it fine. The seismic window would open in half an hour and close fifty minutes later.

Melanie directed Priest down a side turning that crossed

the flat valley floor. It was not really a road, just a track cleared through the boulders and scrub. Although the ground seemed almost level, the main road disappeared from view behind them, and they could see only the tops of high trucks passing.

"Pull up here," Melanie said at last.

Priest stopped the truck, and they both got out. The sun beat down on them from a merciless sky. The 'Cuda pulled up behind them, and Star and Oaktree got out, stretching their arms and legs after the long drive.

"Look at that," Melanie said. "See the dry gulch?"

Priest could see where a stream, long ago dried up, had cut a channel through the rocky ground. But where Melanie was pointing, the gulch came to an abrupt end, as if it had been walled off. "That's strange," Priest said.

"Now look a few yards to the right."

Priest followed her moving finger. The streambed began again just as abruptly and continued toward the middle of the valley. Priest realized what she was pointing out. "That's the fault line," he said. "Last time there was an earthquake, one whole side of this valley picked up its skirts and shifted five yards, then sat down again."

"That's about it."

Oaktree said: "And we're about to make it happen again, is that right?" There was a note of awe in his voice.

"We're going to try," Priest said briskly. "And we don't have much time." He turned to Melanie. "Is the truck in exactly the right place?"

"I guess," she said. "A few yards one way or another up here on the surface shouldn't make any difference five miles down."

"Okay." He hesitated. He almost felt he ought to make a speech. He said: "Well, I'll get started."

He got into the cabin of the truck and settled into the driver's seat, then started the engine that ran the vibrator. He threw the switch that lowered the steel plate to the ground. He set the vibrator to shake for thirty seconds in the middle of its frequency range. He looked through the rear window of the cab and checked the gauges. The readouts were normal. He picked up the remote radio controller and got out of the truck.

"All set," he said.

The four of them got into the 'Cuda. Oaktree took the wheel. They drove back to the road, crossed it, and headed into the scrub on the far side. They went partway up the hillside, then Melanie said: "This is fine."

Oaktree stopped the car.

Priest hoped they were not conspicuous from the road. If they were, there was nothing he could do about it. But the muddy colors of the 'Cuda's paint job blended into the brown landscape.

Oaktree said nervously: "Is this far enough away?"

"I think so," Melanie said coolly. She was not scared at all. Studying her face, Priest saw a hint of mad excitement in her eyes. It was almost sexual. Was she taking her revenge on the seismologists who had rejected her, or the husband who had let her down, or the whole damn world? Whatever the explanation, she was getting a big charge out of this.

They got out and stood looking across the valley. They could just see the top of the truck.

Star said to Priest: "It was a mistake for us both to come. If we die, Flower has no one."

"She has the whole commune," Priest said. "You and I are not the only adults she loves and trusts. We're not a nuclear family, and that's one very good reason why."

Melanie looked annoyed. "We're a quarter of a mile from the fault, assuming it runs along the valley floor," she said in a cut-the-crap tone of voice. "We'll feel the earth move, but we're not in any danger. People who are hurt in earthquakes generally get hit by parts of buildings: falling ceilings, bridges that collapse, flying glass, stuff like that. We're safe here."

Star looked over her shoulder. "The mountain isn't going to fall on us?"

"It might. And we might all be killed in a car wreck driving back to Silver River Valley. But it's so unlikely that we shouldn't waste time worrying about it."

"That's easy for you to say—your child's father is three hundred miles away in San Francisco."

Priest said: "I don't care if I die here. I can't raise my children in suburban America."

Oaktree muttered: "This has to work. This just has to work."

Melanie said: "For God's sake, Priest, we don't have all day. Just press the damn button."

Priest looked up and down the road and waited for a dark green Jeep Grand Cherokee Limited to pass. "Okay," he said when the road was clear. "This is it."

He pressed the button on the remote control.

He heard the roar of the vibrator immediately, though it was muted by distance. He felt the vibration in the soles of his feet, a faint but definite trembling sensation.

Star said: "Oh, God."

A cloud of dust billowed around the truck.

All four of them were taut as guitar strings, their bodies tensed for the first hint of movement in the earth.

Seconds passed.

Priest's eyes raked the landscape, looking for signs of a tremor, though he guessed he would feel it before he saw it.

Come on, come on!

The seismic exploration crews normally set the vibrator for a seven-second "sweep." Priest had set this one for thirty seconds. It seemed like an hour.

At last the noise stopped.

Melanie said: "Goddamn it."

Priest's heart sank. There was no earthquake. It had failed. Maybe it was just a crazy hippie idea, like levitating the Pentagon.

"Try it again," said Melanie.

Priest looked at the remote control in his hand. *Why not?*

There was a sixteen-wheel truck approaching along U.S. 395, but this time Priest did not wait. If Melanie was right, the truck would be unaffected by the tremor. If Melanie was wrong, they would all be dead.

He pressed the button.

The distant roar started up, there was a perceptible vibration in the ground, and a cloud of dust engulfed the seismic vibrator.

Priest wondered if the road would open up under the sixteen-wheeler.

Nothing happened.

The thirty seconds passed more quickly this time. Priest was surprised when the noise stopped. *Is that all?*

Despair engulfed him. Perhaps the Silver River Valley commune was a dream that had come to an end. *What am I going to do? Where will I live? How can I avoid ending up like Bones?*

But Melanie was not ready to give up. "Let's move the truck a ways and try again."

"But you said the exact position doesn't matter," Oaktree pointed out. "'A few yards one way or another up here on the surface shouldn't make any difference five miles down,' that's what you said."

"Then we'll move it more than a few yards," Melanie said angrily. "We're running out of time, let's go!"

Priest did not argue with her. She was transformed. Normally she was dominated by Priest. She was a damsel in distress, he had rescued her, and she was so grateful, she had to be eternally submissive to his will. But now she was in charge, impatient and domineering. Priest could put up with that as long as she could do what she had promised. He would bring her back into line later.

They got into the 'Cuda and drove fast across the baked earth to the seismic vibrator. Then Priest and Melanie climbed into the cab of the truck and she directed him as he drove, while Oaktree and Star followed in the car. They were no longer following the track, but cutting straight through the brush. The truck's big wheels crushed the scrubby bushes and rolled easily over the stones, but Priest wondered if the low-slung 'Cuda would suffer damage. He guessed Oaktree would honk if he had trouble.

Melanie scanned the landscape for the telltale features that showed where the fault line ran. Priest saw no more displaced streambeds. But after half a mile Melanie pointed at what looked like a miniature cliff about four feet high. "Fault scarp," she said. "About a hundred years old."

"I see it," Priest said. There was a dip in the ground, like a bowl; and a break in the rim of the bowl showed where the earth had moved sideways, as if the bowl had cracked and been glued together clumsily.

Melanie said: "Let's try here."

Priest stopped the truck and lowered the plate. Swiftly he rechecked the gauges and set the vibrator. This time he programmed a sixty-second sweep. When all was set he jumped out of the truck.

He checked his watch anxiously. It was two o'clock. They had only twenty minutes left.

Again they drove the 'Cuda across U.S. 395 and up the hill on the far side. The drivers of the few vehicles that passed continued to ignore them. But Priest was nervous. Sooner or later someone would ask what they were doing. He did not want to have to explain himself to a curious cop or a nosy town councilman. He had a plausible story ready, about a university research project on the geology of the dried-up riverbed, but he did not want anyone to remember his face.

They all got out of the car and looked across the valley to

where the seismic vibrator stood near the scarp. Priest wished with all his heart that this time he would see the earth move and open. *Come on, God—give me this one, okay?*

He pressed the button.

The truck roared, the earth trembled faintly, and the dust rose. The vibration went on for a full minute instead of half. But there was no earthquake. They just waited longer for disappointment.

When the noise died away, Star said: "This isn't going to work, is it?"

Melanie threw her a furious look. Turning to Priest, she said: "Can you alter the frequency of the vibrations?"

"Yes," Priest said. "Right now it's set near the middle, so I can go up or down. Why?"

"There's a theory that pitch may be a crucial factor. See, the earth is constantly resounding with faint vibrations. So why aren't there earthquakes all the time? Maybe because a vibration has to be just the right pitch to dislodge the fault. You know how a musical note can shatter a glass?"

"I never saw it happen, except in a cartoon, but I know what you mean. The answer is yes. When they use the vibrator in seismic exploration, they vary the pitch over a seven-second sweep."

"They do?" Melanie was curious. "Why?"

"I don't know, maybe it gives them a better reading on the geophones. Anyway, it didn't seem the right thing for us, so I didn't select that feature, but I can."

"Let's try it."

"Okay—but we need to hurry. It's already five after two."

They jumped into the car. Oaktree drove fast, skidding across the dusty desert. Priest reset the controls of the vibrator for a sweep of gradually increasing pitch over a period of sixty seconds. As they raced back to their observation point, he checked his watch again. "Two-fifteen," he said. "This is our last chance."

"Don't worry," Melanie said. "I'm out of ideas. If this doesn't work, I'm giving up."

Oaktree stopped the car, and they got out again.

The thought of driving all the way back to Silver River with nothing to celebrate depressed Priest so profoundly that he felt he would want to crash the truck on the freeway and end it all. Maybe that was his way out. He wondered if Star would like to die with him. *I can see it now: the two of us, an overdose of painkillers, a bottle of wine to wash down the pills . . .*

"What are you waiting for?" said Melanie. "It's two-twenty. Press the damn button!"

Priest pressed the button.

As before, the truck roared and the ground trembled and a cloud of dust rose from the earth around the pounding steel plate of the vibrator. This time the roar did not stay at the same moderate pitch but started at a profound bass rumble and began slowly to climb.

Then it happened.

The earth beneath Priest's feet seemed to ripple like a choppy sea. Then he felt as if someone took him by the leg and threw him down. He landed flat on his back, hitting the ground hard. It knocked the wind out of him.

Star and Melanie screamed at the same time, Melanie with a high-pitched shriek and Star with a roar of shock and fright. Priest saw them both fall, Melanie next to him and Star a few steps away. Oaktree staggered, stayed on his feet, and fell last.

Priest was silently terrified. *I've had it, this is it, I'm going to die.*

There was a noise like an express train thundering past close by. Dust rose from the ground, small stones flew through the air, and boulders rolled every which way.

The ground continued to move as if someone had hold of the end of a rug and would not stop shaking it. The feeling was unbelievably disorienting, as if the world had suddenly become a completely strange place. It was terrifying.

I'm not ready to die.

Priest caught his breath and struggled to his knees. Then, as he got one foot flat on the ground, Melanie grabbed his arm and pulled him down again. He screamed at her: "Let me go, you dumb cunt!" But he could not hear his own words.

The ground heaved up and threw him downhill, away from the 'Cuda. Melanie fell on top of him. He thought the car might turn over and crush both of them, and he tried to roll out of its path. He could not see Star or Oaktree. A flying thornbush whipped his face, scratching him. Dust got into his eyes, and he was momentarily blinded. He lost all sense of direction. He curled up in a ball, covering his face with his arms, and waited for death.

Christ, if I'm going to die, I wish I could die with Star.

The shaking stopped as suddenly as it had started. He had no idea whether it had lasted ten seconds or ten minutes.

A moment later the noise died away.

Priest rubbed the dust out of his eyes and stood up. His vision cleared slowly. He saw Melanie at his feet. He extended a hand and pulled her up. "Are you okay?" he said.

"I think so," she replied shakily.

The dust in the air thinned, and he saw Oaktree getting to his feet unsteadily. Where was Star? Then he saw her a few steps away. She lay on her back with her eyes closed. His heart lurched. *Not dead, please God, not dead.* He knelt by her side. "Star!" he said urgently. "Are you okay?"

She opened her eyes. "Jesus," she said. "That was a blast!"

Priest grinned, fighting back tears of relief.

He helped Star to her feet. "We're all alive," he said.

The dust was settling fast. He looked across the valley and saw the truck. It was upright and seemed undamaged. A few yards from it there was a great gash in the ground that ran north and south in the middle of the valley as far as he could see.

"Well, I'll be darned," he said quietly. "Look at that."

"It worked," said Melanie.

"We did it," Oaktree said. "Goddamn it, we caused a motherfucking earthquake!"

Priest grinned at them all. "That's the truth," he said.

He kissed Star, then Melanie; then Oaktree kissed them both; then Star kissed Melanie. They all laughed. Then Priest started to dance. He did a red Indian war hop, there in the middle of the broken valley, his boots kicking up the newly settled dust. Star joined in, then Melanie and Oaktree, and the four of them went round and round in a circle, shouting and whooping and laughing until the tears came to their eyes.

PART TWO

Seven Days

8

Judy Maddox was driving home on Friday at the end of the worst week in her FBI career.

She could not figure out what she had done to deserve this. Okay, she had yelled at her boss, but he had been hostile to her before she blew her cool, so there had to be another reason. She had gone to Sacramento yesterday with every intention of making the Bureau look efficient and competent, and somehow she had ended up giving an impression of muddle and impotence. She felt frustrated and depressed.

Nothing good had happened since her meeting with Al Honeymoon. She had been calling seismology professors and interviewing them by phone. She would ask whether the professor was working on locations of critically stressed points on fault lines. If so, who had access to their data? And did any of those people have connections with terrorist groups?

The seismologists had not been helpful. Most of today's academics had been students in the sixties and seventies, when the FBI had paid every creep on campus to spy on the protest movement. It was a long time ago, but they had not forgotten. To them the Bureau was the enemy. Judy understood how they felt, but she wished they would not be passive-aggressive with agents who were working in the public interest.

The Hammer of Eden's deadline ran out today, and there had been no earthquake. Judy was deeply relieved, even though it suggested she had been wrong to take the threat seriously. Maybe this would be the end of the whole thing. She told herself she should have a relaxing weekend. The weather was great, sunny and warm. Tonight she would make stir-fried chicken for Bo and open a bottle of wine. Tomorrow she would have to go to the supermarket, but on Sunday she could drive up the coast to Bodega Bay and sit on the beach reading a book like a normal person. On Monday she would probably be given a new assignment. Maybe she could make a fresh start.

She wondered whether to call her girlfriend Virginia and see if she wanted to go to the beach. Ginny was her oldest friend. Also the daughter of a cop, and the same age as Judy, she was sales director of a security firm. But, Judy realized, it was not feminine company she wanted. It would be nice to lie on the beach beside something with hairy legs and a deep voice. It was a year since she had split up with Don: this was the longest time she had been without a lover since her teens. At college she had been a little wild, almost promiscuous; working at Mutual American Insurance, she had had an affair with her boss; then she had lived with Steve Dolen for seven years and almost married him. She often thought about Steve. He was attractive and smart and kind—too kind, maybe, for in the end she came to think of him as weak. Maybe she asked the impossible. Perhaps all considerate, attentive men were weak, and all the strong ones, like Don Riley, ended up shtupping their secretaries.

Her car phone rang. She did not need to pick up the handset: after two rings it connected automatically in hands-free mode. "Hello," she said. "This is Judy Maddox."

"This is your father."

"Hi, Bo. Will you be home for supper? We could have—"

He interrupted her. "Turn on your car radio, quick," he said. "Tune to John Truth."

Christ, what now? She touched the power switch. A rock music station came on. She jabbed at a preset button and got the San Francisco station that broadcast *John Truth Live.* His nasal twang filled the car.

He was speaking in the ponderously dramatic manner he used to suggest that what he had to say was world-shakingly important. "The California State seismologist has now confirmed that there was an earthquake today—the very day the Hammer of Eden promised it. It took place at twenty minutes after two P.M. in Owens Valley, just as the Hammer of Eden said when they called this show a few minutes ago."

My God—they did it.

Judy was electrified. She forgot her frustration, and her depression vanished. She felt alive again.

John Truth was saying: "But the same state seismologist denied that this or any other earthquake could have been caused by a terrorist group."

Was that true? Judy had to know. What did other seismologists think? She needed to make some calls. Then she heard John Truth say: "In a moment we will play you a recording of the message left by the Hammer of Eden."

They're on tape!

That could be a crucial mistake by the terrorists. They would not know it, but a voice on tape would provide a mass of information when analyzed by Simon Sparrow.

Truth went on: "Meanwhile, what do *you* think? Do you believe the state seismologist? Or do you think he's whistling past the graveyard? Maybe *you* are a seismologist and you have an opinion on the technical possibilities here. Or maybe you're just a concerned citizen and you think the authorities ought to be as worried as you are. Call *John Truth Live* on this number now to tell the world what *you* think."

A commercial for a furniture warehouse came on, and Judy muted the volume. "Are you still there, Bo?"

"Sure."

"They did it, didn't they?"

"Sure looks like it."

She wondered whether he was genuinely uncertain or just being cautious. "What does your instinct say?"

He gave her another ambiguous answer. "That these people are very dangerous."

Judy tried to calm her racing heart and turn her mind to what she should do next. "I'd better call Brian Kincaid—"

"What are you going to tell him?"

"The news . . . Wait a minute." Bo was making a point. "You don't think I should call him."

"I think you should call your boss when you can give him something he can't get from the radio."

"You're right." Judy began to feel calmer as she ran over the possibilities. "I guess I'm going back to work." She made a right turn.

"Okay. I'll be home in an hour or so. Call me if you want supper."

She felt a sudden rush of affection for him. "Thanks, Bo. You're a great daddy."

He laughed. "You're a great kid, too. Later."

"Later." She touched the button that terminated the call, then she turned up the volume on the radio.

She heard a low, sexy voice saying: "This is the Hammer of Eden with a message for Governor Mike Robson."

The picture that came into her mind was of a mature woman with large breasts and a wide smile, likable but kind of off-the-wall.

That's my enemy?

The tone changed, and the woman muttered: "Shit, I didn't expect to be talking to a tape recorder."

She's not the organizational brain behind all this. She's too ditzy. She's taking instructions from someone else.

The woman resumed her formal voice and continued: "Like we promised, we caused an earthquake today, four

weeks after our last message. It happened in Owens Valley
a little after two o'clock, you can check it out."

A faint background noise caused her to hesitate.

What was that?

Simon will find out.

A second later she carried on. "We do not recognize the
jurisdiction of the United States government. Now that you
know we can do what we say, you'd better think again about
our demand. Announce a freeze on construction of new
power plants in California. You have seven days to make up
your mind."

Seven days! Last time they gave us four weeks.

"After that we will trigger another earthquake. But the
next one won't be out in the middle of nowhere. If you force
us, we'll do real damage."

*A carefully calculated escalation of the threat. Jesus,
these people scare me.*

"We don't like it, but it's the only way. Please do as we
say so that this nightmare can end."

John Truth came on. "There it is, the voice of the Hammer of Eden, the group that claims to have triggered the earthquake that shook Owens Valley today."

Judy had to have that tape. She turned down the volume
again and dialed Raja's home number. He was single, he
could give up his Friday evening.

When he answered she said: "Hi, this is Judy."

He said immediately: "I can't, I have tickets for the opera!"

She hesitated, then decided to play along. "What's on?"

"Uh . . . *Macbeth's Wedding.*"

She suppressed a laugh. "By Ludwig Sebastian Wagner?"

"Right."

"No such opera, no such composer. You're working
tonight."

"Shit."

"Why didn't you invent a rock group? I would have
believed you."

"I keep forgetting how old you are."

She laughed. Raja was twenty-six, Judy was thirty-six. "I'll take that as a compliment."

"What's the assignment?" He did not sound too reluctant.

Judy became serious again. "Okay, here it is. There was an earthquake in the eastern part of the state this afternoon, and the Hammer of Eden claim they triggered it."

"Wow! Maybe these people are for real after all!" He sounded pleased rather than scared. He was young and keen, and he had not thought through the implications.

"John Truth just played a recorded message from the perpetrators. I need you to go to the radio station and get the tape."

"I'm on my way."

"Make sure you get the original, not a copy. If they give you a hard time, tell them we can get a court order in an hour."

"Nobody gives me a hard time. This is Raja, remember?"

It was true. He was a charmer. "Take the tape to Simon Sparrow and tell him I need something in the morning."

"You got it."

She broke the connection and turned John Truth up again. He was saying: ". . . a minor earthquake, by the way, magnitude five to six."

How the hell did they do it?

"No one injured, no damage to buildings or other property, but a tremor that was quite definitely felt by the residents of Bishop, Bigpine, Independence, and Lone Pine."

Some of those people must have seen the perpetrators within the last few hours, Judy realized. She had to get over there and start interviewing them as soon as possible.

Where exactly was the earthquake? She needed to talk to an expert.

The obvious choice was the state seismologist. However, he seemed to have a closed mind. He had already ruled out the possibility of a human-made earthquake. That bothered her. She wanted someone who was willing to entertain all possibilities. She thought of Michael Quercus. He could be a pain in the ass, but he was not afraid to speculate. Plus he was just across the bay in Berkeley, whereas the state seismologist was in Sacramento.

If she showed up without an appointment, he would refuse to see her. She sighed and dialed his number.

For a while there was no answer, and she thought he must be out. He picked up after six rings. "Quercus." He sounded annoyed at the interruption.

"This is Judy Maddox from the FBI. I need to talk to you. It's urgent, and I'd like to come to your place right away."

"It's out of the question. I'm with someone."

I might have known you'd be difficult. "Maybe after your meeting is over?"

"It's not a meeting, and it won't be over till Sunday."

Yeah, right.

He had a woman there, Judy guessed. But he had told her at the first meeting that he was not seeing anyone. For some reason she remembered his exact words: "I'm separated from my wife, and I don't have a girlfriend." Perhaps he had lied. Or perhaps this was someone new. It did not sound like a new relationship, if he was expecting her to stay the weekend. On the other hand, he was arrogant enough to assume that a girl would go to bed with him on the first date, and attractive enough that lots of girls probably would.

I don't know why I'm so interested in his love life.

"Have you been listening to the radio?" she asked him. "There's been an earthquake, and the terrorist group we talked about claims to have triggered it."

"Is that so?" He sounded intrigued despite himself. "Are they telling the truth?"

"That's what I need to discuss with you."

"I see."

Come on, you stubborn son of a gun—give in, for once in your life.

"This is really important, Professor."

"I'd like to help you . . . but it's really not possible tonight. . . . No, wait." His voice became muffled as he covered the mouthpiece with his hand, but she could still distinguish his words. "Hey, have you ever met a real-live FBI agent?" She could not hear the reply, but after a moment he said to her: "Okay, my guest would like to meet you. Come on over."

She did not like the idea of being paraded like some kind of circus freak, but at this point she was not going to say so. "Thanks, I'll be there in twenty minutes." She broke the connection.

As she drove over the bridge, she reflected that neither Raja nor Michael had seemed scared. Raja was excited, Michael intrigued. She, too, was electrified by the sudden reanimation of the case; but when she remembered the earthquake of 1989, and the television pictures of rescue workers bringing corpses out of the collapsed double-deck Nimitz Freeway right here in Oakland, and she contemplated the possibility of a terrorist group having the power to do that, her heart felt cold and heavy with foreboding.

To clear her mind she tried to guess what Michael Quercus's girlfriend would be like. She had seen a picture of his wife, a striking redhead with a supermodel figure and a sulky pout. *He seems to like the exotic.* But they had broken up, so perhaps she was not really his type. Judy could see him with a woman professor, in fashionable thin-framed spectacles, with well-cut short hair but no makeup. On the other hand, that type of woman would not cross the street to meet an FBI agent. Most likely he had picked up a sexy airhead who was easily impressed. Judy visualized a girl in tight clothes, smoking and chewing gum at the same time, looking around his apartment and saying: "Have you *read* all these books?"

I don't know why I'm obsessing about his girlfriend when I've got so much else to worry about.

She found Euclid Street and parked under the same magnolia tree as last time. She rang his bell, and he buzzed her into the building. He came to the apartment door barefoot, looking pleasantly weekendish in blue jeans and a white T-shirt. *A girl could have fun spending the weekend fooling around with him.* She followed him into his office-cum–living room.

There, to her astonishment, she saw a little boy of about five, with freckles and fair hair, dressed in pajamas with dinosaurs all over them. After a moment she recognized him as the child in the photograph on the desk. Michael's son. This was his weekend guest. She felt embarrassed about the dumb blonde she had imagined. *I was a little unfair to you, Professor.*

Michael said: "Dusty, meet Special Agent Judy Maddox."

The boy shook hands politely and said: "Are you really in the FBI?"

"Yes, I am."

"Wow."

"Want to see my badge?" She took her shield from her shoulder bag and gave it to him. He held it reverently.

Michael said: "Dusty likes to watch *The X-Files*."

Judy smiled. "I don't work in the Alien Spacecraft Department, I just catch regular earth criminals."

Dusty said: "Can I see your gun?"

Judy hesitated. She knew that boys were fascinated by weapons, but she did not like to encourage such an interest. She glanced at Michael, who shrugged. She unbuttoned her jacket and took the weapon out of its shoulder holster.

As she did so, she caught Michael looking at her breasts, and she felt a sudden sexual frisson. Now that he was not being curmudgeonly, he was kind of appealing, with his bare feet and his T-shirt untucked.

She said: "Guns are pretty dangerous, Dusty, so I'm going to hold it, but you can look."

Dusty's face as he stared at the pistol wore the same expression as Michael's when she opened her jacket. The thought made her grin.

After a minute she holstered the gun.

Dusty said with elaborate politeness: "We were just going to have some Cap'n Crunch. Would you care to join us?"

Judy was impatient to question Michael, but she sensed he would be more forthcoming if she was patient and played along. "How nice of you," she said. "I'm real hungry, I'd love some Cap'n Crunch."

"Come into the kitchen."

The three of them sat at a plastic-topped table in the little kitchen and ate breakfast cereal and milk out of bright blue pottery bowls. Judy realized she was hungry: it was past suppertime. "My goodness," she said. "I'd forgotten how good Cap'n Crunch is."

Michael laughed. Judy was amazed at the difference in him. He was relaxed and amiable. He seemed a different person from the grouch who had forced her to drive back to the office and phone him for an appointment. She was beginning to like him.

When supper was eaten, Michael got Dusty ready for bed. Dusty said to his father: "Can Agent Judy tell me a story?"

Judy suppressed her impatience. *I've got seven days, I can wait another five minutes.* She said: "I think your daddy wants to tell you a story, because he doesn't get to do it as often as he'd like."

"It's okay," Michael said with a smile. "I'll listen in."

They went into the bedroom. "I don't know many stories, but I remember one my mommy used to tell me," Judy said. "It's the legend of the kindly dragon. Would you like to hear it?"

"Yes, please," said Dusty.

"Me too," said Michael.

"Once upon a time, a long, long time ago, there was a kindly dragon who lived in China, where all dragons come from. One day the kindly dragon went wandering. He wandered so far that he left China and got lost in the wilderness.

"After many days he came to another land, far to the south. It was the most beautiful country he had ever seen, with forests and mountains and fertile valleys, and rivers for him to splash about in. There were banana palms and mulberry trees laden with ripe fruit. The weather was always warm with a pleasant breeze.

"But there was one thing wrong. It was an empty land. No one lived there: no people, and no dragons. So although the kindly dragon loved the new land, he was terribly lonely.

"However, he didn't know the way home, so he roamed all around, looking for someone to keep him company. At last, one lucky day, he found the one person who lived there—a fairy princess. She was so beautiful that he fell in love with her at once. Now, the princess was lonely, too, and although the dragon looked fearsome, he had a kind heart, and so she married him.

"The kindly dragon and the fairy princess loved each other, and they had a hundred children. All the children were brave and kindly like their dragon father, and beautiful like their fairy mother.

"The kindly dragon and the fairy princess looked after their children until they were all grown up. Then, suddenly, both parents vanished. They went away to live in love and harmony in the spirit world for all eternity. And their children became the brave, kindly, beautiful people of Vietnam. And that's where my mommy came from."

Dusty was wide-eyed. "Is it true?"

Judy smiled. "I don't know, maybe."

"It's a beautiful story anyway," Michael said. He kissed Dusty good night.

As Judy left the room, she heard Dusty whisper: "She's really nice, isn't she?"

"Yes," Michael replied.

Back in the living room, Michael said: "Thank you for that. You were great with him."

"It wasn't difficult. He's a charmer."

Michael nodded. "Gets it from his mother."

Judy smiled.

Michael grinned and said: "I notice you don't argue with that."

"I've never met your wife. In the picture she looks very beautiful."

"She is. And . . . faithless."

That was an unexpected confidence, coming so suddenly from a man she took to be proud. She warmed to him. But she did not know what to say in reply.

They were both silent for a moment. Then Michael said: "You've had enough of the Quercus family. Tell me about the earthquake."

At last. "It took place in Owens Valley this afternoon at twenty minutes past two."

"Let's get the seismograph." Michael sat at his desk and tapped the keys of his computer. She found herself looking at his bare feet. Some men had ugly feet, but his were well shaped and strong looking, with neatly clipped toenails. The skin was white, and there was a small tuft of dark hair on each big toe.

He did not notice her scrutiny. "When your terrorists made their threat four weeks ago, did they specify the location?"

"No."

"Hmm. In the scientific community, we say that a successful earthquake forecast would have to specify date, location, and magnitude. Your people only gave the date. That's not very convincing. There's an earthquake *somewhere* in California more or less every day. Maybe they just claimed responsibility for something that happened naturally."

"Can you tell me exactly where today's tremor took place?"

"Yes. I can calculate the epicenter by triangulation. Actually, the computer does it automatically. I'll just print out the coordinates." After a moment his printer whirred.

Judy said: "Is there any way of knowing how the earthquake was triggered?"

"You mean, can I tell from the graph whether it was caused by human agency? Yes, I should be able to."

"How?"

He clicked his mouse and turned from the screen to face her. "A normal earthquake is preceded by a gradual buildup of foreshocks, or lesser tremors, which we can see on the seismograph. By contrast, when the earthquake is triggered by an explosion, there is no buildup—the graph begins with a characteristic spike." He turned back to his computer.

He was probably a good teacher, Judy thought. He explained things clearly. But he would be mercilessly intolerant of student foibles. He would give surprise tests and refuse to admit latecomers to his lectures.

"That's odd," he said.

Judy looked over his shoulder at the screen. "What's odd?"

"The seismograph."

"I don't see a spike."

"No. There was no explosion."

Judy did not know whether to feel relieved or disappointed. "So the earthquake happened naturally?"

He shook his head. "I'm not sure. There are foreshocks, yes. But I've never seen foreshocks like this."

Judy was frustrated. He had promised to tell her whether the Hammer of Eden's claim was plausible. Now he was maddeningly uncertain. "What's peculiar about the foreshocks?" she asked.

"They're too regular. They look artificial."

"Artificial?"

He nodded. "I don't know what caused these vibrations, but they don't look natural. I believe your terrorists did *something*. I just don't know what it is."

"Can you find out?"

"I hope so. I'll call a few people. Plenty of seismologists will be studying these readings already. Between us we ought to be able to figure out what they mean."

He didn't sound too sure, but Judy guessed she would have to be content with that for now. She had got all she could out of Michael tonight. Now she needed to get to the scene of the crime. She picked up the sheet that had emerged from the printer. It showed a series of map references.

"Thanks for seeing me," she said. "I appreciate it."

"I enjoyed it." He smiled at her, a big hundred-watt smile showing two rows of white teeth.

"Have a good weekend with Dusty."

"Thanks."

She got in her car and headed back to the city. She would go to the office and look up airline schedules on the Internet, see if there was a flight to somewhere near Owens Valley early tomorrow morning. She would also need to check which FBI field office had jurisdiction over Owens Valley and talk to them about what she was doing. Then she would call the local sheriff and get him on her side.

She reached 450 Golden Gate Avenue, parked in the underground garage, and took the elevator up. As she walked past Brian Kincaid's office, she heard voices. He must be working late.

This was as good a time as any to bring him up to speed. She entered the anteroom and tapped on the open door to the inner office.

"Come in," he called.

She stepped inside. Her heart sank when she saw that Kincaid was with Marvin Hayes. She and Marvin disliked each other intensely. He was sitting in front of the desk, wearing a tan summer suit with a white button-down shirt and a black-and-gold power tie. He was a good-looking man, with bristly dark hair cut short and a neat mustache. He looked the picture of competence, but in fact he was everything a law enforcement officer should not be: lazy, brutal, slapdash, and unscrupulous. For his part, he thought Judy was prissy.

Unfortunately, Brian Kincaid liked him, and Brian was now the boss.

The two men looked startled and guilty when Judy walked in, and she realized they must have been talking about her. To make them feel worse, she said: "Am I interrupting something?"

"We were talking about the earthquake," Brian said. "Did you hear the news?"

"Of course. I've been working on it. I just interviewed a seismologist who says the foreshocks are like nothing he's ever seen before, but he's sure they're artificial. He gave me the map coordinates for the exact location of the tremor. I want to go to Owens Valley in the morning to look for witnesses."

A significant glance passed between the two men. Brian said: "Judy, no one can cause an earthquake."

"We don't know that."

Marvin said: "I've talked to two seismologists myself, tonight, and they both told me it was impossible."

"Scientists disagree—"

Brian said: "We think this group never went near Owens Valley. They found out about the earthquake and claimed credit for it."

Judy frowned. "This is my assignment," she said. "How come Marvin is calling seismologists?"

"This case is becoming very high-profile," Brian said. Suddenly Judy knew what was coming, and her heart filled with impotent fury. "Even though we don't believe the Hammer of Eden can do what they claim, they can get a hell of a lot of publicity. I'm not confident you can deal with that."

Judy struggled to control her rage. "You can't reassign me without a reason."

"Oh, I have a reason," he said. He picked up a fax from his desk. "Yesterday you got into an altercation with a California Highway Patrolman. He stopped you for speeding. According to this, you were uncooperative and abusive, and you refused to show him your license."

"For Christ's sake, I showed him my badge!"

Brian ignored that. Judy realized he was not really interested in the details. The incident with the CHP was just a pretext. "I'm setting up a special squad to deal with the Hammer of Eden," he went on. He swallowed nervously, then lifted his chin in an aggressive gesture and said: "I've asked Marvin to take charge. He won't be needing your help. You're off the case."

9

Priest could hardly believe he had done it.

I caused an earthquake. I really did. Me.

As he drove the truck north on U.S. 395, heading for home, with Melanie beside him and Star and Oaktree in the 'Cuda behind, he let his imagination run riot. He visualized a white-faced TV reporter giving the news that the Hammer of Eden had done what they promised; riots in the streets as people panicked at the threat of another earthquake; and a distraught Governor Robson, outside the Capitol Building, announcing a freeze on the building of new power plants in California.

Maybe that was too optimistic. People might not be ready to panic yet. The governor would not cave in immediately. But he would at least be forced to open negotiations with Priest.

What would the police do? The public would expect them to catch the perpetrators. The governor had called in the FBI. But they had no idea who the Hammer of Eden were, no clues. Their job was next to impossible.

One thing had gone wrong today, and Priest could not help worrying about it. When Star called John Truth, she had not spoken to an individual but had left a message on a machine. Priest would have stopped her, but by the time he realized what was happening it was too late.

An unknown voice on a tape was not much use to the

cops, he figured. All the same he wished they did not have even such a slender lead.

He found it surprising that the world was carrying on as if nothing had happened. Cars and trucks passed up and down the freeway, people parked at Burger King, the Highway Patrol stopped a young man in a red Porsche, a maintenance crew trimmed roadside bushes. They should all have been in shock.

He began to wonder if the earthquake had really happened. Had he imagined the whole thing in a dope dream? He had seen it with his own eyes, the gash in the earth that had opened up in Owens Valley—yet the earthquake seemed more farfetched and impossible now than when it was just an idea. He yearned for public confirmation: a TV news report, a picture on a magazine cover, people talking about it in a bar or the checkout line of a supermarket.

In the late afternoon, while they were on the Nevada side of the border, Priest pulled into a filling station. The 'Cuda followed. Priest and Oaktree filled the tanks, standing in the slanting evening sunlight, while Melanie and Star went to the ladies' room.

"I hope we're on the news," Oaktree said edgily.

He was thinking the same as Priest. "How could we not be?" Priest replied. "We caused an earthquake!"

"The authorities could keep it quiet."

Like a lot of old hippie types, Oaktree believed that the government controlled the news. Priest thought that might be harder than Oaktree imagined. Priest believed the public were their own censors. They refused to buy newspapers or watch TV shows that challenged their prejudices, so they got fed pap.

However, Oaktree's thought worried him. It might not be too difficult to cover up a small earthquake in a lonely place.

He went inside to pay. The air-conditioning made him shiver. The clerk had a radio playing behind the counter. It occurred to Priest that he might hear the news. He asked the time, and the counterman said it was five to six. After he paid, Priest lingered, pretending to study a rack of magazines while he listened to Billy Jo Spears singing " '57 Chevrolet." Melanie and Star came out of the rest room together.

At last the news began.

To give them a reason for hanging around, Priest slowly selected some candy bars and took them to the counter while he listened.

The first item was the wedding of two actors who played neighbors in a TV sitcom. Who could give a shit? Priest listened impatiently, tapping his foot. Then came a report on the president's visit to India. Priest hoped he would learn a mantra. The clerk added up the cost of the candy bars, and Priest paid. Surely the earthquake would come next? But the third story was about a shooting in a school in Chicago.

Priest walked slowly toward the door, followed by Melanie and Star. Another customer finished filling up his Jeep Wrangler and came in to pay.

Finally the newsreader said: "The environmental terrorist group the Hammer of Eden has claimed responsibility for a minor earthquake that took place today in Owens Valley, in eastern California."

Priest whispered, "Yes!" and smacked his left palm with his right fist in a triumphant gesture.

Star hissed, "We're not terrorists!"

The newsreader continued: "The tremor occurred on the day that the group had threatened to trigger one, but state seismologist Matthew Bird denied that this or any other earthquake could be caused by human agency."

"Liar!" Melanie said under her breath.

"The claim was made in a phone call to this station's premier talk show, *John Truth Live*."

Just as Priest reached the exit, he was shocked to hear Star's voice. He stopped dead. She was saying: "We do not recognize the jurisdiction of the United States government. Now that you know we can do what we say, you'd better think again about our demand. Announce a freeze on construction of new power plants in California. You have seven days to make up your mind."

Star exploded: "Jesus Christ—that's me!"

"Hush!" Priest said. He looked over his shoulder. The customer with the Jeep Wrangler was talking while the clerk swiped his credit card through a machine. Neither man seemed to have noticed Star's outburst.

"Governor Mike Robson has not responded to this latest threat. In sports today . . ."

They stepped outside.

Star said: "My God! They broadcast my voice! What am I going to do?"

"Stay calm," Priest told her. He did not feel calm himself, but he was maintaining. As they walked across the asphalt to the vehicles, he said in a low, reasonable voice: "Nobody outside our commune knows your voice. You haven't said more than a few words to an outsider for twenty-five years. And people who might remember you from the Haight-Ashbury days don't know where you're living now."

"I guess you're right," Star said doubtfully.

"The only exception I can think of is Bones. He might hear the tape and recognize your voice."

"He would never betray us. Bones is a Rice Eater."

"I don't know. Junkies will do anything."

"What about the others—like Dale and Poem?"

"Yeah, they're a worry," Priest admitted. There were no radios in the cabins, but there was one in the communal pickup truck, which Dale sometimes drove. "If it happens, we'll just have to level with them." *Or fall back on the Mario solution.*

No, I couldn't do that—not to Dale or Poem.
Could I?

Oaktree was waiting at the wheel of the 'Cuda. "Come on, you guys, what's the holdup?" he said.

Star explained briefly what they had heard. "Luckily, nobody outside the commune knows my voice—Oh, Christ, I just thought of something!" She turned to Priest. "The probation officer—in the sheriff's office."

Priest cursed. Of course. Star had spoken to him only yesterday. Fear gripped his heart. If he heard the radio broadcast and remembered Star's voice, the sheriff and half a dozen deputies might be at the commune right now, just waiting for Star to return.

But maybe he had not heard the news. Priest had to check. But how? "I'm going to call the sheriff's office," he told them.

"But what'll you say?" Star said.

"I don't know, I'll think of something. Wait here."

He went inside, got change from the clerk, and went to the pay phone. He got the Silver City Sheriff's number from California information and dialed. The name of the probation officer came back to him. "I need to speak to Mr. Wicks," he said.

A friendly voice said: "Billy ain't here."

"But I saw him yesterday."

"He caught a plane to Nassau last night. He's lyin' on a beach by now, sippin' a beer and watching the bikinis go by, lucky dog. Back in a couple a weeks. Anyone else help you?"

Priest hung up.

Jesus, what a lucky break.

He went outside. "God's on our side," he told the others.

"What?" Star said urgently. "What happened?"

"The guy went on vacation last night. He's in Nassau for two weeks. I don't think foreign radio stations are likely to broadcast Star's voice. We're safe."

Star slumped with relief. "Thank God for that."

Priest opened the door of the truck. "Let's get back on the road," he said.

It was approaching midnight when Priest steered the seismic vibrator along the rough winding track that led through the forest to the commune. He returned the truck to its hiding place. Although it was dark and they were all exhausted, Priest made sure they covered every square inch of the vehicle with vegetation so that it was invisible from all angles and from the air. Then they all got into the 'Cuda to drive the final mile.

Priest turned on the car radio for the midnight bulletin. This time the earthquake was top of the news. "Our show *John Truth Live* today played a central role in the continuing drama of the Hammer of Eden, the terrorist environmental group that says it can cause earthquakes," said an excited voice. "After a moderate earthquake shook Owens Valley, in the eastern part of California, a woman claiming to represent the group called John Truth and said they had triggered the tremor."

The station then played Star's message in full.

"Shit," Star muttered as she listened to her own voice.

Priest could not help feeling dismayed. Although he felt sure this would not help the police, still he hated to hear Star exposed in this way. It made her seem terribly vulnerable, and he yearned to destroy her enemies and make her safe.

After playing the tape, the newsreader said: "Special Agent Raja Khan tonight took away the recording for analysis by the FBI's experts in psycholinguistics."

That hit Priest like a punch in the stomach. "What the fuck is psycholinguistics?" he said.

Melanie answered: "I never heard the word before, but I guess they study the language you use and draw conclusions about your psychology."

"I didn't know they were that smart," Priest said worriedly.

Oaktree said: "Don't sweat it, man. They can analyze

Star's mind as much as they like, it ain't gonna give them her *address*."

"I guess not."

The newsreader was saying: "No comment yet from Governor Mike Robson, but the head of the FBI's field office in San Francisco has promised a press conference tomorrow morning. In other news—"

Priest switched off. Oaktree parked the 'Cuda next to Bones's carnival ride. Bones had covered the truck with a huge tarpaulin, to protect the colorful paintwork. That suggested he was planning to stay awhile.

They walked down the hill and through the vineyard to the village. The cookhouse and the children's bunkhouse were in darkness. Candlelight flickered behind Apple's window—she was an insomniac and liked to read into the small hours—and soft guitar chords came from Song's place, but the other cabins were dark and silent. Only Spirit, Priest's dog, came to greet them, wagging a happy tail in the moonlight. They said good night quietly and trudged off to their individual homes, too tired to celebrate their triumph.

It was a warm night. Priest lay on his bed naked, thinking. No comment from the governor, but an FBI press conference in the morning. That bothered him. At this point in the game, the governor should be panicking, saying, "The FBI has failed, we can't afford another earthquake, I have to talk to these people." It made Priest uneasy to be so ignorant of what his enemy was thinking. He always got his way by reading people, figuring out what they really wanted from the way they looked and smiled and folded their arms and scratched their heads. He was trying to manipulate Governor Robson, but it was hard without face-to-face contact. And what was the FBI up to? Was there any significance in this talk of psycholinguistic analysis?

He had to find out more. He could not lie here and wait for the opposition to act.

He wondered whether to call the governor's office and try to speak to him. Would he get through to the man himself? And if he did, would he learn anything? It might be worth a try. However, he disliked the position that put him in. He would be a supplicant, asking for the privilege of a conversation with the great man. His strategy was to impose his will on the governor, not beg for a favor.

Then it occurred to him that he could go to the press conference.

It would be dangerous: if he was found out, all would be lost.

But the idea appealed to him. Posing as a reporter was the kind of thing he used to do in the old days. He had specialized in bold strokes: stealing that white Lincoln and giving it to Pigface Riley; knifing Detective Jack Kassner in the toilet of the Blue Light bar; offering to buy the Fourth Street Liquor Store from the Jenkinsons. He had always managed to get away with stuff like that.

Maybe he would pose as a photographer. He could borrow a fancy camera from Paul Beale. Melanie could be the reporter. She was pretty enough to make any FBI agent take his eye off the ball.

What time was the press conference?

He rolled off the bed, stepped into his sandals, and went outside. In the moonlight he found his way to Melanie's cabin. She was sitting on the edge of her bed, naked, brushing her long red hair. As he walked in, she looked up and smiled. The candlelight outlined her body, throwing an aura behind her neat shoulders, her nipples, the bones of her hips, and the red hair in the fork of her thighs. It took his breath away.

"Hello," she said.

It took him a moment to remember why he had come. "I need to use your cell phone," he said.

She pouted. That was not the reaction she wanted from a man who came upon her naked.

He gave her his bad-boy grin. "But I may have to throw you to the ground and ravish you, then use your phone."

She smiled. "It's okay, you can phone first."

He picked up the phone, then hesitated. Melanie had been assertive all day, and he had put up with it because she was the seismologist; but that was over. He did not like her to give him permission for anything. That was not the relationship they were supposed to have.

He lay on the bed, still holding the phone, and guided Melanie's head to his groin. She hesitated, then did what he wanted.

For a minute or so he lay still, enjoying the sensation.

Then he called information.

Melanie stopped what she was doing, but he grasped a coil of her hair and held her head in place. She hesitated, as if contemplating a protest; but after a moment she resumed.

That's better.

Priest got the number of the FBI in San Francisco and dialed it.

A man's voice answered: "FBI."

Inspiration came to Priest, as always. "This is radio station KCAR in Carson City, Dave Horlock speaking," he said. "We want to send a reporter to your press conference tomorrow. Could you give me the address and time?"

"It went out on the wire," the man said.

Lazy bastard. "I'm not in the office," Priest improvised. "And our reporter may have to leave early tomorrow."

"It's at twelve noon, here in the Federal Building at 450 Golden Gate Avenue."

"Do we need an invitation, or can our guy just show up?"

"There are no invitations. All he needs is his regular press accreditation."

"Thanks for your help."

"What station did you say you were from?"

Priest hung up.

Accreditation. How am I going to get around that?

Melanie stopped sucking and said: "I hope they didn't trace that call."

Priest was surprised. "Why would they?"

"I don't know. Maybe the FBI routinely trace all incoming calls."

He frowned. "Can they do that?"

"With computers, sure."

"Well, I wasn't on the line long enough."

"Priest, this isn't the sixties. It doesn't take time, the computer does it in nanoseconds. They just have to check the billing records to find out who owns the number that called at three minutes to one A.M."

Priest had not heard the word "nanosecond" before, but he could guess what it meant. Now he was worried. "Shit," he said. "Can they figure out where you are?"

"Only while the phone is on."

Priest hastily switched it off.

He was beginning to feel unnerved. He had been surprised too often today: by the recording of Star's voice, by the concept of psycholinguistic analysis, and now by the notion of computer tracing of phone calls. Was there anything else he had failed to anticipate?

He shook his head. He was thinking negatively. Caution and worry never got anything done. Imagination and nerve were his strengths. He would show up at the press conference tomorrow, talk his way in, and get a handle on what the enemy was up to.

Melanie lay back on the bed, closed her eyes, and said: "It's been a long day in the saddle."

Priest gazed at her body. He loved to look at her breasts. He liked the way they moved when she walked, with a side-to-side rhythm. He enjoyed seeing her pull a sweater off over her head, the reaching gesture making her tits stick up like pointing guns. He loved to watch her put on a brassiere and adjust her breasts inside the cups to get comfortable.

Now, as she lay on her back, they were slightly flattened, bulging out sideways, and the nipples were soft in repose.

He needed to cleanse his mind of worry. The second-best way of doing that was meditation. The best was in front of him.

He knelt over her. When he kissed her breasts, she sighed contentedly and stroked his hair but did not open her eyes.

Priest saw a movement out of the corner of his eye. He glanced at the door and saw Star, wearing a purple silk robe. He smiled. He knew what she had in mind: she had done this sort of thing before. She raised her eyebrows in an expression of inquiry. Priest nodded assent. She came in and closed the door silently.

Priest sucked Melanie's pink nipple, drawing it into his mouth slowly with his lips, then teasing it with the tip of his tongue as he let it slide back out, again and again with a steady rhythm. She moaned in pleasure.

Star untied her robe and let it fall to the floor, then she stood watching, gently touching her own breasts. Her body was so different from Melanie's, the skin light tan where Melanie's was white, the hips and shoulders wider, the hair dark and thick where Melanie's was red gold and fine. After a few moments she leaned over and kissed Priest's ear, then ran her hand down his back, along his spine, and between his legs, stroking and squeezing.

He began to breathe faster.

Slowly, slowly. Savor the moment.

Star knelt beside the bed and began to caress Melanie's breast while Priest sucked it.

Melanie sensed that something was different. She stopped moaning. Her body stiffened, then she opened her eyes. When she saw Star, she let out a stifled scream.

Star smiled and continued to touch her. "Your body is very beautiful," she said in a low voice. Priest stared, entranced, as she leaned over and took Melanie's other breast into her mouth.

Melanie shoved them both away and sat upright. "No!" she said.

"Relax," Priest told her. "It's okay, really." He stroked her hair.

Star caressed the inside of Melanie's thigh. "You'll like it," she said. "A woman can do some things much better than a man. You'll see."

"No," Melanie said. She pressed her legs together tightly.

Priest could see that this was not going to work. He felt let down. He loved to see Star go down on another woman, driving her wild with pleasure. But Melanie was too spooked.

Star persisted. Her hand slid up Melanie's thigh, and her fingertips lightly brushed the tuft of red hair.

"No!" Melanie slapped Star's hand away.

It was a hard slap, and Star said: "Ow! What did you do that for?"

Melanie pushed Star aside and jumped off the bed. "Because you're fat and old and I don't want to have sex with you!"

Star gasped, and Priest winced.

Melanie stamped to the door and opened it. "Please!" she said. "Leave me alone!"

To Priest's surprise, Star began to cry. Indignantly he said: "Melanie!"

Before Melanie could reply, Star walked out.

Melanie slammed the door.

Priest said to her: "Wow, baby, that was mean."

She opened the door again. "You can go, too, if that's how you feel. Leave me alone!"

Priest was shocked. In twenty-five years no one had ever told him to leave a house here at the commune. Now he was being ordered out by a beautiful naked girl who was flushed with anger or excitement or both. To add to his humiliation, he had a hard-on like a flagpole.

Am I losing my grip?

The thought disturbed him. He could always get people

to do what he wanted, especially here at the commune. He was so taken aback that he almost obeyed her. He walked to the door without speaking.

Then he realized he could not give in. He might never regain dominance if he let her defeat him now. And he needed Melanie under his control. She was crucial to the plan. He would not be able to trigger another earthquake without her help. He could not let her assert her independence in this way. She was too important.

He turned in the doorway and looked at her, standing naked, hands on her hips. What did she want? She had been in control today, in Owens Valley, because of her expertise, and that had given her the courage for this display of bad temper. But in her heart she did not want to be independent—she would not be here if she did. She preferred to be told what to do by someone with power. That was why she had married her professor. Having left him, she had taken up with another authority figure, the leader of a commune. She had revolted tonight because she did not want to share Priest with another woman. She was probably scared Star would take him away from her. But the last thing she wanted was for Priest to walk away.

He closed the door.

He crossed the little room in three paces and stood in front of her. She was still flushed with anger and breathing hard. "Lie down," he commanded.

She looked troubled, but she lay on the bed.

"Open your legs," he said.

After a moment she obeyed.

He lay on her. As he entered her, she suddenly put her arms around him and held him hard. He moved fast inside her, deliberately rough. She lifted her legs around his waist. He felt her teeth on his shoulder, biting. It hurt, but he liked it. She opened her mouth, breathing hard. "Ah, fuck," she said in a low, guttural voice. "Priest, you son of a bitch, I love you."

* * *

When Priest woke up, he went to Star's cabin.

She was lying on her side, eyes open, staring at the wall. When he sat on the bed beside her, she began to cry.

He kissed her tears. He was getting a hard-on. "Talk to me," he murmured.

"Did you know that Flower puts Dusty to bed?"

He had not been expecting *that.* What did it matter? "I didn't know," he said.

"I don't like it."

"Why not?" He tried not to sound irritated. *Yesterday we triggered an earthquake, and today you're crying about the children?* "It's a hell of a lot better than stealing movie posters in Silver City."

"But you have a new family," she burst out.

"What the heck does that mean?"

"You, and Melanie, and Flower, and Dusty. You're like a family. And there's no place in it for me, I don't fit."

"Sure you do," he said. "You're the mother of my child, and you're the woman I love. How could you not fit?"

"I felt so humiliated last night."

He stroked her breasts through the cotton of her nightshirt. She covered his hand with her own and pressed his palm hard against her body.

"The group is our family," he told her. "It's always been that way. We don't suffer with the hang-ups of the suburban mom-and-dad-and-two-kids unit." He was repeating the teachings he had gotten from her years ago. "We're one big family. We love the whole group, and everyone takes care of everyone else. This way, we don't have to lie to each other, or to ourselves, about sex. You can get it on with Oaktree, or Song, and I'll know you still care for me and our child."

"But you know something, Priest—no one ever rejected you or me before now."

There were no rules about who could have sex with whom, but of course no one was obliged to make love if they did not want to. However, now that he thought about it, Priest could not remember an occasion on which a woman had refused him. Obviously it had been the same for Star— until Melanie.

A feeling of panic crept over him. He had felt it several times in the last few weeks. It was the fear that the commune was collapsing, he was losing his grip, and everything he loved was in peril. It was like losing his balance, as if the floor started to move unpredictably and firm ground suddenly became shifting and unreliable, just as it had in Owens Valley yesterday. He fought to suppress his anxiety. He had to stay cool. Only he could keep everyone's loyalty and hold it all together. He had to stay cool.

He lay on the bed beside her and stroked her hair. "It'll be okay," he said. "We scared the shit out of Governor Robson yesterday. He'll do what we want, you'll see."

"Are you sure?"

He took both her breasts in his hands. He felt turned on. "Trust me," he murmured. He pressed against her so that she could feel his erection.

"Make love to me, Priest," she said.

He gave her his roguish grin. "How?"

She smiled back through her tears. "Any damn way you like."

She went to sleep afterward. Lying beside her, Priest worried over the problem of accreditation until he thought of the solution. Then he got up.

He went to the kids' bunkhouse and woke Flower. "I want you to go with me to San Francisco," he said. "Get dressed."

He made toast and orange juice for her in the deserted cookhouse. As she ate, he said: "You remember we talked about you being a writer? And you told me you'd like to work for a magazine?"

"Yes, *Teen* magazine," she said.

"Right."

"But you want me to write poetry so I can live here."

"And I still do, but today you're going to find out what it's like to be a reporter."

She looked happy. "Okay!"

"I'm taking you to an FBI press conference."

"FBI?"

"This is the kind of thing you have to do if you're a reporter."

She wrinkled her nose in distaste. She had picked up her mother's dislike of law enforcement people. "I never read about the FBI in *Teen*."

"Well, Leonardo DiCaprio isn't giving a press conference today, I checked."

She grinned sheepishly. "Too bad."

"But if you just ask the kinds of questions a reporter from *Teen* would think of, you'll be fine."

She nodded thoughtfully. "What's the press conference about?"

"A group who claim they caused an earthquake. Now, I don't want you to tell everyone about this. It has to be a secret, okay?"

"Okay."

He would tell the Rice Eaters about it when he got back, he decided. "It's all right to talk to Mom and Melanie about it, and Oaktree and Song and Aneth and Paul Beale, but no one else. That's really important."

"Gotcha."

He knew he was taking a crazy risk. If things went wrong, he could lose everything. He might even be arrested in front of his daughter. This could end up being the worst day of her life. But mad risks had always been his style.

When he had proposed planting the grapevines, Star

had pointed out that they held their land on a one-year lease. They could break their backs digging and planting and never see the fruits of their labor. She had argued that they should negotiate a ten-year lease before starting work. It sounded sensible, but Priest had known it would be fatal. If they postponed the start, they would never do it. He had persuaded them to take the risk. At the end of that year, the commune had become a community. And the government had renewed Star's lease—that year and every year, until now.

He thought about putting on the navy blue suit. However, it was so old-fashioned that it would be conspicuous in San Francisco, so he wore his usual blue jeans. Although it was warm, he put on a T-shirt and a checked flannel shirt with a long tail, which he wore untucked. From the tool shed he took a heavy knife with a four-inch blade in a neat leather sheath. He stuck it in the waistband of his jeans, at the back, where it was concealed by the tail of his shirt.

He was high on adrenaline throughout the four-hour drive to San Francisco. He had nightmare visions: the two of them being arrested, himself bundled off to a jail cell, Flower sitting alone in an interrogation room at FBI headquarters, being questioned about her parents. But fear gave him a buzz.

They reached the city at eleven A.M. They left the car in a parking lot on Golden Gate. At a drugstore, Priest bought Flower a spiral-bound notebook and two pencils. Then he took her to a coffee shop. While she was drinking her soda, he said, "I'll be right back," and stepped outside.

He walked toward Union Square, scanning the faces of passersby, searching for a man who looked like him. The streets were busy with shoppers, and he had hundreds of faces to pick from. He saw a man with a thin face and dark hair studying the menu outside a restaurant, and for a moment he thought he had found his victim. Feeling wire-taut with tension, he watched for a few seconds; then the guy turned around and Priest saw that his right eye was permanently closed by some kind of injury.

Disappointed, Priest walked on. It was not easy. There were plenty of dark men in their forties, but most of them were twenty or thirty pounds heavier than Priest. He saw another likely candidate, but the guy had a camera around his neck. A tourist was no good: Priest needed someone with local credentials. *This is one of the greatest shopping centers in the world, and it's Saturday morning: there has to be one man here who looks like me.*

He checked his watch: eleven-thirty. He was running out of time.

At last he struck lucky: a thin-faced guy of about fifty, wearing large-framed glasses, walking briskly. He was dressed in navy slacks and a green polo shirt but carried a worn tan attaché case, and looked miserable: Priest guessed he was going to the office to do some Saturday catching up. *Now I need his wallet.* Priest followed him around a corner, psyching himself up, waiting for an opportunity.

I'm angry, I'm desperate, I'm a crazy man escaped from the asylum, I've got to have twenty bucks for a fix, I hate everyone, I want to slash and kill, I'm mad, mad, mad . . .

The man walked past the lot where the 'Cuda was parked and turned into a street of old office buildings. For a moment there was no one else in sight. Priest drew the knife, then ran up to him and said: "Hey!"

The man stopped reflexively and turned.

Priest grabbed the guy by the shirt, shoved the knife in front of his face, and screamed: "GIMME YOUR FUCKIN' WALLET OR I'LL SLIT YOUR FUCKIN' THROAT!"

The guy should have collapsed in terror, but he did not. *Jesus, he's a tough guy.* His face showed anger, not fear.

Staring into his eyes, Priest read the thought *It's only one guy, and he doesn't have a gun.*

Priest hesitated, suddenly fearful. *Shit, I can't afford for this to go wrong.* There was a split-second standoff. *A casu-*

ally dressed man with a briefcase heading for work on Saturday morning ... could he be a police detective?

But it was too late now for second thoughts. Before the guy could move, Priest flicked the blade across his cheek, drawing a thin two-inch line of red blood just below the right lens of his spectacles.

The man's courage evaporated, and all thought of resistance left him. His eyes widened in fear, and his body seemed to sag. "Okay! Okay!" he said in a high-pitched, shaky voice.

Not a cop, after all.

Priest screamed: "NOW! NOW! GIMME IT NOW!"

"It's in my case. . . ."

Priest grabbed the briefcase from the man's hand. At the last minute he decided to take the guy's glasses, too. He snatched them off his face, turned around, and ran away.

At the corner he looked back. The guy was throwing up on the sidewalk.

Priest turned right. He dropped his knife into a garbage bin and walked on. At the next corner he stopped by a building site and opened the case. Inside was a file folder, a notebook and some pens, a paper package that looked as if it contained a sandwich, and a leather billfold. Priest took the billfold and threw the case over the fence into a builder's skip.

He returned to the coffee shop and sat down with Flower. His coffee was still warm. *I haven't lost the touch. Thirty years since I last did that, but I can still scare the shit out of people. Way to go, Ricky.*

He opened the billfold. It contained money, credit cards, business cards, and some kind of identity card with a photo. Priest pulled out a business card and handed it to Flower. "My card, ma'am."

She giggled. "You're Peter Shoebury, of Watkins, Colefax and Brown."

"I'm a lawyer?"

"I guess."

He looked at the photo on the identity card. It was about half an inch square and had been taken in an automatic photo booth. It was about ten years old, he guessed. It did not look exactly like Priest, but neither did it look much like Peter Shoebury. Photos were like that.

Still, Priest could improve the resemblance. Shoebury had straight dark hair, but it was short. Priest said: "Can I borrow your hairband?"

"Sure." Flower took a rubber band out of her hair and shook her locks around her face. Priest did the reverse, pulling his hair back into a ponytail and tying it with the band. Then he put on the glasses.

He showed Flower the photo. "How do you like my secret identity?"

"Hmm." She looked at the back of the card. "This will admit you to the downtown office, but not the Oakland branch."

"I guess I can live with that."

She grinned. "Daddy, where did you get this?"

He raised one eyebrow at her and said: "I borrowed it."

"Did you pick someone's pocket?"

"Sort of." He could see she thought that was roguish rather than wicked. He let her believe what she wanted. He looked at the clock on the wall. It was eleven forty-five. "Are you ready to go?"

"Sure."

They walked along the street and entered the Federal Building, a forbidding gray granite monolith occupying the entire city block. In the lobby they passed through a metal detector, and Priest was glad he had had the forethought to get rid of the knife. He asked the security guard which floor the FBI was on.

They took the elevator up. Priest felt like he was high on cocaine. The danger made him superalert. *If this elevator breaks down, I could power it with my own psychic energy.*

He figured it was okay to be self-confident, maybe even a little arrogant, as he was playing the part of a lawyer.

He led Flower into the FBI office and followed a sign to a conference room off the lobby. There was a table with microphones at the far end of the room. Near the door stood four men, all tall and fit looking, wearing well-pressed business suits, white shirts, and sober ties. They had to be agents.

If they knew who I was, they'd shoot me down without even thinking about it.

Stay cool, Priest—they ain't mind readers, they don't know nothing about you.

Priest was six feet, but they were all taller. He sensed immediately that the leader was the older man whose thick white hair was meticulously parted and combed. He was talking to a man with a black mustache. Two younger men were listening, wearing deferential expressions.

A young woman carrying a clipboard approached Priest. "Hi, can I help you?"

"Well, I sure hope so," Priest said.

The agents noticed him when he spoke. He read their reactions as they looked at him. When they took in his ponytail and blue jeans they became guarded; then they saw Flower and softened again.

One of the younger men said: "Everything okay here?"

Priest said: "My name is Peter Shoebury, I'm an attorney with Watkins, Colefax and Brown here in the city. My daughter Florence is editor of the school newspaper. She heard on the radio about your press conference, and she wanted to cover it for the paper. So I figured hey, it's a public information thing, let's go along. I hope it's okay with you."

Everyone looked at the white-haired guy, confirming Priest's intuition that he was the boss.

There was an awful moment of hesitation.

Hell, boy, you ain't no lawyer! You're Ricky Granger, used to wholesale amphetamines through a bunch of liquor stores in Los Angeles back in the sixties—are you mixed up in this earthquake shit? Frisk him, boys, and cuff his little girl, too. Let's take 'em in, find out what they know.

The white-haired man held out his hand and said: "I'm Associate Special Agent in Charge Brian Kincaid, head of the San Francisco field office of the FBI."

Priest shook hands. "Good to meet you, Brian."

"What firm did you say you're with, sir?"

"Watkins, Colefax and Brown."

Kincaid frowned. "I thought they were real estate brokers, not lawyers."

Oh, shit.

Priest nodded and tried for a reassuring smile. "That's correct, and it's my job to keep them out of trouble." There was a word for a lawyer who was employed by a corporation. Priest searched his memory and found it. "I'm in-house counsel."

"Would you have any kind of ID?"

"Oh, sure." He opened the stolen wallet and took out the card with the photo of Peter Shoebury. He held his breath.

Kincaid looked at it, then checked the resemblance to Priest. Priest could tell what he was thinking: *Could be him, I guess.* He handed it back. Priest breathed again.

Kincaid turned to Flower. "What school are you at, Florence?"

Priest's heart beat faster. *Just make something up, kid.*

"Um. . . ." Flower hesitated. Priest was about to answer for her, then she said: "Eisenhower Junior High."

Priest felt a surge of pride. She had inherited his nerve. Just in case Kincaid should happen to know the schools in San Francisco, he added: "That's in Oakland."

Kincaid seemed satisfied. "Well, we'd be delighted to have you join us, Florence," he said.

We did it!

"Thank you, sir," she said.

"If there are any questions I can answer now, before the press conference starts . . ."

Priest had been careful not to overprepare Flower. If she appeared shy, or fumbled her questions, it would seem only natural, he figured; whereas if she were too poised and seemed well rehearsed, she might arouse suspicion. But now he felt a surge of anxiety on her behalf, and he had to suppress the paternal urge to step in and tell her what to do. He bit his lip.

She opened her notebook. "Are you in charge of this investigation?"

Priest relaxed a little. She would be fine.

"This is only one of many inquiries that I have to keep an eye on," Kincaid answered. He pointed to the man with the black mustache. "Special Agent Marvin Hayes has this assignment."

Flower turned to Hayes. "I think the school would like to know what kind of person you are, Mr. Hayes. Could I ask you some questions about yourself?"

Priest was shocked to observe a hint of coquettishness in the way she tilted her head and smiled at Hayes. *She's too young to flirt with grown men, for God's sake!*

But Hayes bought it. He looked pleased and said: "Sure, go ahead."

"Are you married?"

"Yes. I have two children, a boy around your age and a girl a little younger."

"Do you have any hobbies?"

"I collect boxing memorabilia."

"That's unusual."

"I guess it is."

Priest was both pleased and dismayed by how naturally Flower fell into the role. *She's good at this. Hell, I hope I haven't raised her all these years to become a cheap magazine writer.*

He studied Hayes while the agent answered Flower's

innocent questions. This was his opponent. Hayes was carefully dressed in conventional style. His tan lightweight suit, white shirt, and dark silk tie had probably come from Brooks Brothers. He wore black oxford shoes, highly shined and tightly laced. His hair and mustache were neatly trimmed.

Yet Priest sensed that the ultraconservative look was fake. The tie was too striking, there was an overlarge ruby ring on the pinky of his left hand, and the mustache was a raffish touch. Also, Priest thought that the kind of American Brahmin Hayes was trying to imitate would not be so dressed up on a Saturday morning, even for a press conference.

"What's your favorite restaurant?" Flower asked.

"A lot of us go to Everton's, which is really more of a pub."

The conference room was filling up with men and women with notebooks and cassette recorders, photographers encumbered with cameras and flashguns, radio reporters with large microphones, and a couple of TV crews with handheld videocameras. As they came in, the young woman with the clipboard asked them to sign a book. Priest and Flower seemed to have bypassed that. He was thankful. He could not write "Peter Shoebury" to save his life.

Kincaid, the boss, touched Hayes's elbow. "We need to prepare for our press conference now, Florence. I hope you'll stay to hear what we have to announce."

"Yes, thank you," she said.

Priest said: "You've really been very kind, Mr. Hayes. Florence's teachers will be truly grateful."

The agents moved to the table at the far end. *My God, we fooled them.* Priest and Flower sat at the back and waited. Priest's tension eased. He really had got away with it.

I knew I would.

He had not gained much hard information yet, but that would come with the formal press announcement. What he did have was a sense of the people he was dealing with. He was reassured by what he had learned. Neither Kincaid nor Hayes struck him as brilliant. They seemed like ordinary plodding cops, the kind who got by with a mixture of dogged routine and occasional corruption. He had little to fear from them.

Kincaid stood up and introduced himself. He sounded confident but a touch overassertive. Maybe he had not been the boss very long. He said: "I would like to begin by making one thing very clear. The FBI does not believe that yesterday's earthquake was triggered by a terrorist group."

The flashguns popped, the tapes whirred, and the reporters scribbled notes. Priest tried not to let his anger show on his face. The bastards were refusing to take him seriously—still!

"This is also the opinion of the state seismologist, who I believe is available for interview in Sacramento this morning."

What do I have to do to convince you? I threatened an earthquake, then I made it happen, and still you won't believe I did it! Must I kill people before you'll listen?

Kincaid went on: "Nevertheless, a terrorist threat has been made, and the Bureau intends to catch the people who made it. Our investigation is headed by Special Agent Marvin Hayes. Over to you, Marvin."

Hayes stood up. He was more nervous than Kincaid, Priest saw at once. He read mechanically from a prepared statement. "FBI agents have this morning questioned all five paid employees of the Green California Campaign at their homes. The employees are voluntarily cooperating with us."

Priest was pleased. He had laid a false trail, and the feds were following it.

Hayes went on: "Agents also visited the headquarters of the campaign, here in San Francisco, and examined documents and computer records."

They would be combing the organization's mailing list for clues, Priest guessed.

There was more, but it was repetitive. The assembled

journalists asked questions that added detail and color but did not change the basic story. Priest's tension grew again as he sat waiting impatiently for a chance to leave inconspicuously. He was pleased that the FBI investigation was so far off course—they had not yet come upon his *second* false trail—but he felt angry that they still refused to believe in his threat.

At last Kincaid drew the session to a close and the journalists began to get to their feet and pack up their gear.

Priest and Flower made for the door, but they were stopped by the woman with the clipboard, who smiled brightly and said: "I don't think you two signed in, did you?" She handed Priest a book and a pen. "Just put your names and the organization you represent."

Priest froze with fear. *I can't, I can't!*

Don't panic. Relax.

Ley, tor, pur-doy-cor . . .

"Sir? Would you please sign?"

"Sure." Priest took the book and the pen. Then he handed it to Flower. "I think Florence should sign for us—she's the journalist," he said, reminding her of her false name. It occurred to him that she might have forgotten the school she was supposed to attend. "Put your name, and 'Eisenhower Junior High.' "

Flower did not flinch. She wrote in the book and handed it back to the woman.

Now, for Christ's sake, can we go?

"You, too, sir, please," said the woman, and she gave Priest the book.

He took it reluctantly. Now what? If he just scrawled a squiggle, she might ask him to print his name clearly: that had happened to him before. But maybe he could just refuse and walk out. She was only a secretary.

As he hesitated, he heard the voice of Kincaid. "I hope that was interesting for you, Florence."

Kincaid is an agent—it's his job to be suspicious.

"Yes, sir, it was," Flower said politely.

Priest began to sweat under his shirt.

He drew a scrawl where he was supposed to write his name. Then he closed the book before handing it back to the woman.

Kincaid said to Flower: "Will you remember to send me a copy of your class newspaper when it's printed?"

"Yes, of course."

Let's go, let's go!

The woman opened the book and said: "Oh, sir, pardon me, would you mind printing your name here? I'm afraid your signature isn't really clear."

What am I going to do?

"You'll need an address," Kincaid said to Flower, and he took a business card from the breast pocket of his suit coat. "There you go."

"Thank you."

Priest remembered that Peter Shoebury carried business cards. *That's the answer—thank God!* He opened the wallet and gave one to the woman. "My handwriting is terrible— use this," he said. "We have to run." He shook Kincaid's hand. "You've been wonderful. I'll make sure Florence remembers to send you the clipping."

They left the room.

They crossed the lobby and waited for the elevator. Priest imagined Kincaid coming after him, gun drawn, saying, "What kind of attorney can't write his own god-damn name, asshole?" But the elevator came and they rode down and walked out of the building into the fresh air.

Flower said: "I gotta have the craziest dad in the world."

Priest smiled at her. "That's the truth."

"Why did we have false names?"

"Well, I never like the pigs to get my real name," he said. She would accept that, he thought. She knew how her parents felt about cops.

But she said: "Well, I'm mad at you about it."

He frowned. "Why?"

"I'll never forgive you for calling me Florence," she said.

Priest stared at her for a moment, then they both burst out laughing.

"Come on, kid," Priest said fondly. "Let's go home."

10

Judy dreamed she walked along the seashore with Michael Quercus, and his bare feet left neat, shapely prints in the wet sand.

On Saturday morning she helped out at a literacy class for young offenders. They respected her because she carried a gun. She sat in a church hall beside a seventeen-year-old hoodlum, helping him practice writing the date, hoping that somehow this would make it less likely that in ten years' time she would have to arrest him.

In the afternoon she drove the short distance from Bo's house to Gala Foods on Geary Boulevard and shopped.

The familiar Saturday routines failed to soothe her. She was furious with Brian Kincaid for taking her off the Hammer of Eden case, but there was nothing she could do about it, so she stomped up and down the aisles and tried to turn her mind to Chewy Chips Ahoy, Rice-A-Roni, and Zee "Decor Collection" kitchen towel printed with yellow patterns. In the breakfast cereal aisle she thought of Michael's son, Dusty, and she bought a box of Cap'n Crunch.

But her thoughts kept returning to the case. *Is there really someone out there who can make earthquakes happen? Or am I nuts?*

Back at home, Bo helped her unload the groceries and asked her about the investigation. "I hear Marvin Hayes raided the Green California Campaign."

"It can't have done him much good," she said. "They're all clean. Raja interviewed them on Tuesday. Two men and three women, all over fifty. No criminal records—not a speeding ticket between them—and no association with any suspicious persons. If they're terrorists, I'm Kojak."

"TV news says he's examining their records."

"Right. That's a list of everyone who ever wrote asking them for information, including Jane Fonda. There are eighteen thousand names and addresses. Now Marvin's team has to run each name through the FBI computer to see who's worth interviewing. It could take a month."

The doorbell rang. Judy opened the door to Simon Sparrow. She was surprised but pleased. "Hey, Simon, come on in!"

He was wearing black cycling shorts and a muscle T-shirt with Nike trainers and wraparound sunglasses. However, he had not come by bicycle: his emerald green Honda Del Sol was parked at the curb with the roof down. Judy wondered what her mother would have thought of Simon. "Nice boy," she might have said. "Not very manly, though."

Bo shook hands with Simon, then gave Judy a clandestine look that said *Who the hell is this fruit?* Judy shocked him by saying: "Simon is one of the FBI's top linguistic analysts."

Somewhat bemused, Bo said: "Well, Simon, I'm sure glad to meet you."

Simon was carrying a cassette tape and a manila envelope. Holding them up, he said: "I brought you my report on the Hammer of Eden tape."

"I'm off the case," Judy said.

"I know, but I thought you'd still be interested. The voices on the tape don't match any in our acoustic files, unfortunately."

"No names, then."

"No, but lots of other interesting stuff."

Judy's interest was piqued. "You said 'voices.' I only heard one."

"No, there are two." Simon looked around and saw Bo's radio-cassette on the kitchen counter. It was normally used to play *The Greatest Hits of the Everly Brothers*. He slipped his cassette into the player. "Let me talk you through the tape."

"I'd love you to, but it's Marvin Hayes's case now."

"I'd like your opinion anyway."

Judy shook her head stubbornly. "You should talk to Marvin first."

"I know what you're saying. But Marvin is a fucking idiot. Do you know how long it is since he put a bad guy in jail?"

"Simon, if you're trying to get me to work on this case behind Kincaid's back, forget it!"

"Hear me out, okay? It can't do any harm." Simon turned up the volume control and started the tape.

Judy sighed. She was desperately keen to know what Simon had found out about the Hammer of Eden. But if Kincaid learned that Simon had talked to her before Marvin, there would be hell to pay.

The voice of the woman said: "This is the Hammer of Eden with a message for Governor Mike Robson."

Simon stopped the tape and looked at Bo. "What did you visualize when you first heard that?"

Bo grinned. "I pictured a large woman, about fifty, with a big smile. Kind of sexy. I remember I thought I'd like to"— he glanced at Judy and finished—"meet her."

Simon nodded. "Your instincts are reliable. Untrained people can tell a lot about a speaker just by hearing them. You almost always know if you're listening to a woman or a man, of course. But you can also tell how old they are, and you can generally estimate their height and build pretty accurately. Sometimes you can even guess at their state of health."

"You're right," Judy said. She was intrigued despite herself. "Whenever I hear a voice on the phone, I picture the person, even if I'm listening to a taped announcement."

"It's because the sound of the voice comes from the body. Pitch, loudness, resonance, huskiness, all vocal characteristics have physical causes. Tall people have a longer vocal tract, old people have stiff tissues and creaky cartilage, sick people have inflamed throats."

"That makes sense," Judy said. "I just never really thought about it before."

"My computer picks up the same cues as people do, and is more accurate." Simon took a typed report out of the envelope he had been carrying. "This woman is between forty-seven and fifty-two. She's tall, within an inch of six feet. She's overweight, but not obese: probably just kind of generously built. She's a drinker and a smoker, but healthy despite that."

Judy felt anxious but excited. Although she wished she had not let Simon get started, it was fascinating to learn something about the mystery woman behind the voice.

Simon looked at Bo. "And you're right about the big smile. She has a large mouth cavity, and her speech is underlabialized—she doesn't purse her lips."

"I like this woman," Bo said. "Does the computer say if she's good in bed?"

Simon smiled. "The reason you think she's sexy is that her voice has a whispery quality. This can be a sign of sexual arousal. But when it's a permanent feature, it doesn't necessarily indicate sexiness."

"I think you're wrong," Bo said. "Sexy women have sexy voices."

"So do heavy smokers."

"Okay, that's true."

Simon wound the tape back to the beginning. "Now listen to her accent."

Judy protested. "Simon, I don't think we should—"

"Just listen. Please!"

"Okay, okay."

This time he played the first two sentences. "This is the Hammer of Eden with a message for Governor Mike Robson. Shit, I didn't expect to be talking to a tape recorder."

He stopped the tape. "It's a Northern California accent, of course. But did you notice anything else?"

Bo said: "She's middle class."

Judy frowned. "She sounded upper class to me."

"You're both right," Simon said. "Her accent changes between the first sentence and the second."

"Is that unusual?" said Judy.

"No. Most of us get our basic accent from the social group we grew up with, then modify it later in life. Usually, people try to upgrade: blue-collar people try to make themselves sound more affluent, and the nouveau riche try to talk like old money. Occasionally it goes the other way: a politician from a patrician family might make his accent more down-home, to seem like a man of the people, yuh know what I'm sayin'?"

Judy smiled. "You betcher ass."

"The learned accent is used in formal situations," Simon said as he rewound the tape. "It comes into play when the speaker is poised. But we revert to our childhood speech patterns when we're under stress. Okay so far?"

Bo said: "Sure."

"This woman has downgraded her speech. She makes herself sound more blue-collar than she really is."

Judy was fascinated. "You think she's a kind of Patty Hearst figure?"

"In that area, yes. She begins with a rehearsed formal sentence, spoken in her average-person voice. Now, in American speech, the more high class you are, the more you pronounce the letter 'r.' With that in mind, listen to the way she says the word 'governor' now."

Judy was going to stop him, but she was too interested. The woman on the tape said: "This is the Hammer of Eden with a message for Governor Mike Robson."

"Hear the way she says 'Guvnuh Mike'? This is street talk. But listen to the next bit. The voice mail announcement has put her off guard, and she speaks naturally."

"Shit, I didn't expect to be talking to a tape recorder."

"Although she says 'shit,' she pronounces the word 'recorder' very correctly. A blue-collar type would say 'recawduh,' pronouncing only the first r. The average college graduate says 'recorduh,' pronouncing the second r distinctly. Only very superior people say 'recorder' the way she does, carefully pronouncing all three r's."

Bo said: "Who'd have thought you could find out so much from two sentences?"

Simon smiled, looking pleased. "But did you notice anything about the vocabulary?"

Bo shook his head. "Nothing I can put my finger on."

"What's a tape recorder?"

Bo laughed. "A machine the size of a small suitcase, with two reels on top. I had one in Vietnam—a Grundig."

Judy saw what Simon was getting at. The term "tape recorder" was out of date. The machine they were using today was a cassette deck. Voice mail was recorded on the hard disk of a computer. "She's living in a time warp," Judy said. "It makes me think Patty Hearst again. What happened to her, anyway?"

Bo said: "She served her time, came out of jail, wrote a book, and appeared on *Geraldo*. Welcome to America."

Judy stood up. "This has been fascinating, Simon, but I don't feel comfortable with it. I think you should take your report to Marvin now."

"One more thing I want to show you," he said. He touched the fast-forward button.

"Really—"

"Just listen to this."

The woman's voice said: "It happened in Owens Valley a little after two o'clock, you can check it out." There was a faint background noise, and she hesitated.

Simon paused the tape. "I've enhanced that odd little murmur. Here it is reconstructed."

He released the pause switch. Judy heard a man's voice,

distorted with a lot of background hiss but clear enough to understand, say: "We do not recognize the jurisdiction of the United States government." The background noise returned to normal, and the woman's voice repeated: "We do not recognize the jurisdiction of the United States government." She went on: "Now that you know we can do what we say, you'd better think again about our demand."

Simon stopped the tape.

Judy said: "She was speaking words he had given her, and she forgot something, so he reminded her."

Bo said: "Didn't you figure the original Internet message had been dictated by a blue-collar guy, maybe illiterate, and typed by an educated woman?"

"Yes," Simon said. "But this is a different woman— older."

"So," Bo said to Judy, "now you're beginning to build up profiles of three unknown subjects."

"No, I'm not," she said. "I'm off the case. Come on, Simon, you know this could get me into more trouble."

"Okay." He took the tape out of the machine and stood up. "I've told you all the important stuff, anyway. Let me know if you come up with some brilliant insight that I could pass on to Mogadon Marvin."

Judy saw him to the door. "I'll take my report to the office right now—Marvin will probably still be there," he said. "Then I'm going to sleep. I was up all night on this." He got into his sports car and roared off.

When she came back, Bo was making green tea, looking thoughtful. "So this streetwise guy has a bunch of classy dames to take dictation from him."

Judy nodded. "I believe I know where you're headed."

"It's a cult."

"Yes. I was right to think Patty Hearst." She shivered. The man behind all this must be a charismatic figure with power over women. He was uneducated, but this did not hold him back, for he had others carrying out his orders.

"But something's not right. That demand, for a freeze on new power plants—it's just not wacky enough."

"I agree," Bo said. "It's not showy. I think they have some down-to-earth selfish reason to want this freeze."

"I wonder," Judy mused. "Maybe they have an interest in one particular power plant."

Bo stared at her. "Judy, that's brilliant! Like, it's going to pollute their salmon river or something."

"In there somewhere," she said. "But it hits them really hard." She felt excited. She was on to something.

"The freeze on *all* plant construction is a cover, then. They're afraid to name the one they're really interested in for fear that would lead us to them."

"But how many possibilities can there be? Power plants aren't built every day. And these things are controversial. Any proposal has to have been reported."

"Let's check."

They went into the den. Judy's laptop was on a side table. She sometimes wrote reports in here while Bo was watching football. The TV did not distract her, and she liked to be near him. She switched on the machine. Waiting for it to boot up, she said: "If we put together a list of sites where power plants are to be built, the FBI computer would tell us if there's a cult near any of them."

She accessed the files of the *San Francisco Chronicle* and searched for references to power plants in the last three years. The search produced 117 articles. Judy scanned the headlines, ignoring stories about Pittsburgh and Cuba. "Okay, here's a scheme for a nuclear plant in the Mojave Desert . . ." She saved the story. "A hydroelectric dam in Sierra County . . . an oil-fired plant up near the Oregon border . . ."

Bo said: "Sierra County? That rings some kind of bell. Got an exact location?"

Judy clicked on the article. "Yeah . . . the proposal is to dam the Silver River."

He frowned. "Silver River Valley . . ."

Judy turned from the computer screen. "Wait, this is familiar . . . isn't there a vigilante group that has a big spread there?"

"That's right!" said Bo. "They're called Los Alamos. Run by a speed freak called Poco Latella, who originally came from Daly City. That's how I know about them."

"Right. They're armed to the teeth, and they refused to recognize the U.S. government. . . . Jesus, they even used that sentence on the tape: 'We do not recognize the jurisdiction of the United States government.' Bo, I think we've got 'em."

"What are you going to do?"

Judy's heart sank as she remembered she was off the case. "If Kincaid finds out I've been working this case, he'll bust a gut."

"Los Alamos has to be checked out."

"I'll call Simon." She picked up the phone and dialed the office. The switchboard operator was a guy she knew. "Hey, Charlie, this is Judy. Is Simon Sparrow in the office?"

"He came and went," Charlie said. "Want me to try his car?"

"Yeah, thanks."

She waited. Charlie came back on the line and said: "No answer. I tried his home number, too. Shall I put a message on his pager?"

"Yes, please." Judy recalled that he had said he was going to sleep. "I bet he's turned it off, though."

"I'll send him a message to call you."

"Thanks." She hung up and said to Bo: "I think I have to see Kincaid. I guess if I give him a hot lead, he can't be too mad at me."

Bo just shrugged. "You don't have any choice, do you?"

Judy could not risk people getting killed just because she was afraid to confess what she had been doing. "No, I don't have any choice," she said.

She was wearing narrow black jeans and a strawberry pink T-shirt. The T-shirt was too figure hugging for the office, even on a Saturday. She went up to her room and changed it for a loose white polo shirt. Then she got in her Monte Carlo and drove downtown.

Marvin would have to organize a raid on Los Alamos. There might be trouble: vigilantes were crazy. The raid needed to be heavily manned and meticulously organized. The Bureau was terrified of another Waco. Every agent in the office would be drafted in for it. The Sacramento field office of the FBI would also be involved. They would probably strike at dawn tomorrow.

She went straight to Kincaid's office. His secretary was in the outer room, working at her computer, wearing a Saturday outfit of white jeans and a red shirt. She picked up the phone and said: "Judy Maddox is here to see you." After a moment she hung up and said to Judy: "Go right in."

Judy hesitated at the door to the inner sanctum. The last two times she had entered this office, she had suffered humiliation and disappointment inside. But she was not superstitious. Maybe this time Kincaid would be understanding and gracious.

It still jarred her to see his beefy figure in the chair that used to belong to the slight, dapper Milton Lestrange. She had not yet visited Milt in the hospital, she realized. She made a mental note to go tonight or tomorrow.

Brian's greeting was chilly. "What can I do for you, Judy?"

"I saw Simon Sparrow earlier," she began. "He brought his report to me because he hadn't heard I was off the case. Naturally, I told him to give it to Marvin."

"Naturally."

"But he told me a little of what he had found, and I speculated that the Hammer of Eden is a cult that feels somehow threatened by a planned building project for a power plant."

Brian looked annoyed. "I'll pass this on to Marvin," he said impatiently.

Judy plowed on. "There are several power plant projects in California right now; I checked. And one of them is in

Silver River Valley, where there is a right-wing vigilante group called Los Alamos. Brian, I think Los Alamos must be the Hammer of Eden. I think we should raid them."

"Is that what you think?"

Oh, shit.

"Is there a flaw in my logic?" she said icily.

"You bet there is." He stood up. "The flaw is, you're not on the goddamn case."

"I know," she said. "But I thought—"

He interrupted her, stretching his arm across the big desk and pointing an accusing finger at her face. "You've intercepted the psycholinguistic report and you're trying to sneak your way back on the case—and I know why! You think it's a high-profile case, and you're trying to get yourself noticed."

"Who by?" she said indignantly.

"FBI headquarters, the press, Governor Robson."

"I am not!"

"You just listen up. You are off this case. Do you understand me? O–f–f, off. You don't talk to your friend Simon about it. You don't check power plant schemes. And you don't propose raids on vigilante hangouts."

"Jesus Christ!"

"This is what you do. You go home. And you leave this case to Marvin and me."

"Brian—"

"Good-bye, Judy. Have a nice weekend."

She stared at him. He was red faced and breathing hard. She felt furious but helpless. She fought back the angry retorts that sprang to her lips. She had been forced to apologize for swearing at him once already, and she did not need that humiliation again. She bit her lip. After a long moment she turned on her heel and walked out of the room.

11

Priest parked the old Plymouth 'Cuda at the side of the road in the faint light of early dawn. He took Melanie's hand and led her into the forest. The mountain air was cool, and they shivered in their T-shirts until the effort of walking warmed their bodies. After a few minutes they emerged on a bluff that looked over the width of the Silver River Valley.

"This is where they want to build the dam," Priest said.

At this point the valley narrowed to a bottleneck, so that the far side was no more than four or five hundred yards away. It was still too dark to see the river, but in the morning silence they heard it rushing along below them. As the light strengthened, they could distinguish the dark shapes of cranes and giant earthmoving machines below them, silent and still, like sleeping dinosaurs.

Priest had almost given up hope that Governor Robson would now negotiate. This was the second day since the Owens Valley earthquake, and still there was no word. Priest could not figure out the governor's strategy, but it was not capitulation.

There would have to be another earthquake.

But he was anxious. Melanie and Star might be reluctant, especially as the second tremor would have to do more damage than the first. He had to firm up their commitment. He was starting with Melanie.

"It'll create a lake ten miles long, all the way up the

valley," he told her. He could see her pale oval face become taut with anger. "Upstream from here, everything you see will be under water."

Beyond the bottleneck, there was a broad valley floor. As the landscape became visible, they could see a scatter of houses and some neat cultivated fields, all connected by dirt tracks. Melanie said: "Surely someone tried to stop the dam?"

Priest nodded. "There was a big legal battle. We took no part. We don't believe in courts and lawyers. And we didn't want reporters and TV crews swarming all over our place—too many of us have secrets to keep. That's why we don't even tell people we're a commune. Most of our neighbors don't know we exist, and the others think the vineyard is run from Napa and staffed by transient workers. So we didn't take part in the protest. But some of the wealthier residents hired lawyers, and the environmental groups sided with the local people. It did no good."

"How come?"

"Governor Robson backed the dam and put this guy Al Honeymoon on the case." Priest hated Honeymoon. He had lied and cheated and manipulated the press with total ruthlessness. "He got the whole thing turned around so that the media made folks here look like a handful of selfish types who wanted to deny electric power to every hospital and school in California."

"Like it's your fault that people in Los Angeles put underwater lights in their pools and have electric motors to close their drapes."

"Right. So Coastal Electric got permission to build the dam."

"And all those people will lose their homes."

"Plus a pony-trekking center, a wildlife camp, several summer cabins, and a crazy bunch of armed vigilantes known as Los Alamos. Everyone gets compensation—except us, because we don't own our land, we rent it on a one-year lease. We get nothing—for the best vineyard between Napa and Bordeaux."

"And the only place I ever felt at peace."

Priest gave a murmur of sympathy. This was the way he wanted the conversation to go. "Has Dusty always had these allergies?"

"From birth. He was actually allergic to milk—cow's milk, formula, even breast milk. He survived on goat's milk. That was when I realized. The human race *must* be doing something wrong if the world is so polluted that my own breast milk is poisonous to my child."

"But you took him to doctors."

"Michael insisted. I knew they'd do no good. They gave us drugs that suppressed his immune system in order to inhibit the reaction to allergens. What kind of a way is that to treat his condition? He needed pure water and clean air and a healthy way of life. I guess I've been searching, ever since he was born, for a place like this."

"It was hard for you."

"You have no idea. A single woman with a sick kid can't hold down a job, can't get a decent apartment, can't live. You think America's a big place, but it's all the damn same."

"You were in a bad way when I met you."

"I was about to kill myself, and Dusty, too." Tears came to her eyes.

"Then you found this place."

Her face darkened with anger. "And now they want to take it away from me."

"The FBI is saying we didn't cause the earthquake, and the governor hasn't said anything."

"The hell with them, we'll have to do it again! Only this time make sure they *can't* ignore it."

That was what he wanted her to say. "It would have to cause real damage, bring down some buildings. People might get hurt."

"But we have no choice!"

"We could leave the valley, break up the commune, go back to the old way of life: regular jobs, money, poisoned air, greed, jealousy, and hate."

He had her frightened. "No!" she cried. "Don't say that!"

"I guess you're right. We can't go back now."

"I sure can't."

He took another look up and down the valley. "We'll make certain it stays the way God made it."

She closed her eyes in relief and said: "Amen."

He took her hand and led her through the trees back to the car.

Driving along the narrow road up the valley, Priest said: "Are you going to pick up Dusty from San Francisco today?"

"Yeah, I'll leave after breakfast."

Priest heard a strange noise over the asthmatic throb of the ancient V8 engine. He glanced up out of the side window and saw a helicopter.

"Shit," he said, and stamped on the brake.

Melanie was thrown forward. "What is it?" she said in a frightened voice.

Priest stopped the car and jumped out. The chopper was disappearing northward.

Melanie got out. "What's the matter?"

"What's a helicopter doing here?"

"Oh, my God," she said shakily. "You think it's looking for us?"

The noise faded, then came back. The chopper reappeared suddenly over the trees, flying low.

"I think it's the feds," Priest said. "Damn!" After yesterday's lackluster press conference, he had felt safe for a few more days. Kincaid and Hayes had seemed a long way from tracking him down. Now they were *here*, in the valley.

Melanie said: "What are we going to do?"

"Keep calm. They haven't come for us."

"How do you *know*?"

"I made sure of it."

She became tearful. "Priest, why do you keep talking in riddles?"

"I'm sorry." He remembered that he needed her for what he had to do. That meant he had to explain things to her. He gathered his thoughts. "They can't be coming for us because they don't know about us. The commune doesn't appear on any government records—our land is rented by Star. It's not on police or FBI files because we've never come to their attention. There has never been a newspaper article or TV program about us. We're not registered with the IRS. Our vineyard isn't on any map."

"So why are they here?"

"I think they've come for Los Alamos. Those nutcases must be on file with every law enforcement agency in the continental United States. For God's sake, they stand at their gate holding high-powered rifles, just to make sure that everyone *knows* there's a bunch of dangerous frigging lunatics in there."

"How can you be sure the FBI are after *them*?"

"I made certain of it. When Star called the John Truth show, I had her say the Los Alamos slogan: 'We do not recognize the jurisdiction of the United States government.' I laid a false trail."

"Are we safe, then?"

"Not quite. After they draw a blank at Los Alamos, the feds may take a look at the other people in the valley. They'll see the vineyard from the chopper and pay us a visit. So we'd better get home to warn the others."

He jumped into the car. As soon as Melanie was in, he floored the pedal. But the car was twenty-five years old and had not been designed for speed on winding mountain roads. He cursed its wheezy carburetors and lurching suspension.

As he struggled to maintain speed on the twisting road, he wondered fretfully who at the FBI had ordered this raid. He had not expected Kincaid or Hayes to make the necessary intuitive jump. There had to be someone else on the case. He wondered who.

A black car came up behind, going fast, headlights blazing although it was past daybreak. They were approaching a bend, but the driver honked and pulled out to pass. As it went by, Priest saw the driver and his companion, two burly young men, dressed in casual clothes but clean shaven and short haired.

Immediately afterward a second car came up behind, honking and flashing.

"Fuck this," Priest said. When the FBI was in a hurry, it was best to get out of the way. He braked and pulled over. The nearside wheels of the 'Cuda bumped over the roadside grass. The second car flashed by, and a third came up. Priest brought his car to a halt.

He and Melanie sat and watched a stream of vehicles race past. As well as cars, there were two armored trucks and three minivans full of grim-faced men and a few women. "It's a raid," Melanie said woefully.

"No fucking kidding," Priest said, the tension making him sarcastic.

She did not seem to notice.

Then a car peeled off from the convoy and pulled up right behind the 'Cuda.

Priest was suddenly afraid. He stared at the car in his rearview mirror. It was a dark green Buick Regal. The driver was speaking into a phone. There was another man in the passenger seat. Priest could not make out their faces.

He wished with all his heart that he had not gone to the press conference. One of the guys in the Buick might have been there yesterday. If so, he would be sure to ask what a lawyer from Oakland was doing in Silver River Valley. It could hardly be a coincidence. Any agent with half a brain would immediately put Priest at the top of the suspect list.

The last of the convoy flashed by. In the Buick, the driver put down his phone. Any second now the agents would get out of the car. Priest cast about desperately for a plausible story. *I got so interested in this case, and I remembered a TV show on this vigilante group and their slogan, about not recognizing the government, the same thing the woman said on John Truth's answering machine, so I thought I would, you know, play detective, and check them out myself. . . .* But they would not take his word for it. No matter how plausible his story, they would question him so thoroughly that he could not possibly fool them.

The two agents got out of the car. Priest stared hard at them in his mirror.

He did not recognize either one.

He relaxed a little. There was a film of sweat on his face. He wiped his forehead with the back of his hand.

Melanie said: "Oh, Jesus, what do they want?"

"Stay cool," Priest said. "Don't seem like you want to hurry away. I'm going to pretend I'm real, real interested in them. That'll make them want to get rid of us as fast as they can. Reverse psychology." He jumped out of the car.

"Hey, are you the police?" he said enthusiastically. "Is there something big going down?"

The driver, a thin man with black-framed glasses, said: "We're federal agents. Sir, we checked your plates, and your car is registered to the Napa Bottling Company."

Paul Beale took care of getting the car insured and smogged and other paperwork. "That's my employer."

"May I see your driver's license?"

"Oh, sure." Priest took the license out of his back pocket. "Was that your chopper I saw?"

"Yes, sir, it was." The agent checked his license and handed it back. "And where are you headed this morning?"

"We work at the wine farm up the valley a way. Hey, I hope you've come after those goddamn vigilantes. They got everyone round here scared half to death. They—"

"And where have you been this morning?"

"We were at a party in Silver City last night. It went on kind of late. But I'm sober, don't worry!"

"That's okay."

"Listen, I write paragraphs for the local paper, you know, the *Silver City Chronicle*? Could I get a quote from you, about this raid? It's going to be the biggest news in Sierra County for years!" As the words came out of his mouth, he realized this was a risky pose for a man who could not read or write. He slapped his pockets. "Gee, I don't even have a pencil."

"We can't say anything," the agent said. "You'll have to call the press person at the Sacramento office of the Bureau."

He pretended disappointment. "Oh. Oh, sure, I understand."

"You said you were headed home."

"Yes. Okay, I guess we'll be on our way. Good luck with those vigilantes!"

"Thank you."

The agents returned to their car.

They didn't make a note of my name.

Priest jumped back in his car. In his mirror he watched the agents as they got into their car. Neither one appeared to write anything down.

"Jesus Christ," he breathed gratefully. "They bought my story."

He pulled away, and the Buick followed.

As he approached the entrance to the Los Alamos spread a few minutes later, Priest rolled down his window, listening for gunfire. He heard none. It seemed the FBI had caught Los Alamos sleeping.

He rounded a bend and saw two cars parked near the entrance to the place. The wooden five-bar gate that had blocked the track was smashed to splinters: he guessed the FBI had driven their armored trucks right through it without stopping. The gate was normally guarded—where was the sentry? Then he saw a man in camouflage pants, facedown on the grass, hands cuffed behind his back, guarded by four agents. The feds were taking no chances.

The agents looked up alertly at the 'Cuda, then relaxed when they saw the green Buick following it.

Priest drove slowly, like a curious passerby.

Behind him, the Buick pulled over and stopped near the busted gate.

As soon as he was out of sight, Priest stepped on the gas.

When he got back to the commune he went straight to Star's cabin, to tell her about the FBI.

He found her in bed with Bones.

He touched her shoulder to wake her, then said: "We need to talk. I'll wait outside."

She nodded. Bones did not stir.

Priest stepped outside while she got dressed. He had no objection to Star renewing her relationship with Bones, of course. Priest was sleeping with Melanie regularly, and Star had the right to amuse herself with an old flame. All the same he felt a mixture of curiosity and apprehension. In bed together, were they passionate, hungry for each other—or relaxed and playful? Did Star think of Priest while she was making love to Bones, or did she put all other lovers out of her mind and think only of the one she was with? Did she compare them in her head and notice that one was more energetic, or more tender, or more skillful? These questions were not new. He recalled having the same thoughts whenever Star had a lover. This was just like the early days, except that they were all so much older.

He knew that his commune was not like others. Paul Beale followed the fortunes of other groups. They had all started with similar ideals, but most had compromised. They generally still worshiped together, following a guru or a religious discipline of some kind, but they had reverted to private property and the use of money and no longer practiced complete sexual freedom. They were weak, Priest figured. They had not had the strength of will to stick to their ideals and make them work. In self-satisfied moments he told himself it was a question of leadership.

Star came out in her jeans and a baggy bright blue sweatshirt. For someone who had just got up, she looked great. Priest told her so. "A good fuck does wonders for my complexion," she said. There was just enough of an edge in her voice to make Priest think that Bones was some kind of revenge for Melanie. Was this going to be a destabilizing factor? He already had too much to worry about.

He put that thought aside for the moment. Walking to the cookhouse, he told Star about the FBI raid on Los Alamos. "They may decide to check out the other residences in the valley, and if so, they'll probably find their way here. They won't be suspicious so long as we don't let them know we're a commune. We just have to maintain our usual pretense. If we're itinerant workers, with no long-term interest in the valley, there's no reason we should care about the dam."

She nodded. "You'd better remind everyone at breakfast. The Rice Eaters will know what's really on your mind. The others will think it's just our normal policy of not saying anything that might attract attention. What about the children?"

"They won't question kids. They're the FBI, not the Gestapo."

"Okay."

They went into the cookhouse and started coffee.

It was midmorning when two agents stumbled down the hill with mud on their loafers and weeds clinging to the cuffs of their pants. Priest was watching from the barn. If he recognized anyone from yesterday, he planned to slip away through the cabins and disappear into the woods. But he had never seen these two before. The younger man was tall and broad, with a Nordic look, pale blond hair and fair skin. The older was an Asian man with black hair thinning on top. They were not the two who had questioned him this morning, and he was sure neither had been at the press conference.

Most of the adults were in the vineyard, spraying the vines with diluted hot sauce to keep the deer from eating the new shoots. The children were in the temple, having a Sunday school lesson from Star, who was telling them the story of Moses in the bullrushes.

Despite the careful preparations he had made, Priest felt a stab of sheer terror as the agents approached. For twenty-five years this place had been a secret sanctuary. Until last Thursday, when a cop had come looking for the parents of Flower, no official had ever set foot here: no county surveyor, no mailman, not even a garbage collector. And here was the FBI. If he could have called down a bolt of lightning to strike the agents dead, he would have done it without a second thought.

He took a deep breath, then walked across the slope of the hillside to the vineyard. Dale greeted the two agents, as arranged. Priest filled a watering can with the pepper mixture and began to spray, moving toward Dale so that he could hear the conversation.

The Asian man spoke in a friendly tone. "We're FBI agents, making some routine inquiries in the neighborhood. I'm Bill Ho, and this is John Aldritch."

That was encouraging, Priest told himself. It sounded as though they had no special interest in the vineyard: they were just looking around, hoping to pick up clues. It was a fishing expedition. But the thought did not make him feel much less tense.

Ho looked around appreciatively, taking in the valley. "What a beautiful spot."

Dale nodded. "We're very attached to it."

Take care, Dale—drop the heavy irony. This is not a frigging game.

Aldritch, the younger agent, said impatiently: "Are you in charge here?" He had a southern accent.

"I'm the foreman," Dale said. "How can I help you?"

Ho said: "Do you folks live here?"

Priest pretended to go on working, but his heart was thumping, and he strained to hear.

"Most of us are seasonal workers," Dale said, following the script agreed upon with Priest. "The company provides accommodation because this place is so far from anywhere."

Aldritch said: "Strange place for a fruit farm."

"It's not a fruit farm, it's a winery. Would you like to try a glass of last year's vintage? It's really very good."

"No thanks. Unless you have an alcohol-free product."

"No, sorry. Just the real thing."

"Who owns the place?"

"The Napa Bottling Company."

Aldritch made a note.

Ho glanced toward the cluster of buildings on the far side of the vineyard. "Mind if we take a look around?"

Dale shrugged. "Sure, go ahead." He resumed his work.

Priest watched anxiously as the agents headed off. On the surface, it was a plausible story that these people were badly paid workers living in low-grade accommodation provided by a stingy management. But there were clues here that might make a smart agent ask more questions. The temple was the most obvious. Star had folded up the old banner bearing the Five Paradoxes of Baghram. All the same, someone with an inquiring mind might ask why the schoolroom was a round building with no windows and no furniture.

Also, there were marijuana patches in the woods nearby. The FBI agents were not interested in small-time doping, but cultivation did not fit in with the fiction of a transient population. The free shop looked like any other shop until you noticed that there were no prices on anything and no cash register.

There might be a hundred other ways the pretense would fall apart under thorough investigation, but Priest was hoping the FBI was focused on Los Alamos and just checking out the neighbors as a matter of routine.

He had to fight the temptation to follow the agents. He was desperate to see what they looked at, and hear what they said to each other, as they poked around his home. But he forced himself to keep spraying, glancing up from the vines every minute or two to see where they were and what they were doing.

They went into the cookhouse. Garden and Slow were there, making lasagne for the midday meal. What were the agents saying to them? Was Garden chattering nervously and giving herself away? Had Slow forgotten his instructions and started to jabber enthusiastically about daily meditation?

The agents emerged from the cookhouse. Priest looked hard at them, trying to guess their thoughts; but they were too far away for him to read their faces, and their body language gave nothing away.

They began to wander around the cabins, peeking in. Priest could not guess whether anything they saw would make them suspect that this was anything more than a wine farm.

They checked out the grape press, the barns where the wine was fermented, and the barrels of last year's vintage waiting to be bottled. Had they noticed that nothing was powered by electricity?

They opened the door of the temple. Would they speak to the children, contrary to Priest's prediction? Would Star blow her cool and call them fascist pigs? Priest held his breath.

The agents closed the door without going inside.

They spoke to Oaktree, who was cutting barrel staves in the yard. He looked up at them and answered curtly without stopping his work. Maybe he figured it would look suspicious if he was friendly.

They came across Aneth hanging diapers out to dry. She

refused to use disposable diapers. She was probably explaining this to the agents, saying, "There aren't enough trees in the world for every child to have disposable diapers."

They walked down to the stream and studied the stones in the shallow brook, seeming to contemplate crossing. The marijuana patches were all on the far side. But the agents apparently did not want to get their feet wet, for they turned around and came back.

At last they returned to the vineyard. Priest tried to study their faces without staring. Were they convinced, or had they seen something that made them suspicious? Aldritch seemed hostile, Ho friendly, but that could just be an act.

Aldritch spoke to Dale. "Y'all have some of these cabins tricked out kind of nice, for 'temporary accommodation,' don't you?"

Priest went cold. It was a skeptical question, suggesting that Aldritch did not buy their story. Priest began to wonder if there was any way he could kill both FBI men and get away with it.

"Yeah," Dale said. "Some of us come back year after year." He was improvising: none of this had been scripted. "And a few of us live here all year round." Dale was not a practiced liar. If this went on too long, he would give himself away.

Aldritch said: "I want a list of everyone who lives or works here."

Priest's mind raced. Dale could not use people's communal names, for that would give the game away—and anyway, the agents would insist on real names. But some of the communards had police records, including Priest himself. Would Dale think fast enough to realize he had to invent names for everyone? Would he have the nerve to do it?

Ho added: "We also need ages and permanent addresses." His tone was apologetic.

Shit! This is getting worse.

Dale said: "You could get those from the company's records."

No, they couldn't.

Ho said: "I'm sorry, we need them right now."

Dale looked nonplussed. "Gee, I guess you'll have to go round asking them all. I sure as heck don't know everyone's birthday. I'm their boss, not their granddad."

Priest's mind raced. This was dangerous. He could not allow the agents to question everyone. They would give themselves away a dozen times.

He made a snap decision and stepped forward. "Mr. Arnold?" he said, inventing a name for Dale on the spur of the moment. "Maybe I could assist the gentlemen." Without planning it, he had adopted the persona of a friendly dope, eager to help but not very bright. He addressed the agents. "I've been coming here a few years, I guess I know everybody, and how old they are."

Dale looked relieved to hand the responsibility back to Priest. "Okay, go ahead," he said.

"Why don't you come to the cookhouse?" Priest said to the agents. "If you won't drink wine, I bet you'd like a cup of coffee."

Ho smiled and said: "That'd be real good."

Priest led them back through the rows of vines and took them into the cookhouse. "We got some paperwork to do," he explained to Garden and Slow. "You two take no notice of us, just go on making that great-smelling pasta."

Ho offered Priest his notebook. "Why don't you just write down the names, ages, and addresses right here?"

Priest did not take the notebook. "Oh, my handwriting is the worst in the world," he said smoothly. "Now, you sit yourselves down and write the names while I make you coffee." He put a pot of water on the fire, and the agents sat at the long pine table.

"The foreman is Dale Arnold, he's forty-two." These

guys would never be able to check. No one here was in the phone book or on any kind of register.

"Permanent address?"

"He lives here. Everyone does."

"I thought you were seasonal workers."

"That's right. Most of them will leave, come November, when the harvest is in and the grapes have been crushed; but they ain't the kind of folks who keep two homes. Why pay rent on a place when you're living somewhere else?"

"So the permanent address for everyone here would be . . . ?"

"Silver River Valley Winery, Silver City, California. But people have their mail sent to the company in Napa, it's safer."

Aldritch was looking irritated and slightly bemused, as Priest intended. Querulous people did not have the patience to pursue minor inconsistencies.

He poured them coffee as he made up a list of names. To help him remember who was who, he used variations of their commune names: Dale Arnold, Peggy Star, Richard Priestley, Holly Goldman. He left out Melanie and Dusty, as they were not there—Dusty was at his father's place, and Melanie had gone to fetch him.

Aldritch interrupted him. "In my experience, most transient agricultural workers in this state are Mexican, or at least Hispanic."

"Yeah, and this bunch is everything but," Priest agreed. "The company has a few vineyards, and I guess the boss keeps the Hispanics all together in their own gangs, with Spanish-speaking foremen, and puts everyone else on our team. It ain't racism, you understand, just practical."

They seemed to accept that.

Priest went slowly, dragging out the session as long as possible. The agents could do no harm in the cookhouse. If they got bored and became impatient to leave, so much the better.

While he talked, Garden and Slow carried on cooking. Garden was silent and stone-faced and somehow managed to stir pots in a haughty manner. Slow was jumpy and kept darting terrified glances at the agents, but they did not seem to care. Maybe they were used to people being frightened of them. Maybe they liked it.

Priest took fifteen or twenty minutes to give them the names and ages of the commune's twenty-six adults. Ho was closing his notebook when Priest said: "Now, the children. Let me think. Gee, they grow up so fast, don't they?"

Aldritch gave a grunt of exasperation. "I don't think we need to know the children's names," he said.

"Okay," Priest said equably. "More coffee for you folks?"

"No thanks." Aldritch looked at Ho. "I think we're done here."

Ho said: "So this land is owned by the Napa Bottling Company?"

Priest saw a chance to cover up the slip Dale had made earlier. "No, that ain't exactly right," he said. "The company operates the winery, but I believe the land is owned by the government."

"So the name on the lease would be Napa Bottling."

Priest hesitated. Ho, the friendly one, was asking the really dangerous questions. But how was he to reply? It was too risky to lie. They could check this in seconds. Reluctantly he said: "Matter of fact, I think the name on the lease may be Stella Higgins." He hated to give Star's real name to the FBI. "She was the woman who started the vineyard, years ago." He hoped it would not be of any use to them. He could not see how it gave them any clues.

Ho wrote down the name. "That's all, I think," he said.

Priest hid his relief. "Well, good luck with the rest of your inquiries," he said as he led them out.

He took them through the vineyard. They stopped to thank Dale for his cooperation. "Who are you guys after, anyway?" Dale said.

"A terrorist group that's trying to blackmail the governor of California," Ho told him.

"Well, I sure hope you catch them," Dale said sincerely.

No, you don't.

At last the two agents walked away across the field, stumbling occasionally on the uneven ground, and disappeared into the trees.

"Well, that seemed to go pretty well," Dale said to Priest, looking pleased with himself.

Jesus Christ almighty, if only you knew.

12

Sunday afternoon, Judy took Bo to see the new Clint Eastwood movie at the Alexandria Cinema on the corner of Geary and Eighteenth. To her surprise, she forgot about earthquakes for a couple of hours and had a good time. Afterward they went for a sandwich and a beer at one of Bo's joints, a cops' pub with a TV over the bar and a sign on the door saying "We cheat tourists."

Bo finished his cheeseburger and took a swig of Guinness. "Clint Eastwood should star in the story of my life," he said.

"Come on," Judy said. "Every detective in the world thinks that."

"Yeah, but I even look like Clint."

Judy grinned. Bo had a round face with a snub nose. She said: "I like Mickey Rooney for the part."

"I think people should be able to divorce their kids," Bo said, but he was laughing.

The news came on TV. When Judy saw footage of the raid on Los Alamos, she smiled sourly. Brian Kincaid had screamed at her for interfering—then he had adopted her plan.

However, there was no triumphal interview with Brian. There was film of a smashed five-bar gate, a sign that read "We do not recognize the jurisdiction of the United States government," and a SWAT team in their flak jackets returning from the scene. Bo said: "Looks to me like they didn't find anything."

That puzzled Judy. "I'm surprised," she said. "Los Alamos seemed like really hot suspects." She was disappointed. It seemed her instinct had been completely wrong.

The newscaster was saying that no arrests had been made. "They don't even say they seized evidence," Bo said. "I wonder what the story is."

"If you're about done here, we can go find out," Judy said.

They left the bar and got into Judy's car. She picked up her car phone and called Simon Sparrow's home number. "What do you hear about the raid?" she asked him.

"We got zip."

"That's what I thought."

"There are no computers on the premises, so it's hard to imagine they could have left a message on the Internet. Nobody there even has a college degree, and I doubt if any one of them could *spell* seismologist. There are four women in the group, but none of them matches either of our two female profiles—these girls are in their late teens and early twenties. And the vigilantes have no beef with the dam. They're happy with the compensation they're getting from Coastal Electric for their land, and they're looking forward to moving to their new place. Oh—and on Friday at two-twenty P.M., six of the seven men were at a store called Frank's Sporting Weapons in Silver City, buying ammunition."

Judy shook her head. "Well, whose dumb idea was it to raid them, anyway?"

It had been hers, of course. Simon said: "This morning at the briefing, Marvin claimed it was his."

"Serves him right that it was a flop." Judy frowned. "I don't get it. It seemed like such a good lead."

"Brian has another meeting with Mr. Honeymoon in Sacramento tomorrow afternoon. Looks like he'll go empty-handed."

"Mr. Honeymoon won't like that."

"I hear he's not a real touchy-feely type guy."

Judy smiled grimly. She had no sympathy for Kincaid, but

she could not take pleasure in the failure of the raid. It meant the Hammer of Eden were still out there somewhere, planning another earthquake. "Thanks, Simon. See you tomorrow."

As soon as she hung up, the phone rang. It was the switchboard operator at the office. "A Professor Quercus called with a message he said was urgent. He has some important news for you."

Judy debated calling Marvin and passing the message to him. But she was too curious to know what Michael had to say. She dialed his home.

When he answered, she could hear the soundtrack of a TV cartoon in the background. Dusty was still there, she guessed. "This is Judy Maddox," she said.

"Hi, how are you?"

She raised her eyebrows. A weekend with Dusty had mellowed him out. "I'm fine, but I'm off the case," she said.

"I know that. I've been trying to reach the guy who's taken over, man with a name like a soul singer. . . ."

"Marvin Hayes."

"Right. Like, 'Dancin' in the Grapevine' by Marvin Hayes and the Haystacks."

Judy laughed.

Michael said: "But he doesn't return my calls, so I'm stuck with you."

That was more like Michael. "Okay, what have you got?"

"Can you come over? I really need to show you."

She found herself pleased, even a little excited, at the thought of seeing him again. "Do you have any more Cap'n Crunch?"

"I think there's a little left."

"Okay, I'll be there in fifteen or twenty minutes." She hung up. "I have to go see my seismologist," she said to Bo. "Shall I drop you at the bus stop?"

"I can't ride the bus like Jim Rockford. I'm a San Francisco detective!"

"So? You're a human being."

"Yeah, but the street guys don't know that."

"They don't know you're human?"

"To them I'm a demigod."

He was kidding, but there was some truth in it, Judy knew. He had been putting hoodlums behind bars in this city for almost thirty years. Every kid on a street corner with vials of crack in the pockets of his bomber jacket was afraid of Bo Maddox.

"So you want to ride to Berkeley with me?"

"Sure, why not? I'm curious to meet your handsome seismologist."

She made a U-turn and headed for the Bay Bridge. "What makes you think he's handsome?"

He grinned. "From the way you talked to him," he said smugly.

"You shouldn't use cop psychology on your own family."

"Cop, schmop. You're my daughter, I can read your mind."

"Well, you're right. He's a hunk. But I don't much like him."

"You don't?" Bo sounded skeptical.

"He's arrogant and difficult. He's better when his kid's around, that softens him."

"He's married?"

"Separated."

"Separated is married."

Judy could sense Bo losing interest in Michael. It felt like a drop in the temperature. She smiled to herself. He was still eager to marry her off, but he had old-fashioned scruples.

They reached Berkeley and drove down Euclid Street. There was an orange Subaru parked in Judy's usual space under the magnolia tree. She found another slot.

When Michael opened the door of his apartment, Judy thought he looked strained. "Hi, Michael," she said. "This is my father, Bo Maddox."

"Come in," Michael said abruptly.

His mood seemed to have changed in the short time it

had taken to drive here. When they entered the living room, Judy saw why.

Dusty was on the couch, looking terrible. His eyes were red and watering, and his eyeballs seemed swollen. His nose was running, and he was breathing noisily. A cartoon was playing on TV, but he was hardly paying attention.

Judy knelt beside him and touched his hair. "Poor Dusty!" she said. "What happened?"

"He gets allergy attacks," Michael explained.

"Did you call the doctor?"

"No need. I've given him the drug he needs to suppress the reaction."

"How fast does it work?"

"It's already working. He's past the worst. But he may stay like this for days."

"I wish I could do something for you, little man," Judy said to Dusty.

A female voice said: "I'll take care of him, thank you."

Judy stood up and turned around. The woman who had just walked in looked as if she had stepped off a couturier's catwalk. She had a pale oval face and straight red hair that fell past her shoulders. Although she was tall and thin, her bust was generous and her hips curvy. Her long legs were clad in close-fitting tan jeans, and she wore a fashionable lime green top with a V neck.

Until this moment Judy had felt smartly dressed in khaki shorts, tan loafers that showed off her pretty ankles, and a white polo shirt that gleamed against her café-au-lait skin. Now she felt dowdy, middle-aged, and out of date by comparison with this vision of street chic. And Michael was bound to notice that Judy had a big ass and small tits by comparison.

"This is Melanie, Dusty's mom," Michael said. "Melanie, meet my friend Judy Maddox."

Melanie nodded curtly.

So that's his wife.

Michael had not mentioned the FBI. Did he want Melanie to think Judy was a girlfriend?

"This is my father, Bo Maddox," Judy said.

Melanie did not trouble to make small talk. "I was just leaving," she said. She was carrying a small duffel bag with a picture of Donald Duck on the side, obviously Dusty's.

Judy felt put down by Michael's tall, voguish wife. She was annoyed with herself for the reaction. *Why should I give a damn?*

Melanie looked around the room and said: "Michael, where's the rabbit?"

"Here." Michael picked up a grubby soft toy from his desk and gave it to her.

She looked at the child on the couch. "This never happens in the mountains," she said coldly.

Michael looked anguished. "What am I going to do, not see him?"

"We'll have to meet somewhere out of town."

"I want him to *stay* with me. It's not the same if he doesn't sleep over."

"If he doesn't sleep over, he won't get like this."

"I know, I know."

Judy's heart went out to Michael. He was obviously in distress, and his wife was so cold.

Melanie stuffed the rabbit into the Donald Duck bag and closed the zip. "We have to go."

"I'll carry him to your car." Michael picked up Dusty from the couch. "Come on, tiger, let's go."

When they had left, Bo looked at Judy and said: "Wow. Unhappy families."

She nodded. But she liked Michael better than before. She wanted to put her arms around him and say, *You're doing your best, no one can do more.*

"He's your type, though," Bo said.

"I have a type?"

"You like a challenge."

"That's because I grew up with one."

"Me?" He pretended to be outraged. "I spoiled you rotten."

She pecked his cheek. "You did, too."

When Michael returned he was grim faced and preoccupied. He did not offer Judy and Bo a drink or a cup of coffee, and he had forgotten all about Cap'n Crunch. He sat at his computer. "Look at this," he said without preamble.

Judy and Bo stood behind him and looked over his shoulder.

He put a chart on the screen. "Here's the seismograph of the Owens Valley tremor, with the mysterious preliminary vibrations I couldn't understand—remember?"

"I sure do," Judy said.

"Here's a typical earthquake of about the same magnitude. This has normal foreshocks. See the difference?"

"Yes." The normal foreshocks were uneven and sporadic, whereas the Owens Valley vibrations followed a pattern that seemed too regular to be natural.

"Now look at this." He brought a third chart up on the screen. It showed a neat pattern of even vibrations, just like the Owens Valley chart.

"What made those vibrations?" Judy said.

"A seismic vibrator," Michael announced triumphantly.

Bo said: "What the hell is that?"

Judy almost said, *I don't know, but I think I want one.* She smothered a grin.

Michael said: "It's a machine used by the oil industry to explore underground. Basically, it's a huge jackhammer mounted on a truck. It sends vibrations through the earth's crust."

"And those vibrations triggered the earthquake?"

"I don't think it can be a coincidence."

Judy nodded solemnly. "That's it, then. They really can cause earthquakes." She felt a cold chill descend as the news sank in.

Bo said: "Jesus, I hope they don't come to San Francisco."

"Or Berkeley," said Michael. "You know, although I told you it was possible, I never really believed it, in my heart, until now."

Judy said: "The Owens Valley tremor was quite minor."

Michael shook his head. "We can't take comfort from that. The size of the earthquake bears no relation to the strength of the triggering vibration. It depends on the pressure in the fault. The seismic vibrator could trigger anything from a barely perceptible tremor to another Loma Prieta."

Judy remembered the Loma Prieta earthquake in 1989 as vividly as if it were last night's bad dream. "Shit," she said. "What are we going to do?"

Bo said: "You're off the case."

Michael frowned, puzzled. "You told me that," he said to Judy. "But you didn't say why."

"Office politics," Judy said. "We have a new boss who doesn't like me, and he reassigned the case to someone he prefers."

"I don't believe this!" Michael said. "A terrorist group is causing earthquakes and the FBI is having a family spat about who gets to chase after them!"

"What can I tell you? Do scientists let personal squabbles get in the way of their search for the truth?"

Michael gave one of his sudden unexpected grins. "You bet your ass they do. But listen. Surely you can pass on this information to Marvin Whatever?"

"When I told my boss about Los Alamos, he ordered me not to interfere again."

"This is incredible!" Michael said, becoming angry. "You can't just *ignore* what I've told you."

"Don't worry, I won't do that," Judy said curtly. "Let's keep cool and think for a moment. What's the first thing we need to do with this information? If we can find out where the seismic vibrator came from, we may have a lead on the Hammer of Eden."

"Right," Bo said. "Either they bought it, or more likely they stole it."

Judy asked Michael: "How many of these machines are there in the continental United States? A hundred? A thousand?"

"In there somewhere," he said.

"Anyhow, not many. So the people who manufacture them probably have a record of every sale. I could track them down tonight, get them to make a list. And if the truck was stolen, it may be listed on the National Crime Information Center." The NCIC, run by FBI headquarters in Washington, D.C., could be accessed by any law enforcement agency.

Bo said: "The NCIC is only as good as the information that's put in. We don't have a license plate for this, and there's no telling how it might be categorized on the computer. I could have the San Francisco PD put out a multi-state query on the CLETS Computer." CLETS was the California Law Enforcement Telecommunications System. "And I could get the newspapers to print a picture of one of these trucks, get members of the public looking out for it."

"Wait a minute," Judy said. "If you do that, Kincaid will know I'm behind it."

Michael rolled his eyes in an expression of despair.

Bo said: "Not necessarily. I won't tell the papers that this is connected with the Hammer of Eden. I'll just say we're looking for a stolen seismic vibrator. It's kind of an unusual auto theft, they'll like the story."

"Great," Judy said. "Michael, can I have a printout of the three graphs?"

"Sure." He touched a key and the printer whirred.

Judy put a hand on his shoulder. His skin was warm through the cotton of his shirt. "I sure hope Dusty feels better," she said.

He covered her hand with his own. "Thanks." His touch was light, his palm dry. She felt a frisson of pleasure. Then he took his hand away and said: "Uh, maybe you should give me your pager number, so I can reach you a little faster, if necessary."

She took out a business card. After a moment's thought, she wrote her home number on it before giving it to him.

Michael said: "After you two have made these phone calls . . ." He hesitated. "Would you like to meet for a drink, or maybe dinner? I'd really like to hear how you get on."

"Not me," Bo said. "I have a bowling match."

"Judy, how about you?"

Is he asking me for a date?

"I was planning to visit someone in hospital," she said.

Michael looked crestfallen.

Judy realized that there was not a thing she would rather do this evening than have dinner with Michael Quercus.

"But I guess that won't take me all night," she said. "Okay, sure."

It was only a week since Milton Lestrange's cancer had been diagnosed, but already he looked thinner and older. Perhaps it was the effect of the hospital setting: the instruments, the bed, the white sheets. Or maybe it was the baby blue pajamas that revealed a triangle of pale chest below the neck. He had lost all his power symbols: his big desk, his Mont Blanc fountain pen, his striped silk tie.

Judy was shocked to see him like this. "Gee, Milt, you don't look so great," she blurted.

He smiled. "I knew you wouldn't lie to me, Judy."

She felt embarrassed. "I'm sorry, it just came out."

"Don't blush. You're right. I'm in bad shape."

"What are they doing?"

"They'll operate this week, they haven't said what day. But that's just to bypass the obstruction in the bowel. The outlook is poor."

"What do you mean, poor?"

"Ninety percent of cases are fatal."

Judy swallowed. "Jesus, Milt."

"I may have a year."

"I don't know what to say."

He did not dwell on the grim prognosis. "Sandy, my first wife, came to see me yesterday. She told me you had called her."

"Yeah. I had no idea whether she'd want to see you, but I figured at least she'd like to know you were in the hospital."

He took Judy's hand and squeezed it. "Thank you. Not many people would have thought of that. I don't know how you got to be so wise, so young."

"I'm glad she came."

Milt changed the subject. "Take my mind off my troubles, tell me about the office."

"You shouldn't be concerning yourself—"

"Hell, I won't. Work doesn't worry you much when you're dying. I'm just curious."

"Well, I won my case. The Foong brothers are probably going to spend most of the next decade in jail."

"Well done!"

"You always had faith in me."

"I knew you could do it."

"But Brian Kincaid recommended Marvin Hayes as the new supervisor."

"Marvin? Shit! Brian knows you were supposed to get that job."

"Tell me about it."

"Marvin's a tough guy, but slipshod. He cuts corners."

"I'm baffled," Judy said. "Why does Brian rate him so high? What is it with those two—are they *lovers* or something?"

Milt laughed. "No, not lovers. But one time, years ago, Marvin saved Brian's life."

"No kidding?"

"It was a shoot-out. I was there. We ambushed a boat unloading heroin on Sonoma Beach up in Marin County. It was early one morning in February, and the sea was so cold it hurt. There was no jetty, so the bad guys were stacking kilos of horse on a rubber dinghy to bring them ashore. We let them land the entire cargo, then we moved in." Milt sighed, and a faraway look came into his blue eyes. It occurred to Judy that he would never see another dawn ambush.

After a moment he went on. "Brian made a mistake—he let one of them get too close to him. This little Italian grabbed him and pointed a gun at his head. We all had our weapons out, but if we shot the Italian, he would probably have pulled the trigger before he died. Brian was really scared." Milt lowered his voice. "He pissed himself, we could see the stain on his suit pants. But Marvin was as cool as the devil himself. He starts walking toward Brian and the Italian. 'Shoot me instead,' he says. 'It won't make any difference.' I've never seen anything like it. The Italian fell for it. He swung his gun arm round to aim at Marvin. In that split second, five of our people shot the guy."

Judy nodded. It was typical of the stories that agents told after a few beers in Everton's. But she did not dismiss it as macho bravado. FBI agents did not often get involved in shoot-outs. They never forgot the experience. She could imagine that Kincaid felt intensely close to Marvin Hayes after that. "Well, that explains the trouble I've been having," she said. "Brian gave me a bullshit assignment, and then, when it turned out to be important, he took it from me and gave it to Marvin."

Milt sighed. "I could intervene, I guess. I'm still SAC, technically. But Kincaid is an experienced office politician, and he knows I'm never coming back. He'd fight me. And I'm not sure I have the energy for that."

Judy shook her head. "I wouldn't want you to. I can handle this."

"What's the assignment he gave Marvin?"

"The Hammer of Eden, the people who cause earthquakes."

"The people who *say* they cause earthquakes."

"That's what Marvin thinks. But he's wrong."

Milt frowned. "Are you serious?"

"Totally."

"What are you going to do?"

"Work the case behind Brian's back."

Milt looked troubled. "That's dangerous."

"Yeah," Judy said. "But not as dangerous as a goddamn earthquake."

Michael wore a navy blue cotton suit over a plain white shirt, open at the neck, and no tie. Had he thrown on this ensemble without a moment's thought, Judy wondered, or did he realize it made him look good enough to eat? She had changed into a white silk dress with red polka dots. It was about right for a May evening, and she always turned heads when she was wearing it.

Michael took her to a small downtown restaurant that served vegetarian Indian dishes. She had never tasted Indian food, so she let him order for her. She put her mobile phone on the table. "I know it's bad manners, but Bo promised to call me if he got any information about stolen seismic vibrators."

"Okay by me," Michael said. "Did you call the manufacturers?"

"Yeah. I got a sales director at home watching baseball. He promised me a list of purchasers tomorrow. I tried for tonight but he said it was impossible." She frowned in annoyance. *We don't have much time left—five days, now.* "However, he faxed me a picture." She took a folded sheet of paper from her purse and showed it to him.

He shrugged. "It's just a big truck with a piece of machinery on the back."

"But after Bo puts this picture out on CLETS, every cop in California will be watching for one. And if the newspapers and TV carry the picture tomorrow, half the population will be on the lookout, too."

The food came. It was spicier than she was used to but delicious. Judy ate with gusto. After a few minutes she caught Michael looking at her with a faint smile. She raised an eyebrow. "Did I say something witty?"

"I'm pleased you're enjoying the cuisine."

She grinned. "Does it show?"

"Yeah."

"I'll try to be more dainty."

"Please don't. It's a pleasure to watch you. Besides . . ."

"What?"

"I like your go-for-it attitude. It's one of the things that attracts me to you. You seem to have a big appetite for life. You like Dusty, and you have a good time hanging out with your dad, and you're proud of the FBI, and you obviously love beautiful clothes . . . you even enjoy Cap'n Crunch."

Judy felt herself flush, but she was pleased. She liked the picture he painted of her. She asked herself what it was about *him* that had attracted *her*. It was his strength, she decided. He could be irritatingly stubborn, but in a crisis he would be a rock. This afternoon, when his wife had been so heartless, most men would have quarreled, but he had been concerned only for Dusty.

Plus, I'd really love to get my hands inside his jockey shorts.

Judith, behave.

She took a sip of wine and changed the subject. "We're assuming that the Hammer of Eden have data similar to yours about pressure points along the San Andreas fault."

"They must have, to pick the locations where the seismic vibrator could trigger an earthquake."

"Could you go through the same exercise? Study the data and figure out the best place?"

"I guess I could. Probably there would be a cluster of five or six possible sites." He saw the direction her thoughts were taking. "Then, I suppose, the FBI could stake out the sites and watch for a seismic vibrator."

"Yes—if I were in charge."

"I'll make the list anyway. Maybe I'll fax it to Governor Robson."

"Don't let too many people see it. You might cause a panic."

"But if my forecast turned out to be right, it could give my business a shot in the arm."

"Does it need one?"

"It sure does. I have one big contract that just about pays the rent and the bill for my ex-wife's mobile phone. I borrowed money from my parents to start the business, and I haven't begun to pay it back. I was hoping to land another major client, Mutual American Insurance."

"I used to work for them, years ago. But go on."

"I thought the deal was in the bag, but they're delaying the contract. I guess they're having second thoughts. If they back·out, I'm in trouble. But if I predicted an earthquake and turned out to be right, I think they'd sign. Then I'd be comfortable."

"All the same, I hope you'll be discreet. If everyone tries to leave San Francisco at the same time, there'll be riots."

He gave a devil-may-care grin that was infuriatingly attractive. "Got you rattled, haven't I?"

She shrugged. "I'll admit it. My position at the Bureau is vulnerable. If I'm associated with an outbreak of mass hysteria, I don't think I could survive there."

"Is that important to you?"

"Yes and no. Sooner or later I plan to get out and have children. But I want to quit by my timetable, not someone else's."

"Do you have anyone in mind to have the children with?"

"No." She gave him a candid look. "A good man is hard to find."

"I imagine there'd be a waiting list."

"What a nice compliment." *I wonder if you'd join the line. I wonder if I'd want you to.*

He offered her more wine.

"No thanks. I'd like a cup of coffee."

He waved at a waiter. "Being a parent can be painful, but you never regret it."

"Tell me about Dusty."

He sighed. "I have no pets, no flowers in the apartment, very little dust because of my computers. All the windows are closed tight, and the place is air-conditioned. But we walked down to the bookstore, and on the way home he petted a cat. An hour later he was the way you saw him."

"It's too bad. The poor kid."

"His mother recently moved to a place in the mountains, up near the Oregon border, and since then he's been okay— until today. If he can't visit me without having an attack, I don't know what we'll do. I can't go and live in fucking Oregon; there aren't enough earthquakes there."

He looked so troubled that she reached across the table and squeezed his hand. "You'll work something out. You love him, that's obvious."

He smiled. "Yeah, I do."

They drank their coffee, and he paid. He walked her to her car. "This evening has gone so fast," he said.

I think the guy likes me.

Good.

"Do you want to go to a movie sometime?"

The dating game. It never changes. "Yes, I'd like that."

"Maybe one night this week?"

"Sure."

"I'll call you."

"Okay."

"May I kiss you good night?"

"Yes." She grinned. "Yes, please."

He bent his face to hers. It was a soft, tentative kiss. His lips moved gently against hers, but he did not open his mouth. She kissed him back the same way. Her breasts felt sensitive. Without thinking, she pressed her body against his. He squeezed her briefly, then broke away.

"Good night," he said.

He watched her get into her car and waved as she drew away from the curb.

She turned a corner and pulled up at a stoplight.

"Wow," she said.

On Monday morning Judy was assigned to a team investigating a militant Muslim group at Stanford University. Her first job was to comb computer records of gun licenses, looking for Arab names to check out. She found it hard to concentrate on a relatively harmless bunch of religious fanatics when she knew the Hammer of Eden were planning their next earthquake.

Michael called at five past nine. He said: "How are you, Agent Judy?"

The sound of his voice made her feel happy. "I'm fine, real good."

"I enjoyed our date."

She thought of that kiss, and the corners of her mouth twitched in a private smile. *I'll take another of those, anytime.* "Me, too."

"Are you free tomorrow night?"

"I guess." That sounded too cool. "I mean, yes—unless something happens with this case."

"Do you know Morton's?"

"Sure."

"Let's meet in the bar at six. Then we can pick a movie together."

"I'll be there."

But that was the only bright spot in her morning. By lunchtime she could no longer contain herself, and she called Bo, but he still had nothing. She called the seismic vibrator manufacturers, who said they had almost completed the list and it would be on her fax machine by the end of the business day. *That's another damn day gone! Now we've only got four days to catch these people.*

She was too worried to eat. She went to Simon Sparrow's office. He was wearing a natty English-style shirt, blue with pink stripes. He ignored the unofficial FBI dress code and got away with it, probably because he was so good at his job.

He was talking on the phone and watching the screen of a wave analyzer at the same time. "This may seem like an odd question, Mrs. Gorky, but would you tell me what you can see from your front window?" As he listened to the reply, he watched the spectrum of Mrs. Gorky's voice, comparing it with a printout he had taped to the side of the monitor. After a few moments he drew a line through a name on a list. "Thank you for your cooperation, Mrs. Gorky. I don't need to trouble you any further. Good-bye."

Judy said: "This may seem like an odd question, Mr. Sparrow, but why do you need to know what Mrs. Gorky sees when she looks out the window?"

"I don't," Simon said. "That question generally elicits a response of about the length I need to analyze the voice. By the time she's finished, I know whether she's the woman I'm looking for."

"And who's that?"

"The one who called the John Truth show, of course." He tapped the ring binder on his desk. "The Bureau, the police, and the radio stations that syndicate the show have so far received a total of one thousand two hundred and twenty-nine calls telling us who she is."

Judy picked up the file and leafed through it. Could the vital clue be in here somewhere? Simon had got his secretary to collate the tip-off calls. In most cases there was a name, address, and phone number for the tipster and the same for the suspect. In some cases there was a quote from the caller:

I've always suspected she had Mob connections.
She's one of those subversive types. I'm not surprised she's involved in something like this.

She seems like a regular mom, but it's her voice—I'd swear on the Bible.

One particularly useless tip gave no name but said:

I know I've heard her voice on the radio or something. It was so sexy, I remembered it. But it was a long time ago. Maybe I heard it on a record album.

It *was* a sexy voice, Judy recalled. She had noticed that at the time. The woman could make a fortune as a telephone salesperson, getting male executives to buy advertising space they did not need.

Simon said: "So far today I've eliminated one hundred of them. I think I'm going to need some assistance."

Judy continued leafing through the file. "I'd help you if I could, but I've been warned off the case."

"Gee, thanks, that sure makes me feel better."

"Do you hear how it's going?"

"Marvin's team are calling everyone on the mailing list of the Green California Campaign. He and Brian just left for Sacramento, but I can't imagine what they're going to tell the famous Mr. Honeymoon."

"It's not the goddamn Greens, we all know that."

"He doesn't have any other ideas, though."

Judy frowned, looking at the file. She had come across another call that mentioned a record. As before, there was no name for the suspect, but the caller had said:

I've heard the voice on an album, I'm darn sure. Something from way back, like the sixties.

Judy asked Simon: "Did you notice that two of the tip-offs mention a record album?"

"They do? I missed that!"

"They think they've heard her voice on an old record."

"Is that right?" Simon was instantly animated. "It must be a speech album—bedtime stories, or Shakespeare, or something. A person's speaking voice is quite different from their singing voice."

Raja Khan passed the door and caught her eye. "Oh, Judy, your father called, I thought you were at lunch."

Suddenly Judy felt breathless. She left Simon without a word and rushed back to her desk. Without sitting down, she picked up the phone and dialed Bo's number.

He picked up right away. "Lieutenant Maddox here."

"What have you got?"

"A suspect."

"Jesus—that's great!"

"Get this. A seismic vibrator went missing two weeks ago somewhere between Shiloh, Texas, and Clovis, New Mexico. The regular driver disappeared at the same time, and his burned-out car was found at the local dump, containing what appear to be his ashes."

"He was *murdered* for his damn truck? These people don't take prisoners, do they?"

"The prime suspect is one Richard Granger, aged forty-eight. They called him Ricky, and they thought he was Hispanic, but with a name like that he could be a Caucasian with a tan. And—wait for it—he has a record."

"You're a genius, Bo!"

"A copy should be coming out of your fax machine about now. He was a big-time hoodlum in L.A. around the late sixties, early seventies, in there. Convictions for assault, burglary, grand theft auto. Questioned about three murders, also drug dealing. But he disappeared from the scene in 1972. The LAPD thought he must have been whacked by the Mob—he owed them money—but they never found a body, so they didn't close the file."

"I get it. Ricky ran from the Mob, got religion, and started a cult."

"Unfortunately, we don't know where."

"Except that it's not in Silver River Valley."

"The LAPD can check out his last known address. It's probably a waste of time, but I'll ask them anyway. Guy in Homicide there owes me a favor."

"Do we have a picture of Ricky?"

"There's one in the file, but it's a photo of a nineteen-year-old. He's pushing fifty now, he probably looks completely different. Luckily, the sheriff in Shiloh prepared an E-fit likeness." E-fit was the computer program that had replaced the old-style police artist. "He promised to fax it to me, but it hasn't arrived yet."

"Refax it to me as soon as you get it, would you?"

"Sure. What'll you do?"

"I'm going to Sacramento."

It was four-fifteen when Judy stepped through the door that had GOVERNOR carved in it.

The same secretary sat behind the big desk. She recognized Judy and registered surprise. "You're one of the FBI people, aren't you? The meeting with Mr. Honeymoon started ten minutes ago."

"That's okay," Judy said. "I've brought some important information that came in at the last moment. But before I go into the meeting, did a fax arrive here for me within the last few minutes?" Having left her office before the E-fit picture of Ricky Granger came through, she had called Bo from the car and asked him to fax it to the governor's office.

"I'll check." She spoke into the phone. "Yes, your fax is here." A moment later a young woman appeared from a side door with a sheet of paper.

Judy stared at the face on the fax. This was the man who might kill thousands. Her enemy.

She saw a handsome man who had gone to some trouble to hide the true shape of his face, as if perhaps he had anticipated this moment. His head was covered by a cowboy hat. That suggested that the witnesses who had helped the sheriff create the computer picture had never seen the suspect without a hat. Consequently there was no indication of what his hair was like. If he was bald, or grizzled, or curly, or long haired, he would look different from this picture. And the bottom half of his face was equally well concealed by a bushy beard and mustache. There could be any kind of jaw under there. By now, she guessed, he was clean shaven.

The man had deep-set eyes that stared hypnotically out of the picture. But to the general public, all criminals had staring eyes.

All the same, the picture told her some things. Ricky Granger did not habitually wear spectacles, he was evidently not African American or Asian, and since his beard was dark and luxuriant, he probably had dark hair. From the attached description she learned that he was about six feet tall, slim built, and fit looking, with no noticeable accent. It was not much, but it was better than nothing.

And nothing was what Brian and Marvin had.

Honeymoon's assistant appeared and ushered Judy into the Horseshoe, where the governor and his staff had their offices.

Judy bit her lip. She was about to break the first rule of bureaucracy and make her boss look a fool. It would probably be the end of her career.

Screw it.

All she wanted now was to make her boss get serious about the Hammer of Eden before they killed people. As long as he did that, he could fire her.

They passed the entrance to the governor's personal suite, then the assistant opened the door to Honeymoon's office.

Judy stepped inside.

For a moment she allowed herself to enjoy the shock and dismay on the faces of Brian Kincaid and Marvin Hayes.

Then she looked at Honeymoon.

The cabinet secretary was wearing a pale gray shirt with a subdued black-and-white-dotted tie and dark gray patterned suspenders. He looked at Judy with raised eyebrows and said: "Agent Maddox! Mr. Kincaid just got through telling me he took you off the case because you're a ditz."

Judy was floored. She was supposed to be in control of this scene; she was the one causing consternation. Honeymoon had outdone her. He was not going to be upstaged in his own office.

She recovered fast. *Okay, Mr. Honeymoon, if you want to play hardball, I'll go in to bat.*

She said to him: "Brian's full of shit."

Kincaid scowled, but Honeymoon just raised his eyebrows slightly.

Judy added: "I'm the best agent he has, and I just proved it."

"You did?" Honeymoon said.

"While Marvin has been sitting around with his thumb up his ass pretending there's nothing to worry about, I've solved this case."

Kincaid stood up, his face flushed. He said angrily: "Maddox, just what the hell do you think you're doing here?"

She ignored him. "I know who's sending terrorist threats to Governor Robson," she said to Honeymoon. "Marvin and Brian don't. You can make your own decision about who's the ditz."

Hayes was bright red. He burst out: "What the hell are you talking about?"

Honeymoon said: "Let's all sit down. Now that Ms. Maddox has interrupted us, we may as well hear what she has to say." He nodded to his assistant. "Close the door, John. Now, Agent Maddox, did I hear you say you *know* who's making the threats?"

"Correct." She put a fax picture on Honeymoon's desk. "This is Richard Granger, a hoodlum from Los Angeles who was believed, wrongly, to have been killed by the Mob in 1972."

"And what makes you think he's the culprit?"

"Look at this." She handed him another piece of paper.

"Here's the seismograph of a typical earthquake. Look at the vibrations that precede the tremor. There's a haphazard series of different magnitudes. These are typical foreshocks." She showed him a second sheet. "This is the Owens Valley earthquake. Nothing haphazard here. Instead of a natural-looking mess, there is a neat series of regular vibrations."

Hayes interrupted. "No one can figure out what those vibrations are."

Judy turned to him. "*You* couldn't figure it out, but I did." She put another sheet on Honeymoon's desk. "Look at this chart."

Honeymoon studied the third chart, comparing it with the second. "Regular, just like the Owens Valley graph. What makes vibrations like these?"

"A machine called a seismic vibrator."

Hayes sniggered, but Honeymoon did not crack a smile. "What's that?"

"One of these." She handed him the picture sent to her by the manufacturers. "It's used in oil exploration."

Honeymoon looked skeptical. "Are you saying the earthquake *was* man-made?"

"I'm not theorizing, I'm giving you the facts. A seismic vibrator was used in that location immediately before the earthquake. You can make your own judgment about cause and effect."

He gave her a hard, appraising look. He was asking himself whether she was a bullshitter or not. She stared right back at him. Finally he said: "Okay. How does that lead you to the guy with the beard?"

"A seismic vibrator was stolen a week ago in Shiloh, Texas."

She heard Hayes say: "Oh, shit."

Honeymoon said: "And the guy in the picture . . . ?"

"Richard Granger is the prime suspect in the theft—and in the murder of the truck's regular driver. Granger was working for the oil exploration team that was using the vibrator. The E-fit picture is based on the recollections of his co-workers."

Honeymoon nodded. "Is that it?"

"Isn't it enough?" she expostulated.

Honeymoon did not respond to that. He turned to Kincaid. "What have you got to say about all this?"

Kincaid gave him a shit-eating grin. "I don't think we should bother you with internal disciplinary matters—"

"Oh, I want to be bothered," Honeymoon said. There was a dangerous note in his voice, and the temperature in the room seemed to fall. "Look at it from my angle. You come here and tell me the earthquake definitely was not man-made." His voice became louder. "Now it appears, from this evidence, that it very likely was. So we have a group out there that could cause a major disaster." Judy felt a surge of triumph as it became clear Honeymoon had bought her story. He was furious with Kincaid. He stood up and pointed a finger at Brian. "*You* tell me you can't find the perpetrators, then in walks Agent Maddox with a name, a police record, and a fucking *picture*."

"I think I should say—"

"I feel like you've been dicking me around, Special Agent Kincaid," said Honeymoon, overriding Kincaid. His face was dark with anger. "And when people dick me around I get kind of tetchy."

Judy sat silent, watching Honeymoon destroy Kincaid. *If this is what you're like when you're tetchy, Al, I'd hate to see you when you're real mad.*

Kincaid tried again. "I'm sorry if—"

"I also hate people who apologize," Honeymoon said. "An apology is designed to make the offender feel okay so that he can do it again. Don't be sorry."

Kincaid tried to gather the shreds of his dignity. "What do you want me to say?"

"That you're putting Agent Maddox in charge of this case."

Judy stared at him. This was even better than she had hoped.

Kincaid looked as if he had been asked to strip naked in Union Square. He swallowed.

Honeymoon said: "If you have a problem with that, just say so, and I'll have Governor Robson call the director of the FBI in Washington. The governor could then explain to the director the reasons why we're making this request."

"That won't be necessary," Kincaid said.

"So put Maddox in charge."

"Okay."

"No, not 'okay.' I want you to say it to her, right here, right now."

Brian refused to look at Judy, but he said: "Agent Maddox, you are now in charge of the Hammer of Eden investigation."

"Thank you," Judy said.

Saved!

"Now get out of here," Honeymoon said.

They all got up.

Honeymoon said: "Maddox."

She turned at the door. "Yes."

"Call me once a day."

That meant he would continue to support her. She could talk to Honeymoon any time she liked. And Kincaid knew it. "You got it," she said.

They went out.

As they were leaving the Horseshoe, Judy gave Kincaid a sweet smile and repeated the words he had said to her the last time they were in this building, four days ago. "You did just fine in there, Brian. Don't you worry about a thing."

13

Dusty was sick all day Monday.

Melanie drove into Silver City to pick up more of the allergy drug he needed. She left Dusty being cared for by Flower, who was going through a sudden maternal phase.

She came back in a panic.

Priest was in the barn with Dale. Dale had asked him to taste the blend of last year's wine. It was going to be a nutty vintage, slow to mature but long-lived. Priest suggested using more of the lighter pressing from the lower, shadier slopes of the valley, to make the wine more immediately appealing; but Dale resisted. "This is a connoisseur's wine now," he said. "We don't have to pander to supermarket buyers. Our customers like to keep the wine in their cellars for a few years before drinking it."

Priest knew this was not the real reason Dale wanted to talk to him, but he argued anyway. "Don't knock the supermarket buyers—they saved our lives in the early days."

"Well, they can't save our lives now," Dale said. "Priest, why the fuck are we doing this? We have to be off this land by *next Sunday*."

Priest suppressed a sigh of frustration. *For Christ's sake, give me a chance! I've almost done it—the governor can't ignore earthquakes indefinitely. I just need a little more time. Why can't you have faith?*

He knew that Dale could not be won over by bullying,

cajoling, or bullshit. Only logic would work with him. He forced himself to speak calmly, the epitome of sweet reason. "You could be right," he said magnanimously. Then he could not resist adding a gibe. "Pessimists often are."

"So?"

"All I'm saying to you is, give it those six days. Don't quit *now*. Leave time for a miracle. Maybe it won't happen. But maybe it will."

"I don't know," Dale said.

Then Melanie burst in with a newspaper in her hand. "I have to talk to you," she said breathlessly.

Priest's heart missed a beat. What had happened? It must be about the earthquakes—and Dale was not in on the secret. Priest gave him a grin that said *Ain't women peculiar?* and led Melanie out of the barn.

"Dale doesn't know!" he said as soon as they were out of earshot. "What the hell—"

"Look at this!" she said, waving the paper in front of his eyes.

He was shocked to see a photograph of a seismic vibrator.

He hastily scanned the yard and the nearby buildings, but no one was around. All the same, he did not want to have this conversation with Melanie out in the open. "Not here!" he said fiercely. "Put the damn paper under your arm and let's go to my cabin."

She got a grip on herself.

They walked through the little settlement to his cabin. As soon as they were inside, he took the newspaper from her and looked at the picture again. There was no doubt about it. He could not read the caption or the accompanying story, of course, but the photo was of a truck just like the one he had stolen.

"Shit," he said, and threw the newspaper on the table.

"Read it!" Melanie said.

"It's too dim in here," he replied. "Tell me what it says."

"The police are looking for a stolen seismic vibrator."

"The hell they are."

"It doesn't say anything about earthquakes," Melanie went on. "It's just, like, a funny story—who'd want to steal one of these damn things?"

"I don't buy that," Priest said. "This can't be a coincidence. The story is about us, even if they don't mention us. They know how we made the earthquake happen, but they haven't told the press yet. They're scared of creating a panic."

"So why have they released this picture?"

"To make things hard for us. That picture makes it impossible to drive the truck on the open road. Every Highway Patrol officer in California is on the lookout." He hit the table with his fist in frustration. "Fuck it, I can't let them stop me this easily!"

"What if we drive at night?"

He had thought of that. He shook his head. "Still too risky. There are cops on the road at night."

"I have to go check on Dusty," Melanie said. She was close to tears. "Oh, Priest, he's so sick—we won't have to leave the valley, will we? I'm scared. I'll never find another place where we can be happy, I know it."

Priest hugged her to give her courage. "I'm not beaten yet, not by a long shot. What else does the article say?"

She picked up the paper. "There was a demonstration outside the Federal Building in San Francisco." She smiled through her tears. "A group of people who say the Hammer of Eden are right, the FBI should leave us alone, and Governor Robson should stop building power plants."

Priest was pleased. "Well, what do you know. There are still a few Californians who can think straight!" Then he became solemn again. "But that doesn't help me figure out how to drive the truck without getting pulled over by the first cop who sees it."

"I'm going to Dusty," she said.

Priest went with her. In her cabin, Dusty lay on the bed, eyes streaming, face red, panting for breath. Flower sat beside him, reading aloud from a book with a picture of a giant peach on the cover. Priest touched his daughter's hair. She looked up at him and smiled without pausing in her reading.

Melanie got a glass of water and gave Dusty a pill. Priest felt sorry for Dusty, but he could not help remembering that the boy's illness was a lucky break for the commune. Melanie was caught in a trap. She believed she had to live where the air was pure, but she could not get a job outside the city. The commune was the only answer. If she had to leave here, she might find another, similar commune to take her in—but she might not, and anyway, she was too exhausted and discouraged to hit the road again.

And there was more to it than that, he thought. Deep inside her was a terrible rage. He did not know the source of it, but it was strong enough to make her yearn to shake the earth and burn cities and cause people to run screaming from their homes. Most of the time it was hidden beneath the facade of a sexy but disorganized young woman. But sometimes, when her will was thwarted and she felt frustrated and powerless, the anger showed.

He left them and headed for Star's cabin, worrying over the problem of the truck. Star might have some ideas. Maybe there was a way they could disguise the seismic vibrator so that it looked like some other kind of vehicle, a Coke truck or a crane or something.

He stepped into the cabin. Star was putting a Band-Aid on Ringo's knee, something she had to do about once a day. Priest smiled at his ten-year-old son and said: "What did you do this time, cowboy?" Then he noticed Bones.

He was lying on the bed, fully clothed but fast asleep—or more likely passed out. There was an empty bottle of Silver River Valley chardonnay on the rough wooden table. Bones's mouth was open, and he was snoring softly.

Ringo began to tell Priest a long story about trying to cross the stream by swinging from a tree, but Priest hardly listened. The sight of Bones had given him inspiration, and his mind was working feverishly.

When Ringo's grazed knee had been attended to, and the boy ran out, Priest told Star about the problem of the seismic vibrator. Then he told her the solution.

Priest, Star, and Oaktree helped Bones pull the big tarpaulin off the carnival ride. The vehicle stood revealed in its glorious, gaudy colors: a green dragon breathing red-and-yellow fire over three screaming girls in a spinning seat, and the gaudy lettering that, Bones had told Priest, said "The Dragon's Mouth."

Priest spoke to Oaktree. "We drive this vehicle up the track a way and park it next to the seismic vibrator. Then we take off these painted panels and fix them to our truck, covering the machinery. The cops are looking for a seismic vibrator, not a carnival ride."

Oaktree, who was carrying his toolbox, looked closely at the panels, examining the way they were fixed. "No problem," he said after a minute. "I can do it in a day, with one or two people helping me."

"And can you put the panels back afterward, so that Bones's ride will look the same?"

"Good as new," Oaktree promised.

Priest looked at Bones. The great snag with this scheme was that Bones had to be in on it. In the old days Priest would have trusted Bones with his life. He was a Rice Eater, after all. Perhaps he could not be relied upon to show up for his own wedding, but he could keep a secret. However, since Bones had become a junkie, all bets were off. Heroin lobotomized people. A junkie would steal his mother's wedding ring.

But Priest had to take the risk. He was desperate. He had promised an earthquake four days from now, and he had to carry out his threat. Otherwise all was lost.

Bones agreed readily to the plan. Priest had half expected him to demand payment. However, he had been living free at the commune for four days, so it was too late for him to put his relationship with Priest on a commercial footing. Besides, as a communard Bones knew that the greatest imaginable sin was to value things in money terms.

Bones would be more subtle. In a day or two he would ask Priest for cash to go score some smack. Priest would cross that bridge when he came to it.

"Let's get to it," he said.

Oaktree and Star climbed into the cab of the carnival ride with Bones. Melanie and Priest took the 'Cuda for the mile-long ride to where the seismic vibrator was hidden.

Priest wondered what else the FBI knew. They had figured out that the earthquake had been triggered using a seismic vibrator. Had they progressed any further? He turned on the car radio, hoping for a bulletin. He got Connie Francis singing "Breakin' in a Brand New Broken Heart," an oldie even by his standards.

The 'Cuda bumped along the muddy track through the forest behind Bones's truck. Bones handled the big rig confidently, Priest observed, even though he had only just been roused from a drunken sleep. There was a moment when Priest felt sure the carnival ride was going to get stuck in a mudslide, but it pulled through without stopping.

The news came on just as they drew near the hiding place of the seismic vibrator. Priest turned up the volume.

What he heard turned him pale with shock.

"Federal agents investigating the Hammer of Eden terrorist group have issued a photographic likeness of a suspect," the newsreader said. "He has been named as Richard or Ricky Granger, aged forty-eight, formerly of Los Angeles."

Priest said: "Jesus *Christ!*" and slammed on the brakes.

"Granger is also wanted for a murder in Shiloh, Texas, nine days ago."

"What?" No one knew he had killed Mario, not even Star.

The Rice Eaters were desperately keen to cause an earthquake that might kill hundreds, but all the same they would be appalled to know he had battered a man to death with a wrench. People were inconsistent.

"That's not true," Priest said to Melanie. "I didn't kill anyone."

Melanie was staring at him. "Is that your real name?" she said. "Ricky Granger?"

He had forgotten that she did not know. "Yeah," he said. He racked his brains to think who knew his real name. He had not used it for twenty-five years, except in Shiloh. Suddenly he remembered that he had gone to the sheriff's office in Silver City, to get Flower out of jail, and his heart stopped for a moment; then he recalled that the deputy had assumed he had the same name as Star and called him Mr. Higgins. Thank God.

Melanie said: "How did they get a photo of you?"

"Not a photo," he said. "A *photographic likeness*. That must mean one of those Identikit pictures that they make up."

"I know what you mean," she said. "Only they use a computer program now."

"There's a computer program for every goddamn thing," Priest muttered. He was now very glad he had changed his appearance before taking the job in Shiloh. It had been worth the time it took to grow a beard, the bother of pinning up his hair every day, and the nuisance of having to wear a hat all the time. With luck, the photographic likeness would not remotely resemble the way he looked now.

But he needed to be sure.

"I need to get to a TV," he said.

He jumped out of the car. The carnival ride had pulled over near the hiding place of the seismic vibrator, and Oaktree and Star were getting out. In a few words he explained the situation to them. "You make a start here while I drive into Silver City," he said. "I'll take Melanie—I want her opinion, too."

He got back in the car, drove out of the woods, and headed for Silver City.

On the outskirts of the small town there was an electronics store. Priest parked and they got out.

Priest looked around nervously. It was still light. What if he should meet someone who had seen his face on TV? Everything hung on whether the picture was like him. He had to know. He had to take a chance. He approached the store.

The window displayed several TV sets all showing the same picture. The program was some kind of game show. A silver-haired host in a powder blue suit was joshing a middle-aged woman wearing too much eyeliner.

Priest glanced up and down the sidewalk. There was no one else about. He looked at his watch: almost seven. The news would be on in a few seconds.

The silver-haired host put his arm around the woman and spoke to the camera. There was a shot of an audience applauding with hysterical enthusiasm. Then the news came on. There were two anchors, a man and a woman. They spoke for a few seconds.

Then the multiple screens showed a black-and-white picture of a heavily bearded man in a cowboy hat.

Priest stared at it.

The picture did not look like him at all.

"What do you think?" he said.

"Even I wouldn't know it was supposed to be you," Melanie said.

Relief washed over him in a tidal wave. His disguise had worked. The beard changed the shape of his face, and the hat hid his most distinctive feature, the long, thick, wavy hair. Even he might not have recognized the picture if he had not known it was supposed to be him.

He relaxed. "Thank you, god of the hippies," he said.

The screens all flickered, and another picture appeared. Priest was shocked to see, reproduced a dozen times, a police photo of himself at nineteen. He was so thin, his face looked like a skull. He was trim now, but in those days,

doping and drinking and never eating a regular meal, he had
been a skeleton. His face was drawn, his expression sullen.
His hair was lank and dull, with a Beatles haircut that must
have been out of date even then.

Priest said: "Would you recognize me?"

"Yes," she said. "By the nose."

He looked again. She was right; the picture showed his
distinctive narrow nose, like a curved knife.

Melanie added: "But I don't think anyone else would
know you, certainly not strangers."

"That's what I thought."

She put an arm around his waist and squeezed affection-
ately. "You looked like such a bad boy when you were
young."

"I guess I was."

"Where did they get that picture, anyway?"

"From my police record, I'm assuming."

She looked up at him. "I didn't know you had a police
record. What did you do?"

"You want a list?"

She seemed shocked and disapproving. *Don't get moral
on me, baby—remember who told us how to cause an earthquake.* "I gave up the life of crime when I came to the
valley," he said. "I didn't do anything wrong for the next
twenty-five years—until I met you."

A frown wrinkled her brow. She did not think of herself
as a criminal, he realized. In her own eyes she was a normally respectable citizen who had been driven to commit a
desperate act. She still believed she was of a different race
from people who robbed and murdered.

Work it out any way you like, honey—just stay with the plan.

The two anchors reappeared, then the scene shifted to a
skyscraper. A line of words appeared at the bottom of the
screen. Priest did not need to be able to read them: he recognized the place. It was the Federal Building, where the FBI
had its San Francisco office. A demonstration was going on,

and Priest recalled Melanie reading about it in the news-paper. They were demonstrating in support of the Hammer of Eden, she had said. A bunch of people with placards and bullhorns were haranguing a group entering the building.

The camera focused on a young woman with an Asian cast to her features. She caught Priest's eye because she was beautiful in the exotic way that strongly appealed to him. She was slender and dressed in an elegant dark pantsuit, but she had a formidable don't-fuck-with-me look on her face, and she elbowed her way through the crowd with a calm ruthlessness.

Melanie said: "Oh, my God, it's her!"

Priest was startled. "You know that woman?"

"I met her on Sunday!"

"Where?"

"At Michael's apartment, when I went to get Dusty."

"Who is she?"

"Michael just introduced her as Judy Maddox, he didn't say anything about her."

"What's she doing at the Federal Building?"

"It says, right there on the screen: 'FBI agent Judy Maddox, in charge of Hammer of Eden case.' She's the detective who's after us!"

Priest was fascinated. Was this his enemy? She was gor-geous. Just looking at her on TV made him want to touch her golden skin with his fingertips.

I should be scared, not turned on. She's a hell of a detec-tive. She caught on about the seismic vibrator, found out where it came from, and got my name and picture. She's smart and she works fast.

"And you met her at Michael's place?"

"Yes."

Priest was spooked. She was too close. She had met Melanie! His intuition told him he was in great danger from this agent. The fact that he was so attracted to her, after seeing her only briefly on TV, made it worse. It was as if she had some kind of power over him.

Melanie went on: "Michael didn't say she was with the FBI. I thought she was a new girlfriend, so I kind of froze her out. She brought this older guy with her, said he was her father, though he didn't look Asian."

"Girlfriend or not, I don't like her getting this close to us!" He turned away from the store and walked slowly back to the car. His brain was racing. Maybe it was not so surprising that the agent on the case had consulted a leading seismologist. Agent Maddox had talked to Michael for the same reason Priest had: he knew about earthquakes. Priest guessed it was Michael who had helped her make the link to the seismic vibrator.

What else had he told her?

They sat in the car, but Priest did not start the engine. "This is bad for us," he said. "Very bad."

"What's bad?" Melanie said defensively. "It's okay if Michael wants to screw around with an FBI agent. Maybe she sticks her gun up his ass. I don't care."

It was not like her to talk dirty. *She's really shook.* "What's bad is, Michael could give her the same information he gave us."

Melanie frowned. "I don't get it."

"Think about it. What's on Agent Maddox's mind? She's asking: 'Where will the Hammer of Eden strike next?' Michael can help her with that. He can look at his data, same way you did, and figure out the most likely places for an earthquake. Then the FBI can stake out those locations and watch for a seismic vibrator."

"I never thought of that." Melanie stared at him. "My fucking bastard husband and his FBI floozie are going to screw this up for us, is that what you're telling me?"

Priest glanced at her. She looked about ready to cut his throat. "Calm down, will you?"

"God *damn.*"

"Wait a minute." Priest was getting an idea. Melanie was the link. Maybe she could find out what Michael had told the beautiful FBI agent. "There could be a way around this. Tell me something, how do you feel about Michael now?"

"Like, nothing. It's over, and I'm glad. I just hope we can work out our divorce without too much hostility, is all."

Priest studied her. He did not believe her. What she felt for Michael was rage. "We have to know whether the FBI has staked out possible earthquake locations—and if so, which ones. I think he might tell you."

"Why would he do that?"

"I believe he's still carrying a torch for you, sort of."

She stared at him. "Priest, what the hell is this about?"

Priest took a deep breath. "He'd tell you anything, if you slept with him."

"Fuck you, Priest, I won't do it. Fuck you!"

"I hate to ask you." It was true. He did not want her to sleep with Michael. He believed that no one should have sex unless they wanted to. He had learned from Star that the most disgusting thing about marriage was the right it gave one person to have sex with another. So this whole scheme was a betrayal of his beliefs. "But I have no choice."

"Forget it," Melanie said.

"Okay," he said. "I'm sorry I asked." He started the car. "I just wish I could think of some other way."

They were silent for a few minutes, driving through the mountains.

"I'm sorry, Priest," she said eventually. "I just can't do it."

"I told you, don't worry about it."

They turned off the road and drove down the long, rough track toward the commune. The carnival ride was no longer visible from the track; Priest guessed that Oaktree and Star had concealed it for the night.

He parked in the cleared circle at the end of the track. As they walked through the woods to the village in the twilight, he took Melanie's hand. After a moment's hesitation she moved closer to him and squeezed his hand fondly.

Work in the vineyard was over. Because of the warm weather, the big table had been dragged out of the cookhouse into the yard. Some of the children were putting out plates and cutlery while Slow sliced a long loaf of home-baked bread. There were bottles of the commune's own wine on the table, and a spicy aroma was drifting over the scene.

Priest and Melanie went to Melanie's hut to check on Dusty. They saw immediately that he was better. He was sleeping peacefully. The swelling had gone down, his nose had stopped running, and he was breathing normally. Flower had gone to sleep in the chair beside the bed, with the book open on her lap.

Priest watched as Melanie tucked in the sheet around the sleeping boy and kissed his forehead. She looked up at Priest and whispered: "This is the only place he's ever been okay."

"It's the only place *I've* ever been okay," Priest said quietly. "It's the only place the *world* has ever been okay. That's why we have to save it."

"I know," she said. "I know."

14

The Domestic Terrorism squad of the San Francisco FBI worked in a narrow room along one side of the Federal Building. With its desks and room dividers it looked like a million other offices, except that the shirtsleeved young men and smart-suited women wore guns in holsters on their hips or under their arms.

At seven o'clock on Tuesday morning they were standing, sitting on desk corners, or leaning against the wall, some sipping coffee from Styrofoam containers, others holding pens and pads, ready to take notes. The whole squad, except for the supervisor, had been put under Judy's orders. There was a low buzz of conversation.

Judy knew what they were talking about. She had gone up against the acting SAC—and won. It did not happen often. In an hour the entire floor would be alive with rumor and gossip. She would not be surprised to hear by the end of the day that she had prevailed because she was having an affair with Al Honeymoon.

The noise died away when she stood up and said: "Pay attention, everyone."

She looked over the group for a moment and experienced a familiar thrill. They were all fit, hardworking, well dressed, honest, and smart, the smartest young people in America. She felt proud to work with them.

She began to speak. "We're going to divide into two

teams. Peter, Jack, Sally, and Lee will check out tips based on the pictures we have of Ricky Granger." She handed out a briefing sheet that she had worked on overnight. A list of questions would enable the agents to eliminate most of the tips and assess which ones merited a visit by an agent or neighborhood cop. Many of the men identified as "Ricky Granger" could be ruled out fast: African Americans, men with foreign accents, twenty-year-olds, short men. On the other hand, the agents would be quick to visit any suspect who fit the description and had been away from home for the two-week period during which Granger had worked in Shiloh, Texas.

"Dave, Louise, Steve, and Ashok will form the second team. You'll work with Simon Sparrow, checking tip-offs based on the recorded voice of the woman who phoned John Truth. By the way, some of the tip-offs Simon is working on mention a pop record. We asked John Truth to flag that up on his show last night." She had not done this personally: the office press person had spoken to Truth's producer. "So we may get calls about it." She handed out a second briefing sheet with different questions.

"Raja."

The youngest member of the team grinned his cocky grin. "I was afraid you'd forgotten about me."

"In my dreams," she said, and they all laughed. "Raja, I want you to prepare a short briefing to go out to all police departments, and especially the California Highway Patrol, telling them how to recognize a seismic vibrator." She held up a hand. "And no vibrator jokes, please." They laughed again.

"Now I'm going to get us some extra manpower and more work space. Meanwhile, I know you'll do your best. One more thing."

She paused, choosing her words. She needed to impress them with the importance of their work—but she felt she had to avoid coming right out and saying that the Hammer of Eden could cause earthquakes.

"These people are trying to blackmail the governor of California. They *say* they can make earthquakes happen." She shrugged. "I'm not telling you they can. But it's not as impossible as it sounds, and I'm sure as hell not telling you they *can't*. Either way, you need to understand that this assignment is very, very serious." She paused again, then finished: "Let's get to it."

They all moved to their seats.

Judy left the room and walked briskly along the corridor to the SAC's office. The official start of the workday was eight-fifteen, but she was betting Brian Kincaid had come in early. He would have heard that she had called her team to a seven o'clock briefing, and he would want to know what was happening. She was about to tell him.

His secretary was not yet at her desk. Judy knocked on the inner door and went in.

Kincaid was sitting in the big chair with his suit coat on, looking as if he had nothing to do. The only items on his desk were a bran muffin with one bite taken out of it, and the paper bag it had come in. He was smoking a cigarette. Smoking was not allowed in FBI offices, but Kincaid was the boss, so there was no one to tell him to stop. He gave Judy a hostile glare and said: "If I asked you to make me a cup of coffee, I guess you'd call me a sexist pig."

There was no way she was going to make his coffee. He would take it as a sign that he could carry on walking all over her. But she wanted to be conciliatory. "I'll get you coffee," she said. She picked up his phone and dialed the DT squad secretary. "Rosa, would you come to the SAC's office and put on a pot of coffee for Mr. Kincaid? . . . Thank you."

He still looked angry. Her gesture had done nothing to win him over. He probably felt that by getting him coffee without actually making it herself, she had in a way out-witted him.

Bottom line, I can't win.

She got down to business. "I have more than a thousand

leads to follow up on the voice of the woman on tape. I'm guessing we'll get even more calls about the picture of Ricky Granger. I can't begin to evaluate them all by Friday with nine people. I need twenty more agents."

He laughed. "I'm not putting twenty people on this bullshit assignment."

She ignored that. "I've notified the Strategic Information Operations Center." SIOC was an information clearinghouse that operated from a bombproof office in the Hoover Building in Washington, D.C. "I'm assuming that as soon as the news gets around headquarters, they'll send some people here—if only to take the credit for any success we have."

"I didn't tell you to notify SIOC."

"I want to convene the Joint Terrorist Task Force so we'll have delegates here from police departments, Customs, and the U.S. Federal Protective Service, all of whom will need somewhere to sit. And starting from sundown on Thursday, I plan to stake out the likeliest locations for the next earthquake."

"There isn't going to be one!"

"I'll need extra personnel for that, too."

"Forget it."

"There isn't a room big enough here at the office. We're going to have to set up our emergency operations center someplace else. I checked out the Presidio buildings last night." The Presidio was a disused military base near the Golden Gate Bridge. The officers' club was habitable, though a skunk had been living there and the place smelled foul. "I'm going to use the ballroom of the officers' club."

Kincaid stood up. "You are like hell!" he shouted.

Judy sighed. There was no way to get this done without making a lifetime enemy of Brian Kincaid. "I have to call Mr. Honeymoon soon," she said. "Do you want me to tell him you're refusing to give me the manpower I need?"

Kincaid was red with fury. He stared at Judy as if he

wanted to pull out his gun and blow her away. At last he said: "Your FBI career is over, you know that?"

He was probably right, but it hurt to hear him say it. "I never wanted to fight with you, Brian," she said, striving to keep her voice low and reasonable. "But you dicked me around. I deserved a promotion after putting the Foong brothers away. Instead you promoted your buddy and gave me a bullshit assignment. You shouldn't have done that. It was unprofessional."

"Don't tell me how to—"

She overrode him. "When the bullshit assignment turned into a big case, you took it away from me, then screwed it up. Every bad thing that's happened to you is your own damn fault. Now you're sulking. Well, I know your pride is wounded, and I know your feelings are hurt, and I just want you to understand that I don't give a flying fuck."

He stared at her with his mouth half-open.

She went to the door.

"Now I'm going to talk to Honeymoon at nine-thirty," she said. "By then I'd like to have a senior logistics person assigned to my team with the authority to organize the manpower I need and set up a command post at the officers' club. If I don't, I'll tell Honeymoon to call Washington. Your move." She went out and slammed the door.

She felt the exhilaration that comes from a reckless act. She would have to fight every step, so she might as well fight hard. She would never be able to work with Kincaid again. The Bureau's top brass would side with the superior officer in a situation like this. She was almost certainly finished. But this case was more important than her career. Hundreds of lives might be at stake. If she could prevent a catastrophe and capture the terrorists, she would retire proudly, and to hell with them all.

The DT squad secretary was in Kincaid's outer office, filling the coffee machine. "Thanks, Rosa," Judy said as she passed through. She returned to the DT office. The phone on her desk was ringing. She picked up. "Judy Maddox."

"John Truth here."

"Hello!" It was weird to hear the familiar radio voice on the other end of a phone. "You're at work early!"

"I'm at home, but my producer just called me. My voice mail at the radio station was maxed with overnight calls about the Hammer of Eden woman."

Judy was not supposed to talk to the media herself. All such contacts should go through the office media specialist, Madge Kelly, a young agent with a journalism degree. But Truth was not asking her for a quote, he was giving her information. And she was in too much of a hurry to tell Truth to call Madge. "Anything good?" she asked.

"You bet. I got two people who remembered the name of the record."

"No kidding!" Judy was thrilled.

"This woman was reading poetry over a background of psychedelic music."

"Yuck."

"Yeah." He laughed. "The album was called *Raining Fresh Daisies.* That also seems to be the name of the band, or 'group,' as they used to call them then."

He seemed pleasant and friendly, nothing like the spiteful creep he was on air. Maybe that was just an act. But you could never trust media people. Judy said: "I never heard of them."

"Me either. Before my time, I guess. And we sure don't have the disk at the radio station."

"Did either of your callers give you a catalog number, or even the name of the record label?"

"Nope. My producer called both people back, but they don't actually have the record, they just remember it."

"Damn. I guess we'll just call every record company. I wonder if they keep files that far back. . . ."

"The album may have come out on a minor-league label

that no longer exists—it sounds like that kind of far-out stuff. Want to know what I'd do?"

"Sure."

"Haight-Ashbury is full of secondhand record stores with clerks who live in a time warp. I'd check them out."

"Good idea—thanks."

"You're welcome. Now, how's the investigation going otherwise?"

"We're making some progress. Can I get our press officer to call you later with details?"

"Come on! I've just done you a favor, haven't I?"

"You sure have, and I wish I could give you an interview, but agents aren't allowed to talk directly to the media. I'm really sorry."

His tone turned aggressive. "Is this the thanks you give to our listeners for calling in with information for you?"

A dreadful thought struck her. "Are you taping this?"

"You don't mind, do you?"

She hung up. *Shit.* She had been trapped. Talking to the media without authorization was what the FBI called a "bright-line issue," meaning you could be fired for it. If John Truth played his tape of their conversation over the air, Judy would be in trouble. She could argue that she had urgently needed the information Truth offered, and a decent boss would probably let her off with a reprimand, but Kincaid would make the most of it.

Heck, Judy, you're already in so much trouble, this won't make any difference.

Raja Khan walked up to her desk with a sheet of paper in his hand. "Would you like to see this before it goes out? It's the memo to police officers about how to recognize a seismic vibrator."

That was quick. "What took you so long?" she said, joshing him.

"I had to look up how to spell 'seismic.'"

She smiled and glanced over what he had written. It was

fine. "This is great. Send it out." She handed back the sheet. "Now I have another job for you. We're looking for an album called *Raining Fresh Daisies*. It's from the sixties."

"No kidding."

She grinned. "Yeah, it does have kind of a hippie feel to it. The voice on the record is the Hammer of Eden woman, and I'm hoping we'll get a name for her. If the label still exists, we might even get a last known address. I want you to contact all the major recording companies, then call stores that sell rare records."

He looked at his watch. "It's not yet nine, but I can start with the East Coast."

"Get to it."

Raja went to his desk. Judy picked up the phone and dialed police headquarters. "Lieutenant Maddox, please." A moment later he came on the line. She said: "Bo, it's me."

"Hi, Judy."

"Cast your mind back to the late sixties, when you knew what music was hip."

"I'd have to go further. Early sixties, late fifties, that's my era."

"Too bad. I think the Hammer of Eden woman made a record with a band called Raining Fresh Daisies."

"My favorite groups were called things like Frankie Rock and the Rockabillies. I never liked acts with flowers in their names. Sorry, Jude, I never heard of your outfit."

"Well, it was worth a try."

"Listen, I'm glad you called. I've been thinking about your guy, Ricky Granger—he's the man behind the woman, right?"

"That's what we think."

"You know, he's so careful, he's such a planner, he must be dying to know what you're up to."

"Makes sense."

"I think the FBI has probably talked to him already."

"You do?" That was hopeful, if Bo was right. There was a type of perpetrator who insinuated himself into the investigation, approaching the police as a witness or a kindly neighbor offering coffee, then tried to befriend officers and chat to them about the progress of the case. "But Granger also seems ultracareful."

"There's probably a war going on inside him, between caution and curiosity. But look at his behavior—he's daring as all hell. My guess is, curiosity will win out."

Judy nodded into the phone. Bo's intuitions were worth listening to: they came from thirty years of police experience. "I'm going to review every interview in the case."

"Look for something off-the-wall. This guy never does the normal thing. He'll be a psychic offering to divine where the next earthquake will come, or like that. He's imaginative."

"Okay. Anything else?"

"What do you want for supper?"

"I probably won't be home."

"Don't overdo it."

"Bo, I have three days to catch these people. If I fail, hundreds of people could die! I'm not thinking about supper."

"If you get tired, you'll miss the crucial clue. Take breaks, eat lunch, get the sleep you need."

"Like you always did, huh?"

He laughed. "Good luck."

"Bye." She hung up, frowning. She would have to go over every interview Marvin's team had done with the Green California Campaign people, plus all the notes from the raid on Los Alamos and anything else in the file. It should all be on the office computer network. She touched her keyboard and called up the directory. As she scanned the material, she realized there was far too much for her to review personally. They had interviewed every householder in Silver River Valley, more than a hundred people. When she got her extra personnel, she would put a small team on it. She made a note.

What else? She had to arrange stakeouts on likely earthquake sites. Michael had said he could make a list. She was glad to have a reason to call him. She dialed his number.

He sounded pleased to hear from her. "I'm looking forward to our date tonight."

Shit—I forgot all about it. "I've been put back on the Hammer of Eden case," she told him.

"Does that mean you can't make it tonight?" He sounded crestfallen.

She certainly could not contemplate dinner and a movie. "I'd like to see you, but I won't have much time. Could we meet for a drink, maybe?"

"Sure."

"I'm really sorry, but the case is developing fast. I called you about that list you promised, of likely earthquake sites. Did you make it?"

"No. You got anxious about the information getting out to the public and causing a panic, and that made me think the exercise might be dangerous."

"Now I need to know."

"Okay, I'll look at the data."

"Could you bring the list with you tonight?"

"Sure. Morton's at six?"

"See you there."

"Listen . . ."

"Still here."

"I'm really glad you're back on the case. I'm sorry we can't have dinner together, but I feel safer knowing you're after the bad guys. I mean it."

"Thanks." As she hung up, she hoped she merited his confidence.

Three days left.

By midafternoon the emergency operations center was up and running.

The officers' club looked like a Spanish villa. Inside, it was a gloomy imitation of a country club, with cheap paneling, bad murals, and ugly light fixtures. The smell of the skunk had not gone away.

The cavernous ballroom had been fitted out as a command post. In one corner was the head shed, a top table with seats for the heads of the principal agencies involved in managing the crisis, including the San Francisco police, firefighters and medical people, the mayor's office of emergency services, and a representative of the governor. The experts from headquarters, who were even now flying from Washington to San Francisco in an FBI jet, would sit here.

Around the room, groups of tables were set up for the different teams that would work on the case: intelligence and investigation, the core of the effort; negotiation and SWAT teams that would be called in if hostages were taken; an administration and technical support team that would grow if the crisis escalated; a legal team to expedite search warrants, arrest warrants, or wiretaps; and an evidence response team, which would enter any crime scene after the event and collect evidence.

Laptop computers on each table were linked in a local network. The FBI had long used a paper-based information control system called Rapid Start, but now it had developed a computerized version, using Microsoft Access software. But paper had not disappeared. Around two sides of the room, notice boards covered the walls: lead status boards, event boards, subject boards, demand boards, and hostage boards. Key data and clues would be written up here so that everyone could see them at a glance. Right now the subject board had one name—Richard Granger—and two pictures. The lead status board had a picture of a seismic vibrator.

The room was big enough for a couple of hundred people, but so far there were only about forty. They were mostly grouped around the intelligence and investigation table, speaking into phones, tapping keyboards, and reading files on screen. Judy had divided them into teams, each with a leader who monitored the others, so that she could keep track of progress by talking to three people.

There was an air of subdued urgency. Everyone was calm,

but they were concentrating hard and working intensely. No one stopped for coffee or schmoozed over the photocopier or went outside for a cigarette. Later, if the situation developed into a full-blown crisis, the atmosphere would change, Judy knew: people would be yelling into phones, the expletive quotient would multiply, tempers would fray, and it would be her job to keep the lid on the cauldron.

Remembering Bo's tip, she pulled up a chair next to Carl Theobald, a bright young agent in a fashionable dark blue shirt. He was the leader of the team reviewing Marvin Hayes's files. "Anything?" she said.

He shook his head. "We don't really know what we're looking for, but whatever it is, we haven't found it yet."

She nodded. She had given this team a vague task, but she could not help that. They had to look for something out of the ordinary. A lot depended on the intuition of the individual agent. Some people could smell deceit even in a computer.

"Are we sure we have *everything* on file?" she asked.

Carl shrugged. "We should."

"Check whether they kept any paper records."

"They're not supposed to. . . ."

"But people do."

"Okay."

Rosa called her back to the head shed for a phone call. It was Michael. She smiled as she picked up. "Hi."

"Hi. I've got a problem tonight. I can't make it."

She was shocked by his tone. He sounded curt and unfriendly. For the last few days he had been warm and affectionate. But this was the original Michael, the one who had turned her away from his door and told her to make an appointment. "What is it?" she said.

"Something came up. I'm sorry to cancel on you."

"Michael, what the hell is wrong?"

"I'm in kind of a rush. I'll call you."

"Okay," she said.

He hung up.

She cradled the phone, feeling hurt. "Now, what was all that about?" she said to herself. *Just as I was getting fond of the guy. What is it with him? Why can't he stay the way he was on Sunday night? Or even when he called me this morning?*

Carl Theobald interrupted her thoughts. He looked troubled. "Marvin Hayes is giving me a hard time," he said. "They do have some paper records, but when I said I needed to see them, he pretty much told me to shove it."

"Don't worry, Carl," Judy said. "These things are sent by heaven to teach us patience and tolerance. I'll just go and tear his balls off."

The agents nearby heard her and laughed.

"Is that what patience and tolerance means?" Carl said with a grin. "I must remember that."

"Come with me, I'll show you," she said.

They went outside and jumped in her car. It took fifteen minutes to reach the Federal Building on Golden Gate Avenue. As they went up in the elevator, Judy wondered how to deal with Marvin. Should she tear his balls off or be conciliatory? The cooperative approach worked only if the other party was willing. With Marvin she had probably gone past that point forever.

She hesitated outside the door to the Organized Crime squad room. *Okay, I'll be Xena, the warrior princess.*

She went in, and Carl followed.

Marvin was on the phone, grinning broadly, telling a joke. "So the barman says to the guy, there's a badger in the back room that gives the best blow job—"

Judy leaned on his desk and said loudly: "What's this crap you're giving Carl?"

"Someone's interrupting me, Joe," he said. "I'll call you right back." He hung up. "What can I do for you, Judy?"

She leaned closer, putting herself in his face. "Stop dicking around."

"What is it with you?" he said, sounding aggrieved. "What

do you mean by going over my records as if I must have made some goddamn mistake?"

He had not necessarily made a mistake. When the perpetrator presented himself to the investigating team in the guise of a bystander or witness, he generally tried to make sure that they did not suspect him. It was not the fault of the investigators, but it was bound to make them feel foolish.

"I think you may have talked to the perpetrator," she said. "Where are these paper records?"

He smoothed his yellow tie. "All we have are some notes from the press conference that never got keyed into the computer."

"Show me."

He pointed to a box file on a side table against the wall. "Help yourself."

She opened the file. On top was an invoice for the rental of a small public address system with microphones.

"You won't find a damn thing," Marvin said.

He might be right, but she had to try, and it was dumb of him to obstruct her. A smarter man would have said, "Hey, if I overlooked something, I sure hope you find it." Everyone made mistakes. But Marvin was now too defensive to be gracious. He just had to prove Judy wrong.

It would be embarrassing if she *was* wrong.

She rifled through the papers. There were some faxes from newspapers asking for details of the press conference, a note about how many chairs would be needed, and a guest list, a form on which the journalists attending the press conference had been asked to put their names and the publications or broadcasters they represented. Judy ran her eye down the list.

"What the hell is this?" she said suddenly. "Florence Shoebury, Eisenhower Junior High?"

"She wanted to cover the press conference for the school newspaper," Marvin said. "What should we do, tell her to fuck off?"

"Did you check her out?"

"She's a kid!"

"Was she alone?"

"Her father brought her."

There was a business card stapled to the form. "Peter Shoebury, from Watkins, Colefax and Brown. Did you check *him* out?"

Marvin hesitated for a long moment, realizing he had made a mistake. "No," he said finally. "Brian decided to let them into the press conference, and afterward I never followed up."

Judy handed the form with the business card to Carl. "Call this guy right away," she said.

Carl sat at the nearest desk and picked up the phone.

Marvin said: "Anyway, what makes you so sure we talked to the subject?"

"My father thinks so." As soon as the words were out of her mouth she realized she had made a mistake.

Marvin sneered. "Oh, so your *daddy* thinks so. Is that the level we've sunk to? You're checking on me because your *daddy* told you to?"

"Knock it off, Marvin. My father was putting bad guys in jail when you were still wetting your bed."

"Where are you going with this, anyway? Are you trying to set me up? You looking for someone to blame when you fail?"

"What a great idea," she said. "Why didn't I think of it?"

Carl hung up the phone and said: "Judy."

"Yeah."

"Peter Shoebury has never been inside this building, and he has no daughter. But he was mugged on Saturday morning two blocks from here, and his wallet was stolen. It contained his business cards."

There was a moment's silence, then Marvin said: "Fuck it."

Judy ignored his embarrassment. She was too excited by the news. This could be a whole new source of information. "I guess he didn't look like the E-fit picture we got from Texas."

"Not a bit," Marvin said. "No beard, no hat. He had big glasses and long hair in a ponytail."

"That's probably another disguise. What about his build, and like that?"

"Tall, slim."

"Dark hair, dark eyes, about fifty?"

"Yes, yes, and yes."

Judy almost felt sorry for Marvin. "It was Ricky Granger, wasn't it?"

Marvin looked at the floor as if he wanted it to open up and swallow him. "I guess you're right."

"I would like you to produce a new E-fit, please."

He nodded, still not looking at her. "Sure."

"Now, what about Florence Shoebury?"

"Well, she kind of disarmed us. I mean, what kind of terrorist brings a little girl along with him?"

"One who is completely ruthless. What did the kid look like?"

"White girl about twelve, thirteen. Dark hair, dark eyes, slim build. Pretty."

"Better do an E-fit of her, too. Do you think she really is his daughter?"

"Oh, sure. That's how they seemed. She showed no signs of being under coercion, if that's what you're thinking."

"Yes. Okay, I'm going to assume they're father and daughter, for now." She turned to Carl. "We're out of here."

They went out. In the corridor Carl said: "Wow. You really did tear off his balls."

Judy was jubilant. "But we've got another suspect—the kid."

"Yeah. I just hope you never catch *me* making a mistake."

She stopped and looked at him. "It wasn't the mistake, Carl. Anyone can screw up. But he was willing to impede the investigation in order to cover up. That's where he went wrong. And that's why he looks like such an asshole now. If you make a mistake, admit it."

"Yeah," Carl said. "But I think I'll keep my legs crossed, too."

Late that evening Judy got the first edition of the *San Francisco Chronicle* with the two new pictures: the E-fit of Florence Shoebury and the new E-fit of Ricky Granger disguised as Peter Shoebury. Earlier she had only glanced at the pictures before asking Madge Kelly to get them to the newspapers and TV stations. Now, studying them by the light of her desk lamp, she was struck by the resemblance between Granger and Florence. *They're father and daughter, they have to be. I wonder what will happen to her if I put her daddy in jail?*

She yawned and rubbed her eyes. Bo's advice came back to her. "Take breaks, eat lunch, get the sleep you need." It was time to go home. The overnight shift was already here.

Driving home, she reviewed the day and what she had achieved. Sitting at a stoplight, looking at twin rows of streetlights converging to infinity along Geary Boulevard, she realized that Michael had not faxed her the promised list of likely earthquake sites.

She dialed his number on the car phone, but there was no answer. For some reason that bothered her. She tried again at the next red light, and the number was busy. She called the office switchboard and asked them to check with Pacific Bell and find out whether there were voices on the line. The operator called her back and said there were not. The phone had been taken off the hook.

So he was home, but not picking up.

He had sounded odd when he called to cancel their date. He was like that; he could be charming and kind, then change abruptly and be difficult and arrogant. But why was his phone off the hook? Judy felt uneasy.

She checked the dashboard clock. It was just before eleven.

Two days left.

I don't have time to screw around.

She turned the car around and headed for Berkeley.

She reached Euclid Street at eleven-fifteen. There were lights on in Michael's apartment. Outside was an old orange Subaru. She had seen the car before but did not know whose it was. She parked behind it and rang Michael's doorbell.

There was no answer.

Judy was troubled. Michael had crucial information. Today, on the very day she had asked him a key question, he had abruptly canceled an appointment, then had become incommunicado.

It was suspicious.

She wondered what to do. Maybe she should call for police backup and break in. He could be tied up or dead in there.

She returned to her car and picked up the two-way radio, but she hesitated. When a man took the phone off the hook at eleven P.M., it might mean a variety of things. He might want to sleep. He might be getting laid, although Michael seemed too interested in Judy to play around—he was not the type to sleep with a different woman every night, she thought.

While she was wavering, a young woman with a brief-case approached the building. She looked like an assistant professor returning home from a late evening at the lab. She stopped at the door and fumbled in her briefcase for keys.

Impulsively Judy jumped out of her car and walked quickly across the lawn to the entrance. "Good evening," she said. She showed her badge. "FBI special agent Judy Maddox. I need access to this building."

"Something wrong?" the woman said anxiously.

"I hope not. If you go to your apartment and close the door, you'll be just fine."

They went in together. The woman entered a ground-floor apartment, and Judy went up the stairs. She rapped on Michael's door with her knuckles.

There was no reply.

What was going on? He was in there. He must have heard her ring and knock. He knew no casual caller would be so persistent at this time of night. Something was wrong, she felt sure.

She knocked again, three times, hard. Then she put her ear to the door and listened.

She heard a scream.

That did it. She took a step back and kicked the door as hard as she could. She was wearing loafers, and she hurt the underside of her right foot, but the wood around the lock splintered: thank God he did not have a steel door. She kicked it again. The lock seemed almost to break. She ran at the door with her shoulder, and it burst open.

She drew her gun. "FBI!" she shouted. "Drop your weapons and put up your hands!" There was another scream. It sounded like a woman, she realized in the back of her mind, but there was no time to figure out what that signified. She stepped into the entrance lobby.

Michael's bedroom door was open. She dropped to one knee with her arms extended and aimed into the room.

What she saw stunned her.

Michael was on the bed, naked, perspiring. He was on top of a thin woman with red hair who was breathing hard. It was his wife, Judy realized.

They were making love.

They both stared at Judy in fear and disbelief.

Then Michael recognized her and said: "Judy? What the hell . . . ?"

She closed her eyes. She had never felt like such a fool in her life.

"Oh, shit," she said. "I'm sorry. Oh, shit."

15

Early on Wednesday Priest stood beside the Silver River, looking at the way the morning sky was reflected in the broken planes of the water's shifting surface, marveling at the luminosity of blue and white in the dawn light. Everyone else was asleep. His dog sat beside him, panting quietly, waiting for something to happen.

It was a tranquil moment, but Priest's soul was not at peace.

His deadline was only two days away, and still Governor Robson had said nothing.

It was maddening. He did not want to trigger another earthquake. This one would have to be more spectacular, destroying roads and bridges, bringing skyscrapers tumbling down. People would die.

Priest was not like Melanie, thirsting for revenge upon the world. He just wanted to be left alone. He was willing to do anything to save the commune, but he knew it would be smarter to avoid killing if he could. After this was all over, and the project to dam the valley had been canceled, he and the commune wanted to live in peace. That was the whole point. And their chances of staying here undisturbed would be greater if they could win without killing innocent California citizens. What had happened so far could be forgotten soon enough. It would drop out of the news, and no one would care what became of the nutcases who said they could trigger earthquakes.

As he stood musing, Star appeared. She slipped out of her purple robe and stepped into the cold river to wash. Priest looked hungrily at her voluptuous body, familiar but still desirable. He had shared his bed with no one last night. Star was still spending her nights with Bones, and Melanie was with her husband in Berkeley. *So the great cocksman sleeps alone.*

While she was toweling herself dry, Priest said: "Let's go get a newspaper. I want to know if Governor Robson said anything last night."

They got dressed and drove to a gas station. Priest filled the tank of the 'Cuda while Star got the *San Francisco Chronicle*.

She came back white-faced. "Look," she said, showing him the front page.

There was a picture of a young girl who looked familiar. After a moment he realized with horror that it was Flower.

Stunned, he picked up the newspaper.

Beside the picture of Flower was one of himself.

Both were computer-generated images. The one of Priest was based on his appearance at the FBI press conference, when he had been disguised as Peter Shoebury, with his hair pulled back and wearing large glasses. He did not think anyone would recognize him from that.

Flower had not been in disguise. Her computer picture was like a poorly drawn portrait—not *her*, but *like* her. Priest felt cold. He was not used to fear. He was a daredevil who enjoyed risk. But this was not about him. He had put his daughter in danger.

Star said angrily: "Why the hell did you have to go to that press conference?"

"I had to know what they were thinking."

"It was so dumb!"

"I've always been rash."

"I know." Her voice softened, and she touched his cheek. "If you were timid, you wouldn't be the man I love."

A month ago it would not have mattered: no one outside

the commune knew Flower, and no one inside read newspapers. But she had been going secretly to Silver City to meet boys; she had stolen a poster from a store; she had been arrested; and she had spent a night in custody. Would the people she had met remember her? And if so, would they recognize the picture? The probation officer might remember her, but luckily he was still on vacation in the Bahamas, where he was unlikely to see the *San Francisco Chronicle*. But what about the woman who had guarded her overnight? A schoolteacher who was also the sheriff's sister, Priest recalled. Her name came back: Miss Waterlow. She saw hundreds of little girls presumably, but she might remember their faces. Maybe she had a bad memory. Maybe she had gone on vacation, too. Maybe she had not read today's *Chronicle*.

And maybe Priest was finished.

There was nothing he could do about it. If the schoolteacher saw the picture and recognized Flower and called the FBI, a hundred agents would descend on the commune and it would be all over.

He stared at the paper while Star read the text. "If you didn't know her, would you recognize her?"

Star shook her head. "I don't think so."

"I don't either. But I wish I were sure."

"I didn't think the feds were this goddamn smart," Star said.

"Some are, some aren't. It's this Asian girl that worries me. Judy Maddox." Priest recalled the TV pictures of her, so slender and graceful, pushing through a hostile crowd with a look of bulldog determination on her delicate features. "I got a bad feeling about her," he said. "A real bad feeling. She keeps coming up with leads—first the seismic vibrator, then the picture of me in Shiloh, now Flower. Maybe that's why Governor Robson hasn't said anything. She's got him hoping we'll be caught. Is there a statement from the governor in the paper?"

"No. According to this report, a lot of people are saying

Robson should give in and negotiate with the Hammer of Eden, but he refuses to comment."

"This is no good," he said. "I've got to find a way to talk to him."

When Judy woke up she could not remember why she felt so bad. Then the whole ghastly scene came back in a dreadful rush.

Last night she had been paralyzed with embarrassment. She had mumbled an apology to Michael and run out of the building, burning with shame. But this morning her mortification had been replaced by a different feeling. Now she just felt sad. She had thought Michael might become part of her life. She had been looking forward to getting to know him, growing more fond of him, making love to him. She had imagined that he cared for her. But the relationship had crashed and burned in no time.

She sat up in bed and looked at the collection of Vietnamese water puppets she had inherited from her mother, arranged on a shelf above the chest of drawers. She had never seen a puppet show—had never been to Vietnam—but her mother had told her how the puppeteers stood waist deep in a pond, behind a backdrop, and used the surface of the water as their stage. For hundreds of years such painted wooden toys had been used to tell wise and funny tales. They always reminded Judy of her mother's tranquility. What would she say now? Judy could hear her voice, low and calm. "A mistake is a mistake. Another mistake is normal. Only the same mistake twice makes you a fool."

Last night had just been a mistake. Michael had been a mistake. She had to put all that behind her. She had two days to prevent an earthquake. That was *really* important.

On the TV news, people were arguing about whether the Hammer of Eden might really be able to trigger an earthquake. The believers had formed a pressure group to urge Governor Robson to give in. But, as she got dressed, Judy's mind kept returning to Michael. She wished she could speak to her mother about it. She could hear Bo stirring, but this was not the kind of thing to tell your father about. Instead of making breakfast she called her friend Virginia. "I need someone to talk to," she told her. "Have you had breakfast yet?"

They met at a coffee shop near the Presidio. Ginny was a petite blonde, funny and honest. She would always tell Judy exactly what she thought. Judy ordered two chocolate croissants to make herself feel better, then related what had happened last night.

When she came to the part where she burst in with her gun in her hand and found them screwing, Ginny practically fell down laughing. "I'm sorry," she said, and got a piece of toast stuck in her throat.

"I guess it is kind of funny," Judy said, smiling. "But it didn't seem that way last night, I can tell you."

Ginny coughed and swallowed. "I don't mean to be cruel," she said when she had recovered. "I can see it wasn't too hilarious at the time. What he did was really sleazy, dating you and sleeping with his wife."

"To me, it shows that he's not over her," Judy said. "So he's not ready for a new relationship."

Ginny made a doubtful face. "I don't necessarily buy that."

"You think it was like a good-bye, one last embrace for old times' sake?"

"Maybe even simpler. You know, men almost never say no to a fuck if it's offered to them. It sounds as if he's been living the life of a monk since she left him. His hormones are probably giving him hell. She's attractive, you say?"

"Very sexy looking."

"So if she walked in wearing a tight sweater and started making moves on him, he probably couldn't help getting a hard-on. And once that happens, a man's brain cuts out and the autopilot in his dick takes control."

"You think so?"

"Listen, I've never met Michael, but I've known some men, good and bad, and that's my take on the scenario."

"What would you do?"

"I'd talk to him. Ask him why he did it. See what he says. See if I believed him. If he gave me a line of bullshit, I'd forget him. But if he seemed honest, I'd try to make some kind of sense of the whole incident."

"I have to call him anyway," Judy said. "He still hasn't sent me that list."

"So call. Get the list. Then ask him what he thinks he's doing. You're feeling embarrassed, but he has something to apologize for, too."

"I guess you're right."

It was not yet eight o'clock, but they were both in a hurry to get to work. Judy paid the check, and they went out to their cars. "Boy," Judy said, "I'm beginning to feel better about this. Thank you."

Ginny shrugged. "What are girlfriends for? Let me know what he says."

Judy got into her car and dialed Michael's number. She was afraid he might be asleep and she would find herself talking to him while he was in bed with his wife. However, his voice sounded alert, as if he had been up for a while. "I'm sorry about your door," she said.

"Why did you do it?" He sounded more curious than angry.

"I couldn't understand why you didn't answer. Then I heard a scream. I thought you must be in some kind of trouble."

"What brought you here so late?"

"You didn't send me that list of earthquake sites."

"Oh, that's right! It's on my desk. I just forgot. I'll fax it now."

"Thanks." She gave him the fax number of the new emergency operations center. "Michael, there's something I have to ask you." She took a deep breath. Asking this question was harder than she had anticipated. She was no shrinking violet, but she was not as brash as Ginny. She swallowed and said: "You gave me the impression you were growing fond of me. Why did you sleep with your wife?" There. It was out.

At the other end of the line there was a long silence. Then he said: "This is not a good time."

"Okay." She tried to keep the disappointment out of her voice.

"I'll send that list right away."

"Thanks."

She hung up and started the engine. Ginny's idea had not been so great after all. It took two to talk, and Michael was not willing.

When she reached the officers' club, Michael's fax was waiting for her. She showed it to Carl Theobald. "We need surveillance teams at each of these locations, watching out for a seismic vibrator," she said. "I was hoping to use the police, but I don't think we can. They might talk. And if local people find out that we think they're a target, they'll panic. So we have to use FBI personnel."

"Okay." Carl frowned at the sheet. "You know, these locations are awful big. One team can't really watch an area a mile square. Should we put on multiple teams? Or could your seismologist narrow it down?"

"I'll ask him." Judy picked up the phone and dialed Michael again. "Thanks for the fax," she said. She explained the problem.

"I'd have to visit the sites myself," he said. "Signs of earlier earthquake activity, such as dried-up streambeds or fault scarp, would give me a more precise fix."

"Would you do that today?" she said immediately. "I can take you to all the locations in an FBI helicopter."

"Uh . . . sure, I guess," he said. "I mean, of course I will."

"You could be saving lives."

"Exactly."

"Can you find your way to the officers' club in the Presidio?"

"Sure."

"By the time you get here, the chopper will be waiting."

"Okay."

"I appreciate this, Michael."

"You're welcome."

But I'd still like to know why you slept with your wife.

She hung up.

It was a long day. Judy, Michael, and Carl Theobald covered a thousand miles in the helicopter. By nightfall they had set up round-the-clock surveillance at the five locations on Michael's list.

They returned to the Presidio. The helicopter landed on the deserted parade ground. The base was a ghost town, with its moldering office buildings and rows of vacant houses.

Judy had to go into the emergency operations center and report to a big shot from FBI headquarters in Washington who had shown up at nine o'clock that morning with a take-charge air. But first she walked Michael to his car in the darkened parking lot. "What if they slip through the surveillance?" she said.

"I thought your people were good."

"They're the best. But what if? Is there some way I can get notified real fast if there's a tremor anywhere in California?"

"Sure," he said. "I could set up on-line seismography right here at your command post. I just need a computer and an ISDN phone line."

"No problem. Would you do it tomorrow?"

"Okay. That way, you'll know immediately if they start the seismic vibrator someplace that's not on the list."

"Is that likely?"

"I don't think so. If their seismologist is competent, he'll pick the same places I picked. And if he's incompetent, they probably won't be able to trigger an earthquake."

"Good," she said. "Good." She would remember that. She could tell the Washington big shot that she had the crisis under control.

She looked up at Michael's shadowed face. "Why did you sleep with your wife?"

"I've been thinking about that all day."

"Me, too."

"I guess I owe you some kind of explanation."

"I think so."

"Until yesterday I was sure it was over. Then, last night, she reminded me of the things that had been good about our marriage. She was beautiful, fun, affectionate, and sexy. More important, she made me forget all the things that were bad."

"Such as?"

He sighed. "I think Melanie is drawn to authority figures. I was her professor. She wants the security of being told what to do. I expected an equal partner, someone who would share decisions and take responsibility. She resented that."

"I get the picture."

"And there's something else. Deep down, she's mad as hell at the whole world. Most of the time she hides it, but when she's frustrated she can be violent. She would throw things at me, heavy things, like a casserole dish one time. She never hurt me, she's just not strong enough, though if there was a gun in the house, I'd be scared. But that level of hostility is hard to live with."

"And last night . . . ?"

"I forgot all that. She seemed to want to try again, and I thought maybe we should, for Dusty's sake. Plus . . ."

She wished she could read his expression, but it was too dark. "What?"

"I want to tell you the truth, Judy, even though you'll be

offended by it. So I have to admit that it wasn't as rational and decent as I'm pretending. Part of it was that she's a beautiful woman and I wanted to fuck her. Now I've said it."

She smiled in the dark. Ginny had been half-right, anyway. "I knew that," she said. "But I'm glad you told me. Good night." She walked away.

"Good night," he said, sounding bewildered.

A few moments later he called after her: "Are you angry?"

"No," she said over her shoulder. "Not anymore."

Priest expected Melanie to return to the commune around midafternoon. When suppertime came and she still had not arrived, he started to worry.

By nightfall he was frantic. What had happened to her? Had she decided to go back to her husband? Had she confessed everything to him? Was she even now spilling the beans to Agent Judy Maddox in an interrogation room at the Federal Building in San Francisco?

He could not sit still in the cookhouse or lie on his bed. He took a candle lamp and walked across the vineyard and through the woods to the parking circle and waited there, listening for the engine of her old Subaru—or the throb of the FBI helicopter that would herald the end of everything.

Spirit heard it first. He cocked his ears, tensed, then ran up the mud road, barking. Priest stood up, straining his hearing. It was the Subaru. Relief swamped him. He watched the lights approach through the trees. He had the beginnings of a headache. He had not had a headache for years.

Melanie parked erratically, got out, and slammed the car door.

"I hate you," she said to Priest. "I hate you for making me do that."

"Was I right?" he said. "Is Michael making a list for the FBI?"

"Fuck you!"

Priest realized he had goofed. He should have been understanding and sympathetic. For a moment he had allowed his anxiety to cloud his judgment. Now he would have to spend time talking her around. "I asked you to do it because I love you, don't you understand that?"

"No, I don't. I don't understand anything." She folded her arms across her chest and turned away from him, staring into the darkness of the woods. "All I know is, I feel like a prostitute."

Priest was bursting to know what she had found out, but he made himself calm. "Where have you been?" he said.

"Driving around. I stopped for a drink."

He was silent for a minute. Then he said: "A prostitute does it for money—then she spends the money on stupid clothes and drugs. You did it to save your child. I know you feel bad, but you're not bad. You're good."

At last she turned to him. There were tears in her eyes. "It's not just that we had sex," she said. "It's worse than that. I liked it. That's what makes me feel ashamed. I came. I really did. I screamed."

Priest felt a hot wave of jealousy and strained to suppress it. He would make Michael Quercus suffer for that one day. But now was not the time to say so. He needed to cool things down here. "It's okay," he murmured. "Really, it's okay. I understand. Weird things happen." He put his arms around her and hugged her.

Slowly she relaxed. He could feel the tension leaving her bit by bit. "You don't mind?" she said. "You're not mad?"

"Not a bit," he lied, stroking her long hair. *Come on, come on!*

"You were right about the list," she said.

At last.

"That FBI woman had asked Michael to work out the best locations for an earthquake, just the way you imagined it."

Of course she did. I'm so damn smart.

Melanie went on: "He was sitting at his computer when I got there, just finishing."

"So what happened?"

"I made him dinner, and like that."

Priest could imagine. If Melanie decided to be seductive, she was irresistible. And she was at her most alluring when she wanted something. She probably took a bath and put on a robe, then moved around the apartment smelling of soap and flowers, pouring wine or making coffee, letting the robe fall open now and again to show him tantalizing glimpses of her long legs and her soft breasts. She would have asked Michael questions and listened intently to his answers, smiling at him in a way that said *I like you so much, you can do anything you want with me.*

"When the phone rang I told him not to answer, then I took it off the hook. But the damn woman came over anyway, and when Michael didn't answer the door she broke it down. Boy, did she have a shock." Priest figured she needed to get all this off her chest, so he did not hurry her. "She almost died of embarrassment."

"Did he give her the list?"

"Not then. I guess she was too confused to ask. But she called this morning, and he faxed it to her."

"And did you get it?"

"While he was in the shower, I got to his computer and printed out another copy."

So where the hell is it?

She reached into the back pocket of her jeans, pulled out a single sheet of paper folded in four, and gave it to Priest.

Thank God.

He unfolded it and looked at it in the light of the lamp. The typed letters and numbers meant nothing to him. "These are the places he's told her to watch?"

"Yes, they're going to stake out each of these locations, looking for a seismic vibrator, just the way you predicted."

Judy Maddox was clever. The FBI surveillance would

make it very difficult for him to operate the seismic vibrator, especially if he had to try several different locations, as he had in Owens Valley.

But he was even cleverer than Judy. He had anticipated this move by her. And he had thought of a way around it. "You understand how Michael picked these sites?" he said.

"Sure. They're the places where the tension in the fault is highest."

"So you could do the same thing."

"I already have. And I picked the same places he did."

He folded the paper and gave it back to her. "Now, listen very carefully. This is important. Could you look over the data again and pick the five *next* best locations?"

"Yes."

"And could we cause an earthquake at one of them?"

"Probably," she said. "It's maybe not as sure, but the chances are good."

"Then that's what we'll do. Tomorrow we'll take a look at the new sites. Right after I talk to Mr. Honeymoon."

16

At five A.M., the guard at the entrance to the Los Alamos place was yawning.

He became alert when Melanie and Priest pulled up in the 'Cuda. Priest got out of the car. "How are you, buddy?" he said as he walked across to the gate.

The guard hefted his rifle, assumed a mean expression, and said: "Who are you and what do you want?"

Priest hit him in the face very hard, crushing his nose. Blood spurted. The guard cried out, his hands flying to his face. Priest said: "Ow!" His fist hurt. It was a long time since he had punched anyone.

His instincts took over. He kicked the guard's legs from under him. The man fell on his back, and his rifle went flying through the air. Priest kicked him in the ribs three or four times, fast and hard, trying to break the bones. Then he kicked his face and head. The man curled up in a ball, sobbing in pain, helpless with fear.

Priest stopped, breathing hard. It all came back to him in a flood of remembered excitement. There had been a time when he had done this sort of thing every day. It was so easy to frighten people when you knew how.

He knelt and took the handgun from the man's belt. This was what he had come for.

He looked at the weapon in disgust. It was a reproduction of a long-barreled .44-caliber Remington revolver originally manufactured in the days of the Wild West. It was a stupid, impractical firearm, the kind owned by collectors and kept in a felt-lined display case in the den. It was not for shooting people.

He broke it open. It was loaded.

That was all he really cared about.

He returned to the car and got in. Melanie was at the wheel. She was pale and bright-eyed, breathing fast, as if she had just taken cocaine. Priest guessed she had never witnessed serious violence. "Will he be okay?" she said in an excited voice.

Priest glanced back at the guard. He was lying on the ground, his hands to his face, rocking slightly. "Sure he will," Priest said.

"Wow."

"Let's go to Sacramento."

Melanie pulled away.

After a while she said: "Do you really think you can talk this Honeymoon guy around?"

"He's got to see sense," Priest said, sounding more confident than he felt. "Look at the choice he has. Number one, an earthquake that will do millions of dollars of damage. Or, number two, a sensible proposal to reduce pollution. Plus, if he picks number one, he faces the same choice all over again two days later. He has to take the easy road."

"I guess," Melanie said.

They reached Sacramento a few minutes before seven A.M. The state capital was quiet this early. A few cars and trucks moved unhurriedly along the broad, empty boulevards. Melanie parked near the Capitol Building. Priest put on a baseball cap and tucked his long hair up inside it. Then he donned sunglasses. "Wait for me right here," he said. "I may be a couple of hours."

Priest walked around the Capitol block. He had hoped there would be a surface-level parking lot, but he was disappointed. The ground around was all garden, with magnificent trees. On either side of the building, a ramp led down to an underground garage. Both ramps were monitored by security guards in sentry booths.

Priest approached one of the large, imposing doors. The building was open, and there was no security check at the entrance. He went into a grand hall with a mosaic-tiled floor.

He took off the sunglasses, which looked conspicuous indoors, and followed a staircase down to the basement. There was a coffee shop where a few early workers were getting a charge of caffeine. He walked past them, looking as if he belonged here, and followed a corridor he thought must lead to the parking garage. As he approached the end of the corridor, a door opened and a fat man in a blue blazer came through. Behind the man, Priest saw cars.

Bingo.

He slipped into the garage and looked around. It was almost empty. There were a few cars, a sport utility, and a sheriff's car parked in the marked spaces. He saw no one.

He slipped behind the back of the sport utility. It was a Dodge Durango. From here, peering through the car windows, he could see the entrance to the garage and the door that led inside the building. Other cars parked on either side of the Durango would shield him from the gaze of new arrivals.

He settled to wait. *This is their last chance. There's still time to negotiate and avoid a catastrophe. But if this doesn't work . . . boom.*

Al Honeymoon was a workaholic, Priest figured. He would arrive early. But there was a lot that could go wrong. Honeymoon could be spending the day at the governor's residence. He might call in sick today. Perhaps he had meetings in Washington; maybe he was on a trip to Europe; his wife could be having a baby.

Priest did not think he would have a bodyguard. He was not an elected official, just a government employee. Would he have a chauffeur? Priest had no idea. That would spoil everything.

A car pulled in every few minutes. Priest studied the drivers from his hiding place. He did not have to wait long. At seven-thirty a smart dark blue Lincoln Continental drove in. Behind the wheel was a black man in a white shirt and tie. It was Honeymoon: Priest recognized him from the newspaper photos.

The car pulled into a slot near the Durango. Priest put on his sunglasses, crossed the garage swiftly, opened the near-side door of the Lincoln, and slid into the passenger seat before Honeymoon could get his seat belt off. He showed him the gun. "Pull out of the garage," he said.

Honeymoon stared at him. "Who the hell are you?"

Arrogant son of a bitch in a chalk-stripe suit with a pin through the collar of your shirt, I'll ask the frigging questions.

Priest cocked the hammer of the revolver. "I'm the maniac who's going to put a bullet in your guts unless you do as I say. Now drive."

"Fuck," Honeymoon said feelingly. "Fuck." Then he started the car and pulled out of the garage.

"Smile nicely at the security guard and drive slowly by," Priest said. "You say one word to him and I'll kill him."

Honeymoon did not reply. He slowed the car as it approached the sentry booth. For a moment, Priest thought he was going to try something. Then they saw the guard, a middle-aged black man with white hair. Priest said: "If you want this brother to die, just go ahead with what's on your mind."

Honeymoon cursed under his breath and drove on.

"Take Capitol Mall out of town," Priest told him.

Honeymoon drove around the Capitol Building and headed west on the broad avenue that led to the Sacramento River. "What do you want?" he said. He hardly seemed afraid—more impatient.

Priest would have liked to shoot him. This was the asshole who had made the dam possible. He had done his best to ruin Priest's life. And he was not a bit sorry. He really did not care. A bullet in the guts was hardly punishment enough.

Controlling his anger, Priest said: "I want to save people's lives."

"You're the Hammer of Eden guy, right?"

Priest did not answer. Honeymoon was staring at him. Priest guessed he was trying to memorize his features. *Smart-ass.* "Watch the goddamn road."

Honeymoon looked ahead.

They crossed the bridge. Priest said: "Take I-80 toward San Francisco."

"Where are we going?"

"You ain't going nowhere."

Honeymoon pulled onto the freeway.

"Drive at fifty in the slow lane. Why the hell won't you give me what I'm asking for?" Priest had intended to stay cool, but Honeymoon's arrogant calm enraged him. "Do you *want* a frigging earthquake?"

Honeymoon was deadpan. "The governor can't give in to blackmail, you must know that."

"You can get around that problem," Priest argued. "Give out that you were planning a freeze anyway."

"No one would believe us. It would be political suicide for the governor."

"It would like hell. You can fool the public. What are spin doctors for?"

"I'm the best there is, but I can't do miracles. This is too high-profile. You shouldn't have brought John Truth into it."

Priest said angrily: "No one listened to us until John Truth got on the case!"

"Well, whatever the reason, this is now a public face-off, and the governor can't back down. If he did, the state of California would be open to blackmail by every idiot with a hunting rifle in his hand and a bug up his ass about some damn cause. But *you* could back off."

The bastard is trying to talk me around!

Priest said: "Take the first exit and head back into town."

Honeymoon indicated right and went on talking: "Nobody knows who you people are or where to find you. If you drop the whole thing now, you can get away with it. No real harm has been done. But if you set off another earthquake, you'll have every law enforcement agency in the United States after you, and they won't give up until they find you. No one can hide forever."

Priest was angered. "Don't you threaten me!" he yelled. "I'm the one with the motherfucking gun!"

"I haven't forgotten that. I'm trying to get us both out of this without further damage."

Honeymoon had somehow taken control of the conversation. Priest felt sick with frustration. "You listen to me," he said. "There's only one way out of this. Make an announcement, today. No more power plant building in California."

"I can't do that."

"Pull over."

"We're on the freeway."

"Pull the fuck over!"

Honeymoon slowed the car and stopped on the shoulder of the road.

The temptation to shoot was strong, but Priest resisted it. "Get out of the car."

Honeymoon put the shift in park and got out.

Priest slid over behind the wheel. "You got until midnight to see sense," he said. He pulled away.

In the rearview mirror he saw Honeymoon try to wave down a passing car. It drove right by. He tried again. No one would stop.

Seeing the big man in his expensive suit and shiny shoes, standing at the dusty roadside trying to get a ride, gave Priest a small measure of satisfaction and helped to quell the nagging suspicion that Honeymoon had somehow got the better of the encounter, even though Priest had held the gun.

Honeymoon gave up waving at cars and began to walk.

Priest smiled and drove on into town.

Melanie was waiting where he had left her. He parked the Lincoln, leaving the keys in, and got into the 'Cuda.

"What happened?" Melanie said.

Priest shook his head in disgust. "Nothing," he said angrily. "It was a waste of time. Let's go."

She started the car and pulled away.

Priest rejected the first location Melanie took him to.

It was a small seaside town fifty miles north of San Francisco. They parked on the cliff top, where a stiff breeze rocked the old 'Cuda on its tired springs. Priest rolled down the window to smell the sea. He would have liked to take off his boots and walk barefoot along the beach, feeling the damp sand between his toes, but there was no time.

The location was very exposed. The truck would be too conspicuous here. It was a long distance from the freeway, so there could be no quick getaway. Most important of all, there was not much of value here to be destroyed—just a few houses clustered around a harbor.

Melanie said: "An earthquake sometimes does the greatest damage many miles from its epicenter."

"But you can't be sure of that," Priest said.

"True. You can't be sure of anything."

"Still, the best way to bring down a skyscraper is to have an earthquake underneath it, am I right?"

"All other things being equal, yes."

They drove south through the green hills of Marin County and across the Golden Gate Bridge. Melanie's second location was in the heart of the city. They followed Route 1 through the Presidio and Golden Gate Park and pulled up not far from the San Francisco campus of Cal State University.

"This is better," Priest said immediately. All around him were homes and offices, stores and restaurants.

"A tremor with its epicenter here would cause the most damage at the marina," Melanie said.

"How come? That's miles away."

"It's all reclaimed land. The underlying sedimentary deposits are saturated with water. That amplifies the shaking. Whereas the ground here is probably solid. And these buildings look strong. Most buildings survive an earthquake. The ones that fall down are made of unreinforced masonry— typically low-income housing—or concrete-frame structures without bracing."

This was all quibbling, Priest decided. She was just nervous. *An earthquake is a frigging earthquake, for Christ's sake. No one knows what's going to fall down. I don't care, so long as something does.*

"Let's look at another place," he said.

Melanie directed him south on Interstate 280. "Right where the San Andreas fault crosses Route 101, there's a small town called Felicitas," she said.

They drove for twenty minutes. They almost passed the exit ramp for Felicitas. "Here, here!" Melanie yelled. "Didn't you see the sign?"

Priest wrenched the wheel to the right and made the ramp. "I wasn't looking," he said.

The exit led to a vantage point overlooking the town. Priest stopped the car and got out. Felicitas was laid out in front of him like a picture. Main Street ran from left to right across his field of vision, lined with low clapboard stores and offices, a few cars parked slantwise in front of the buildings. There was a small wooden church with a bell tower. North and south of the main drag was a neat grid of tree-lined streets. All the houses were one story. At either end of the town, the street became a pre-freeway country road and disappeared among fields. The landscape north of the town was split by a meandering river like a jagged crack in a window. In the distance was a railway track as straight as a

draftsman's line from east to west. Behind Priest, the
freeway ran along a viaduct on high concrete arches.

Stepping down the hill was a cluster of six huge bright
blue pipes. They dipped under the freeway, passed the town
to the west, and disappeared over the horizon, looking like
an infinite xylophone. "What the hell is that?" Priest said.

Melanie thought for a moment. "I think it must be a gas
pipeline."

Priest breathed a long sigh of satisfaction. "This place is
perfect," he said.

They made one more stop that day.

After the earthquake, Priest would need to hide the
seismic vibrator. His only weapon was the threat of more
earthquakes. He had to make Honeymoon and Governor
Robson believe he had the power to do this again and again
until they gave in. So it was crucial that he kept the truck
hidden away.

It was going to become more and more difficult to drive
the vibrator on public roads, so he needed to hide it someplace where he could, if necessary, trigger a third earthquake without moving far.

Melanie directed him to Third Street, which ran parallel
with the shore of the huge natural harbor that was San Francisco Bay. Between Third and the waterfront was a run-
down industrial neighborhood. There were disused railway
tracks along the potholed streets; rusting, derelict factories;
empty warehouses with smashed windows; and dismal
yards full of pallets, tires, and wrecked cars.

"This is good," Priest said. "It's only half an hour from
Felicitas, and it's the kind of district where nobody takes
much interest in their neighbors."

Realtors' signs were optimistically fixed to some of the
buildings. Melanie, posing as Priest's secretary, called the
number on one of the signs and asked if they had a warehouse to rent, real cheap, about fifteen hundred square feet.

An eager young salesman drove out to meet them an hour later. He showed them a crumbling cinder-block ruin with holes in the corrugated roof. There was a broken sign over the door, which Melanie read aloud: "Perpetua Diaries." There was plenty of room to park the seismic vibrator. The place also had a working bathroom and a small office with a hot plate and a big old Zenith TV left by the previous tenant.

Priest told the salesman he needed a place to store barrels of wine for a month or so. The man did not give a damn what Priest wanted to do with the space. He was delighted to get some rent on a near valueless property. He promised to have the power and water turned on by the following day. Priest paid him four weeks' rent in advance, cash, from the secret stash he kept in his old guitar.

The salesman looked like it was his lucky day. He gave Melanie the keys, shook hands, and hurried away before Priest could change his mind.

Priest and Melanie drove back to Silver River Valley.

Thursday evening, Judy Maddox took a bath. Lying in the water, she remembered the Santa Rosa earthquake that had so frightened her when she was in first grade. It came back to her as vividly as if it were yesterday. Nothing could be more terrifying than to find that the ground beneath your feet was not fixed and stable, but treacherous and deadly. Sometimes, in quiet moments, she saw nightmare visions of multiple car wrecks, bridges collapsing, buildings falling down, fires and floods—but none of these were as dreadful to her as the recollection of her own terror at six years of age.

She washed her hair and thrust the memory to the back of her mind. Then she packed an overnight bag and went back to the officers' club at ten P.M.

The command post was quiet, but the atmosphere was tense. Still no one knew for certain whether the Hammer of Eden could cause an earthquake. But since Ricky Granger had abducted Al Honeymoon at gunpoint in the garage of the Capitol Building and left him stranded on I-80, everyone was sure these terrorists were dead serious.

There were now more than a hundred people in the old ballroom. The on-scene commander was Stuart Cleever, the big shot who had flown in from Washington Tuesday night. Despite Honeymoon's orders, there was no way the Bureau was going to let a lowly agent take overall charge of something this big. Judy did not want total control, and she had not argued about it. However, she had been able to ensure that neither Brian Kincaid nor Marvin Hayes was directly involved.

Judy's title was investigative operations coordinator. That gave her all the control she needed. Alongside her was Charlie Marsh, emergency operations coordinator, in command of the SWAT team on standby in the next room. Charlie was a man of about forty-five with a grizzled crewcut. He was ex-army, a fitness freak and a gun collector, not the type Judy normally liked, but he was straightforward and reliable, and she could work with him.

Between the head shed and the investigation team table were Michael Quercus and his young seismologists, sitting at their screens, watching for signs of earthquake activity. Michael had gone home for a couple of hours, like Judy. He came back wearing clean khakis and a black polo shirt, carrying a sports duffel, ready for a long spell.

They had talked, during the day, about practical matters as he set up his equipment and introduced his helpers. At first they had been awkward with each other, but Judy realized he was quickly getting over his feelings of anger and guilt about Tuesday's incident. She felt she ought to sulk about it for a day or two, but she was too busy. So the whole thing got shoved to the back of her mind, and she found herself enjoying having Michael around.

She was trying to think of an excuse to talk to him when the phone on her desk rang.

She picked it up. "Judy Maddox."

The operator said: "A call for you from Ricky Granger."

"Trace it!" she snapped. It would take the operator only seconds to contact Pacific Bell's twenty-four-hour security center. She waved at Cleever and Marsh, indicating that they should listen.

"You got it," the operator said. "Shall I connect you or leave him on hold?"

"Put him on. Tape the call." There was a click. "Judy Maddox here."

A male voice said: "You're smart, Agent Maddox. But are you smart enough to make the governor see sense?"

He sounded irate, frustrated. Judy imagined a man of about fifty, thin, badly dressed, but accustomed to being listened to. He was losing his grip on life and feeling resentful, she speculated.

She said: "Am I speaking to Ricky Granger?"

"You know who you're speaking to. Why are they forcing me to cause another earthquake?"

"*Forcing* you? Are you kidding yourself that all this is someone *else's* fault?"

This seemed to make him angrier. "It's not me who's using more and more electric power every year," he said. "I don't want more power plants. I don't use electricity."

"You don't?" *Really?* "So what's powering your phone—steam?" *A cult that doesn't use electricity. That's a clue.* While she taunted him, she was trying to figure out what this meant. *But where are they?*

"Don't fuck with me, Judy. You're the one that's in trouble."

Next to her, Charlie's phone rang. He snatched it up and wrote in large letters on his notepad: "Pay phone— Oakland—I-980 & I-580—Texaco."

"We're all in trouble, Ricky," she said in a more reasonable voice. Charlie went to the map on the wall. She heard him say the word "roadblocks."

"Your voice changed," Granger said suspiciously. "What happened?"

Judy felt out of her depth. She had no special training in negotiating skills. All she knew was that she had to keep him on the phone. "I suddenly thought what a catastrophe there will be if you and I don't manage to come to some agreement," she said.

She could hear Charlie giving urgent orders in a low voice: "Call the Oakland PD, Alameda County Sheriff's Office, and the California Highway Patrol."

"You're bullshitting me," Granger said. "Have you traced this call already? Jeez, that was fast. Are you trying to keep me on the line while your SWAT team comes after me? Forget it! I got a hundred and fifty ways out of here!"

"But only one way out of the jam you're in."

"It's past midnight," he said. "Your time is up. I'm going to cause another earthquake, and there's not one damn thing you can do to stop me." He hung up.

Judy slammed down the phone. "Let's go, Charlie!" She ripped the E-fit picture of Granger off the subject board and ran outside. The helicopter was waiting on the parade ground, its rotors turning. She jumped in, with Charlie close behind.

As they took off, he put on headphones and motioned to her to do the same. "I figure it'll take twenty minutes to get the roadblocks in place," he said. "Assume he's driving at sixty, to avoid being stopped for speeding, he could be twenty miles away by the time we're ready for him. So I've ordered the major freeways closed in a twenty-five-mile radius."

"What about other roads?"

"We have to hope he's going a long way. If he gets off the freeway, we lose him. This is one of the busiest road networks in California. You couldn't seal it off watertight if you had the goddamn U.S. Army."

Turning onto I-80, Priest heard the throb of a helicopter and looked up to see it passing overhead, coming from San

Francisco across the bay toward Oakland. "Shit," he said. "They can't be after us, can they?"

"I told you," Melanie said. "They can trace phone calls like, instantly."

"But what are they going to do? They don't even know which way we headed when we left the gas station!"

"They could close the freeway, I guess."

"Which one? Nine-eighty, eight-eighty, five-eighty, or eighty? North or south?"

"Maybe all of them. You know cops, they do what they like."

"Shit." Priest put his foot down.

"Don't get stopped for goddamn speeding."

"Okay, okay!" He slowed down again.

"Can't we get off the freeway?"

He shook his head. "No other way home. There are side roads, but they don't cross the water. All we could do is hole up in Berkeley. Park somewhere and sleep in the car. But we don't have time, we have to get home to get the seismic vibrator." He shook his head. "Nothing to do but run for it."

The traffic thinned as they left Oakland and Berkeley behind. Priest peered into the darkness ahead, alert for flashing lights. He was relieved to reach the Carquinez Bridge. Once they were across the water, they could use country roads. It might take them half the night to get home, but they would be out of danger.

He approached the toll plaza slowly, scanning for signs of police activity. Only one booth was open, but that was not surprising after midnight. No blue lights, no cruisers, no cops. He pulled up and fished in his jeans pocket for change.

When he looked up he saw a Highway Patrol officer.

Priest's heart seemed to stop.

The cop was in the booth, behind the attendant, staring at Priest with a surprised expression.

The toll attendant took Priest's money but did not turn on the green light.

The officer stepped quickly out of the booth.

Melanie said: "Shit! What now?"

Priest considered making a run for it but quickly decided against it. That would just start a chase. His old car could not outrun the cops.

"Good evening, sir," the officer said. He was a fat man of about fifty wearing a bulletproof vest over his uniform. "Please pull over to the right side of the road."

Priest did as he said. A Highway Patrol car was parked beside the road, where it could not be seen from the other side of the toll plaza.

Melanie whispered: "What are you going to do?"

"Try to stay calm," Priest said.

There was another officer waiting in the parked car. He got out when he saw Priest pull up. He, too, was wearing a bullet-proof vest. The first officer came over from the tollbooth.

Priest opened the glove compartment and took out the revolver he had stolen that morning from Los Alamos.

Then he got out of the car.

It took Judy only a few minutes to reach the Texaco gas station from which the phone call had been made. The Oakland police had moved fast. In the parking lot, four cruisers were parked at the corners of a square, facing inward, their blue roof lights flashing, their headlights illuminating a cleared landing space. The chopper came down.

Judy jumped out. A police sergeant greeted her. "Take me to the phone," she said. He led her inside. The pay phone was in a corner next to the rest rooms. Behind the counter were two clerks, a middle-aged black woman and a young white man with an earring. They looked scared. Judy asked the sergeant: "Have you questioned them at all?"

"Nope," he said. "Just told them it was a routine search."

They would have to be dumb to believe that, Judy thought,

with four police cars and an FBI helicopter outside. She introduced herself and said: "Did you notice anyone using that phone around"—she checked her watch—"fifteen minutes ago?"

The woman said: "A lot of people use the phone." Judy instantly got the sense that she did not like cops.

Judy looked at the young man. "I'm talking about a tall white man about fifty."

"There was a guy like that," he replied. He turned to the woman. "Didn't you notice him? He looked kind of like an old hippie."

"I never saw him," she replied stubbornly.

Judy produced the E-fit picture. "Could this be him?"

The young man looked dubious. "He didn't have glasses. And his hair was real long. That's why I thought he must be a hippie." He looked more closely. "It could be him, though."

The woman looked hard at the picture. "I remember now," she said. "I believe that is him. Skinny guy wearing a blue jean shirt."

"That's really helpful," Judy said gratefully. "Now, this question is really important. What kind of car was he driving?"

"I didn't look," the man said. "You know how many cars come through here every day? And it's dark now."

Judy looked at the woman, who shook her head sadly. "Honey, you're asking the wrong person—I can't tell the difference between a Ford and a Cadillac."

Judy could not hide her disappointment. "Hell," she said. She pulled herself together. "Thanks anyway, folks."

She stepped outside. "Any other witnesses?" she said to the sergeant.

"Nope. There may have been other customers in here at the same time, but they're long gone. Only those two work here."

Charlie Marsh came hurrying up with a mobile phone to

his ear. "Granger's been spotted," he said to Judy. "Two CHPs stopped him at the toll plaza at Carquinez Bridge."

"Incredible!" Judy said. Then something about Charlie's face made her realize the news could not be good. "We have him in custody?"

"No," Charlie said. "He shot them. They were wearing vests, but he shot them both in the head. He got away."

"Did we get a make on his car?"

"No. Tollbooth attendant didn't notice."

Judy could not keep the note of despair out of her voice. "Then he's got clean away?"

"Yeah."

"And the two Highway Patrol officers?"

"Both dead."

The police sergeant paled. "God rest their souls," he whispered.

Judy turned away, sick with disgust. "And God help us catch Ricky Granger," she said. "Before he kills anyone else."

17

Oaktree had done a great job of making the seismic vibrator look like a carnival ride.

The gaily painted red-and-yellow panels of The Dragon's Mouth completely concealed the massive steel plate,
the large vibrating engine, and the complex of tanks and
valves that controlled the machine. As Priest drove across
the state on Friday afternoon, from the foothills of the Sierra
Nevada through the Sacramento valley to the coastal range,
other drivers smiled and honked in a friendly way, and children waved from the rear windows of station wagons.

The Highway Patrol ignored him.

Priest drove the truck with Melanie beside him. Star and
Oaktree followed in the old 'Cuda. They reached Felicitas
in the early evening. The seismic window would open a few
minutes after seven P.M. It was a good time: Priest would
have twilight for his getaway. Plus, the FBI and the cops
had now been on alert for eighteen hours—they should be
getting tired, their reactions slow. They might already be
starting to believe there would be no earthquake.

He pulled off the freeway and stopped the truck. At the
end of the exit ramp there was a gas station and a Big Ribs
restaurant where several families were eating dinner. The
kids stared through the windows at the carnival ride. Next to
the restaurant was a field with five or six horses grazing;
then came a low glass office building. The road leading

from here into town was lined with houses, and Priest could also see a school and a small wood-frame building that looked like a Baptist chapel.

Melanie said: "The fault line runs right across Main Street."

"How can you tell?"

"Look at the sidewalk trees." There was a line of mature pines on the far side of the street. "The trees at the western end stand about five feet farther back than those to the east."

Sure enough, Priest saw that the line was broken about halfway along the street. West of the break, the trees grew in the middle of the sidewalk instead of at the curb.

Priest turned on the truck's radio. The John Truth show was just beginning. "Perfect," he said.

The newsreader said: "A top aide to Governor Mike Robson was abducted in Sacramento in a bizarre incident yesterday. The kidnapper accosted cabinet secretary Al Honeymoon in the parking garage of the Capitol Building, forced him to drive out of town, then abandoned him on I-80."

Priest said: "You notice they don't mention the Hammer of Eden? They know that was me in Sacramento. But they're trying to pretend it had nothing to do with us. They think they're preventing panic. They're wasting their time. In twenty minutes there's going to be the biggest panic California has ever seen."

"All right!" Melanie said. She was tense but excited, her face flushed, her eyes bright with hope and fear.

But, secretly, Priest was full of doubt. *Will it work this time? Only one way to find out.*

He put the truck in gear and drove down the hill.

The link road from the freeway looped around and joined the old country road leading into the town from the east. Priest swung onto Main Street. There was a coffee shop right on the fault line. Priest pulled onto the parking apron in front. The 'Cuda slid in beside the truck. "Go buy some doughnuts," he told Melanie. "Look natural."

She jumped out and sauntered across to the coffee shop.

Priest engaged the parking brake and flicked the switch that lowered the hammer of the seismic vibrator to the ground.

A uniformed cop came out of the coffee shop.

Priest said: "Shit."

The cop was carrying a paper bag and heading purposefully across the lot. Priest guessed he had stopped off to get coffee for himself and his partner. But where was the patrol car? Priest looked around and spotted the blue-and-white roof light of a car that was mostly concealed by a minivan. He had not noticed it as he drove in. He cursed himself for inattention.

But it was too late for regrets. The cop spotted the truck, changed direction, and came over to Priest's window.

"Hi, how you doin' today?" the cop said in a friendly tone. He was a tall, thin boy in his early twenties with short fair hair.

"I'm just fine," Priest said. *Small-town cops, they act like they're everyone's next-door neighbor.* "How are you?"

"You know you can't operate that ride without a permit, don't you?"

"Same everywhere," Priest told him. "But we're aiming to set up in Pismo Beach. We just stopped for coffee, same as you."

"Okay. Enjoy the rest of your day."

"You, too."

The cop walked off, and Priest shook his head in amazement. *If you realized who I am, buddy, you'd choke on your chocolate-frosted doughnut.*

He looked through the rear window and checked the dials of the vibrating mechanism. Everything was green.

Melanie reappeared. "Go get in the car with the others," Priest told her. "I'll be right there."

He set the machine to vibrate on a signal from the remote control, then jumped out, leaving the engine running.

Melanie and Star were in the backseat of the 'Cuda, sitting as far apart as they could: they were polite, but they could not hide their hostility to each other. Oaktree was at the wheel. Priest jumped into the front passenger seat. "Drive back up the hill to where we stopped before," he said.

Oaktree pulled away.

Priest turned on the radio and tuned to John Truth.

"Seven twenty-five on Friday evening, and the threat of an earthquake by the terrorist group the Hammer of Eden has failed to materialize, heaven be praised. What's the scariest thing that ever happened to *you*? Call John Truth now and tell us. It could be something dumb, like a mouse in your refrigerator, or maybe you were the victim of a robbery. Share your thoughts with the world, on *John Truth Live* tonight."

Priest turned to Melanie. "Call him on your cell phone."

"What if they trace the call?"

"It's a radio station, not the goddamn FBI, they can't trace calls. Go ahead."

"Okay." Melanie tapped out the number John Truth was repeating on the radio. "It's busy."

"Keep trying."

"This phone has automatic redial."

Oaktree stopped the car at the top of the hill, and they looked down on the town. Priest anxiously scanned the parking area in front of the coffee shop. The cops were still there. He did not want to start the vibrator while they were so close—one of them might have the presence of mind to jump into the cab and switch off the engine. "Those damn cops!" he muttered. "Why don't they go catch some criminals?"

"Don't say that—they might come after us," Oaktree joked.

"We're not criminals," Star said forcefully. "We're trying to save our country."

"Damn right," Priest said with a smile, and he punched the air.

"I mean it," she said. "In a hundred years' time, when

people look back, they'll say we were the rational ones, and the government was insane for letting America be destroyed by pollution. Like deserters in World War One—they were hated then, but nowadays everybody says the men who ran away were the only ones who weren't mad."

Oaktree said: "That's the truth."

The police cruiser pulled away from the coffee shop.

"I got through!" Melanie said. "I got through to— Hello? Yes, I'll hold for John Truth. . . . He says to turn off the radio, you guys. . . ." Priest snapped off the car radio. "I want to talk about the earthquake," Melanie went on, answering questions. "It's . . . Melinda. Oh! He's gone. Fuck, I nearly told him my name!"

"It wouldn't matter, there must be a million Melanies," Priest said. "Give me the phone."

She handed it over, and Priest put it to his ear. He heard a commercial for a Lexus dealership in San Jose. It seemed the station played the show to people waiting on hold. He watched the police cruiser come up the hill toward him. It went past the truck, pulled onto the freeway, and disappeared.

Suddenly he heard: "And Melinda wants to talk about the earthquake threat. Hello, Melinda, you're on *John Truth Live!*"

Priest said: "Hello, John, this isn't Melinda, it's the Hammer of Eden."

There was a pause. When Truth spoke again, his voice had taken on the portentous tone he used for announcements of great gravity. "Buddy, you better not be kidding, because if you are, you could go to jail, you know?"

"I guess I could go to jail if I'm *not* kidding," Priest said.

Truth did not laugh. "Why are you calling me?"

"We just want to be sure, this time, that everyone knows the earthquake was caused by us."

"When will it happen?"

"Within the next few minutes."

"Where?"

"I can't tell you that, because it might give the FBI the jump on us, but I'll tell you something no one could possibly guess. It will take place right on Route 101."

Raja Khan jumped on a table in the middle of the command post. "Everyone, shut up and listen!" he yelled. They all heard the shrill note of fear in his voice, and the room went dead. "A guy claiming to be from the Hammer of Eden is on *John Truth Live*."

There was a burst of noise as everyone asked questions. Judy stood up. "Quiet, everyone!" she shouted. "Raja, what did he say?"

Carl Theobald, who was sitting with his ear close to the speaker of a portable radio, answered her question. "He just said the next earthquake will take place on Route 101 within a few minutes."

"Well done, Carl! Turn up the volume." Judy swung around. "Michael—does that fit any of the locations we have under surveillance?"

"Nope," he said. "Shit, I guessed wrong!"

"Then guess again! Try to figure out where these people might be!"

"All right," he said. "Stop yelling." He sat at his computer and put his hand on the mouse.

On Carl Theobald's radio a voice said: "Here it comes now."

An alarm sounded on Michael's computer.

Judy said: "What's that? Is it a tremor?"

Michael clicked his mouse. "Wait, it's just coming on screen. . . . No, it's not a tremor. It's a seismic vibrator."

Judy looked over his shoulder. On the screen she saw a pattern just like the one he had shown her on Sunday. "Where is it?" she said. "Give me a location!"

"I'm working on it," he snapped back. "Shouting at me won't make the computer triangulate faster."

How could he be so damn touchy at a time like this? "Why is there no earthquake? Maybe their method isn't working!"

"In Owens Valley it didn't work the first time."

"I didn't know that."

"Okay, here are the coordinates."

Judy and Charlie Marsh went to the wall map. Michael sang out coordinates. "Here!" Judy said triumphantly. "Right on Route 101, south of San Francisco. A town called Felicitas. Carl, call the local police. Raja, notify the Highway Patrol. Charlie, I'm coming with you in the chopper."

"This is not pinpoint accurate," Michael warned. "The vibrator could be anywhere within a mile or so of the coordinates."

"How can we narrow it down?"

"If I look at the landscape, I can spot the fault line."

"You better come in the helicopter. Grab a bulletproof vest. Let's go!"

"It's not working!" Priest said, trying to control his alarm.

Melanie said: "It didn't work the first time in Owens Valley, don't you remember?" She sounded exasperated. "We had to move the truck and try again."

"Shit, I hope we have time," Priest said. "Drive, Oaktree! Back to the truck!"

Oaktree put the old car in drive and tore down the hill.

Priest turned and shouted to Melanie over the roar of the engine. "Where do you think we should move it to?"

"There's a side street almost opposite the coffee shop—go down there about four hundred yards. That's where the fault line runs."

"Okay."

Oaktree stopped the car in front of the coffee shop. Priest leaped out. A heavy middle-aged woman stood in front of him. "Did you hear that noise?" she said. "It seemed to be coming from your truck. It was earsplitting!"

"Get out of my way or I'll split your fucking head,"

Priest said. He jumped into the truck. He raised the plate, put the transmission in drive, and pulled away. He shot out onto the street in front of a big old station wagon. The wagon screeched to a halt, and the driver honked indignantly. Priest headed down the side street.

He drove four hundred yards and stopped outside a neat one-story house with a fenced garden. A small white dog barked fiercely at him through the fence. Working with feverish haste, he again lowered the plate of the vibrator and checked its dials. He set it to remote operation, jumped out, and got back into the 'Cuda.

Oaktree screeched around in a U-turn and tore off. As they raced along Main Street, Priest observed that their activities were beginning to attract attention. They were watched by a couple carrying shopping bags, two boys on mountain bikes, and three fat men who came out of a bar to see what was going on.

They came to the end of Main Street and turned up the hill. "This is far enough," Priest said. Oaktree stopped the car, and Priest activated the remote control.

He could hear the truck vibrating six blocks away.

Star said shakily: "Are we safe here?"

They were silent, frozen in suspense, waiting for the earthquake.

The truck vibrated for thirty seconds, then stopped.

"Too safe," Priest said to Star.

Oaktree said: "It ain't fucking working, Priest!"

"This happened last time," Priest said desperately. "It's gonna work!"

Melanie said: "You know what I think? The earth here is too soft. The town is close to the river. Soft, wet ground soaks up vibrations."

Priest turned to her accusingly. "Yesterday you told me earthquakes cause *more* damage on wet ground."

"I said that buildings on wet soil are more likely to be damaged, because the ground underneath them moves more.

But for transmitting shock waves to the fault, rock should be better."

"Skip the goddamn lecture!" Priest said. "Where do we try next?"

She pointed up the hill. "Where we came off the freeway. It's not directly on the fault line, but the ground should be rock."

Oaktree raised an eyebrow at Priest. Priest said: "Back to the truck, go!"

They raced back along Main Street, watched now by more people. Oaktree screeched into the side street and skidded to a halt next to the seismic vibrator. Priest jumped into the truck, raised the plate, and pulled away, flooring the gas pedal.

The truck moved with painful slowness through the town and crawled up the hill.

When it was halfway up, the police car they had seen earlier came off the freeway ramp, lights flashing and siren sounding, and sped past them, heading into town.

At last the truck arrived at the spot from which Priest had first looked over the town and pronounced it perfect. He stopped across the road from the Big Ribs restaurant. For the third time, he lowered the vibrator's plate.

Behind him he could see the 'Cuda. Coming back up the hill from the town was the police cruiser. Glancing up, he spotted a helicopter in the distant sky.

He had no time to get clear of the truck and use the remote. He would have to activate the vibrator sitting here in the driver's seat.

He put his hand on the control, hesitated, and pulled the lever.

From the helicopter, Felicitas looked like a town asleep.

It was a bright, clear evening. Judy could see Main Street and the grid of streets around it, the trees in the gardens and the cars in the driveways, but nothing seemed to be moving. A man watering flowers was so motionless, he seemed to be a statue; a woman in a big straw hat stood still on the sidewalk; three teenage girls on a street corner were frozen in place; two boys had stopped their bicycles in the middle of the road.

There was movement on the freeway that flew past the town on the elegant arches of a viaduct. As well as the usual mixture of cars and trucks, she spotted two police cruisers a mile or so away, approaching the town at high speed, coming, she assumed, in response to her emergency call.

But in the town no one moved.

After a moment she figured out what was going on.

They were listening.

The roar of the helicopter prevented her from hearing what they were listening to, but she could guess. It had to be the seismic vibrator.

But where was it?

The chopper flew low enough for her to identify the makes of cars parked on Main Street, but she could not see a vehicle big enough to be a seismic vibrator. None of the trees that partly obscured the side streets seemed big enough to hide a full-size truck.

She spoke to Michael over the headset. "Can you see the fault line?"

"Yes." He was studying a map and comparing it with the landscape beneath. "It crosses the railroad, the river, the freeway, and the gas pipeline. Dear God almighty, there's going to be some damage."

"But where's the vibrator?"

"What's that on the hillside?"

Judy followed his pointing finger. Above the town, close to the freeway, she saw a small cluster of buildings: a fast-food restaurant of some kind, a glass-walled office building, and a small wooden structure, probably a chapel. On the road near the restaurant were a mud-colored coupé that looked like an old muscle car from the early seventies, a police cruiser pulling up behind it, and a large truck painted all over with dragons in livid red and acid yellow. She made out the words "The Dragon's Mouth." "It's a carnival ride," she said.

"Or a disguise," he suggested. "That's about the right size for a seismic vibrator."

"My God, I bet you're right!" she said. "Charlie, are you listening?"

Charlie Marsh was sitting beside the pilot. Six members of his SWAT team were seated behind Judy and Michael, armed with stubby MP-5 submachine guns. The rest of the team were hurtling down the freeway in an armored truck, their mobile tactical operations center. "I'm listening," Charlie said. "Pilot, can you put us down near that carnival truck on the hill?"

"It's awkward," the pilot replied. "The hillside slopes steeply, and the road forms a narrow ledge. I'd rather come down in the parking lot of that restaurant."

"Do it," Charlie said.

"There isn't going to be an earthquake, is there?" the pilot said.

Nobody answered him.

As the chopper came down, a figure jumped out of the truck. Judy peered at it. She saw a tall, thin man with long dark hair, and she felt immediately that this had to be her enemy. He stared up at the chopper, and it seemed as if his eyes were on her. She was too far away to see his features clearly, but she felt sure he was Granger.

Stay right there, you son of a bitch, I'm coming to get you.

The helicopter hovered over the parking lot and began to descend.

Judy realized that she and everyone with her could die in the next few seconds.

As the helicopter touched the ground, there was a noise like the crack of doom.

*　*　*

The bang was a thunderclap so loud, it drowned the roar of the seismic vibrator and the thrash of the helicopter rotors.

The ground seemed to rise up and hit Priest like a fist. He was watching the chopper land in the Big Ribs parking lot, thinking that the vibrator was pounding away in vain, his scheme had failed, and he would now be arrested and thrown in jail. The next moment he was flat on his face, feeling as if he had been punched out by Mike Tyson.

He rolled over, gasping for breath, and saw the trees all around him bending and twisting as if a hurricane were blowing.

A moment later he came to his senses and realized—it had worked! He had caused an earthquake.

Yes!

And he was in the middle of it.

Then he was afraid for his life.

The air rang with a terrifying rumbling sound like rocks being shaken in a giant pail. He scrambled to his knees, but the ground would not stay still, and in trying to stand up, he fell over again.

Oh, shit, I'm done for.

He rolled over and managed to sit upright.

He heard a sound like a hundred windows breaking. Looking over to his right, he saw that was exactly what was happening. The glass walls of the office building were all shattering at the same time. A million shards of glass flowed like a waterfall off the building.

Yes!

The Baptist chapel farther down the road seemed to fall over sideways. It was a flimsy wooden building, and its thin walls went down in a cloud of dust and lay flat on the ground, leaving a massive carved-oak lectern standing in the middle of the wreckage.

I did it! I did it!

The windows of Big Ribs smashed, and the screams of terrified children pierced the air. One corner of the roof sagged, then dropped on a group of five or six teenagers, crushing them and their table and their rib dinners. The other patrons rose in a wave and surged toward the now-glassless windows as the rest of the roof started to come down on them.

The air was full of the pungent smell of gasoline. The tremor had ruptured the tanks at the filling station, Priest thought. He looked across and saw a sea of fuel spilling over the forecourt. An out-of-control motorcycle came off the road, weaving from side to side, until the rider fell off and the machine slid across the concrete, striking sparks. The spilling gas caught a light with a *whoosh,* and a second later the entire plaza was ablaze.

Jesus Christ!

The fire was frighteningly close to the 'Cuda. He could see the car rocking up and down, and the terrified face of Oaktree behind the wheel.

He had never seen Oaktree scared.

The horses from the field next to the restaurant burst through the broken fence and galloped full-tilt along the road toward Priest, eyes staring, mouths open, terrified. Priest had no time to get out of the way. He covered his head with his hands. They raced by either side of him.

Down in the town, the church bell was ringing madly.

The helicopter lifted again a second after it had touched down. Judy saw the ground beneath her shimmer like a block of Jell-O. Then it fell away fast as the chopper gained height. She gasped to see the glass walls of the little office building turn to something that looked like surf and fall in a great wave to the ground. She saw a motorcyclist crash into the filling station, and she cried out in grief as the gasoline caught on fire and the flames engulfed the fallen rider.

The helicopter swung around, and her view changed. Now she saw across the flat plain. In the distance, a freight train was crossing the fields. At first she thought it had

escaped damage, then she realized it was slowing harshly. It
had come off the rails, and as she watched, horrified, the
locomotive plowed into the field alongside the track. The
loaded wagons began to snake as they piled into the back of
the engine. Then the chopper swung around again, still
rising.

Now Judy could see the town. It was a shocking sight. Desperate, panicky people were running into the street, mouths
open in screams of terror that she could not hear, trying to
escape as their houses collapsed, walls cracking open and
windows exploding and roofs lurching terrifyingly sideways and falling into neat gardens and crushing cars in
driveways. Main Street seemed to be on fire and flooded
with water at the same time. Cars had crashed in the streets.
There was a flash like lightning, then another, and Judy
guessed power lines were snapping.

As the helicopter gained height, the freeway came into
view, and Judy's hands flew to her mouth in horror as she
saw that one of the giant arches supporting the viaduct had
twisted and snapped. The roadbed had cracked, and a
tongue of road now stuck out into midair. At least ten cars
had piled up on either side of the break, and several were on
fire. And the carnage was not over. Even as she watched, a
big old Chevrolet with fins hurtled toward the precipice,
skidding sideways as the driver tried in vain to stop. Judy
heard herself scream as the car flew off the edge. She could
see the terrified face of the driver, a young man, as he realized he was about to die. The car tumbled over and over in
the air, with ghastly slowness, and finally crashed on the
roof of a house below, bursting into flames and setting the
building on fire.

Judy buried her face in her hands. It was too dreadful to
watch. But then she remembered she was an FBI agent. She
forced herself to look again. Cars on the freeway were now
slowing early enough to stop before crashing, she saw. But
Highway Patrol vehicles and the SWAT truck that was on

its way would not be able to reach Felicitas from the freeway.

A sudden wind blew away the cloud of black smoke over the filling station, and Judy saw the man she thought was Ricky Granger.

You did this. You killed all these people. You piece of shit, I'm going to put you in jail if it's the last thing I do.

Granger struggled to his feet and ran to the brown coupé, shouting and gesticulating to the people inside.

The police cruiser was right behind the coupé, but the cops seemed slow to act.

Judy realized the terrorists were about to flee.

Charlie came to the same conclusion. "Go down, pilot!" he yelled through the headset.

"Are you out of your mind?" he shouted back.

"Those people did this!" Judy screamed, pointing over the pilot's shoulder. "They caused all this carnage and now they're getting away!"

"Shit," the pilot said, and the helicopter swooped toward the ground.

Priest yelled at Oaktree through the open window of the 'Cuda. "Let's get out of here!"

"Okay—which way?"

Priest pointed along the road that led to the town. "Take this road, but instead of going left into Main Street, turn right along the old country road—it leads back toward San Francisco, I checked."

"Okay!"

Priest saw the two local cops getting out of their cruiser.

He leaped into the truck, raised the plate, and pulled away, heaving on the steering wheel. Oaktree scorched a U-turn in the 'Cuda and headed down the hill. Priest turned the truck around more slowly.

One of the cops was standing in the middle of the road, pointing his gun at the truck. It was the thin youngster who had told Priest to enjoy the rest of his day. Now he was shouting: "Police! Stop!"

Priest drove right at him.

The cop let off a wild shot, then dived out of the way.

The road ahead skirted the town to the east, avoiding the worst of the damage, which was in the town center. Priest had to swing around a pair of crashed cars outside the destroyed glass office building, but after that the road looked clear. The truck picked up speed.

We're going to make it!

Then the FBI helicopter landed in the middle of the road a quarter of a mile ahead.

Shit.

Priest saw the 'Cuda screech to a halt.

Okay, assholes, you asked for it.

Priest floored the gas pedal.

Agents in SWAT gear, armed to the teeth, leaped out of the chopper one by one and began to take cover at the roadside.

Priest in his truck careered down the hill, gathering speed, and roared past the stopped 'Cuda.

"Now follow me," Priest muttered, hoping Oaktree would guess what was expected of him.

He saw Judy Maddox jump out of the chopper. A bullet-proof vest hid her graceful body, and she was holding a shotgun. She knelt behind a telegraph pole. A man tumbled out after her, and Priest recognized Melanie's husband, Michael.

Priest glanced in his side mirrors. Oaktree had the 'Cuda tucked in right behind him, making it a difficult target. He had not forgotten everything he had learned in the marines.

Behind the 'Cuda, a hundred yards back but going like a blue streak and gaining fast, was the police cruiser.

Priest's truck was twenty yards from the agents, heading straight for the chopper.

An FBI agent stood up at the roadside and aimed a stubby machine gun at the truck.

Jesus, I hope the feds don't have grenade launchers.
The chopper lifted off the ground.

Judy cursed. The helicopter pilot, bad at taking orders, had landed too close to the approaching vehicles. There was hardly time for the SWAT team and the other agents to spill out and take positions before the carnival truck was on them.

Michael staggered to the side of the road. "Lie flat!" Judy screamed at him. She saw the driver of the truck duck behind the dash as one of the SWAT team opened fire with his submachine gun. The windshield frosted, and holes appeared in the fenders and the hood, but the truck did not stop. Judy cried out with frustration.

She hastily aimed her M870 five-chamber shotgun and fired at the tires, but she was off balance and her shot went wide.

Then the truck was alongside her. All firing stopped: the agents were fearful of hitting one another.

The chopper was lifting out of the way—but then Judy saw, to her horror, that the pilot had been a split second too slow. The roof of the truck's cab clipped the undercarriage of the helicopter. The aircraft tilted suddenly.

The truck charged on, unaffected. The brown 'Cuda raced by, close behind the truck.

Judy fired wildly at the retreating vehicles.

We let them get by!

The helicopter seemed to wobble in midair as the pilot tried to correct its lurch. Then a rotor blade touched the ground.

"Oh, no!" Judy cried. "Please, no!"

The tail of the machine swung around and up. Judy could see the frightened expression of the pilot as he fought the controls. Then, suddenly, the helicopter nose-dived into the middle of the road. There was a heavy *crump!* of deforming metal and, immediately afterward, the musical crash of shattering glass. For a moment the chopper stood on its nose. Then it began to fall slowly sideways.

The pursuing police cruiser, traveling at maybe a hundred miles an hour, braked desperately, skidded, and smashed into the crashed helicopter.

There was a deafening bang, and both vehicles burst into flame.

Priest saw the crash in his side mirrors and let out a victory whoop. Now the FBI looked stuck: no helicopter, no cars. For the next few minutes they would be trying desperately to rescue the cops and the pilot from the wreckage in case they were still alive. By the time one of them thought of commandeering a car from a nearby house, Priest would be miles away.

He pushed out the frosted glass of his shot-up windshield without slowing the truck.

My God, I think we made it!

Behind him, the 'Cuda was swaying in a peculiar way. After a minute he figured it must have a flat. It was still traveling, so the flat must be a rear tire. Oaktree could keep going for a mile or two like that.

They reached the crossroads. Three cars had piled up at the junction: a Toyota minivan with a baby seat in the back, a battered Dodge pickup, and an old white Cadillac Coupe de Ville. Priest looked hard at them. None was badly damaged, and the minivan's engine was still running. He could not see the drivers anywhere. They must have gone looking for a phone.

He steered around the pileup and turned right, away from the town. He pulled up around the first bend. They were now more than a mile from the FBI team and well out of sight. He thought he was safe for a minute or two. He jumped out of the truck.

The 'Cuda pulled up behind, and Oaktree jumped out. He was grinning broadly. "Mission successfully completed, General!" he said. "I never saw anything like that in the goddamn military!"

Priest gave him a high five. "But we need to get away from the battlefield, and fast," he said.

Star and Melanie got out of the car. Melanie's cheeks were pink with exhilaration, almost as if she were sexually aroused. "My God, we did it, we did it!" she said.

Star bent over and threw up at the roadside.

Charlie Marsh was talking into a mobile phone. "The pilot is dead, and so are two local cops. There's a hell of a pileup on Route 101, which needs to be closed. Here in Felicitas we have car wrecks, fires, flooding, a busted gas pipeline, and a train wreck. You'll need to call in the Governor's Office of Emergency Management, no question."

Judy motioned for him to give her the phone.

He nodded to her and said into the mouthpiece: "Put one of Judy's people on the line." He handed her the phone.

"This is Judy, who's that?" she said rapidly.

"Carl. How the hell are you?"

"Okay, but mad at myself for losing the suspects. Put out a call for two vehicles. One is a truck painted with red and yellow dragons, looks like a carnival ride. The other is a brown Plymouth 'Cuda twenty-five or thirty years old. Also, send out another chopper to look for the vehicles on the roads leading from Felicitas." She looked up into the sky. "It's almost too dark already, but do it anyway. Any vehicle of either description should be stopped and the occupants questioned."

"And if one of them could conceivably fit the description of Granger . . . ?"

"Bring him in and nail him to the floor until I get there."

"What are you going to do?"

"I guess we'll commandeer some cars and come back to the office. Somehow . . ." She stopped and fought off a wave of exhaustion and despair. "Somehow, we've got to stop this from happening again."

* * *

"It's not over yet," Priest said. "In an hour or so, every cop in California will be looking for a carnival ride called 'The Dragon's Mouth.' " He turned to Oaktree. "How fast could we get these panels off?"

"In a few minutes, with a couple of good hammers."

"The truck has a tool kit."

Working fast, the two of them took the carnival panels off the truck and tossed them over a wire fence into a field. With luck, in the confusion following the earthquake, it would be a day or two before anyone took a close look at them.

"What the hell you going to tell Bones?" Oaktree said as they worked.

"I'll think of something."

Melanie helped, but Star stood with her back to them, leaning against the trunk of the 'Cuda. She was crying. She was going to make trouble, Priest knew, but there was no time to gentle her now.

When they had finished with the truck, they stood back, panting with the effort. Oaktree said worriedly: "Now the damn thing looks like a seismic vibrator again."

"I know," Priest said. "Nothing I can do about that. It's getting dark, I don't have far to go, and every cop within fifty miles is going to be conscripted into rescue work. I'm just hoping to be lucky. Now get out of here. Take Star."

"First I need to change a wheel—I have a flat."

"Don't bother," Priest said. "We gotta ditch the 'Cuda anyway. The FBI saw it, they'll be looking for it." He pointed back toward the crossroads. "I saw three vehicles back there. Grab yourself a new ride."

Oaktree hurried off.

Star looked at Priest with accusing eyes. "I can't believe we did this," she said. "How many people have we killed?"

"We had no choice," he said angrily. "You told me you'd do *anything* to save the commune—don't you remember?"

"But you're so calm about it. All these people killed,

more injured, families who have lost their homes—aren't you *heartsick*?"

"Sure."

"And her." She nodded at Melanie. "Look at her face. She's so up. My God, I think she *likes* all this."

"Star, we'll talk later, okay?"

She shook her head as if amazed. "I spent twenty-five years with you and never really knew you."

Oaktree came back driving the Toyota. "Nothing wrong with this but dents," he said.

Priest said to Star: "Go with him."

She hesitated for a long moment, then she got in the car. Oaktree pulled away and disappeared fast.

"Get in the truck," Priest said to Melanie. He got behind the wheel and reversed the seismic vibrator to the crossroads. They both jumped out and looked at the remaining two cars. Priest liked the look of the Cadillac. Its trunk was smashed in, but the front end was undamaged, and the keys were in the ignition. "Follow me in the Caddy," he said to Melanie.

She got in the car and turned the key. It started right away. She said: "Where are we headed?"

"Perpetua Diaries warehouse."

"Okay."

"Give me your phone."

"Who are you going to call? Not the FBI."

"No, just the radio station."

She handed over her phone.

As they were about to leave, there was a huge explosion in the distance. Priest looked back toward Felicitas and saw a jet of flame shoot high in the sky.

Melanie said: "Wow, what's that?"

The flame receded and became a bright glow in the evening sky.

"I guess the gas pipeline just caught on fire," Priest said. "Now, that's what I call fireworks."

* *- *

Michael Quercus was sitting on a patch of grass at the side of the road, looking shocked and helpless.

Judy went over to him. "Get up," she said. "Pull yourself together. People die every day."

"I know," he said. "It's not the killings—although they're enough. It's something else."

"What?"

"Did you see who was in the car?"

"The 'Cuda? There was a black guy driving it."

"But in the back?"

"I didn't notice anyone else."

"I did. A woman."

"Did you recognize her?"

"I sure did," he said. "It was my wife."

It took twenty minutes of redialing on Melanie's cell phone before Priest got through to the John Truth show. By the time he heard the ringing tone, he was on the outskirts of San Francisco.

The show was still on the air. Priest said he was from the Hammer of Eden and got connected right away.

"You have done a terrible thing," Truth said. He was using his most portentous voice, but Priest could tell that underneath the solemn tone the man was exultant. The earthquake had practically happened on his show. This would make him the most famous radio personality in America. Move over, Howard Stern.

"You're wrong," Priest told him. "The people who are turning California into a poison wasteland have done a terrible thing. I'm just trying to stop them."

"By killing innocent people?"

"Pollution kills innocent people. Automobiles kill innocent people. Call that Lexus dealer that advertises on your show and tell him he did a terrible thing selling five cars today."

There was a moment's silence. Priest grinned. Truth was not sure how to answer him. He could not start discussing the ethics of his sponsors. He quickly changed the subject. "I appeal to you to turn yourself in, right now."

"I have one thing to say to you and the people of California," Priest said. "Governor Robson must announce a statewide freeze on power plant building—otherwise there will be another earthquake."

"You would do this *again*?" Truth sounded genuinely shocked.

"You bet I would. And—"

Truth tried to interrupt him. "How can you claim—"

Priest overrode him. "—the next earthquake will be worse than this one."

"Where will it strike?"

"I can't tell you that."

"Can you say when?"

"Oh, sure. Unless the governor changes his mind, another earthquake will take place in two days' time." He paused for dramatic effect. "Exactly," he added.

He hung up.

"Now, Mister Governor," he said aloud. "Tell the people not to panic."

PART THREE

Forty-eight Hours

18

Judy and Michael got back to the emergency operations center a few minutes before midnight.

She had been awake for forty hours, but she did not feel sleepy. The horror of the earthquake was still with her. Every few seconds she would see, in her mind's eye, one of the nightmare pictures of those few seconds: the train wreck, the screaming people, the helicopter bursting into flames, or the old Chevy tumbling over and over in the air. She was spooked and jittery as she walked into the old officers' club.

But Michael's revelation had given her new hope. It was a shock to learn that his wife was one of the terrorists, but it was also the most promising lead yet. If Judy could find Melanie, she could find the Hammer of Eden.

And if she could do it in two days, she could prevent another earthquake.

She went into the old ballroom that had become the command post. Stuart Cleever, the big shot from Washington who had taken control, stood at the head shed. He was a neat, orderly guy, immaculately dressed in a gray suit with a white shirt and a striped tie.

Beside him stood Brian Kincaid.

The bastard has wormed his way back onto the case. He wants to impress the guy from Washington.

Brian was ready for her. "What the hell went wrong?" he said as soon as he saw her.

"We were too late, by a few seconds," she said wearily.

"You told us you had all the sites under surveillance," he snapped.

"We had the likeliest. But they knew that. So they picked a secondary site. It was a risk for them—more chance of failure—but their gamble paid off."

Kincaid turned to Cleever with a shrug, as if to say, *"Believe that and you'll believe anything."*

Cleever said to Judy: "As soon as you've made a full report, I want you to go home and get some rest. Brian will take charge of your team."

I knew it. Kincaid has poisoned Cleever against me.

Time to go for broke.

Judy said: "I'd like a break, but not just yet. I believe I will have the terrorists under arrest within twelve hours."

Brian let out an exclamation of surprise.

Cleever said: "How?"

"I've just developed a new lead. I know who their seismologist is."

"Who?"

"Her name is Melanie Quercus. She's the estranged wife of Michael, who's been helping us. She got the information about where the fault is under tension from her husband— stole it off his computer. And I suspect she also stole the list of sites we had under surveillance."

Kincaid said: "Quercus should be a suspect, too! He could be in cahoots with her!"

Judy had anticipated this. "I'm sure he's not," she said. "But he's taking a lie detector test right now, just to make sure."

"Good enough," Cleever said. "Can you find the wife?"

"She told Michael she was living in a commune in Del Norte County. My team are already searching our databases for communes there. We have a two-man resident agency in that neighborhood, in a town called Eureka, and I've asked them to contact the local police."

Cleever nodded. He gave Judy an appraising look. "What do you want to do?"

"I'd like to drive up there now. I'll sleep on the way. By the time I get there the local guys will have the addresses of all communes in the area. I'd like to raid them all at dawn."

Brian said: "You don't have enough evidence for search warrants."

He was right. The mere fact that Melanie had said she was living in a commune in Del Norte County did not constitute probable cause. But Judy knew the law better than Brian. "After two earthquakes, I think we have exigent circumstances, don't you?" That meant that people's lives were in danger.

Brian looked baffled, but Cleever understood. "The legal desk can solve that problem, it's what they're here for." He paused. "I like this plan," he said. "I think we should do it. Brian, do you have any other comment?"

Kincaid looked sulky. "She better be right, that's all."

Judy rode north in a car driven by a woman agent she did not know, one of several dozen drafted in from FBI offices in Sacramento and Los Angeles to help in the crisis.

Michael sat beside Judy in the back. He had begged to come. He was worried sick about Dusty. If Melanie was part of a terrorist group causing earthquakes, what kind of danger might their son be in? Judy had got Cleever's agreement by arguing that someone had to take care of the boy after Melanie was arrested.

Shortly after they crossed the Golden Gate Bridge, Judy took a call from Carl Theobald. Michael had told them which of the five hundred or so American cell-phone companies Melanie used, and Carl had got hold of her call records. The phone company had been able to identify the general area from which each call had been made, because of roaming charges.

Judy was hoping most of them had been made from Del Norte County, but she was disappointed.

"There's really no pattern at all," Carl said wearily. "She made calls from the Owens Valley area, from San Francisco, from Felicitas, and from various places in between; but all that tells us is that she's been traveling all over the state, and we knew that already. There are no calls from the part of the state you're headed for."

"That suggests she has a regular phone there."

"Or she's cautious."

"Thanks, Carl. It was worth a try. Now get some sleep."

"You mean this isn't a dream? Shit."

Judy laughed and hung up.

The driver tuned the car radio to an easy-listening station, and Nat Cole sang "Let There Be Love" as they sped through the night. Judy and Michael could talk without being overheard.

"The terrible thing about it is that I'm not surprised," Michael said after a thoughtful silence. "I guess I sort of always knew Melanie was crazy. I should never have let her take him away—but she's his mother, you know?"

Judy reached for his hand in the dark. "You did your best, I guess," she said.

He squeezed her hand gratefully. "I just hope he's okay now."

"Yeah."

Drifting off to sleep, Judy kept hold of his hand.

They all met up at five A.M. in the Eureka office of the FBI. As well as the local resident agents, there were representatives from the town's police department and the county sheriff's office. The FBI always liked to involve local law enforcement personnel in a raid—it was a way of maintaining good relations with people whose help they often needed.

There were four residential communes in Del Norte

County listed in *Communities Directory: A Guide to Cooperative Living*. The FBI database had revealed a fifth, and local knowledge had added two more.

One of the local FBI agents pointed out that the commune known as Phoenix Village was only eight miles from the site of a proposed nuclear power plant. Judy's pulse accelerated when she heard that, and she led the group that raided Phoenix.

As she approached the location, in a Del Norte County sheriff's cruiser at the head of a convoy of four cars, her tiredness fell away. She felt keen and energetic again. She had failed to prevent the Felicitas earthquake, but she could make sure there was not another.

The entrance to Phoenix was a side turning off a country road, marked by a neat painted sign showing a bird rising from flames. There was no gate or guard. The cars roared into the settlement on a well-made road and pulled up around a traffic circle. The agents leaped out of the cars and fanned out through the houses. Each had a copy of the picture of Melanie and Dusty that Michael kept on his desk.

She's here, somewhere, probably in bed with Ricky Granger, sleeping after the exertions of yesterday. I hope they're having bad dreams.

The village looked peaceful in the early light. There were several barnlike buildings plus a geodesic dome. The agents covered front and back entrances before knocking on the doors. Near the traffic circle, Judy found a map of the village painted on a board, listing the houses and other buildings. There was a shop, a massage center, a mailroom, and an auto repair shop. As well as fifteen houses, the map showed pasture, orchards, playgrounds, and a sports field.

It was cool in the morning this far north, and Judy shivered, wishing she had worn something heavier than her linen pantsuit.

She waited for the shout of triumph that would tell her an agent had identified Melanie. Michael paced around the traffic circle, his whole body stiff with tension. *What a shock, to learn that your wife has become a terrorist, the kind of person a cop would shoot and everyone would cheer. No wonder he's tense. It's a miracle he isn't banging his head against the wall.*

Next to the map was a village notice board. Judy read about a folk dance workshop that was being organized to raise funds for the Expanding Light Fireplace fund. These people had an air of harmlessness that was remarkably plausible.

The agents entered every building and looked in every room, moving rapidly from house to house. After a few minutes a man came out of one of the larger houses and walked across to the traffic circle. He was about fifty, with disheveled hair and beard, wearing homemade leather sandals and a rough blanket around his shoulders. He said to Michael: "Are you in charge here?"

Judy said: "I'm in charge."

He turned to her. "Would you please tell me what the hell is going on?"

"I'd be glad to," she said crisply. "We're looking for this woman." She held out the photo.

The man did not take it from her. "I've already seen that," he said. "She's not one of us."

Judy had a depressing feeling that he was telling the truth.

"This is a religious community," he said with mounting indignation. "We're law-abiding citizens. We don't use drugs. We pay our taxes and obey local ordinances. We don't deserve to be treated like criminals."

"We just have to be sure this woman is not hiding out here."

"Who is she, and why do you think she's here? Or is it just that you assume people who live in communes are suspect?"

"No, we don't make that assumption," Judy said. She

was tempted to snap at the guy, but she reminded herself that *she* had woken *him* up at six o'clock in the morning. "This woman is part of a terrorist group. She told her estranged husband she was living in a commune in Del Norte County. We're sorry we have to wake up everyone in every commune in the county, but I hope you can understand that it is very important. If it wasn't, we wouldn't have disturbed you, and, frankly, we wouldn't have put ourselves to so much trouble."

He looked at her keenly, then nodded, his attitude changing. "Okay," he said. "I believe you. Is there anything I can do to make your job easier?"

She thought for a moment. "Is every building in your community marked on this map?"

"No," he said. "There are three new houses on the west side just beyond the orchard. But please try to be quiet—there's a new baby in one of them."

"Okay."

Sally Dobro, a middle-aged woman agent, came up. "I think we've checked every building here," she said. "There's no sign of any of our suspects."

Judy said: "There are three houses west of the orchard—did you find those?"

"No," Sally said. "Sorry. I'll do it right away."

"Go quietly," Judy said. "There's a new baby in one."

"You got it."

Sally went off, and the man in the blanket nodded his appreciation.

Judy's mobile phone rang. She answered and heard the voice of Agent Frederick Tan. "We've just checked out every building in the Magic Hill commune. Zilch."

"Thanks, Freddie."

In the next ten minutes the other raid leaders called her.

They all had the same message.

Melanie Quercus was not to be found.

Judy sank into a pit of despair. "Hell," she said. "I screwed it up."

Michael was equally dismayed. He said fretfully: "Do you think we've missed a commune?"

"Either that, or she lied about the location."

He looked thoughtful. "I'm just remembering the conversation," he said. "I asked *her* where she was living, but *he* answered the question."

Judy nodded. "I think he lied. He's smart like that."

"I've just remembered his name," Michael said. "She called him Priest."

19

On Saturday morning at breakfast, Dale and Poem stood up in the cookhouse in front of everyone and asked for quiet. "We have an announcement," Poem said.

Priest thought she must be pregnant again. He got ready to cheer and clap and make the short congratulatory speech that would be expected of him. He felt full of exuberance. Although he had not yet saved the commune, he was close. His opponent might not be out for the count, but he was down on the canvas, struggling to stay in the fight.

Poem hesitated, then looked at Dale. His face was solemn. "We're leaving the commune today," he said.

There was a shocked silence. Priest was dumbstruck. People did not leave, not unless he wanted them to. These folk were under his spell. And Dale was the oenologist, the key man in winemaking. They could not afford to lose him.

And today of all days! If Dale had heard the news—as Priest had, an hour ago, sitting in a stationary car listening to the radio—he would know that California was in a panic. The airports were mobbed, and the freeways were jammed with people fleeing the cities and all neighborhoods close to the San Andreas fault. Governor Robson had called out the National Guard. The vice president was on a plane, coming to inspect the damage at Felicitas. More and more people— state senators and assemblymen, city mayors, community leaders, and journalists—were urging the governor to give in to the demand made by the Hammer of Eden. But Dale knew nothing of all this.

Priest was not the only one to be shocked by the announcement. Apple burst into tears, and at that Poem started crying, too. Melanie was the first to speak. She said: "But Dale—why?"

"You know why," he said. "This valley is going to be flooded."

"But where will you go?"

"Rutherford. It's in Napa Valley."

"You have a regular job?"

Dale nodded. "In a winery."

It was no surprise that Dale had been able to get a job, Priest thought. His expertise was priceless. He would probably make big money. The surprise was that he wanted to go back to the straight world.

Several of the women were crying now. Song said: "Can't you wait and hope, like the rest of us?"

Poem answered her tearfully. "We have three children. We have no right to take risks with their lives. We can't stay here, hoping for a miracle, until the waters start rising around our homes."

Priest spoke for the first time. "This valley is not going to be flooded."

"You don't know that," Dale said.

The room went quiet. It was unusual for someone to contradict Priest so directly.

"This valley is not going to be flooded," Priest repeated.

Dale said: "We all know that something's been going on, Priest. In the last six weeks you've been away more than you've been home. Yesterday four of you were out until midnight, and this morning there's a dented Cadillac up there in the parking circle. But whatever you're up to, you haven't shared it with us. And I can't risk the future of my children on your faith. Shirley feels the same."

Poem's real name was Shirley, Priest recalled. For Dale

to use it meant he was already detaching himself from the commune.

"I'll tell you what will save this valley," Priest said. *Why not tell them about the earthquake—why not? They should be pleased—proud!* "The power of prayer. Prayer will save us."

"I'll pray for you," Dale said. "So will Shirley. We'll pray for all of you. But we're not staying."

Poem wiped her tears on her sleeve. "I guess that's it. We're sorry. We packed last night, not that we have much. I hope Slow will drive us to the bus station in Silver City."

Priest stood up and went to them. He put one arm around Dale's shoulders and the other around Poem's. Hugging them to him, he said in a low, persuasive voice: "I understand your pain. Let's all go to the temple and meditate together. After that, whatever you decide to do will be the right thing."

Dale moved away, detaching himself from Priest's embrace. "No," he said. "Those days are gone."

Priest was shocked. He was using his full persuasive power, and it was not working. Fury rose inside him, dangerously uncontrollable. He wanted to scream at Dale's faithlessness and ingratitude. He would have killed them both if he could. But he knew that showing his anger would be a mistake. He had to maintain the facade of calm control.

However, he could not summon up the grit to bid them a gracious farewell. Torn between rage and the need for restraint, he walked silently, with as much dignity as he could muster, out of the cookhouse.

He returned to his cabin.

Two more days and it would have been okay. One day!

He sat on the bed and lit a cigarette. Spirit lay on the floor, watching him mournfully. They were both silent and still, brooding. Melanie would follow him in a minute or two.

But it was Star who came in.

She had not spoken to him since she and Oaktree had driven away from Felicitas last night in the Toyota minivan.

He knew she was angered and distressed by the earthquake. He had not yet had time to talk her down.

She said: "I'm going to the police."

Priest was astonished. Star loathed cops passionately. For her to enter a precinct house would be like Billy Graham going to a gay club. "You're out of your mind," he said.

"We killed people yesterday," she said. "I listened to the radio on the drive back. At least twelve people died, and more than a hundred were hospitalized. Babies and children were hurt. People lost their homes, everything they had—poor people, not just rich. And we did that to them."

Everything is falling apart—just when I'm about to win!

He reached for her hand. "Do you think I *wanted* to kill people?"

She backed away, refusing to take his hand. "You sure as hell didn't look sad when it happened."

I've got to hold it together for just a little longer. I must.

He made himself look penitent. "I was happy the vibrator worked, yes. I was glad we were able to carry out our threat. But I didn't intend to hurt anyone. I knew there was a risk, and I decided to take it, because what was at stake was so important. I thought you made the same decision."

"I did, and it was a bad decision, a wicked decision." Tears came to her eyes. "For Christ's sake, can't you see what's happened to us? We were the kids who believed in love and peace—now we're killing people! You're just like Lyndon Johnson. He bombed the Vietnamese and justified it. We said he was full of shit, and he was. I've dedicated my whole life to *not* being like that!"

"So you feel you made a mistake," Priest said. "I can understand that. What's hard for me to dig is that you want to redeem yourself by punishing me and the whole commune. You want to betray us to the cops."

She was taken aback. "I hadn't looked at it that way," she said. "I don't want to punish anyone."

He had her now. "So what do you really want?" He did

not give her time to answer for herself. "I think you need to be sure it's over."

"I guess so, yeah."

He reached out to her, and this time she let him hold her hands. "It's over," he said softly.

"I don't know," she said.

"There will be no more earthquakes. The governor will give in. You'll see."

Speeding back to San Francisco, Judy was diverted to Sacramento for a meeting at the governor's office. She grabbed another three or four hours' sleep in the car, and when she arrived at the Capitol Building she felt ready to bite the world.

Stuart Cleever and Charlie Marsh had flown there from San Francisco. The head of the FBI's Sacramento office joined them. They met at noon in the conference room of the Horseshoe, the governor's suite. Al Honeymoon was in the chair.

"There's a twelve-mile traffic jam on I-80 with people trying to get away from the San Andreas fault," Honeymoon said. "The other major freeways are almost as bad."

Cleever said: "The president called the director of the FBI and asked him about public order." He looked at Judy as if all this was her fault.

"He called Governor Robson, too," Honeymoon said.

"As of this moment, we do not have a serious public order problem," Cleever said. "There are reports of looting in three neighborhoods in San Francisco and one in Oakland, but it's sporadic. The governor has called out the National Guard and stationed them in the armories, although we don't need them yet. However, if there should be another earthquake . . ."

The thought made Judy feel ill. "There can't be another earthquake," she said.

They all looked at her. Honeymoon made a sardonic face. "You have a suggestion?"

She did. It was a poor one, but they were desperate.

"There's only one thing I can think of," she said. "Set a trap for him."

"How?"

"Tell him Governor Robson wants to negotiate with him personally."

Cleever said: "I don't believe he'd fall for it."

"I don't know." Judy frowned. "He's smart, and any smart person would suspect a trap. But he's a psychopath, and they just love controlling others, calling attention to themselves and their actions, manipulating people and circumstances. The idea of personally negotiating with the governor of California is going to tempt him mightily."

Honeymoon said: "I guess I'm the only person here who's met him."

"That's right," Judy said. "I've seen him, and spoken to him on the phone, but you spent several minutes in a car with him. What was your impression?"

"You've summed him up about right—a smart psychopath. I believe he was angry with me for not being more impressed by him. Like I should have been, I don't know, more deferential."

Judy suppressed a grin. Honeymoon did not defer to many people.

Honeymoon went on: "He understood the political difficulties of what he was asking for. I told him the governor could not give in to blackmail. He'd thought of that already, and he had his answer prepared."

"What was it?"

"He said we could deny what really happened. Announce a freeze on power plant building and say it had nothing to do with the earthquake threat."

"Is that a possibility?" Judy said.

"Yes. I wouldn't recommend it, but if the governor put it to me as a plan, I'd have to say it could be made to work. However, the question is academic. I know Mike Robson, and he won't do it."

"But he could pretend," Judy said.

"What do you mean?"

"We could tell Granger the governor is willing to announce the freeze, but only under the right conditions, as he has to protect his political future. He wants to talk personally with Granger to agree to those conditions."

Stuart Cleever put in: "The Supreme Court has ruled that law enforcement personnel may use trickery, ruse, and deceit. The only thing we're not permitted to do is threaten to take away the suspect's children. And if we promise immunity from prosecution, it sticks—we can't prosecute. But we can certainly do what Judy suggests without violating any laws."

"Okay," Honeymoon said. "I don't know if this is going to work, but I guess we have to try. Let's do it."

Priest and Melanie drove into Sacramento in the dented Cadillac. It was a sunny Saturday afternoon, and the town was thronged with people.

Listening to the car radio soon after midday, Priest had heard the voice of John Truth, although it was not time for his show. "Here is a special message for Peter Shoebury of Eisenhower Junior High," Truth had said. Shoebury was the man whose identity Priest had borrowed for the FBI press conference, and Eisenhower was the imaginary school attended by Flower. Priest realized the message was for him. "Would Peter Shoebury please call me at the following number," Truth had said.

"They want to make a deal," he had said to Melanie "That's it—we've won!"

While Melanie drove around downtown, surrounded by hundreds of cars and thousands of people, Priest made the call from her mobile phone. Even if the FBI was tracing the call, he figured, they would not be able to pick one car out of the traffic.

His heart was in his mouth as he listened to the ringing tone. *I won the lottery and I'm here to pick up my check.*

The call was answered by a woman. "Hello?" She sounded guarded. Maybe she had received a lot of crank calls in response to the radio spot.

"This is Peter Shoebury from Eisenhower Junior High."

The response was instant. "I'm going to connect you with Al Honeymoon, the governor's cabinet secretary."

Yes!

"I just need to verify your identity first."

It's a trick. "How do you propose to do that?"

"Would you mind giving me the name of the student reporter who was with you a week ago?"

Priest remembered Flower saying, "I'll never forgive you for calling me Florence."

Warily he said: "It was Florence."

"Connecting you now."

No trick—just a precaution.

Priest scanned the streets anxiously, alert for a police car or a bunch of FBI men bearing down on his car. He saw nothing but shoppers and tourists. A moment later the deep voice of Honeymoon said: "Mr. Granger?"

Priest got right to the point. "Are you ready to do the sensible thing?"

"We're ready to talk."

"What does that mean?"

"The governor wants to meet with you today, with the object of negotiating a resolution to this crisis."

Priest said: "Is the governor willing to announce the freeze we want?"

Honeymoon hesitated. "Yes," he said reluctantly. "But there must be conditions."

"What kind?"

"When you and I spoke in my car, and I told you that the governor could not give in to blackmail, you mentioned spin doctors."

"Yes."

"You're a sophisticated individual, you understand that the governor's political future is at risk here. The announcement of this freeze will have to be handled very delicately."

Honeymoon had changed his tune, Priest thought with satisfaction. The arrogance was gone. He had developed respect for his opponent. That was gratifying. "In other words, the governor has to cover his ass and he wants to make sure I won't blow it for him."

"You might look at it that way."

"Where do we meet?"

"In the governor's office here at the Capitol Building."

You're out of your frigging mind.

Honeymoon went on: "No police, no FBI. You would be guaranteed freedom to leave the meeting without hindrance, regardless of the outcome."

Yeah, right.

Priest said: "Do you believe in fairies?"

"What?"

"You know, little flying people that can do magic? You believe they exist?"

"No, I guess I don't."

"Me either. So I'm not going to fall into your trap."

"I give you my word—"

"Forget it. Just forget it, okay?"

There was silence at the other end.

Melanie turned a corner, and they drove past the grand classical facade of the Capitol Building. Honeymoon was in there somewhere, talking on the phone, surrounded by FBI men. Looking at the white columns and the dome, Priest said: "I'll tell you where we'll meet, and you'd better make notes. Are you ready?"

"Don't worry, I'm taking notes."

"Set up a little round table and a couple of garden chairs in front of the Capitol Building, on the lawn there, right in the middle. It'll be like a photo opportunity. Have the governor sitting there at three o'clock."

"Out in the open?"

"Hey, if I was going to shoot him, I could do it easier than this."

"I guess so. . . ."

"In his pocket the governor must have a signed letter guaranteeing me immunity from prosecution."

"I can't agree to all this—"

"Talk to your boss. He'll agree."

"I'll talk to him."

"Have a photographer there with one of them instant cameras. I want a picture of him handing me the letter of immunity, for proof. Got that?"

"Got it."

"You better play this straight. No tricks. My seismic vibrator is already in place, ready to trigger another earthquake. This one will strike a major city. I'm not saying which one, but I'm talking thousands of deaths."

"I understand."

"If the governor doesn't appear today at three o'clock . . . *bang*."

He broke the connection.

"Wow," said Melanie. "A meeting with the governor. Do you think it's a trap?"

Priest frowned. "It might be," he said. "I don't know. I just don't know."

Judy could not fault the setup. Charlie Marsh had worked on it with the Sacramento FBI. There were at least thirty agents within sight of the white garden table with the umbrella that sat prettily on the lawn, but she could not see any of them. Some stood behind the windows of the surrounding government offices, others crouched in cars and vans on the street and in the parking lot, more lurked in the pillared cupola of the Capitol Building. All were heavily armed.

Judy herself was playing the part of the photographer, with cameras and lenses around her neck. Her gun was in a camera bag slung from her shoulder. While she waited for the governor to appear, she looked through her viewfinder at the table and chairs, pretending to frame a shot.

In the hopes Granger wouldn't recognize her, she wore a blond wig. It was one she kept permanently in her car. She used it a lot on surveillance work, especially if she spent several days following the same targets, to reduce the risk that she might be noticed and recognized. She had to put up with a certain amount of teasing when she wore it. *Hey, Maddox, send the cute blonde over to my car, but you can stay where you are.*

Granger was watching, she knew. No one had spotted him, but he had called, an hour ago, to protest against the erection of crowd barriers around the block. He wanted the public using the street, and visitors touring the building, just as normal.

The barriers had been taken away.

There was no other fence around the grounds, so tourists were wandering freely across the lawns, and tour parties were following their prescribed routes around the Capitol, its gardens, and the elegant government buildings on adjacent streets. Judy surreptitiously studied everyone through her lens. She ignored superficial appearances and concentrated on features that could not easily be disguised. She scrutinized every tall, thin man of middle age, regardless of hair, face, or dress.

At one minute to three she still had not seen Ricky Granger.

Michael Quercus, who had met Granger face-to-face, was also watching. He was in a surveillance van with blacked-out windows parked around the corner. He had to stay out of sight, for fear Granger would recognize him and be spooked.

Judy spoke into a little microphone under her shirt,

clipped to her bra. "My guess is that Granger won't show until after the governor appears."

A tiny speaker behind her ear crackled, and she heard Charlie Marsh reply. "We were just saying the same thing. I wish we could have got this done without exposing the governor."

They had talked about using a body double, but Governor Robson himself had nixed that plan, saying he would not allow someone else to risk dying in his place.

Now Judy said: "But if we can't . . ."

"So be it," said Charlie.

A moment later the governor emerged from the grand front entrance of the building.

Judy was surprised that he was a little below average height. Seeing him on television, she had imagined him a tall man. He looked bulkier than usual on account of the bulletproof vest under his suit coat. He walked across the lawn with a relaxed, confident stride and sat at the little table under the umbrella.

Judy took a few pictures of him. She kept her camera bag slung from her shoulder so that she could get to her weapon quickly.

Then, out of the corner of her eye, she saw movement.

An old Chevrolet Impala was approaching slowly on Tenth Street.

It had a faded two-tone paint job, sky blue and cream, rusting around the wheel arches. The face of the driver was in shade.

She darted a glance around. Not a single agent was in sight, but everyone would be watching the car.

It stopped at the curb right opposite Governor Robson.

Judy's heart beat faster.

"I guess this is him," said the governor in a remarkably calm voice.

The door of the car opened.

The figure that stepped out wore blue jeans, a checked

workshirt open over a white T-shirt, and sandals. When he stood upright, Judy saw that he was about six feet tall, maybe a little more, and thin, with long, dark hair.

He wore large-framed sunglasses and a colorful cotton scarf as a headband.

Judy stared at him, wishing she could see his eyes.

Her earpiece crackled. "Judy? Is it him?"

"I can't tell!" she said. "It could be."

He looked around. It was a big lawn, and the table had been placed twenty or thirty yards back from the curb. He started toward the governor.

Judy could feel everyone's eyes on her, waiting for her sign.

She moved, placing herself between him and the governor. The man noticed her move, hesitated, then continued walking.

Charlie spoke again. "Well?"

"I don't know!" she whispered, trying not to move her lips. "Give me a few more seconds!"

"Don't take too long."

"I don't think it's him," Judy said. All the pictures had shown a nose like the blade of a knife. This man had a broad, flat nose.

"Sure?"

"It's not him."

The man was within touching distance of Judy. He stepped around her and approached the governor. Without pausing in his stride, he put his hand inside his shirt.

In her earpiece Charlie said: "He's reaching for something!"

Judy dropped to one knee and fumbled for the pistol in her camera bag.

The man began to pull something out of his shirt. Judy saw a dark-colored cylinder, like the barrel of a gun. She yelled: "Freeze! FBI!"

Agents burst out of cars and vans and came running from the Capitol Building.

The man froze.

Judy pointed her gun at his head and said: "Pull it out real slow and pass it to me."

"Okay, okay, don't shoot me!" The man drew the object out of his shirt. It was a magazine, rolled up into a cylinder, with a rubber band around it.

Judy took it from him. Still pointing her gun at him, she examined the magazine. It was this week's *Time*. There was nothing inside the cylinder.

The man said in a frightened voice: "Some guy gave me a hundred dollars to hand it to the governor!"

Agents surrounded Mike Robson and bundled him back into the Capitol Building.

Judy looked around, scanning the grounds and the streets. *Granger is watching this, he has to be. Where the hell is he?* People had stopped to stare at the running agents. A tour group was coming down the steps of the grand entrance, led by a guide. As Judy watched, a man in a Hawaiian shirt peeled off from the group and walked away, and something about him caught Judy's eye.

She frowned. He was tall. Because the shirt was baggy and hung loose around his hips, she could not tell whether he was thin or fat. His hair was covered by a baseball cap.

She went after him, walking fast.

He did not seem to be in a hurry. Judy did not raise the alarm. If she got every agent here chasing some innocent tourist, that might permit the real Granger to get away. But instinct made her quicken her pace. She had to see this man's face.

He turned the corner of the building. Judy broke into a run.

She heard Charlie's voice in her earpiece. "Judy? What's up?"

"Just checking someone out," she said, panting a little. "Probably a tourist, but get a couple of guys to follow me in case I need backup."

"You got it."

She reached the corner and saw the Hawaiian shirt pass

through a pair of tall wood doors and disappear into the Capitol Building. It seemed to her that he was walking more briskly. She looked back over her shoulder. Charlie was talking to a couple of youngsters and pointing at her.

On the side street across the garden, Michael jumped out of a parked van and came running toward her. She pointed into the building. "Did you see that guy?" she yelled.

"Yes, that was him!" he called back.

"You stay here," she shouted. He was a civilian; she did not want him involved. "Keep the hell out of this!" She ran into the Capitol Building.

She found herself in a grand lobby with an elaborate mosaic floor. It was cool and quiet. Ahead of her was a broad carpeted staircase with an ornately carved balustrade. Did he go left or right, up or down? She chose left. The corridor dog-legged right. She raced past an elevator bank and found herself in the rotunda, a circular room with some kind of sculpture in the middle. The room extended up two floors to a richly decorated dome. Here she faced another choice: had he gone straight ahead, turned right toward the Horseshoe, or gone up the stairs on her left? She looked around. A tour group stared fearfully at her gun. She glanced up to the circular gallery at second-floor level and caught a glimpse of a brightly colored shirt.

She bounded up one of the paired grand staircases.

At the top of the stairs she looked across the gallery. On the far side was an open doorway leading to a different world, a modern corridor with strip lighting and a plastic-tiled floor. The Hawaiian shirt was in the corridor.

He was running now.

Judy went after him. As she ran, she spoke into her bra mike, panting. "It's him, Charlie! What the hell happened to my backup?"

"They lost you, where are you?"

"On the second floor in the office section."

"Okay."

The office doors were shut, and there was no one in the corridors: it was Saturday. She followed the shirt around a corner, then another, and a third. She was keeping him in view but not gaining on him.

The bastard is very fit.

Coming full circle, he returned to the gallery. She lost sight of him momentarily and guessed he had gone up again.

Breathing hard, she went up another ornate staircase to the third floor.

Helpful signs told her that the senate gallery was to her right, the assembly to her left. She turned left, came to the door of the gallery, and found it locked. No doubt the other would be the same. She returned to the head of the staircase. Where had he gone?

In a corner she noticed a sign that read "North Stair—No Roof Access." She opened it and found herself in a narrow functional stairwell with plain floor tiles and an iron balustrade. She could hear her quarry clattering down the stairs, but she could not see him.

She hurtled down.

She emerged at ground level in the rotunda. She could not see Granger, but she spotted Michael, looking around distractedly. He caught her eye. "Did you see him?" she called.

"No."

"Stay back!"

From the rotunda, a marble corridor led to the governor's quarters. Her view was obscured by a tour party being shown the door to the Horseshoe. Was that a Hawaiian shirt beyond them? She was not sure. She ran after it, along the marble hall, past framed displays featuring each county in the state. To her left, another corridor led to an exit with a plate-glass automatic door. She saw the shirt going out.

She followed. Granger was darting across L Street, dodging perilously through the impatient traffic. Drivers swerved to avoid him and honked indignantly. He jumped on the hood of a yellow coupé, denting it. The driver opened the door and leaped out in a rage, then saw Judy with her gun and hastily got back in his car.

She sprinted across the street, taking the same mad risks with the traffic. She darted in front of a bus that pulled up with a screech of brakes, ran across the hood of the same yellow coupé, and forced a stretch limousine to swerve across three lanes. She was almost at the sidewalk when a motorcycle came speeding up the inside lane straight at her. She stepped back, and he missed her by an inch.

Granger sped along Eleventh Street, then dodged into an entrance. Judy flew after him. He had gone into a parking garage. She turned into the garage, going as fast as she could, and something hit her, a mighty blow in the face.

Pain exploded in her nose and forehead. She was blinded. She fell on her back, hitting the concrete with a crash. She lay still, paralyzed by shock and pain, unable even to think. A few seconds later she felt a strong hand behind her head and heard, as if from a great distance, the voice of Michael saying: "Judy, for God's sake, are you alive?"

Her head began to clear, and her vision came back. Michael's face swam into focus.

"Speak to me, say something!" Michael said.

She opened her mouth. "It hurts," she mumbled.

"Thank God!" He pulled a handkerchief from the pocket of his khakis and wiped her mouth with surprising gentleness. "Your nose is bleeding."

She sat upright. "What happened?"

"I saw you turning inside, going like greased lightning, then the next minute you were flat on the ground. I think he was waiting for you and hit you as you came around the corner. If I get my hands on him . . ."

Judy realized she had dropped her weapon. "My gun . . ."

He looked around, picked it up, and handed it to her.

"Help me up."

He pulled her to her feet.

Her face hurt like hell, but she could see clearly and her legs felt steady. She tried to think straight.

Maybe I haven't lost him yet.

There was an elevator, but he could not have had time to take it. He must have gone up the ramp. She knew this garage—she parked here herself when she came to see Honeymoon—and she recalled that it spanned the width of the block, with entrances on Tenth and Eleventh Streets. Maybe Granger knew that, too, and was already getting away by the Tenth Street door.

There was nothing to do but follow.

"I'm going after him," she said.

She ran up the ramp. Michael followed. She let him. She had twice ordered him to stay back, and she could not spare the breath to tell him again.

They reached the first parking level. Judy's head started throbbing, and her legs suddenly felt weak. She knew she could not go much farther. They started across the floor.

Suddenly a black car shot out of its parking slot straight at them.

Judy leaped sideways, fell to the ground, and rolled, frantically fast, until she was underneath a parked car.

She saw the wheels of the black car as it turned with a squeal of tires and accelerated down the ramp like a shot from a gun.

Judy stood up, searching frantically for Michael. She had heard him shout with surprise and fear. Had the car hit him?

She saw him a few yards from her, on his hands and knees, white with shock.

"Are you all right?" she said.

He got to his feet. "I'm fine, just shook up."

Judy looked to see the make of the black car, but it had disappeared.

"Shit," she said. "I lost him."

20

As Judy was entering the officers' club at seven P.M., Raja Khan came running out.

He stopped when he saw her. "What happened to you?"

What happened to me? I failed to prevent the earthquake, I made a wrong guess about where Melanie Quercus was hiding out, and I let Ricky Granger slip through my fingers. I blew it, and tomorrow there will be another earthquake, and more people will die, and it will be my fault.

"Ricky Granger punched me in the nose," she said. She had a bandage across her face. The pills they had given her at the hospital in Sacramento had eased the pain, but she felt battered and dispirited. "Where are you going in such a hurry?"

"We were looking for a record album called *Raining Fresh Daisies*, remember?"

"Sure. We hoped it might give us a lead on the woman that called the John Truth show."

"I've located a copy—and it's right here in town. A store called Vinyl Vic's."

"Give that agent a gold star!" Judy felt her energy returning. This could be the lead she needed. It wasn't much, but it filled her with hope again. Perhaps there was still a chance she could prevent another earthquake. "I'm coming with you."

They jumped into Raja's dirty Dodge Colt. The floor was littered with candy bar wrappers. Raja tore out of the parking lot and headed for Haight-Ashbury. "The guy who owns the store is called Vic Plumstead," he said as he drove. "When I called a couple of days ago, he wasn't there, and I got a part-time kid who said he didn't think they had the record but he would ask the boss. I left a card, and Vic called me five minutes ago."

"At last, a piece of luck!"

"The record was released in 1969 on a San Francisco label, Transcendental Tracks. It got some publicity and sold a few copies in the Bay Area, but the label never had another success and went out of business after a few months."

Judy's elation cooled. "That means there are no files we can search for clues to where she might be now."

"Maybe the album itself will give us something."

Vinyl Vic's was a small store stuffed to bursting with old records. A few conventional sales racks in the middle of the floor had been swamped by cardboard boxes and fruit crates stacked to the ceiling. The place smelled like a dusty old library. There was one customer, a tattooed man in leather shorts, studying an early David Bowie album. At the back, a small, thin man in tight blue jeans and a tie-dyed T-shirt stood beside a cash register, sipping coffee from a mug that said "Legalize it!"

Raja introduced himself. "You must be Vic. I spoke to you on the phone a few minutes ago."

Vic stared at them. He seemed surprised. He said: "Finally, the FBI hits my place, and it's two Asians? What happened?"

Raja said: "I'm the token nonwhite, and she's the token woman. Every FBI office has to have one of each, it's a rule. All the other agents are white men with short haircuts."

"Oh, right." Vic looked baffled. He didn't know whether Raja was kidding or not.

Judy said impatiently: "What about this record?"

"Here it is." Vic turned to one side, and Judy saw he had a turntable behind the cash register. He swung the arm over the disk and lowered the stylus. A burst of manic guitar introduced a surprisingly laid-back jazz-funk track with piano chords over a complex drumbeat. Then the woman's voice came in:

I am melting
Feel me melting
Liquefaction
Turning softer

"I think it's quite meaningful, actually," Vic said.

Judy thought it was crap, but she did not care. It was the voice on the John Truth tape, without question. Younger, clearer, gentler, but with that same unmistakable low, sexy tone. "Do you have the sleeve?" she said urgently.

"Sure." He handed it to her.

It was curling at the corners, and the transparent plastic coating was peeling off the glossy paper. The front had a swirling multicolored design that induced eyestrain. The words "Raining Fresh Daisies" could just be discerned. Judy turned it over. The back was grubby, and there was a coffee ring in the top right-hand corner.

The sleeve notes began: "Music opens the doors that lead to parallel universes. . . ."

Judy skipped over the words. At the bottom was a row of five monochrome photographs, just head and shoulders, four men and a woman. She read the captions:

Dave Rolands, keyboards
Ian Kerry, guitar
Ross Muller, bass
Jerry Jones, drums
Stella Higgins, poetry

Judy frowned. "Stella Higgins," she said excitedly. "I believe I've heard that name before!" She felt sure, but she could not remember where. Maybe it was wishful thinking. She stared at the small black-and-white head shot. She saw a girl of about twenty with a smiling, sensual face framed by wavy dark hair and the wide, generous mouth Simon Sparrow had predicted. "She was beautiful," Judy murmured, almost to herself. She searched the face for the craziness that would make a person threaten an earthquake, but she could see no sign of it. All she saw was a young woman full of vitality and hope. *What went wrong with your life?*

"Can we borrow this?" Judy said.

Vic looked sulky. "I'm here to sell records, not lend them," he said.

She was not going to argue. "How much?"

"Fifty bucks."

"Okay."

He stopped the turntable, picked up the disk, and slipped it into its paper cover. Judy paid him. "Thank you, Vic. We appreciate your help."

Driving back in Raja's car, she said: "Stella Higgins. Where have I seen that name?"

Raja shook his head. "It doesn't ring any bells with me."

As they got out of the car, she gave him the album. "Make blowups of her photo and circulate them to police departments," she said. "Give the record to Simon Sparrow. You never know what he might come up with."

They entered into the command post. The big ballroom now looked crowded. The head shed had been augmented by another table. Among the people crowded around would be several more suits from FBI headquarters in Washington, Judy assumed, plus people from the city, state, and federal emergency management agencies.

She went to the investigation team table. Most of her people were working the phones, running down leads. Judy spoke to Carl Theobald. "What are you on?"

"Sightings of tan Plymouth 'Cudas."

"I've got something better for you. We have the California

phone book on CD-ROM here somewhere. Look up the name Stella Higgins."

"And if I find her?"

"Call her and see if she sounds like the woman on the John Truth tape."

She sat at a computer and initiated a search of criminal records. There was a Stella Higgins in the files, she found. The woman had been fined for possession of marijuana and been given a suspended sentence for assaulting a police officer at a demonstration. Her date of birth was about right, and her address was on Haight Street. There was no picture in the database, but it sounded like the right woman.

Both convictions were dated 1968, and there was nothing since.

Stella's record was like that of Ricky Granger, who had dropped off the radar in the early seventies. Judy printed the file and pinned it to the suspect board. She sent an agent to check out the Haight Street address, though she felt sure Higgins would not be there thirty years later.

She felt a hand on her shoulder. It was Bo. His eyes were full of concern. "My baby, what happened to your face?" He touched the bandage on her nose with gentle fingertips.

"I guess I was careless," she said.

He kissed the top of her head. "I'm on duty tonight, but I had to stop by and see how you are."

"Who told you I was hurt?"

"That married guy, Michael."

That married guy. She grinned. *Reminding me that Michael belongs to someone else.* "There's no real damage, but I guess I'm going to have two beautiful black eyes."

"You got to get some rest. When are you going home?"

"I don't know. I just made a breakthrough. Take a seat." She told him about *Raining Fresh Daisies.* "The way I see it, she's a beautiful girl living in San Francisco in the sixties, going on demos, smoking dope, and hanging out with rock bands. The sixties turn into the seventies, she becomes disillusioned or maybe just bored, and she hooks up with a charismatic guy who is on the run from the Mob. The two of them start a cult. Somehow the group survives, making jewelry or whatever, for three decades. Then something goes wrong. Somehow, their existence is threatened by a plan to build a power plant. As they face the ruin of everything they've worked for and built up over the years, they cast about for some way, any way, to block this power plant. Then a seismologist joins the group and comes up with a crazy idea."

Bo nodded. "It makes sense, or a kind of sense, the kind that appeals to wackos."

"Granger has the criminal experience to steal the seismic vibrator, and the personal magnetism to persuade other cult members to go along with the scheme."

Bo looked thoughtful. "They probably don't own their home," he said.

"Why?"

"Well, imagine they live someplace close to where this nuclear plant is going, so they have to move away. If they owned their house, or farm, or whatever, they'd get compensation, and they could start again somewhere else. So I'm guessing they have a short lease, or maybe they're squatters."

"You're probably right, but it doesn't help. There's no statewide database of land leases."

Carl Theobald came up with a notebook in his hand. "Three hits in the phone book. Stella Higgins in Los Angeles is a woman of about seventy with a quavery voice. Mrs. Higgins in Stockton has a strong accent from some African country, maybe Nigeria. And S. J. Higgins in Diamond Heights is a man called Sidney."

"Damn," Judy said. She explained to Bo: "Stella Higgins is the voice on the John Truth tape—and I'm sure I've seen the name before."

Bo said: "Try your own files."

"What?"

"If the name seems familiar, that could be because it has already come up during this investigation. Search the case files."

"Good idea."

"I gotta go," he said. "With all these people getting out of the city and leaving their homes empty, the San Francisco PD is going to have a busy night. Good luck—and get some rest."

"Thanks, Bo." Judy activated the find function on the computer and had it search the entire Hammer of Eden directory for "Stella Higgins."

Carl watched over her shoulder. It was a big directory, and the search took a while.

Finally the screen flickered and said:

1 file(s) found

Judy felt a burst of elation.

Carl shouted: "Christ! The name is already in the computer!"

Oh, my God, I think I've found her.

Two more agents looked over Judy's shoulder as she opened the file.

It was a large document containing all the notes made by agents during the abortive raid on Los Alamos six days ago.

"What the hell?" Judy was mystified. "Was she at Los Alamos and we missed her?"

Stuart Cleever appeared at her side. "What's all the fuss about?"

"We've found the woman who called John Truth!" Judy said.

"Where?"

"Silver River Valley."

"How did she slip through your fingers?"

It was Marvin Hayes, not me, who organized that raid. "I

don't know, I'm working on it, give me a minute!" She used the search function to locate the name in the notes.

Stella Higgins had not been at Los Alamos. That was why they had missed her.

Two agents had visited a winery a few miles up the valley. The site was rented from the federal government, and the name of the tenant was Stella Higgins.

"Damn, we were so close!" Judy cried in exasperation. "We almost had her a week ago!"

"Print this so everyone can see it," Cleever said.

Judy hit the print button and read on.

The agents had conscientiously noted the name and age of every adult at the winery. Some were couples with children, Judy saw, and most gave their address as that of the winery. So they were living there.

Maybe it was a cult, and the agents simply had not realized that.

Or the people had been careful to conceal the true nature of their community.

"We've got them!" Judy said. "We were sidetracked, the first time by Los Alamos, who seemed perfect suspects. Then, when they turned out to be clean, we thought we must be barking up the wrong tree. That made us careless about checking for *other* communes in that valley. So we overlooked the real perpetrators. But we've found them now."

Stuart Cleever said: "I think you're right." He turned to the SWAT team table. "Charlie, call the Sacramento office and organize a joint raid. Judy has the location. We'll hit them at first light."

Judy said: "We should raid them now. If we wait until morning, they may be gone."

"Why would they leave now?" Cleever shook his head. "Nighttime is too risky. The suspects can slip away in the darkness, especially in the countryside."

He had a point, but instinct told Judy not to wait. "I'd

rather take that risk," she said. "Now that we know where they are, let's go get 'em."

"No," he said decisively. "No further discussion, please, Judy. We raid at dawn."

She hesitated. She was sure it was the wrong decision. But she was too tired to argue anymore. "So be it," she said. "What time do we head out, Charlie?"

Marsh looked at his watch. "Leaving here at two A.M."

"I may grab a couple of hours' rest."

She seemed to remember parking her car outside on the parade ground. It felt like months ago, but in fact it had been Thursday night, only forty-eight hours ago.

On the way out she met Michael. "You look exhausted," he said. "Let me drive you home."

"Then how will I get back here?"

"I'll nap on your couch and drive you back."

She stopped and looked at him. "I have to tell you, my face is so sore I don't think I could kiss, let alone anything else."

"I'll settle for holding your hand," he said with a smile.

I'm beginning to think this guy cares for me.

He raised a questioning eyebrow. "Well, what do you say?"

"Will you tuck me into bed, and bring me hot milk and aspirins?"

"Yes. Will you let me watch you sleep?"

Oh, boy, I'd like that better than anything in the world.

He read her expression. "I think I'm hearing yes," he said. She smiled. "Yes."

Priest was mad as hell when he got back from Sacramento. He had been sure the governor was going to make a deal. He felt he was on the very brink of victory. He had been congratulating himself already. And it had all been a sham. Governor Robson had had no thought of making a deal. The whole thing had been a setup. The FBI had imagined they could catch him in a dumb-ass trap like some two-bit crook. It was the disrespect that really got to him. They thought he was some dope.

They would learn the truth. And the lesson would be dear.

It would cost them another earthquake.

Everyone at the commune was still stunned by the departure of Dale and Poem. It had reminded them of something they had been pretending to forget: that tomorrow they were all supposed to leave the valley.

Priest told the Rice Eaters how much pressure they had put on the governor. The freeways were still jammed with minivans full of kids and suitcases escaping from the earthquake to come. In the semideserted neighborhoods they had left behind, looters were walking out of suburban homes loaded with microwave ovens and CD players and computers.

But they also knew the governor showed no signs of giving in.

Although it was Saturday night, nobody wanted to party. After supper and evening worship, most of them retired to their cabins. Melanie went to the bunkhouse to read to the children. Priest sat outside his cabin, watching the moon go down over the valley, and slowly calmed down. He opened a five-year-old bottle of his own wine, a vintage with the smoky flavor he loved.

It was a battle of nerves, he told himself when he was able to think calmly. Who could tough it out longer, him or the governor? Which of them could best keep their people under control? Would the earthquakes bring the state government to its knees before the FBI could track Priest down to his mountain lair?

Star came into view, backlit by moonlight, walking barefoot and smoking a joint. She took a deep pull on the joint, bent over Priest, and kissed him, opening her mouth. He inhaled the intoxicating smoke from her lungs. He breathed out, smiled, and said: "I remember the first time you did that. It was the sexiest thing that ever happened to me."

"Really?" she said. "Sexier than a blow job?"

"A lot. Remember, when I was seven years old I saw my mother giving a blow job to a john. She never kissed them, though. I was the only person she kissed. She told me that."

"Priest, what a hell of a life you've had."

He frowned. "You make it sound as if it's over."

"This part of it is over, though, isn't it?"

"No!"

"It's almost midnight. Your deadline is about to run out. The governor isn't going to give in."

"He has to," Priest said. "It's only a matter of time." He stood up. "I have to listen to the radio news."

She walked with him as he crossed the vineyard in the moonlight and climbed the track to the cars. "Let's go away," she said suddenly. "Just you and me and Flower. Let's get in a car, right now, and leave. We won't say good-bye, or pack a bag, or even take spare clothes or anything. We'll just take off, the way I did when I left San Francisco in 1969. We'll go where the mood takes us—Oregon, or Las Vegas, or even New York. What about Charleston? I've always wanted to see the South."

Without answering, he got in the Cadillac and turned on the radio. Star sat beside him. Brenda Lee was singing "Let's Jump the Broomstick."

"Come on, Priest, what do you say?"

The news came on, and he turned up the volume.

"Suspected Hammer of Eden terrorist leader Richard Granger slipped through the fingers of the FBI in Sacramento today. Meanwhile, residents fleeing neighborhoods near the San Andreas fault have brought traffic to a standstill on many freeways within the San Francisco Bay Area, with miles of cars blocking long sections of Interstate Routes 280, 580, 680, and 880. And a Haight-Ashbury rare-record dealer claims FBI agents bought from him an album with a photograph of another terrorist suspect."

"Album?" Star said. "What the fuck . . . ?"

"Store owner Vic Plumstead told reporters the FBI called him in to help track down a sixties album, which they believed featured the voice of one of the Hammer of Eden suspects. After days of effort, he said, he found the album, by an obscure rock band, *Raining Fresh Daisies*."

"Jesus Christ! I'd almost forgotten them myself!"

"The FBI would not confirm or deny they are seeking the vocalist, Stella Higgins."

"Shit!" Star burst out. "They know my name!"

Priest's mind was racing. How dangerous was this? The name was not much use to them. Star had not used it for almost thirty years. No one knew where Stella Higgins lived.

Yes, they did.

He suppressed a groan of despair. The name Stella Higgins was on the lease for this land. And he had said that to the two FBI agents who had come here on the day they raided Los Alamos.

This changed everything. Sooner or later someone at the FBI would make the connection.

And if by some mischance the FBI failed to figure it out, there was a Silver City sheriff's deputy, currently on vacation in the Bahamas, who had written the name "Stella Higgins" on a file that was due to come up in court in a couple of weeks' time.

Silver River Valley was a secret no more.

The thought made him unbearably sad.

What could he do?

Maybe he *should* run away with Star now. The keys were in the car. They could be in Nevada in a couple of hours. By midday tomorrow they would be five hundred miles away.

Hell, no. I'm not beat yet.

He could still hold things together.

His original plan had been that the authorities would never know who the Hammer of Eden were or why they had demanded a ban on new power plants. Now the FBI was about to find out—but maybe they could be forced to keep it secret. That could become part of Priest's demand. If they could bring themselves to agree to the freeze, they could swallow this, too.

Yes, it was outrageous—but this whole thing was outrageous. He could do it.

But he would have to stay out of the clutches of the FBI.

He opened the car door and got out. "Let's go," he said to Star. "I've got a lot to do."

She got out slowly. "You won't run away with me?" she said sadly.

"Hell, no." He slammed the door and walked away.

She followed him across the vineyard and back to the settlement. She went to her cabin without saying good night.

Priest went to Melanie's cabin. She was asleep. He shook her roughly to wake her. "Get up," he said. "We have to go. Quickly."

Judy watched and waited while Stella Higgins cried her heart out.

She was a big woman, and though she might have been attractive in different circumstances, she now looked destroyed. Her face was contorted with grief, her old-fashioned eye makeup was running down her cheeks, and her heavy shoulders shook with sobs.

They sat in the tiny cabin that was her home. All around were medical supplies: boxes of bandages, cartons of aspirin and Rolaids, Tylenol and Trojans, bottles of colic water, cough syrup, and iodine. The walls were decorated with kids' drawings of Star taking care of sick children. It was a primitive building, without electric power or running water, but it had a happy feel.

Judy went to the door and looked out, giving Star a minute to recover her composure. The place was beautiful in the pale sunlight of early morning. The last ribbons of a light mist were vanishing from the trees on the steep hillsides, and the river flashed and glittered in the fork of the valley.

On the lower slopes was a neat vineyard, the ordered rows of vines with their shoots tied to wooden trellises. For a moment Judy was taken by a sense of spiritual peace, a feeling that here in this place things were as they should be, and it was the rest of the world that was weird. She shook herself to get rid of the spooky sensation.

Michael appeared. Once again he had wanted to be here to take care of Dusty, and Judy had told Stuart Cleever that he should be indulged because his expertise was so important to the investigation. He was leading Dusty by the hand. "How is he?" Judy asked.

"He's just fine," Michael said.

"Have you found Melanie?"

"She's not here. Dusty says there's a big girl called Flower who's been looking after him."

"Any idea where Melanie went?"

"No." He nodded toward Star. "What does she say?"

"Nothing, yet." Judy went back inside and sat on the edge of the bed. "Tell me about Ricky Granger," she said.

"There's good in him as well as bad," Star said as her weeping subsided. "He was a hoodlum before, I know, he's even killed people, but in all the time we were together, more than twenty-five years, he didn't once hurt anyone, until now, until someone thought up the idea of this stupid fucking dam."

"All I want to do," Judy said gently, "is find him before he hurts any more people."

Star nodded. "I know."

Judy made Star look at her. "Where did he go?"

"I'd tell you if I knew," Star said. "But I don't."

21

Priest and Melanie drove to San Francisco in the commune's pickup truck. Priest figured the dented Cadillac was too conspicuous, and the police might be looking for Melanie's orange Subaru.

All the traffic was heading in the opposite direction, so they were not much delayed. They reached the city a little after five on Sunday morning. A few people were on the streets: a teenage couple embracing at a bus stop, two nervy crackheads buying one last rock from a dealer in a long coat, a helpless drunk zigzagging across the road. However, the waterfront district was deserted. The derelict industrial landscape looked bleak and eerie in the early-morning light. They found the Perpetua Diaries warehouse, and Priest unlocked the door. The real-estate agent had kept his promise: the electric power was on, and there was water in the rest room.

Melanie drove the pickup inside, and Priest checked the seismic vibrator. He started the engine, then lowered and raised the plate. Everything worked.

They lay down to sleep on the couch in the small office, close together. Priest stayed awake, running over his position again and again. No matter how he looked at it, the only smart thing for Governor Robson to do was give in. Priest found himself making imaginary speeches on the John Truth show, pointing out how dumb the governor was being. *He could stop the earthquakes with one word!* After an hour of this he realized it was pointless. Lying on his back, he went through the relaxation ritual he used for meditation. His body became still, his heartbeat calmed, his mind emptied, and he went to sleep.

When he woke it was ten o'clock in the morning.

He put a pan of water on the hot plate. He had brought from the commune a can of organic ground coffee and some cups.

Melanie turned on the TV. "I miss the news, living at the commune," she said. "I used to watch it all the time."

"I hate the news, normally," Priest said. "It gets you worried about a million things you can't do nothing about." But he watched with her, to see if there was anything about him.

It was *all* about him.

"Authorities in California are taking seriously the threat of an earthquake today as the terrorist deadline looms closer," said the anchor, and there was footage of city employees erecting a tent hospital in Golden Gate Park.

The sight made Priest angry. "Why don't you just give us what we want?" he said to the TV.

The next clip showed FBI agents raiding log cabins in the mountains. After a moment Melanie said: "My God, it's our commune!"

They saw Star, wrapped in her old purple silk robe, her face a picture of grief, being walked out of her cabin by two men in bulletproof vests.

Priest cursed. He was not surprised—it was the possibility of a raid that had led him to leave so hastily last night—but all the same he found himself plunged into rage and despair by the sight. His home had been violated by these self-righteous bastards.

You should have left us alone. Now it's too late.

He saw Judy Maddox, looking grim. *You were hoping to catch me in your net, weren't you?* She was not so pretty today. She had two black eyes and a large Band-Aid across her nose. *You lied to me and tried to trap me, and you got a bloody nose for it.*

But in his heart he was daunted. All along he had underestimated the FBI. When he started out he had never dreamed that he would see agents invade the sanctuary of the valley that had been a secret place for so many years. Judy Maddox was smarter than he had imagined.

Melanie gasped. There was a shot of her husband, Michael, carrying Dusty. "Oh, no!" she said.

"They're not arresting Dusty," Priest said impatiently.

"But where will Michael take him?"

"Does it matter?"

"It does if there's going to be an earthquake!"

"Michael knows better than anyone where the fault lines are! He won't be anywhere dangerous."

"Oh, God, I hope not, especially if he has Dusty with him."

Priest had watched enough TV. "Let's go out," he said. "Bring your phone."

Melanie drove the pickup out, and Priest locked the warehouse behind them. "Head for the airport," he told her as he got in.

Avoiding the freeways, they got close to the airport before they were stuck in traffic. Priest figured there had to be thousands of people using phones in the vicinity—trying to get flights, calling their families, checking how big the traffic jam was. He called the John Truth show.

John Truth himself answered. Priest figured he was hoping for this call. "I have a new demand, so listen carefully," Priest said.

"Don't worry, I'm taping this," Truth said.

"I guess I'll be on your show tonight, huh, John?" Priest said with a smile.

"I hope you'll be in goddamn jail," Truth said nastily.

"Well, fuck you, too." There was no need for the guy to

get pissy. "My new demand is a presidential pardon for everyone in the Hammer of Eden."

"I'll let the president know."

Now it was like he was being sarcastic. Didn't he understand how important this was? "That's as well as the freeze on new power plants."

"Wait a minute," Truth said. "Now that everyone knows where your commune is, you don't need a statewide freeze. You just want to stop your valley from being flooded, don't you?"

Priest considered. He had not thought of this, but Truth was right. Still, he decided not to agree. "Hell, no," he said. "I've got principles. California needs less electric power, not more, if it's going to be a decent place for my grand-children to live in. Our original demand stands. There will be another earthquake if the governor doesn't agree."

"How can you do this?"

The question took Priest by surprise. "What?"

"How can you do this? How can you bring such suffering and misery to so many people—killing, wounding, damaging property, making people flee their homes in fear. . . . How will you ever sleep?"

The question angered Priest. "Don't make like *you're* the ethical one," he said. "I'm trying to save California."

"By killing people."

Priest lost patience. "Shut the fuck up and listen," he said. "I'm going to tell you about the next earthquake." According to Melanie, the seismic window would open at six-forty P.M. "Seven o'clock," Priest said. "It will hit at seven tonight."

"Can you tell me—"

Priest broke the connection.

He was silent for a while. The conversation left him with an uneasy feeling. Truth should have been scared to death, but he had almost bantered with Priest. He had treated Priest like a loser, that was it.

They came to a junction. "We could turn here and head back," Melanie said. "No traffic the other way."

"Okay."

She made the turn. She was thoughtful. "Will we ever go back to the valley?" she said. "Now that the FBI and everyone knows about it?"

"Yes!" he said.

"Don't shout!"

"Yes, we will," he said more quietly. "I know it looks bad, and we may have to stay away for a while. I'm sure we'll lose this year's vintage. The media will crawl all over the place for weeks. But they will forget about us, eventually. There'll be a war, or an election, or a sex scandal, and we'll be old news. Then we can slip quietly back, and move into our homes, and get the vines back in shape, and grow a new crop."

Melanie smiled. "Yeah," she said.

She believes it. I'm not sure I do. But I'm not going to think about it anymore. Fretting will sap my will. No doubts now. Just action.

Melanie said: "You want to go back to the warehouse?"

"No. I'll go crazy shut up in that hole all day. Head for the city and see if we can find a restaurant that's serving brunch. I'm starving."

Judy and Michael took Dusty to Stockton, where Michael's parents lived. They went in a helicopter. Dusty was thrilled. It landed on the football field of a high school in the suburbs.

Michael's father was a retired accountant, and they had a neat suburban house that backed onto a golf course. Judy drank coffee in the kitchen while Michael settled Dusty in. Mrs. Quercus said worriedly: "Maybe this dreadful affair will give the business a boost, anyway—it's an ill wind that blows nobody any good." Judy recalled that they had put money into Michael's consultancy, and he was worried about paying them back. But Mrs. Quercus was right—his being the FBI's earthquake expert might help.

Judy's mind was on the seismic vibrator. It was not in Silver River Valley. It had not been sighted since Friday evening, though the panels that made it look like a carnival ride had been found at the roadside by one of the hundreds of rescue workers still clearing up the mess at Felicitas.

She knew what Granger was driving. She had found out by asking the commune members what cars they had and checking which was missing. He was using a pickup truck, and she had put out an all-points bulletin on it. In theory every cop in California should be looking for it, although most of them would be too busy coping with the emergency.

She was tantalized unbearably by the thought that she might have caught Granger at the commune if she had fought harder and persuaded Cleever to raid the place last night instead of this morning. But she had just been too tired. She felt better today—the raid had pumped adrenaline into her system and given her energy. But she was bruised physically and mentally, running on empty.

A small TV set on the kitchen counter was on with the sound muted. The news came on, and Judy asked Mrs. Quercus to turn up the volume. There was an interview with John Truth, who had spoken on the phone to Granger. He played an extract from his tape of the conversation. "Seven o'clock," Granger said on the tape. "It will hit at seven tonight."

Judy shivered. He meant it. There was no regret or remorse in his voice, no sign that he hesitated to risk the lives of so many people. He sounded rational, but there was a flaw in his humanity. He did not really care about the suffering of others. It was the characteristic of psychopaths.

She wondered what Simon Sparrow would make of the voice. But it was too late now for psycholinguistics. She went to the kitchen door and called: "Michael! We have to go!"

She would have liked to leave Michael here with Dusty,

where they would both be safe. But she needed him at the command post. His expertise might be crucial.

He came in with Dusty. "I'm about ready," he said. The phone rang and Mrs. Quercus picked it up. After a moment she held out the receiver to Dusty. "Someone for you," she said.

Dusty took the phone and said tentatively: "Hello?" Then his face brightened. "Hi, Mom!"

Judy froze.

It was Melanie.

Dusty said: "I woke up this morning and you were gone! Then Daddy came to get me!"

Melanie was with Priest and the seismic vibrator, almost certainly. Judy grabbed her mobile and dialed the command post. She got Raja and said quietly: "Trace a call. Melanie Quercus is calling a number in Stockton." She read the number off the instrument Dusty was using. "Call started a minute ago, still in progress."

"I'm on it," Raja said.

Judy broke the connection.

Dusty was listening, nodding and shaking his head occasionally, forgetting that his mother could not see his movements.

Then he abruptly offered the phone to his father. "She wants you."

Judy whispered to Michael: "For God's sake, find out where she is!"

He took the phone from Dusty and held it against his chest, muffling it. "Pick up the bedroom extension."

"Where?"

Mrs. Quercus said: "Just across the hall, dear."

Judy darted into the bedroom, threw herself across the flowered bedspread, and grabbed the phone from the bedside table, covering the mouthpiece with her hand.

She heard Michael say: "Melanie—where the hell are you?"

"Never mind," Melanie replied. "I saw you and Dusty on TV. Is he okay?"

So she's been watching TV, wherever she is.

"Dusty's fine," Michael said. "We just got here."

"I was hoping you'd be there."

Her voice was low, and Michael said: "Can you speak up?"

"No, I can't, so just listen harder, okay?"

She doesn't want Granger to hear her. That's good—it may be a sign that they're beginning to disagree.

"Okay, okay," Michael said.

"You're going to stay there with Dusty, right?"

"No," Michael said. "I'm going into the city."

"What? For God's sake, Michael, it's dangerous!"

"Is that where the earthquake will be—in San Francisco?"

"I can't tell you."

"Will it be on the peninsula?"

"Yes, on the peninsula, so keep Dusty away!"

Judy's cell phone beeped. Keeping the mouthpiece of the bedroom phone tightly covered, she put the cell phone to her other ear and said: "Yeah."

It was Raja. "She's calling on her mobile. It's in downtown San Francisco. They can't do better than that for a digital phone."

"Get some people out in the streets looking for that pickup!"

"You got it."

Judy broke the connection.

Michael was saying: "If you're so worried, why don't you just tell me where the seismic vibrator is?"

"I can't do that!" Melanie hissed. "You're out of your mind!"

"Come on. *I'm* out of my mind? You're the one who's causing earthquakes!"

"I can't talk anymore." There was a click.

Judy replaced the handset on the bedside phone and rolled over onto her back, her mind racing. Melanie had given away a great deal of information. She was somewhere in downtown San Francisco, and although that did not make her easy to find, it was a smaller haystack than the whole of California. She had said the earthquake would be triggered somewhere on the San Francisco peninsula, the broad neck of land between the Pacific Ocean and the San Francisco Bay. The seismic vibrator had to be somewhere in that area. But most intriguing, to Judy, had been the hint of some division between Melanie and Granger. She had obviously been making the call without telling him, and she had seemed to be afraid he might overhear. That was hopeful. There might be a way Judy could take advantage of a split.

She closed her eyes, concentrating. Melanie was worried about Dusty. That was her weakness. How could it be used against her?

She heard footsteps and opened her eyes. Michael came into the room. He gave her a strange look.

"What?" she said.

"This may seem inappropriate, but you look great lying on a bed."

She remembered she was in his parents' house. She stood up.

He wrapped his arms around her. It felt good. "How's your face?" he said.

She looked up at him. "If you're very gentle . . ."

He kissed her lips softly.

If he wants to kiss me when I look this bad, he must really like me.

"Mm," she said. "When this is all over . . ."

"Yes."

She closed her eyes for a moment.

Then she started thinking about Melanie again.

"Michael . . ."

"Still here."

She detached herself from his embrace. "Melanie is worried that Dusty might be in the earthquake zone."

"He's going to be here."

"But you didn't confirm that. She asked you, but you said if she was worried, she should tell you where the seismic vibrator is, and you never answered her question properly."

"Still, the implication . . . I mean, why would I take him into danger?"

"I'm just saying, she may have a nagging doubt. And, wherever she is, there's a TV."

"She leaves the news on all day sometimes—it relaxes her."

Judy felt a stab of jealousy. *He knows her so well.* "What if we had a reporter interview you, at the emergency operations center in San Francisco, about what you're doing to help the Bureau . . . and Dusty was, like, just in the background somewhere?"

"Then she'd know he was in San Francisco."

"And what would she do?"

"Call me and scream at me, I guess."

"And if she couldn't reach you . . ."

"She'd be real scared."

"But would she stop Granger from operating the seismic vibrator?"

"Maybe. If she could."

"Is it worth a try?"

"Is there another choice?"

Priest had a do-or-die feeling. Maybe the governor and the president would not give in to him, even after Felicitas. But tonight there would be a third earthquake. Then he would call John Truth and say: "I'll do it again! Next time it could be Los Angeles, or San Bernardino, or San Jose. I can do this as often as I like. I'm going to keep on until you give in. The choice is yours!"

Downtown San Francisco was a ghost town. Few people wanted to shop or sightsee, though plenty were going to church. The restaurant was half-empty. Priest ordered eggs and drank three Bloody Marys. Melanie was subdued, worrying about Dusty. Priest thought the kid would be fine, he was with his father.

"Did I ever tell you why I'm called Granger?" he said to Melanie.

"It's not your parents' name?"

"My mother called herself Veronica Nightingale. She told me my father's name was Stewart Granger. He had gone on a long trip, she said, but one day he would come back, in a big limousine loaded with presents—perfume and chocolates for her, and a bicycle for me. On rainy days, when I couldn't play in the streets, I used to sit at the window watching for him, hour after hour."

For a moment Melanie seemed to forget her own problems. "Poor kid," she said.

"I was about twelve when I realized that Stewart Granger was a big movie star. He played Allan Quatermain in *King Solomon's Mines* just about the time I was born. I guess he was my mother's fantasy. Broke my heart, I can tell you. All those hours looking out the damn window." Priest smiled, but the memory hurt.

"Who knows?" Melanie said. "Maybe he *was* your father. Movie stars go to hookers."

"I guess I should ask him."

"He's dead."

"Is he? I didn't know that."

"Yeah, I read it in *People* magazine, a few years ago."

Priest felt a pang of loss. Stewart Granger was the nearest thing to a father he had ever had. "Well, now I'll never know." He shrugged and called for the bill.

When they left the restaurant, Priest did not want to return to the warehouse. He could easily sit doing nothing when he was at the commune, but in a dingy room in an industrial wasteland he would get cabin fever. Twenty-five years of living in Silver River Valley had spoiled him for the city. So he and Melanie walked around Fisherman's Wharf, making like tourists, enjoying the salty breeze off the bay.

They had altered their appearance, as a precaution. She had put up her distinctive long red hair and concealed it under a hat, and she wore sunglasses. Priest had greased his dark hair and plastered it to his head, and he had three days' growth of dark stubble on his cheeks, giving him a Latin lover air that was quite different from his usual aging-hippie look. No one gave them a second glance.

Priest listened in to the conversations of the few people walking around. Everyone had an excuse for not leaving town.

"I'm not worried, our building is earthquake-proof. . . ."

"So's mine, but at seven o'clock I'm going to be in the middle of the park. . . ."

"I'm a fatalist; either this earthquake has my name on it or it doesn't. . . ."

"Exactly, you could drive to Vegas and get killed in a car wreck. . . ."

"I've had my house retrofitted. . . ."

"No one can cause earthquakes, it was a coincidence. . . ."

They got back to the car a few minutes after four.

Priest did not see the cop until it was almost too late.

The Bloody Marys had made him strangely calm, and he felt almost invulnerable, so he was not looking out for the police. He was only eight or ten feet from the pickup truck when he noticed a uniformed San Francisco cop staring at the license plate and speaking into a walkie-talkie.

Priest stopped dead and grabbed Melanie's arm.

A moment later he realized that the smart thing to do was walk right by; but by then it was too late.

The cop glanced up from the license plate and caught Priest's eye.

Priest looked at Melanie. She had not seen the cop. He almost said, *Don't look at the car,* but just in time he realized that would be sure to make her look. Instead he said the next thing that came into his head. "Look at my hand." He turned his palm up.

She stared at it, then looked at him again. "What am I supposed to see?"

"Keep looking at my hand while I explain."

She did as he said.

"We're going to walk right past the car. There's a cop taking the number. He's noticed us; I can see him out of the corner of my eye."

She looked up from his hand to his face. Then, to his astonishment, she slapped him.

It hurt. He gasped.

Melanie cried: "And now you can just go back to your dumb blonde!"

"What?" he said angrily.

She walked on.

He watched her in astonishment. She strode past the pickup truck.

The cop looked at Priest with a faint grin.

Priest walked after Melanie, saying: "Now just wait a minute!"

The cop returned his attention to the license plate.

Priest caught up with Melanie, and they turned a corner.

"Very cute," he said. "But you didn't have to hit me so hard."

A powerful portable spotlight shone on Michael, and a miniature microphone was clipped to the front of his dark green polo shirt. A small television camera on a tripod was aimed at him. Behind him, the young seismologists he had brought in worked at their screens. In front of him sat Alex Day, a twentysomething television reporter with a fashionably short haircut. He was wearing a camouflage jacket, which Judy thought was overly dramatic.

Dusty stood beside Judy, holding her hand trustingly, watching his daddy being interviewed.

Michael was saying: "Yes, we can identify locations where an earthquake could most easily be triggered—but, unfortunately, we can't tell which one the terrorists have chosen until they start up their seismic vibrator."

"And what's your advice to citizens?" Alex Day asked. "How can they protect themselves if there is an earthquake?"

"The motto is 'Duck, cover, and hold,' and that's the best counsel," he replied. "Duck under a table or desk, cover your face to protect yourself from flying glass, and hold your position until the shaking stops."

Judy whispered to Dusty: "Okay, go to Daddy."

Dusty walked into the shot. Michael lifted the boy onto his knee. On cue Alex Day said: "Anything special we can do to protect youngsters?"

"Well, you could practice the 'Duck, cover, and hold' drill with them right now, so they'll know what to do if they feel a tremor. Make sure they're wearing sturdy shoes, not thongs or sandals, because there will be a lot of broken glass around. And keep them close, so you don't have to go searching for them afterward."

"Anything people should avoid?"

"Don't run out of the house. Most injuries in earthquakes are caused by falling bricks and other debris from damaged buildings."

"Professor Quercus, thank you for being with us today."

Alex Day smiled at Michael and Dusty for a long frozen moment, then the cameraman said: "Great."

Everyone relaxed. The crew started rapidly packing up their equipment.

Dusty said: "When can I go to Grandma's in the helicopter?"

"Right now," Michael told him.

Judy said: "How soon will that be on the air, Alex?"

"It hardly needs editing, so it will go right out. Within half an hour, I'd say."

Judy looked at the clock. It was five-fifteen.

* * *

Priest and Melanie walked for half an hour without seeing a taxi. Then Melanie called a cab service on her mobile phone. They waited, but no car came.

Priest felt as if he was going mad. After all he had done, his great scheme was in jeopardy because he could not find a goddamn taxi!

But at last a dusty Chevrolet pulled up at Pier 39. The driver had an unreadable Central European name, and he seemed stoned. He understood no English except "left" and "right," and he was probably the only person in San Francisco who had not heard about the earthquake.

They got back to the warehouse at six-twenty.

At the emergency operations center, Judy slumped in her chair, staring at the phone.

It was six twenty-five. In thirty-five minutes Granger would start up his seismic vibrator. If it worked as well as it had the last two times, there would be an earthquake. But this one would be the worst. Assuming Melanie had told the truth, and the vibrator was somewhere in the San Francisco peninsula, the quake would almost certainly hit the city.

Around two million people had fled the metropolitan area since Friday night, when Granger had announced on the John Truth show that the next earthquake would hit San Francisco. But that left more than a million men, women, and children who were unable or unwilling to leave their homes: the poor, the old, and the sick, plus all the cops, firefighters, nurses, and city employees waiting to begin rescue work. And that included Bo.

On the TV screen, Alex Day was speaking from a temporary studio set up at the mayor's emergency command center on Turk Street, a few blocks away. The mayor was wearing a hard hat and a purple vest and telling citizens to duck, cover, and hold.

The interview with Michael ran every few minutes on all

channels: the television editors had been told its real purpose.

But it seemed Melanie was not watching.

Priest's pickup had been found parked at Fisherman's Wharf at four o'clock. It was under surveillance, but he had not returned to it. Right now, every garage and parking lot in the neighborhood was being searched for a seismic vibrator.

The ballroom of the officers' club was full of people. There were at least forty suits around the head shed. Michael and his helpers were clustered around their computers, waiting for the inappropriately cheerful musical warning sound that would be the first sign of the seismic tremor they all feared. Judy's team was still working the phones, following up sightings of people who looked like Granger or Melanie, but there was an increasingly desperate tone to their voices. Using Dusty in the TV interview with Michael had been their last shot, and it seemed to have failed.

Most of the agents working in the EOC had homes in the Bay Area. The admin desk had organized the evacuation of all their families. The building they were in was considered as safe as any: it had been retrofitted by the military to make it earthquake-resistant. But they could not flee. Like soldiers, like firefighters, like cops, they had to go where the danger was. It was their job. Outside, on the parade ground, a fleet of helicopters stood ready, with their rotors turning, waiting to take Judy and her colleagues into the earthquake zone.

Priest went to the bathroom. While he was washing his hands, he heard Melanie scream.

He ran to the office with wet hands. He found her staring at the TV. "What is it?" he said.

Her face was white, and her hand covered her mouth. "Dusty!" she said, pointing at the screen.

Priest saw Melanie's husband being interviewed. He had their son on his knee. A moment later the picture changed, and a female anchor said: "That was Alex Day, interviewing

one of the world's leading seismologists, Professor Michael
Quercus, at the FBI's emergency operations center in the
Presidio."

"Dusty's in San Francisco!" Melanie said hysterically.

"No, he's not," Priest said. "Maybe he *was,* when the
interview was filmed. By now he's miles away."

"You don't know that!"

"Of course I do. So do you. Michael's going to take care
of his kid."

"I wish I could be sure," Melanie said in a shaky voice.

"Make a cup of coffee," Priest said, just to give her
something to do.

"Okay." She took the pan from the hot plate and went to
fill it with water in the rest room.

Judy looked at the clock. It was six-thirty.

Her phone rang.

The room fell silent.

She snatched up the handset, dropped it, cursed, picked it
up again, and held it to her ear. "Yes?"

The switchboard operator said: "Melanie Quercus asking
for her husband."

Thank God! Melanie pointed at Raja. "Trace the call."

He was already speaking into his phone.

Judy said to the operator: "Put her on."

All the suits from the head shed gathered around Judy's
chair. They stood silent, straining to hear.

This could be the most important phone call of my life.

There was a click on the line. Judy tried to make her
voice calm and said: "Agent Maddox here."

"Where's Michael?"

Melanie sounded so frightened and lost that Judy felt a
surge of compassion for her. She seemed no more than a
foolish mother worried about her child.

Get real, Judy. This woman is a killer.

Judy hardened her heart. "Where are *you,* Melanie?"

"Please," Melanie whispered. "Just tell me where he's taken Dusty."

"Let's make a deal," Judy said. "I'll make sure Dusty's okay—if you tell me where the seismic vibrator is."

"Can I speak to my husband?"

"Are you with Ricky Granger? I mean Priest?"

"Yes."

"And you have the seismic vibrator, wherever you are?"

"Yes."

Then we've almost got you.

"Melanie—do you really want to kill all those people?"

"No, but we have to. . . ."

"You won't be able to take care of Dusty while you're in jail. You'll miss watching him grow up." Judy heard a sob at the other end of the line. "You'll only ever see him through a glass partition. By the time they let you out, he'll be a grown man who doesn't know you."

Melanie was crying.

"Tell me where you are, Melanie."

In the big ballroom, the silence was total. No one moved.

Melanie whispered something, but Judy could not hear it.

"Speak up!"

At the other end of the line, in the background, a man shouted: "Who the fuck are you calling?"

Judy said: "Quickly, quickly! Tell me where you are!"

The man roared: "Give me that goddamn phone!"

Melanie said: "Perpetua—" Then she screamed.

A moment later the connection was broken.

Raja said: "She's somewhere on the Bay Shore, south of the city."

"That's not good enough!" Judy cried.

"They can't be more precise!"

"Shit!"

Stuart Cleever said: "Quiet, everybody. We'll play the tape back in a moment. First, Judy, did she give you any clues?"

"She said something at the end. It sounded like "Perpetual.' Carl, check for a street called Perpetual."

Raja said: "We should check for a company, too. They could be in the garage of an office building."

"Do that."

Cleever pounded the table in frustration. "What made her hang up?"

"I think Granger found her calling and took the phone away."

"What do you want to do now?"

"I'd like to get in the air," Judy said. "We can fly down the shoreline. Michael can come with me and point out where fault lines run. Maybe we'll spot the seismic vibrator."

"Do it," Cleever said.

Priest stared at Melanie in fury as she cowered up against the grimy washbasin. She had tried to betray him. He would have shot her right there and then if he had had a gun. But the revolver he had taken from the guard at Los Alamos was in the seismic vibrator, under the driver's seat.

He switched off Melanie's phone, dropped it into his shirt pocket, and tried to make himself calm. This was something Star had taught him. As a young man he had given way to his rages, knowing that they frightened others, because people were easier to deal with when they were scared. But Star had taught him to breathe right and relax and *think*, which was better in the long run.

Now he considered the damage Melanie had done. Had the FBI been able to trace her phone? Could they find out where a mobile was calling from? He had to assume they could. If so, they would soon be cruising the neighborhood, looking for a seismic vibrator.

He had run out of time. The seismic window opened at six-forty. He looked at his watch: it was six thirty-five. To hell with his seven o'clock deadline—he had to trigger the earthquake right now.

He ran out of the restroom. The seismic vibrator stood in the middle of the empty warehouse, facing the high entrance doors. He jumped up into the driver's cabin and started the engine.

It took a minute or two for pressure to build up in the vibrating mechanism. He watched the gauges impatiently. *Come on, come on!* At last the readings went green.

The passenger door of the truck opened, and Melanie climbed in. "Don't do it!" she yelled. "I don't know where Dusty is!"

Priest reached out to the lever that lowered the plate of the vibrator to the ground.

Melanie knocked his hand aside. "Please, don't!"

Priest hit her backhanded across the face. She screamed, and blood came from her lip. "Stay out of the damn way!" he yelled. He pulled the lever, and the plate descended.

Melanie reached across and threw the lever back to its start position.

Priest saw red. He hit her again.

She cried out and covered her face with her hands, but she did not flee.

Priest returned the lever to the down position.

"Please," she said. "Don't."

What am I going to do with this stupid bitch? He remembered the gun. It was under his seat. He reached down and snatched it up. It was too big, a clumsy weapon in such a small space. He pointed it at Melanie. "Get out of the truck," he said.

To his surprise she reached across him again, pressing her body against the barrel of the gun, and threw the lever.

He pulled the trigger.

The bang was deafening in the little cabin of the truck.

For a split second, a small part of his mind felt a shock of grief that he had ruined her beautiful body; but he dismissed the feeling.

She was thrown back across the cab. The door was still open, and she fell out and tumbled down, hitting the floor of the warehouse with a sickening thud.

Priest did not stop to see if she was dead.

For the third time, he pulled the lever.

Slowly the plate descended to the ground.

When it made contact, Priest started the machine.

The helicopter was a four-seater. Judy sat next to the pilot, Michael behind. As they flew south along the shore of the San Francisco Bay, Judy heard in her headphones the voice of one of Michael's student assistants, calling from the command post. "Michael! This is Paula! It's started up—a seismic vibrator!"

Judy went cold with fear. *I thought I had more time!* She checked her watch: it was six forty-five. Granger's deadline was still fifteen minutes away. Melanie's phone call must have made him start early.

Michael was saying: "Any tremors on the seismograph?"

"No—just the seismic vibrator, so far."

No earthquake yet. Thank God.

Judy shouted into her microphone: "Give us the location, quickly!"

"Wait a minute, the coordinates are coming up now."

Judy grabbed a map.

Hurry, hurry!

A long moment later Paula read the numbers on her screen. Judy found the location on her map. She said to the pilot: "Due south two miles, then about five hundred yards inland."

Her stomach lurched as the chopper dived and picked up speed.

They were flying over the old waterfront neighborhood, full of derelict factories and car dumps. It would have been quiet on a normal Sunday: today it was empty. Judy scanned the horizon, looking for a truck that could be the seismic vibrator.

To the south she saw two police patrol cars speeding toward the same location. Looking west, she spotted the FBI SWAT wagon approaching. Back at the Presidio, the other helicopters would be lifting off, full of armed agents. Soon half the law enforcement vehicles in Northern California would be heading for the map coordinates Paula had given out.

Michael said into his microphone: "Paula! What's happening on your screens?"

"Nothing—the vibrator is operating, but it's not having any effect."

"Thank God!" Judy said.

Michael said: "If he follows his previous pattern, he'll move the truck a quarter of a mile and try again."

The pilot said: "This is it. We've arrived at the coordinates." The helicopter began to circle.

Judy and Michael stared out, searching frantically for the seismic vibrator.

On the ground, nothing moved.

Priest cursed.

The vibrating machinery was operating, but there was no earthquake.

This had happened before, both times. Melanie had said she did not really understand why it worked in some locations but not others. It probably had something to do with different kinds of subsoil. Both times the vibrator had triggered an earthquake on the third try. But today Priest really needed to be lucky the first time.

He was not.

Boiling with frustration, he turned off the mechanism and raised the plate.

He had to move the truck.

He jumped out. Stepping over Melanie, who was crumpled up against the wall, bleeding onto the concrete floor, he ran to the entrance. There was a pair of old-fashioned high doors that folded back to admit big vehicles. Inset into one panel was a small, people-size door. Priest threw it open.

Over the entrance to a small warehouse Judy saw a sign that read "Perpetua Diaries."

She had thought Melanie was saying "Perpetual."

"That's the place!" she yelled. "Go down!"

The helicopter descended rapidly, avoiding a power line that ran from pole to pole along the side of the road, and touched down in the middle of the deserted street.

As soon as she felt the bump of contact with the ground, Judy opened the door.

Priest looked out.

A helicopter had landed in the road. As he watched, someone jumped out. It was a woman with a wound dressing on her face. He recognized Judy Maddox.

He screamed a curse that was lost in the noise of the chopper.

There was no time to open the big doors.

He dashed back to the truck, got in, and rammed the shift into reverse. He backed as far as he could into the warehouse, stopping when the rear bumper hit the wall. Then he engaged first gear. He revved the engine high, then let out the clutch with a jerk. The truck lurched forward.

Priest pressed the pedal to the floor. Engine screaming, the big truck gathered speed the length of the warehouse, then crashed into the old wooden door.

Judy Maddox was standing right in front of the door, gun in hand. Shock and fear showed on her face as the truck burst through the door. Priest grinned savagely as he bore down on her. She dived sideways, and the truck missed her by an inch.

The helicopter was in the middle of the road. A man was getting out. Priest recognized Michael Quercus.

He steered toward the helicopter, changed up a gear, and accelerated.

Judy rolled over, aimed at the driver's door, and squeezed off two shots. She thought she might have hit something, but she failed to stop the truck.

The chopper lifted quickly.

Michael ran to the side of the road.

Judy guessed that Granger was hoping to clip the helicopter's undercarriage, as he had in Felicitas, but this time the pilot was too quick for him and lifted high as the truck charged the space where the aircraft had been.

But, in his haste, the pilot forgot the roadside power lines.

There were five or six cables stretched between tall poles. The rotor blade caught in the lines, slicing through some. The helicopter's engine faltered. One of the poles tilted under the strain and fell. The rotor blade began to spin freely again, but the chopper had lost lift, and it fell to the ground with a mighty crash.

Priest had one hope left.

If he could drive a quarter of a mile, then get the plate down and the vibrator operating, he might yet trigger an earthquake before the FBI could get to him. And in the chaos of an earthquake, he might escape, as he had before.

He wrenched the wheel around and headed down the road.

Judy fired again as the truck swung away from the downed helicopter. She was hoping to hit either Granger or some essential part of the engine, but she was unlucky. The truck lumbered down the potholed road.

She looked at the crashed helicopter. The pilot was not

moving. She looked back to the seismic vibrator as it gradually gathered speed.

I wish I had a rifle.

Michael ran up to her. "Are you okay?"

"Yes," she said. She made a decision. "You see if you can help the pilot—I'll go after Granger."

He hesitated, then said: "Okay."

Judy holstered her pistol and ran after the truck.

It was a sluggish vehicle, taking long moments to accelerate. At first she closed the distance rapidly. Then Granger changed gear, and the truck picked up speed. Judy ran as fast as she could, heart pounding, chest aching. The tail of the truck carried a huge spare wheel. She was still gaining on it, but not so rapidly. Just when she thought she would never catch it, Granger shifted gears again, and in the momentary slowdown, Judy put on a burst of speed and leaped for the tailgate.

She got one foot on the bumper and grabbed the spare wheel. For a frightening moment she thought she would slip and fall; and she looked down to see the road speeding beneath her. But she managed to hold on. She clambered onto the flatbed among the tanks and valves of the machinery. She staggered to keep her balance, almost fell, and righted herself.

She did not know whether Granger had seen her.

He could not operate the vibrator while the truck was in motion, so she remained where she was, heart thumping, waiting for him to stop.

But he had seen her.

She heard glass shatter and saw the barrel of a gun poke through the rear window of the driver's cabin. She ducked instinctively. The next moment she heard a slug ricochet off a tank beside her. She leaned to the left so that she was directly behind Granger, and crouched low, heart in her mouth. She heard another shot and cringed, but it missed her. Then he seemed to give up.

But he had not.

The truck braked fiercely. Judy was thrown forward, banging her head painfully against a pipe. Then Granger swerved violently to the right. Judy swung sideways and thought for a terrifying moment that she would be hurled to her death on the hard surface of the road, but she managed to hang on. She saw that Granger was heading suicidally straight for the brick front of a disused factory. She clung to a tank.

At the last moment he braked hard and swerved, but he was a fraction of a second too late. He averted a head-on smash, but the offside fender plowed into the brickwork with a crash of crumpling metal and breaking glass. Judy felt an agonizing pain in her ribs as she was crushed against the tank she was holding. Then she was thrown into the air.

For a dizzy moment she was totally disoriented. Then she hit the ground, landing on her left side. All the breath was knocked out of her body so that she could not even yell with pain. Her head banged against the road, her left arm went numb, and panic filled her mind.

Her head cleared a second or two later. She hurt, but she could move. Her bulletproof jacket had helped to protect her. Her black corduroys were ripped and one knee was bleeding, but not badly. Her nose was bleeding, too: she had reopened the wound Granger had given her yesterday.

She had fallen near the rear corner of the truck, close to its enormous double wheels. If Granger reversed a yard, he would kill her. She rolled sideways, staying behind the truck but getting away from its giant tires. The effort sent sharp pain through her ribs, and she cursed.

The truck did not reverse. Granger was not trying to run her over. Perhaps he had not seen where she had fallen.

She looked up and down the street. She could see Michael struggling to get the pilot out of the crashed helicopter, four hundred yards away. In the other direction, there was no sign of the SWAT wagon or the police cars she had spotted from the air, or of the other FBI helicopters. They were probably seconds away—but she did not have seconds to spare.

She got to her knees and drew her weapon. She expected Granger to jump out of the cabin and shoot at her, but he did not.

She struggled painfully to her feet.

If she approached on the driver's side of the truck, he would surely see her in his side-view mirror. She went to the other side and risked a peek around the rear corner. There was a big mirror on this side, too.

She dropped to her knees, lay flat on her belly, and crawled under the truck.

She wriggled forward until she was almost beneath the driver's cab.

She heard a new noise above her and wondered what it was. Glancing up, she saw a huge steel plate above her.

It was being lowered onto her.

Frantically she rolled sideways. Her foot caught on one of the rear wheels. For a few horrendous seconds she struggled to free herself as the massive plate moved inexorably down. It would crush her leg like a plastic toy. At the last moment she pulled her foot out of her shoe and rolled clear.

She was out in the open. Granger would see her at any second. If he leaned out of the passenger door now, gun in hand, he could shoot her easily.

There was a blast like a bomb in her ears, and the ground beneath her shook violently. He had started the vibrator.

She had to stop it. She thought momentarily of Bo's house. In her mind she saw it crumble and fall, then the whole street collapse.

Pressing her left hand to her side to ease the pain, she forced herself to her feet.

Two paces took her to the nearside door. She needed to

open it with her right hand, so she shifted the gun to her left—she could shoot with either—and pointed it up to the sky.

Now.

She jumped onto the step, grabbed the door handle, and flung it open.

She came face-to-face with Richard Granger.

He looked as scared as she felt.

She pointed the gun at him with her left hand. "Turn it off!" she screamed. "Turn it *off*!"

"Okay," he said, and he grinned and reached beneath his seat.

The grin alerted her. She knew he was not going to turn off the vibrator. She got ready to shoot him.

She had never shot anyone before.

His hand came up holding a revolver like something out of the Wild West.

As the long barrel swung toward her, she aimed her pistol at his head and squeezed the trigger.

The bullet hit him in the face, beside the nose.

He shot her a split second later. The flash and noise of the double gunshot was terrific. She felt a burning pain across her right temple.

Years of training came into play. She had been taught always to fire twice, and her muscles remembered. Automatically she pulled the trigger again. This time she hit his shoulder. Blood spurted immediately. He spun sideways and fell back against the door, dropping the gun from limp fingers.

Oh, Jesus, is that what it's like when you kill someone?

Judy felt her own blood course down her right cheek. She fought a wave of faintness and nausea. She held the gun pointed at Granger.

The machine was still vibrating.

She stared at the mass of switches and dials. She had just shot the one person who knew how to turn the thing off. Panic swept over her. She fought it down. *There must be a key.*

There was.

She reached over the inert body of Ricky Granger and turned it.

Suddenly there was quiet.

She glanced along the street. Outside the Perpetua Diaries warehouse, the helicopter was on fire.

Michael!

She opened the door of the truck, fighting to stay conscious. She knew there was something she ought to do, something important, before she went to help Michael, but she could not think what it was. She gave up trying to remember and climbed out of the truck.

A distant police siren came closer, and she saw a patrol car approaching. She waved it down. "FBI," she said weakly. "Take me to that chopper." She opened the door and fell into the car.

The cop drove the four hundred yards to the warehouse and pulled up a safe distance from the burning aircraft. Judy got out. She could not see anyone inside the helicopter. "Michael!" she yelled. "Where are you?"

"Over here!" He was behind the busted doors of the warehouse, bending over the pilot. Judy ran to him. "This guy needs help," Michael said. He looked at her face. "Jesus, so do you!"

"I'm all right," she said. "Help is on the way." She pulled out her cell phone and called the command post. She got Raja. He said: "Judy, what's happening?"

"You tell me, for Christ's sake!"

"The vibrator stopped."

"I know, I stopped it. Any tremors?"

"No. Nothing at all."

Judy slumped with relief. She had stopped the machine in time. There would be no earthquake.

She leaned against the wall. She felt faint. She struggled to stay upright.

She felt no triumph, no sense of victory. Perhaps that

would come later, with Raja and Carl and the others, in Everton's bar. For now she was drained empty.

Another patrol car pulled up, and an officer got out. "Lieutenant Forbes," he said. "What the hell went on here? Where's the perpetrator?"

Judy pointed along the street to the seismic vibrator. "He's in the front of that truck," she said. "Dead."

"We'll take a look." The lieutenant got back in his car and tore off down the street.

Michael had disappeared. Looking for him, Judy stepped inside the warehouse.

She saw him sitting on the concrete floor in a pool of blood. But he was unhurt. In his arms he held Melanie. Her face was even paler than usual, and her skimpy T-shirt was soaked with blood from a grisly wound in her chest.

Michael's face was contorted with grief.

Judy went to him and knelt beside him. She felt for a pulse in Melanie's neck. There was none.

"I'm sorry, Michael," she said. "I'm so sorry."

He swallowed. "Poor Dusty," he said.

Judy touched his face. "It will be all right," she said.

A few moments later Lieutenant Forbes reappeared. "Pardon me, ma'am," he said politely. "Did you say there was a dead man in that truck?"

"Yes," she said. "I shot him."

"Well," the cop said, "he ain't there now."

22

Star was jailed for ten years.

At first, prison was torture. The regimented existence was hell for someone whose whole life had been about freedom. Then a pretty wardress called Jane fell in love with her and brought her makeup and books and marijuana, and things began to look up.

Flower was placed with foster parents, a Methodist minister and his wife. They were kindhearted people who could not begin to understand where Flower was coming from. She missed her parents, did poorly at school, and got in more trouble with the police. Then, a couple of years later, she found her grandma. Veronica Nightingale had been thirteen when she gave birth to Priest, so she was only in her mid-sixties when Flower found her. She was running a store in Los Angeles selling sex toys, lingerie, and porno videos. She had an apartment in Beverly Hills and drove a red sports car, and she told Flower stories about her daddy when he was a little boy. Flower ran away from the minister and his wife and moved in with her grandma.

Oaktree disappeared. Judy knew there had been a fourth person in the 'Cuda at Felicitas, and she had been able to piece together his role in the affair. She even got a full set of fingerprints from his woodwork shop at the commune. But no one knew where he had gone. However, his prints showed up a couple of years later, on a stolen car that had been used in an armed robbery in Seattle. The police did not suspect him, because he had a solid alibi, but Judy was automatically notified. When she reviewed the file with the U.S. attorney—her old friend Don Riley, now married to an insurance saleswoman—they realized they had only a weak case against Oaktree for his part in the Hammer of Eden, and they decided to let him be.

Milton Lestrange died of cancer. Brian Kincaid retired. Marvin Hayes resigned and became security director for a supermarket chain.

Michael Quercus became moderately famous. Because he was nice looking and good at explaining seismology, TV shows always called him first when they wanted a quote about earthquakes. His business prospered.

Judy was promoted to supervisor. She moved in with Michael and Dusty. When Michael's business started to make real money, they bought a house together and decided to have a baby. A month later she was pregnant, so they got married. Bo cried at the wedding.

Judy figured out how Granger had got away.

The wound to his face was nasty but not serious. The bullet to his shoulder had nicked a vein, and the sudden loss of blood caused him to lose consciousness. Judy should have checked his pulse before going to help Michael, but she was weakened by her injuries and confused because of loss of blood, and she failed to follow routine.

Granger's slumped position caused his blood pressure to rise again, and he came around a few seconds after she left. He crawled around the corner to Third Street, where he was lucky enough to find a car waiting at a stoplight. He got in, pointed his gun at the driver, and demanded to be taken to the city. En route he used Melanie's mobile to call Paul Beale, the wine bottler who was a criminal associate of Granger's from the old days. Beale had given him the address of a crooked doctor.

Granger made the driver drop him at a corner in a grungy

neighborhood. (The traumatized citizen drove home, called the local police precinct house, got a busy signal, and did not get around to reporting the incident until the next day.) The doctor, a disbarred surgeon who was a morphine addict, patched Granger up. Granger stayed at the doctor's apartment overnight, then left.

Judy never found out where he went after that.

The water is rising fast. It has flooded all the little wooden houses. Behind the closed doors, the homemade beds and chairs are floating. The cookhouse and the temple are also awash.

He has waited weeks for the water to reach the vineyard. Now it has, and the precious plants are drowning.

He had been hoping he might find Spirit here, but his dog is long gone.

He has drunk a bottle of his favorite wine. It is difficult for him to drink or eat, because of the wound to his face, which has been sewn up badly by a doctor who was stoned. But he has succeeded in pouring enough down his throat to make himself drunk.

He throws the bottle away and takes from his pocket a big joint of marijuana laced with enough heroin to knock him out. He lights it, takes a puff, and walks down the hill.

When the water is up to his thighs, he sits down.

He takes a last look around his valley. It is almost unrecognizable. There is no tumbling stream. Only the roofs of the buildings are visible, and they look like upturned shipwrecks floating on the surface of a lagoon. The vines he planted twenty-five years ago are now submerged.

It is not a valley anymore. It has become a lake, and everything that was here has been killed.

He takes a long pull on the joint between his fingers. He draws the deadly smoke deep into his lungs. He feels the rush of pleasure as the drug enters his bloodstream and the chemicals flood his brain. *Little Ricky, happy at last,* he thinks.

He rolls over and falls in the water. He lies face down, helpless, stoned out of his mind. Slowly his consciousness fades, like a distant lamp becoming dimmer, until, at last, the light goes out.

Acknowledgments

I am grateful to the following people for help with this book:

Governor Pete Wilson of California; Jonathan R. Wilcox, deputy director, Office of Public Affairs, Office of Governor Pete Wilson; Andrew Poat, chief deputy director, Department of Transportation;

Mark D. Zoback, professor of geophysics, chairman, Department of Geophysics, Stanford University;

In the San Francisco field office of the FBI: Special Agent George E. Grotz, director of press relations and public affairs, who opened many doors; Special Agent Candice DeLong, profiling coordinator, who generously spent much time helping me with the details of an agent's life and work; Bob Walsh, special agent in charge; George Vinson, assistant special agent in charge; Charles W. Matthews III, associate special agent in charge; Supervising Special Agent John Gray, crisis management coordinator; Supervising Special Agent Don Whaley, chief division counsel; Supervising Special Agent Larry Long, Tech squad; Special Agent Tony Maxwell, evidence response team coordinator; Dominic Gizzi, administrative officer;

In the Sacramento field office of the FBI: Special Agent Carole Micozzi; Special Agent Mike Ernst;

Pearle Greaves, computer specialist, Information Resources Division, FBI headquarters;

Sierra County sheriff Lee Adams;

Lucien G. Canton, director, Mayor's Office of Emergency Services, San Francisco;

James F. Davis, Ph.D., California State geologist; Ms. Sherry Reser, information officer, Department of Conservation;

Charles Yanez, manager, South Texas, Western Geophysical; Janet Loveday, Western Geophysical; Rhonda G. Boone, manager, corporate communications, Western Atlas International; Donnie McLendon, Western Geophysical, Freer, Texas; Mr. Jesse Rosas, bulldozer driver;

Seth Rosing DeLong;

Dr. Keith J. Rosing, director of emergency services, Irvine Medical Center;

Brian Butterworth, professor of cognitive neuropsychology, University College, London.

Most of the above were found for me by Dan Starer, of Research for Writers, New York City.

As always, my outlines and drafts were read and criticized constructively by my agent, Al Zuckerman; my editors, Ann Patty in New York and Suzanne Baboneau in London; and numerous friends and relatives, including George Brennan, Barbara Follett, Angus James, Jann Turner, and Kim Turner.

Visit the Ken Follett Web site at http://www.ken-follett. com

From internationally bestselling author

Ken Follett

*comes an epic saga of young lovers
in an age of riot and revolution.*

A PLACE CALLED FREEDOM

Sentenced to a life of misery in the brutal coal mines of Scotland, Mack McAsh hungers for escape. His only ally is the beautiful, high-born Lizzie Hallim, who is trapped in her own kind of hell. From the teeming streets of London to a sprawling Virginia plantation circa 1766, these two restless young people, separated by politics and position, are bound by their passionate search for a place called freedom....

Published by The Ballantine Publishing Group.
Available in bookstores everywhere.

And don't miss this thrilling
New York Times *bestseller by*

Ken Follett

THE THIRD TWIN

Using a restricted FBI database, genetic researcher Jeannie Ferrami has located identical twins *born to different mothers*. Frightened by her bizarre discovery, she is determined to discover the truth at any cost—until she finds herself at the center of a scandal that could ruin her career. With growing horror, she uncovers a cynical, far-reaching conspiracy involving some of the most powerful men in America—men who will kill to keep their secrets concealed.

Published by The Ballantine Publishing Group.
Available in bookstores everywhere.

Look for these novels by
bestselling author

KEN FOLLETT

——◆——

Published by The Ballantine Publishing Group.
Available in your local bookstore.